# THE Perfect PLAY

BOOK FIVE
NOLAN
U

*Katy ♡ xoxo Archer*

# KATY ARCHER

THE PERFECT PLAY
Nolan U Football #5
© Copyright 2025 Katy Archer
www.katyarcher.com

———

———

Cover Design © Designed with Grace

———

———

ISBN: 978-1-991403-09-4 (Kindle e-book)
ISBN: 978-1-991403-10-0 (paperback)

Archer Street Romance
www.katyarcher.com

# A SPECIAL GIFT FOR YOU...

Would you like to become an honorary member of Nolan University?

For special access to the NOLAN U LOCKER ROOM, you can sign up for exclusive content, character interviews, bonus scenes and a bunch of special goodies.

**Get your exclusive content here!**
www.katyarcher.com/nolan-u-locker-room-sign-up

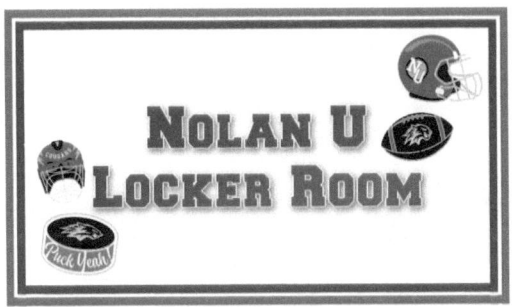

# CHAPTER 1
## DANI

Offside is busy for a Monday night. It makes me grateful that I've got the next two days off. Two years ago, if you'd told me I was going to be tending bar in a small town like Nolan, I would have laughed in your face.

But a lot can change in two years.

The glass in my hand starts to slip, and I squeeze it a little tighter, focusing on the beer I'm pulling and not the man I'm desperately trying to escape. He haunts my every day, and that's why I moved.

That's why I packed my bags, hugged my family goodbye, and took a job with Tobin's boyfriend. It was the out I'd been waiting for. And now I have to make the most of it.

Tobin and I grew up together—next-door neighbors and elementary school buddies. I'm so glad I kept in touch with him, even after he left for college. When he suggested I come to Nolan for a change of scenery, I initially said no, but it took all of three days for me to change my mind.

And here I am.

"There you go." I place the beer down with a bright smile, handing over the card reader so the sexy man across the bar can tap his Visa card.

Damn, he is fine.

I take in his stunning smile—all straight white teeth—and those glittery blue eyes.

It's impossible not to grin back.

This is exactly what I need.

Some hot guy giving me a flirty smile, distracting me, pulling me away from a life I can't live anymore.

That's why I'm here.

Fresh start.

New beginnings.

All that shit.

I can't keep being single, pining for a man I can never have.

Because I can seriously *never* be with Atlas again. He's gone. Died in my arms. And I've spent too many days, weeks, *months* mourning him. If I didn't make a drastic change, I was going to wake up from my stupor in fifty years and realize life had passed me by.

I can't keep doing this anymore.

And so I'm here, with my heart held together by string and duct tape, barely hanging on while I try to let go of the man I thought I'd marry. My one true love.

Clearing my throat, I try to shake off the blues and flash this guy another bright smile.

"You let me know if you need anything else." I raise my voice to be heard above the guy crooning on the stage and the cacophony of voices surrounding the bar.

He raises his glass and smiles at me. "I will definitely be calling you over again."

My smile grows while my nerves flail.

*Yes, you want this, Dani. You* need *this!*

*Ask for his number. Be bold. I dare you.*

Brushing my teeth over my lower lip, I go against every grain in my body and rest my elbows on the bar. I know the move squishes my boobs together, because his eyes dart south for a second before popping back up to my face.

A sizzle rushes through me.

I haven't had sex since Atlas died. My wasted body is like the Sahara Desert, and although the idea of sleeping with some random guy doesn't sit well with me, a primal part of me needs to get laid.

My insides tremble as I run my fingertip across the bar and force myself to say it. "Maybe I can give you my number... and you can call me if you need me."

*Ugh! I can't believe you just said that.*

My entire body is cringing as he lets out a soft laugh and snatches a napkin from next to the bowl of pretzels. "How about I give you mine?"

Pulling a pen from my apron, I hand it over, and he scribbles down his number before handing it to me.

It flops in front of my hand, and I have to tell myself to take it, to read the name beneath those digits.

"Nice to meet you, Sutton."

"You too, Dani." He points to my name tag, and yeah, I really do hate wearing one, even if it does mean I don't have to introduce myself to people. "You give me a call and maybe we can hang out sometime."

I nod, slipping the number into my back pocket. "I'll do that."

His smile grows a little wider, and I have that second of doubt—will he answer if I call? Will he reply if I text?

Shit, this dating thing sucks!

Atlas and I met in high school. Everything about it was so natural and simple and easy.

Now I'm trying to get back into the world, and it all feels impossible.

I'll love Atlas forever, but it's time to move on, and I had no idea how challenging that would be. Putting myself out there is terrifying. But if I don't start living again... I'm gonna shrivel up and die.

I want to love my life again.

I want to *feel* something other than despair... or that hollow numbness that's been feasting on me for way too long now.

So, I will call Sutton. And I'll ask him out on a date, and I'll go to that damn thing, and I'll enjoy it. Because I have to.

Because I need—

"Dani!"

I turn to see who just shouted my name... and the air in my lungs goes still, my eyes bulging as I stare down the bar and double-check that I am in fact seeing what I'm seeing.

*No way.*

*No freaking way.*

My lips part, my heart catapulting into my throat as that tall glass of water at the end of the bar raises his hand and gives me a shy smile.

It's still the same.

Even after all this time.

He may look stronger, tougher even... but that smile hasn't changed.

"Tyrell Jackson," I whisper under my breath as a force I can't counter drags me down toward Atlas's best friend.

A giddy feeling I wasn't expecting fills me up, bubbling and bursting in my chest. And before I know it, a laugh is punching out of me. "Tyrell Jackson? No way!" I slap the bar. "What are you doing here?"

"What are *you* doing here?" He points at me.

I tip my head back with another laugh, still surprised by just how happy I am to see him. It's taking everything in me not to climb over the counter and give him a big ol' hug. From memory, Tyrell always gave the best hugs, those full-body, hold-you-close kinds.

He was like that with everybody, which is probably why he always had a gaggle of girls chasing after him. He was always so oblivious to it, though.

*Tyrell Jackson.*

Nostalgia sweeps through me as I try to answer his question without my voice shaking. "I just moved here in January. New year. Fresh start. You know how it is." My throat closes up, because he does know. If anyone in this town gets it, it's him.

Shit, there's so much history between us.

So much knowledge. Memory.

My chest starts to hurt as he leans against the bar, watching me with those deep brown eyes of his. "So... you doing okay?"

I have to give him an honest smile—none of that bright, plastic cheese will work on him. I shrug and throw it back on him. "How about you?"

"Yeah." He nods, then licks his bottom lip and swallows. "Nolan's good. 'Bout to finish my senior year."

I should be too.

So should Atlas.

Shit, life did not turn out at all how we'd planned.

"Congratulations," I croak, my eyes dipping to the counter as memories try to take me out. It suddenly hurts to look at him.

"You ever gone back?" I murmur, unable to recall seeing him around.

I can't picture his face since the funeral, so he must have come back up to Nolan and just stayed away. I'd forgotten that he moved up here for college. I didn't realize he'd stayed. Maybe I assumed his life would have screeched to a halt the way mine did... and he'd crawled into a dark cave to lick his wounds and try to recover.

"My family's in Texas now, so..."

"Okay." I nod, my chin still dipped as I pick at the counter between us. "Yeah, I stayed for a while, but you know, he was just everywhere. It didn't matter how much time passed, I couldn't dodge the memories." My eyes start to burn as I look up and take in his sad expression.

Shit. Does he miss Atlas as much as I do?

They were best friends. Closer than brothers.

They grew up together. Tyrell was always there—the quiet one, happy to stay in the background while Atlas took center stage. Happy to follow his buddy around, keep him safe.

Until he moved to Nolan and only came back for special occasions. Atlas missed him so bad but didn't want to say anything. He got worse after Tyrell left... and I couldn't control him. He started hanging out with his band *all the time*, and from the outside, that probably seemed like a good thing, but he wasn't the same without Tyrell's calm presence. There was no one there to check his wild side.

That was why I'd been so relieved that Tyrell was coming down for the show. He was gonna be there backstage with me and then come to the after-party. Maybe if he had, things wouldn't have turned to shit.

*He was there. He was just late.*

*Too late.*

My aching chest starts to throb with a dull, familiar beat that makes my legs want to buckle.

Crossing my arms, I suck in a breath and try to dodge images of Atlas's pale face, those eyes that kept staring at nothing.

He wouldn't blink.

I couldn't make him blink.

"It's been…"

"Two years, three months, and ten days," he finishes for me, and I can tell that night is still burned into his memory as clearly as it's burned into mine.

I try to smile, but who knows what the hell my face is doing. With a slow nod, I force myself to admit, "It's been really hard to move on, you know?"

"Yeah," he rasps. "I get it."

"But I have to learn to live without him." I shrug, almost feeling bad for saying it. Tyrell was Atlas's *best friend*. Will this feel like a betrayal to him? Atlas's girl moving on? "I'm hoping a change of scenery will help," I finish in a rush.

"It will," he assures me. "I wouldn't have survived if I hadn't had this place. I would have… drowned in

Colorado Springs. He would have haunted me around every corner. Being up here has... helped me... move on."

My eyes shoot up to meet his tortured gaze. "Yet you still know exactly how long it's been since that night."

His forehead wrinkles, and I can feel his pain, still so raw. I get it. We can try to wrap our wounds, cover them with Band-Aids, but you peel back that tape and it's still just below the surface, fresh and painful.

"Hey, Dani! We've got people waiting," Jed calls. "Can I get a hand down here?"

"Sure thing." I hold up my finger, relief flooding me. "One second." Looking back up at the tall man in front of me, I give him a smile—a familiar affection pulsing inside me. "It's nice to see you again, Ty."

And I mean it. Although his presence brings with it a plethora of painful memories, there are also a bunch of happy ones in there too. This nostalgic feeling is kinda nice.

"Yeah, you too, Dani."

I spin and walk back down the bar, heading for the group of girls—a giggling clump out for a good time.

Taking their orders, I focus back on opening bottles and mixing cocktails.

I force myself not to search the space for Tyrell. I don't want to look at him again tonight.

As nice as it is to see him, it's also a knife right through the chest. It took all of two seconds for us to start talking about Atlas, reliving our shared pain as if it only happened yesterday. Do I really want to be hanging around someone like that?

It's like intentionally putting myself in the line of fire, and... well, I came to this place to move on.

How could I forget that Tyrell had come here to play football?

I still remember when Atlas found out he'd gotten in. He'd been gutted. He wanted his best friend to play at Denver U, but the boy got a scholarship to Nolan instead, and he took it.

Atlas never once let it show, but he turned up at my house the night Tyrell told him with tears in his eyes. All I could do was hold him tight. He spent the night in my bed, glued to my side, and I didn't know what to say to make him feel better.

Shit. If I'd remembered Tyrell was here, would I have taken Tobin up on the invite to move in with him and Jed? Would I have taken this job at Offside?

The truth is... probably not.

Because I'm trying to put my past behind me... and Tyrell Jackson is a glaring reminder of everything I lost.

Thank God graduation isn't too far away. Hopefully he'll be leaving town. Maybe he'll move to Texas to be close to his family.

I don't know, and I can't care.

As long as he leaves Nolan, everything will be okay.

All I have to do is avoid him for the next couple of months... and maybe then I'll have a shot at leaving Atlas behind me and creating a life with someone new.

# CHAPTER 2
## TYRELL

I weave my way back to the table, knowing I'll be facing a plethora of questions the second my ass touches the chair. Thankfully, only Wily and Satch are still at the table, but that doesn't last long.

Within a minute of taking a seat, the pool game is abandoned, and I'm surrounded by six sets of curious eyes. Shit... I'm gonna have to say something.

"An old friend from high school." I point over my shoulder, hoping that's enough of an explanation... but knowing it's not.

Sienna grins. "She's cute."

I shake my head. "It's not like that."

"More like a sister?" Satch asks.

"Yeah?" I hitch my shoulder, but I'll never think about Dani the way I think about my kid sister, Lacey.

"Was that supposed to be a question?" Nylah laughs at me. "You're not sure how you feel about her?"

I groan and tip my head back. "It's complicated, you guys."

"You seemed pretty happy to talk to her." Nylah wiggles her eyebrows at me while Carson swings his arm across the back of her chair and eyes me up, quietly demanding an explanation.

They're not going to let this go, and there's only one thing I can do to shut this conversation up.

"She dated my best friend in high school. We hung out *a lot*, so I know her, and she's awesome. But it's not like that between us. It never will be. She was my best friend's girl."

"You just said *was*." Sienna points at me, and I internally cringe, realizing that none of the women at this table know, because I made the guys promise never to breathe a word.

They know better than to talk about Atlas.

When I first lost him, I was a wreck.

They kept me afloat. Stopped me from dropping out of college, leaving football for good. They offered me a place in Football Frat—anything to keep me grounded. And once I'd processed the worst of my grief, they knew better than to bring him up again.

But I have to mention him tonight.

It's the only way to shut down this inquisition.

Clearing my throat, I dart a glance at Zander, whose expression tells me he already knows what I'm about to spill. "He died."

I say it simply, because that's the only way to do it.

"In my sophomore year at college, he—" I swallow. "He died."

"Oh my gosh, I'm so sorry." Satch reaches across the table, resting her hand on my forearm and giving it a squeeze. "That must have been awful."

"It was." I nod. "Devastating."

"For her too, I'm guessing." Nylah gazes across the crowded room, obviously looking for Dani behind the bar.

"Yeah." I can't help looking for her too. "Broke her up pretty bad."

"Was she with him when he died?" Why Sienna would ask that, I have no idea, but she's right on the money, and I can't picture Atlas's pale, dead face right now.

Squeezing my eyes shut, I pinch the bridge of my nose and rise from my seat. "I'm gonna head home."

"I'm sorry. I didn't mean to pry," Sienna rushes out.

I open my eyes in time to see her guilt-ridden expression and quickly shake my head.

"It's all good," I assure her, forcing myself to smile.

But it's not good.

It's heavy and painful and... I need to get the fuck out of here.

"We can give you a ride."

"No, I..." Shaking my head, I step away from the table, pushing in my chair and glancing around at my buddies.

They know.

They saw me fall apart.

They heard the harrowing recount.

"I'm gonna walk."

"'Kay, man." Carson nods, not needing anything more from me.

I take my cue and make a beeline for the exit.

I can't look back and try to spot Dani one last time. I'm suddenly wrecked all over again, and I just need to walk this shit off.

The others are no doubt talking about me, explaining to their girls how we were down in Denver for the weekend...

It was an end-of-season game, and we won. Just. It'd been a tough fight, but we'd hung on to that last play, and damn if Grady didn't find the perfect gap and punch right through it. He got a touchdown with eight seconds left in the fourth quarter, and we came away victorious. The coaches were pumped, the team was beyond ecstatic, and I lost track of time as we celebrated the win.

I'd arranged with the coaches to leave right after the game so I could drive to Colorado Springs and watch my best friend's band play. They'd even let me drive down from Nolan so I could have my own car. I was kind of bummed out that I couldn't go on the bus, but a few of the offensive linemen jumped in with me, and we drove down together. It was nice of the coaches and team to accommodate me this way.

Atlas knew I was gonna be late, but I'd promised him I'd be there for the final set and the after-party.

But I got busy jumping around a locker room and singing stupid songs. I got busy laughing and whooping with my football team. I was having way too much fun to notice the time, and when Grady finally asked me if I was supposed to be somewhere else, I felt a rush of disappointment. I didn't want to leave my team to go to the concert, but I'd promised Atlas.

I hadn't seen him in over a month. Football season was busy, and it'd been getting really hard to fit in visits with him and Dani... and my family. Last time, Atlas had come up to hang with me, but it'd been kind of awkward. Our lives, which used to be so cohesive and in sync, were starting to splinter. He was getting heavy into the punk rock world, and football was becoming king for me.

But he was still my best friend.

And so I left the football celebrations. Admittedly, I was dragging my feet, and by the time I got into my car, I was running over an hour late.

I'd missed his final set, and he'd no doubt be pissed about it. I spent the drive south formulating a decent apology, hoping he'd get how epic this win was and how much it meant to me.

The after-party was happening above the bar they performed in, and I got through without too many problems. Had to have one small argument with a bouncer who couldn't find my name on the list to start with. At first, I thought Atlas had scrubbed it because he was pissed off that I hadn't made it. But then the bouncer checked again, and I was finally let through.

I was nearly two hours later than I said I'd be, and I did feel bad about that... and it was made a million times worse the second I wove my way into the crowd and heard the screaming.

A jolt ran through my body, my blood turning to ice when I heard a woman wail, "Wake up! Atlas! Wake! Up!"

"Dani," I whispered, shoving my way through the crowd as fear wrapped its bony fingers around my neck and started to squeeze.

I punched through the crowd gathering in the hallway, wrestling past bodies until I reached the bathroom.

The door was ajar, and I shoved it open the second I

spotted Dani on her knees, Atlas's floppy head resting in her lap.

She was tapping his face, sobbing and shaking him, but he was unresponsive.

He was dead.

I knew it the second I looked at those lifeless eyes, gazing up at the ceiling... and seeing nothing.

His skin was so pale, his lips blue, and I knew. In my gut, I *knew* he was gone, but I still shoved my way into the cramped space.

"Call 9-1-1!" I shouted, hoping someone would as I checked Atlas's vitals and pulled him onto the floor.

I didn't know much about first aid, but we'd learned CPR in high school PE class, and I attempted to revive my friend while Dani stayed on the floor beside me, sobbing and whimpering into her hands.

"He's dead," she kept saying, rocking back and forth and crying.

It fucking killed me.

But I couldn't stop trying to revive him.

When the paramedics arrived, my body was aching from the effort. They gently moved me aside, calmly asking me questions I could barely answer.

They tried the defibrillator. It didn't work, so they loaded him onto a stretcher, rushing him out to the ambulance, where they would no doubt try to revive him again.

It wouldn't work. I knew it in my crushed soul.

So instead of running after them, I flopped onto my ass, my back slumping against the wall, a numb chill sweeping through my body.

Someone rushed in and coaxed Dani to her feet.

I think it was her sister.

They followed Atlas's body out of the place, but I stayed on that bathroom floor, staring at the wall, everything turning to a white, hot blur.

I can't really remember much else after that.

Shoving my hands into my jeans pockets, I hunch my shoulders against the spring breeze and walk the familiar path back to Football Frat.

My brain did a pretty good job of blocking out the harrowing days following that night. There was the funeral. Atlas's dad came back for it. He sat in that front pew and quietly cried, couldn't say a damn word to anybody.

He'd left the family a month after Atlas's fourteenth birthday. Had some kind of mental breakdown and skipped town. He was useless at keeping in touch, and it'd hurt Atlas pretty bad. In fact, I don't know if my friend ever really got over it.

Is that why he got into drugs?

Or was it because of the band life? Those guys knew how to party.

During our high school days, I was there to keep an eye on him.

But then I left for Nolan, and Dani stepped up. She was always glued to his side. She was his girl, his agent, his manager. She sought out gigs for the band, then made sure they got there on time. She'd walk miles posting flyers and telling people to come see them play. She'd argue with venue owners until they'd capitulate and supply the band with everything they needed to be successful. She'd help with setup and make sure the sound was as perfect as it could be.

She was there for every single show.

She'd watch from the side of the stage or just in front, singing along and dancing. She was Atlas's biggest cheerleader... and when I left, she had to become his protector too.

She had a way of coaxing him into leaving places when things got too intense. She could pull a joint from between his lips and throw it away when no one else could. She could tell him "No more shots," distracting him with kisses.

Atlas did anything for Dani.

But not that night.

I never found out exactly what happened.

Dani was a wreck at the funeral, and I couldn't talk to her, because I was a wreck too.

My best friend had overdosed... and I hadn't been there to stop him.

He got reckless and made a mistake. Atlas's mom told me that the autopsy report came back indicating that her son's poor body had been riddled with a blend of fentanyl-laced drugs and alcohol. He never stood a chance.

But he would have if I'd been there.

She didn't say it, but I knew she was thinking it.

I'd always been the guy to keep him safe. But then I moved to Nolan, abandoned him just the way his daddy had.

Mom told me that was bullshit when I let it slip.

"You didn't do anything wrong by taking a great

scholarship to a great school. And you kept in touch with Atlas. You are nothing like that boy's father. Nothing!"

She'd gotten all riled up, and Dad had to calm her down.

I just stood there, not believing a fucking word.

I'd told Atlas I'd be there.

And I wasn't.

And now he's dead.

# CHAPTER 3
## DANI

"Okay, who was that?" Jed asked me the second I got back down to his end of the bar... and he hasn't stopped asking since.

Thankfully, we had a rush, and I could avoid the question while we filled food and drink orders.

But things are quieting down now, and there my roommate goes again, asking away.

"You know I'm not a quitting man, Dani Girl. You better tell me who that hunk of handsome was."

"Hey." I frown at him. "You have a boyfriend."

"And if he wasn't studying for an exam right now, I'd be calling his fine ass down here so we could drool over that man together. My boy knows fine when he sees it. Why do you think he's with me?" Jed flicks a hand down his tall body, and I can't help snorting with laughter.

I can see why Tobin fell in love with him.

He's about as tall as Tyrell, although I doubt he's sporting the same chiseled muscles under that shirt of his. He may be bulky, but it's soft bulk. Tyrell, on the other hand... hmmmm. If he's anything like he was in high school—and I can only imagine he's gotten more cut with age—then he'll be like 8 percent body fat, meaning he's got an eight-pack to drool over, and the rest... well, I can imagine the girls still flock around him just like they used to.

They would have flocked around Atlas too, but they knew better than to look at my man.

My stomach pinches into a tight knot. Atlas is with me more than usual tonight, and I'm holding Tyrell responsible.

"So..." Jed lightly flicks my arm with the back of his hand.

"Stop," I grumble, then force a smile. "What can I get you tonight, sir?"

A man steps up to the bar, looking over his shoulder and holding up two fingers before nodding, then turning back to me. "Gimme two Coors Lights and a Coke, thanks."

Jed moves to pour the Coke while I grab two bottles of Coors from the fridge. As soon as the payment has gone through and the man is walking away, Jed's back by my side.

"Tell me. Tell me, tell me, tell me."

"Stop." I laugh as he bats his eyelashes at me, then turn and start walking away. "Ouch!" I let out a little squawk when he gets me on the ass with a flick of that dish towel he always has draped over his shoulders. "Boy!" I spin with a growl. "You are gonna pay for that."

He lets out his standard giggle—it's this high-pitched musical sound that does not match his six-foot, three-inch massive frame, but it makes me laugh every single time.

Sometimes, Jed is a twelve-year-old boy hiding inside a twenty-five-year-old man's body.

Seriously.

"Just tell me and I'll stop harassing you."

Resting my hands on my hips, I narrow my eyes at him. "I'm filing a formal complaint with Tobin. You know he's gonna side with me."

"Ahhh—bullshit. He's gonna want deets and every single one of them. You better tell me somethin' so I can deliver for my man."

I roll my eyes. "I never should have moved in with you guys."

"Oh, girl, please. You love living with us." He waves a hand through the air. "Now spill your guts or I'm flicking you again."

"You better not." I point at him, checking the bar for any new patrons.

Dammit. Everyone seems perfectly fine.

Willing the rush of people back, I inch toward my roommate and finally settle beside him.

"Oh, Dani Girl, your Jed, your Jed is calling." He starts singing some old-time tune from like World War II or something.

I think it's supposed to be "Danny Boy" and something about pipes, but he's adapted the lyrics for me. He thinks it's hilarious, and dammit, he's just gonna keep on singing.

"Okay, fine!" I raise my hands in defeat. "His name's Tyrell, and I knew him in high school." My shoulders sag. "He was Atlas's best friend."

Jed soaks that in for a second, then lets out a gentle "Oh."

"Right?" I raise my eyebrows while he nods... and then proves he doesn't get it.

"He's hot."

Rolling my eyes again, I lurch forward the second someone approaches the bar. I try to take my time filling her order, but Jed helps me out, and we're soon back to being able to chat again.

"I say you go for it."

"What?" I balk. "Are you crazy? I'm not dating my dead boyfriend's best friend. That's just weird."

"Why? You think Atlas would have a problem with it?"

"If he was alive, he sure would!"

Jed's expression softens, his smile kind when he rests his huge hand on my petite shoulder. "But he's not... and you're trying to move on. Why not do that with a man Atlas obviously loved? You said they were besties, right?"

I cringe, already shaking my head. "They grew up together. They were like brothers. It... there's no way... I..." Shaking my head some more, I give him an emphatic look. "It's never gonna happen. I don't even know if I want to see him again."

"Why not? You two looked like you were having a great catch-up." Jed lifts his chin toward the bar where I'd smiled up at Tyrell, nostalgia swamping me.

"Yeah, I mean..." I rub my forehead. "It was nice to see him again, but it just brings it all back, you know?"

Jed pauses for a second, then rests his elbow on the bar so he can bend down and look me in the eye. "I get it. Probably hurts, right?"

I nod, my throat swelling.

"But there must have been good times too. Maybe it's worth remembering those, you know?"

"Excuse me?" A woman with a black bob cut raises her hand. "Can I get a drink, please?"

"Sure thing." Jed pulls the towel off his shoulder, looking like an old-timey bartender as he wipes down the counter and memorizes the woman's order.

I stay where I am, watching him fulfill it and trying to dodge a million different memories. All those laughs we had in high school. All those good times we shared. It was awesome... until it wasn't.

Until Tyrell moved away and Atlas just got worse and worse.

I don't blame Tyrell. He had to follow his path.

I just wish I could have been strong enough to keep Atlas on track by myself.

But I wasn't.

And then I got all shitty and stormed away from him.

Shit, I'll regret that night forever.

"I get that you don't want to be romantic with the guy, even though I think you're totally missing out there." Jed makes an appreciative sound as he leans back against the counter. "But what about just hanging with him for old times' sake?"

"I don't know." I shrug, then grip the counter in front of me, needing it to help me stay upright.

"Okay." Jed nods. "Well, I'm gonna keep bugging you about this, because you told us you wanted to move on, find yourself a guy. Maybe Tyrell can be your in-betweener, you know? Nothing romantic, just a friend to chill with. Although, damn, girl." He bulges his eyes at me. "That boy be fine."

I let out a soft laugh, because Jed's right. Tyrell Jackson is one hot specimen. "Yeah, I get it. I'm sorry he's not gay. At least I don't think he is."

"He's not." Jed pouts. "I can sense these things."

"Okay." I grin up at him.

"And besides, I'm in love with Tobin. I might appreciate the view in this place sometimes, but my heart belongs to that boy forever."

My smile grows. "I know. You two are perfect for each other."

His eyes start to sparkle the way they always do when Tobin comes up in conversation. They got together about eighteen months ago, within weeks of Tobin starting at Nolan U. When my old neighbor found out I was wanting a change of scenery, he invited me to come live with him and Jed... and I couldn't think of a good reason to say no.

The day I arrived, they introduced me to their other roommate, Nix, and the three of them then peppered me about how I was going to make the most out of my time in Nolan.

I made the mistake of telling them everything and confessing that this was my big attempt to move on, find love again, start living the life of a woman in her early twenties.

Well, I've been here for over three months now, and no matter how many times they've tried to push me out the door, I've failed to take the big step.

"You know, you could maybe have coffee with him, get used to hanging out with a straight guy again, and that will give you the push you need to ask someone else out...

or say yes when some guy asks *you* out." Jed catches my eye, his dark eyebrows rising. "You feel me? It's a good plan, right?"

"Actually." I reach for my back pocket and pull out the napkin. "I got someone's number tonight. All by myself, before I even noticed Tyrell."

"You did?" Jed perks up. "Who? Is he still here?"

I scan the sports bar, my eyes eventually landing on Sutton. He's near the dartboard, laughing with a couple of other guys. "Over there." I point. "The guy with the curly hair. Sandy brown."

"Hmmm." Jed assesses him with narrowed eyes. "Not bad for a white boy."

"Oh stop." I flick his arm with the backs of my fingers. "He's cute. And he's got a great smile."

"Okay, okay." Jed nods.

"Do you know him?"

"I've seen him around."

"Do you think he's safe enough to go out with?"

Jed eyes him up for a minute before nodding. "Yeah. I think you're good. Just choose somewhere public for your first date, and make sure you've got some pepper spray."

"Seriously?"

"You know Tobin's gonna say the same thing." He nudges me with his elbow. "We'll help you find some good spots."

Nerves rush through me at the thought of actually going through with this thing. Do I honestly want to go out with some guy I met at a bar?

*How else are you planning on meeting them?*

Shit, why is putting myself out there so damn hard?

"Still think it's a damn shame you won't consider the

Black god, but if you've made up your mind about that, then the skinny white boy is probably a safe enough choice."

My eyebrows dip into a V. "He's not that skinny."

"Compared to Shango he is."

I can't help a soft snicker. Jed comparing Tyrell to the Yoruba deity of strength, lightning, and thunder is... well, from a physical point of view, it's completely appropriate.

Atlas always used to joke that Tyrell Jackson was like a Black Jack Reacher.

He was Atlas's bodyguard. His wingman... his protector.

When he first introduced me to the shy fourteen-year-old, he called him Black Jack. Even then Tyrell was taller than everybody else in the class. He was strong and powerful, yet quiet and calm.

There was a shy sweetness to him that countered Atlas's sometimes reckless side.

They were the perfect pair, always laughing and joking together.

Atlas took the lead, and Black Jack would be right behind him, following in his wake, scanning for dangers on all sides.

Looking up from the bar, I dart my eyes across the room, seeking him out, but I can't see him anywhere.

He must have left already, quietly slipped out the door when I wasn't looking.

I wonder where he is right now.

I wonder where he lives.

I wonder if he's happy, the way I so desperately want to be.

# CHAPTER 4
## TYRELL

Football Frat is quiet when I get back.

I don't know where Grady and Blake went off to, but I was half expecting to see Wily's truck in the driveway. It wasn't.

I'm all alone.

And that's kind of the way I want it, even though the house is unnervingly quiet as I climb the stairs to my room.

I can't believe I only have a couple of months left in this place. Feels weird to know I'll be moving out soon. It's been a good home for the last two years. It's kept me sane on those days I wanted to lose it.

I love my brothers at Football Frat. I would have quit without them, and the idea that we'll all be going our separate ways soon is... It's weird.

Who knows where we'll all end up. I mean, Grady and Carson are sticking around, but Zander and Wily? I guess we'll find out after the draft at the end of this month. Man, they are both so tense over that one.

Zander's confident he'll get picked up by someone, so his tension is laced with excitement. But he has no idea who'll sign him, and this of course affects Sienna and Zoey. They'll be shifting to be with him, and upcoming change can be disconcerting.

Satch, on the other hand, who knows what she'll do. We still don't know if a team will take Wily on with his injury, so his tension has a negative edge to it... and we're all feeling it.

At this stage, my plan is to move to Dallas, spend my summer there, try to find myself a job, then figure out my next steps.

As much as I've enjoyed playing college ball, after Atlas died, I lost the dream of going pro. I don't even know why, but the idea of playing for the NFL, all the attention and the pro life... I just couldn't do it anymore. It's been hard enough getting through the last two seasons. I avoid interviews as much as I can. I even dropped my agent last year, finally convinced him that I wouldn't be changing my mind.

I'll have my degree in civil engineering, and I'll find a job somewhere, start at the bottom and work my way up. Dad's got a connection, and I keep promising him I'll look into it, try to set up an initial meeting, but...

My insides deflate, the idea hardly inspiring.

Trudging up the last few steps, I head down the hallway and slip into my room.

I don't even bother turning on the light. I haven't changed up the furniture once in the time I've been here, and my body knows the exact path to walk.

Slumping down on the edge of my bed, I grip the mattress and stare into the darkness, memories swamping me. They dance through my mind, a cacophony of good and bad—laughter and goofing around with my best friend, arguments and play fights, whispering in the dark for the countless sleepovers we had growing up. Atlas consumes me as I travel back through the years, then work my way forward to high school and the day Dani came on the scene.

Atlas spotted her from across the room, and he was gone. It was love at first sight—for both of them. I found it hilarious. Dani was cute, definitely. I could see the appeal, but Atlas was gone for that girl. Like seriously gone!

They became obsessed with each other pretty damn fast, and for a minute there, I thought I'd lost my friend. But that season only lasted a few months before they quickly settled into "couple mode" and I was brought back into the picture. The three of us used to hang out a lot, and I really liked Dani. She was funny and cool and had this awesome effect on Atlas. She could calm him in a way I couldn't.

Besides, I was getting big into football, and she was a great buffer. I appreciated that there'd always be someone to keep an eye on my friend.

"Should I be keeping an eye on *her* now?" I whisper into the darkness.

With a frown, I lean forward and flick on my bedside lamp.

An orange glow illuminates the space around me as I open the top drawer of my nightstand and pull out a framed photo of Atlas and me. It was taken when we were thirteen, about three months before Atlas's dad bailed. It was one of my favorite summers. We were old enough to bike everywhere on our own, and the freedom was awesome. We spent every day together, hanging out, riding around town, getting into mischief and escaping before we got caught. We flirted with the girls, played arcade games, swam in the waterhole, walked around the mall. The days just disappeared, and every day, Atlas and I were together.

I gaze down at my friend, his arm slung around my shoulders. He was always so skinny compared to me. Our contrasting skin color is so marked, yet we had the same hair—black and curly. Sure, mine were Afro curls, but still, when we introduced ourselves as brothers and people balked like we were crazy, we'd always laugh and say, "Can't you tell? We've got the same hair."

He grew it out in high school. Dani loved his hair, and it ended up longer than hers. He'd tie it up in a top knot or a low ponytail when he was performing onstage, and Dani and I would stand off to the side, or right in the front row, cheering him on.

Until I left.

"Fuck." I scrub a hand down my face, digging out the other framed photo I always keep in that drawer.

It's a shot after Atlas won our high school talent show. It was senior year, and he'd performed an acoustic cover of "Perfect" by Simple Plan. He'd been epic, his voice carrying across the gym, where a stage had been set up in the middle. The entire crowd got into it, and out of all the performances, his felt most like a concert. Dani and I had rushed him after the announcement, and someone snapped a pic—the three of us, standing in a row with beaming smiles. Atlas was between Dani and me. He was sandwiched by my towering body and her petite one, and all three of us looked so damn happy.

Brushing my thumb over his smile, I softly murmur, "Miss you, man." My throat swells, and I have to clear it before I continue. "She does too. It's so obvious. She's tryin' to move on, but you'll be with her for life, brah. You always had that effect on people. You stay with them, you know?"

Swallowing, I stare at my buddy.

I've done this before, spoken to his photograph, just needing that connection.

Lying down on my back, I cross my ankles, holding the photo above me and talking to him as if he's right here in the room.

"She looks good. Her hair's shorter than it was last time, but it really suits her. She's got it up just above her shoulders, and it makes her curls look all springy and bouncy, you know? But it's cut in like this cool, edgy way." My lips twitch. "She always was cool. Made your skinny white ass cool too." I snicker. "Do you remember your *loose tie* phase? I think you were vibing off Kevin Bacon in *Footloose* or some shit, but brah, it did not fly. I tried to tell you, but you wouldn't listen. And then when she came along, you tried to bring it back, and she shot that shit down." I start laughing. "Damn, man. She took you from try-hard musician to legit sex symbol in our school. Do you have any idea how many girls wanted to be her after that?"

My laughter fades as the echoing silence reminds me that he's not here. If he had been, he'd be punching my arm and telling me I'm a douchebiscuit or shitwhistle. Those were his two favorite insults because he thought they were funny. Dani did too. Every time he used them, she'd get the giggles, and then we'd try to come up with similar insults, laughing our asses off with how ridiculous they got. But we always came back to those two.

I can picture Atlas laughing, wrapping his arm around Dani and pulling her close. He was never shy about kissing her, never shy about looking at her like she was the only girl on the planet...

"What should I do, man? I mean, I had no idea she was even in Nolan. And I can keep playin' that I don't know." I sigh, scrubbing a hand down my face. "But I do. I know. And..." I swallow. "Do I keep in touch? Do you want me to reconnect with her or leave her alone? Because I'm telling you, seeing her just... It hurt, you know? Every time I look at her, I'm gonna think of you, and I'm trying to move on. Forget." I wince, hoping he's not offended by that.

*He's not here! How can he be offended!*

But if he was.

If he knew that Dani was in Nolan and he couldn't be here, he'd want me to watch out for her.

He was always protective of his girl.

Is that my job now?

*She's a grown woman. She doesn't need you* protecting *her.*

But Atlas would want me to. I know he would. And maybe it's a way for me to make amends for letting him down so badly.

Licking my bottom lip, I look at them in the photo, so loved-up and happy. My sigh is heavy as I finally nod.

"Okay. If she needs me, I'll step up. I'm not gonna get up in her face or insert myself into her life, but I'll... I'll keep an eye out. I'm only here for a couple more months, but I'll watch her back if you want me to."

He does. I can sense it.

I know that he'll be gutted about Dani moving to Nolan, possibly not knowing anyone. Trying to move on with her life.

So, I'll be there for her.

Although, I have no idea how because I don't even have her number.

I doubt she's kept her old one. I don't even know if I have it anymore.

Slipping the photo back into the drawer, I dig out my phone and search my Contacts. Her name pops up, and I stare at the screen, wondering if I should text her. Test it out and see. But...

With a wince, I lay the phone down beside me.

Not tonight.

Maybe tomorrow.

Rolling onto my side, I reach for my lamp and switch it off, plunging myself back into the darkness and trying not to remember, not to relive, every damn day of my past.

# CHAPTER 5
## DANI

Jed was on closing tonight, so I waited around and helped, then jumped into his car and drove home with him. When I first took this job, I was a little worried that living and working with the same person might be too much, but Jed's a breeze, and we're so busy tending bar most nights that we barely have a chance to talk some shifts.

Man, my feet are killing me.

I'm so relieved I have tomorrow off.

I'm gonna sleep in, maybe go for an amble around town or meet up with Tobin for lunch or something. Whatever it is, it's gonna be chill.

Music drifts over us as we drive to the apartment building about ten minutes off campus. It's an old, five-story orange-brick building that's been restored. Who knows when it was built, but I love the historic edge to the architecture.

We're on the fourth floor, and Jed always likes to climb the stairs, so I follow him up. He's got this theory that always taking the stairs will keep him fit and healthy. It's actually Tobin's theory, and I don't know how accurate it is, but I do know it's healthier than taking the elevator.

"We're home," Jed sings the second we walk through the door.

Tobin jumps up from the couch, grinning at us both but making a beeline for his boyfriend.

"Hey." Jed's voice gets all soft, the way it only ever does with Tobs.

"Hey, you." Tobin grins up at him, and they share a kiss.

It's never some sweet little peach with those two. They always go for it—tongues and passion and …

I look away, laughing to myself as I slip off my shoes… until I remember that Atlas and I used to be like that. Damn, we were hot for each other, especially that summer when we first crossed the line and slept together. We'd been dating for over a year, and I finally felt ready. We were both sixteen, and that summer, I gave him his first blow job. He went down on me a few days later, and about a week after that, I gave my V-card away and never looked back.

I've never slept with another man, and it kinda kills me that if I do want to move on with my life, I'm gonna have to come to terms with the fact that Atlas will no longer be my one and only.

*You could stay single for the rest of your life.*

The thought sits like a mossy stone in my stomach, and I shake off that idea. I can't. I can't keep living this way. I want love again. I want to walk in the door and have someone say, "Hey, you," like I matter and then kiss me—all tongues and passion.

Dropping my bag onto the end of my bed, I walk back into the open-plan living/kitchen area to make myself a cup of chamomile tea. I've been drinking the stuff every night before bed since Atlas died. It's a habit I can't break.

Jed and Tobin have moved to the couch, their fingers threaded together as they talk about their days.

I tense, just waiting for Jed to spill the tea on Tyrell, but he's busy listening to Tobin's story about the girl in his class who was brought down a peg or two by the professor and just how satisfying that was.

"She's the worst." Tobin rolls his eyes, then starts to laugh. "Babe, you should have seen her face when the professor corrected her. It was the most rewarding part of my day." His voice softens. "Until now."

Jed grins at him, kissing his knuckles before asking about the rest of his day.

I get busy making tea and am just sitting down to drink it when Nix walks in the front door.

Her full name is Phoenix, but I've never heard her called anything but Nix. It suits her. She's like a little fairy, always flittering around everywhere. She's petite and energetic, her dark auburn hair short at the back and long and messy at the front. Thick tendrils frame her face, and she's constantly tucking them behind her ears or brushing them back, but she swears short hair is easier than long. I don't know if that's true, but all I can say is that her straight hair is definitely easier to manage than my Afro curls.

"Hey, peeps," she sings, skipping into the kitchen and kissing my cheek before spinning to grin at the boys.

"Hey, Nixie-Noo." Tobin smiles up at her. "How's my favorite fairy?"

"Oh, shut up." She laughs, flopping onto the couch and rolling her eyes when we all laugh.

But it's true. If Tinker Bell was ever made into a live-action, Nix would be perfectly cast. The only thing she's missing is a set of wings, and I'm pretty sure Tobin has made it his mission to remind her of that… for the rest of her life.

"You seem happy." I swivel in my chair, looking down on my roommates from my perch on the stool. "Did you have a good night?"

Nix's smile gives it all away, her euphoric look letting us know without a doubt that this new man she's started dating is a keeper.

"He's perfect." She swoons.

"What's his name again?" Jed asks.

"Ricky." Even saying his name makes her smile. "He took me out for ice cream, and then we strolled around town and ended up at that park near Greek Row. It was empty, of course, no kids at this time of night, so we played on the equipment." She giggles. "He nearly got stuck coming down the slide. He's way too big for it." Her head tips back as another giddy laugh pops out of her. "And then we made out on the grass and…" She finishes her sentence with a dreamy sigh.

I share a grin with my roomies.

"Someone's in love." Jed sings the last word.

"I am," she admits. "I know it's fast, but I don't give a shit. I love that boy and he loves me, and it's bliss!" She stretches her arms wide and sinks into the couch cushions, one happy little fairy.

It's nice to see her this way. When I first moved in, Tobin took me aside and warned me that Nix was awesome but guarded. "Sometimes she's a little bitch, but don't worry, it's all bark and no bite. She's a really good person who has been through some tough shit, so it makes her a little hard. But give it time, okay? She'll warm to you, and once she likes you, she'll be loyal for life."

It was a little disconcerting, knowing I was moving in with a yappy dog who may not like me, but she actually warmed up faster than I was expecting.

It took about two months. She was kind of surly and borderline rude to start with, but I just kept being nice, and each week another layer of her ice wall would melt away. And then, there she was—the girl Tobin promised me was in there. And she really is awesome.

I love all three of the people I live with, and I can't believe I waited so long to make this big change in my life.

Moving to Nolan has been the best decision.

Or has it?

Seeing Tyrell tonight has really thrown me.

I grip my mug of tea, letting the hot ceramic warm my fingers. I did go over three months without seeing him, so the chance of bumping into him again could be slim. But he knows where I work now. Will he come back to visit? Does he want to connect again?

I'm not sure I can handle that.

I've moved here to start fresh, leave the past behind me.

"Should we?" Tobin whispers.

My eyes dart his way, and I catch the tail end of Tobin and Jed's hushed conversation.

"It's okay, babe. We're all here now. Let's just do it."

"Do what?" Nix's head pops off the couch, her eyes narrowing in suspicion.

"Um..." Jed licks his lower lip before glancing at me, then looking back to his boyfriend.

Tobin grins. "Jed has some exciting news. He only found out last month, and we've just been waiting for everything to fall into place so we could tell you."

"What?" Nix isn't smiling. She's gone all tense, her petite features dropping into a guarded frown.

I hold my breath, feeding off her immediate stress and tension.

"Well..." Jed's lips twitch. "I've been offered..." He glances at Tobin again.

"Offered what?" Nix barks. "Just spit it out, man!"

Tobin glares at Nix for a hot second, then spills the beans. "My highly talented, amazing boyfriend has been offered the chance to work at a restaurant in New York City, baby!"

My heart stops beating for a second.

"That's right. His uncle is opening a super-classy, high-end restaurant in Manhattan, and he wants Jed to be in charge of the bar."

My mouth pops open while Nix shifts on the couch, perching on her knees and staring at Jed. "You're moving to New York?"

"*We're* moving to New York," Tobin corrects her. "I just found out this morning that I've been accepted to New York University!"

"Isn't that place stupidly expensive and hard to get into?" Nix's expression bunches into a skeptical frown.

"The stars have aligned, my love. The universe acquiesced to my request, and I got in!"

"And as for cash," Jed continues. "He doesn't need to worry about housing, because he'll be living with me, and he only has one year left of study, so between our two families, we've been able to borrow what we need."

"An interest-free loan." Tobin grins, then flashes a smile at Jed. "I love your parents so much. I've told you that, right?"

"All the time." Jed laughs. "And I love your parents too. I still can't believe they went for it without even blinking an eye."

"They love us and want us to be happy." Tobin leans forward and kisses his boyfriend again while I sit there blinking in shock.

"Wow," I finally choke out, knowing I should be jumping up and celebrating with these two, but I'm also crushed.

They're leaving?

Nix blinks at them, obviously feeling exactly the same way I am.

"Aw, you guys." Tobin's expression crumples. "I know this is unexpected. We're having the best time together here, but this opportunity is just too good to pass up."

I nod, knowing it is, but still struggling to find my voice.

"And we'll keep in touch," Jed promises. "You guys can come visit."

"And we'll get the lease for this place transferred over to you. All you need is a couple more roommates and you can totally cover the rent. We'll even help you find some people before the summer break."

"When are you leaving?" Nix's expression has softened, although she's still frowning.

"After the school year finishes," Jed answers, reaching out to brush his fingers down her arm.

She flinches away from his touch, then slumps back with a sigh. "I'm happy for you guys," she grumbles. "I swear I am. I'm just bummed out that you're leaving. You're like the perfect roommates, and I don't want to replace you with new randos. I want this place to stay the same."

"I know." Tobin gives her a sad pout. "Leaving you two is going to suck."

I swallow and force a smile. "But moving to New York is going to be epic."

"It is." Tobin lets out this excited laugh before lurching forward and kissing Jed yet again.

Jed cups his face, his big hands swamping Tobin's cheeks. I glance away from them, trying to catch Nix's eye, but she's busy on her phone.

Maybe she's texting Ricky, telling him the news.

Maybe she'll invite him to come live here.

Or maybe he'll invite her to move in with him. She said they're in love. It could be an option.

And where does that leave me?

All alone.

Shit.

Jumping off the stool, I leave Jed and Tobs to their kiss-fest and slip into my bedroom. The door clicks shut behind me and I lean against it, staring up at the ceiling with a heavy sigh.

I should not be so gutted about this.

I should be celebrating for both of them. It's such an amazing opportunity.

It's just...

*Just what?*

*You can't use them as crutches.*

I came here to make a big change. To start fresh and move on.

I came here to find love again, and I can't keep standing on the sidelines or hiding behind my room-mates. I have to throw myself out there.

Like I did with that guy tonight.

Pinging up straight, I pull the napkin out of my back pocket.

"Sutton," I whisper, brushing my thumb over his phone number.

Chewing on my bottom lip, I stare down at those terrifying digits and feel my hand start to shake.

"You can do this. Just go out with him. One date. Who knows where it could lead." I try to encourage myself.

Thinking about Nix and her loved-up blissfulness, I start to nod. Yes. I want that again. I'm going to *need* it with Jed and Tobin leaving.

With my breath on hold, I grab my phone and carefully punch in Sutton's number, sending him a text.

*Hey. "Fancy a date sometime?" asks the girl from the bar.*

Is that too bold? Too forward?

I frown, deleting it and trying several different versions before growling in frustration and going back to what I originally had, then adding a few emojis to make the tone playful and fun.

Squeezing my eyes shut, I send it and then wait

against the door, staring down at the screen for those little dots to appear.

I only have to wait a few moments and... there they are.

I let out a relieved sigh, gripping the phone and waiting... waiting...

*Sutton (from the bar): You bet I do. I'm free tomorrow night. Where should we meet?*

Tomorrow night?

That's fast.

Um... okay?

Yes, okay.

Okay!

"I can do this," I remind myself, texting back and suggesting the Mexican place Tobin and Jed took me to a few weeks ago. It was super delicious and had a nice vibe.

*Sutton (from the bar): Perfect. I'll see you there at seven. Looking forward to it.*

I read his text, letting out a shaky laugh while hearting the message.

Am I looking forward to it?

I really don't know.

This is my first date since Atlas died, and I'm freaking terrified!

But I have to do this.

I can't stay on the sidelines watching everyone else get on with their lives. I made a big change by coming to Nolan, and it's time to make another one and go out on a date.

"I can do this," I say yet again, finally stepping away from my bedroom door and inhaling a full breath. "I can do this."

# CHAPTER 6
## TYRELL

"I can't do this!" the girl in front of me wails.

"Would you calm down?" her friend mutters. "It's a coffee order. For fuck's sake, girl, pull yourself together."

"How am I supposed to decide between a mocha latte and a frappé? They both sound like exactly what I need."

"Then get both." Her friend is on her phone and barely paying attention now.

"And turn into some hyper, jittery mess?" the girls squeaks. "You are no help at all."

With a huff, the girl in front of me slips her phone away and turns to eyeball her friend. "It's a coffee order. You should never be this stressed over something so simple. Flip a coin or something. It's not that hard."

With a whimpering sigh, the girl's shoulders deflate, and she stares up at the order board with an exaggerated pout.

Clearing my throat, I give away the fact that I was listening in and softly tell her, "The mocha lattes here are really good. That's what I'd go for."

Spinning with a little gasp, she looks up at me, her surprise morphing into a flirtatious smile.

Oh shit. I should have kept my mouth shut.

"Well, thank you." She brushes her teeth over her bottom lip.

I reply with a polite smile. "You're welcome."

"I'm totally gonna get that now." She places her index finger on my arm. "Because you said I should."

"Okay." I nod, tucking my hand into my pocket so it's out of reach of her long fingernails. Those things are like talons. And they're painted red too, so it looks like she's gone on some killing spree and clawed up a bunch of bad guys.

"You're really sweet, you know that?"

"Aw... nah, I'm just trying to be helpful."

"Well, you are." She giggles.

Her friend has turned to eye me up as well. Shit, I really should have kept my fucking mouth shut!

"The Silent Knight, right?" She wiggles her eyebrows at me.

I cringe, remembering that interview published in the *Nolan U Sports Digest* at the beginning of the football season. Ugh. So painful. The interviewer called me the Silent Knight, like I was some god among my team or some shit. I'm nothing special, and I didn't win that game. *We* won the game. The *entire team* won that game. I didn't want any glory for it, but she labeled me, and that frickin' nickname stuck for way too long.

The guys hassled the shit out of me, and it took months of low growls and cringing frowns before people finally dropped it.

My body tenses at the thought of having to counter that shit with these two.

Thankfully, the line moves forward, and I can point ahead of me and indicate that the girls need to turn around and place their order.

They get distracted with that and I breathe a sigh of relief, pulling out my phone and trying to look busy so they hopefully won't attempt to reengage.

*What are you doing?*

*Aren't you trying to find yourself a girl?*

*What's wrong with the two hotties in front of you?*

I frown at my phone screen, wondering where I should start.

Talon nails?

Indecisive?

Too flirty?

*You are one picky MOFO, you know that?*

"So, the Silent Knight, huh?" An amused voice behind my back has me spinning with a jolt.

Smirking up at me with those sparkling brown eyes of hers is Dani Hill.

She snickers. "You must love that one."

"Hate it with every fiber of my being," I grumble.

She snorts and shakes her head, no doubt thinking that Atlas would have had a field day with it.

"I'm pretty sure they don't." She lifts her chin at the two girls who are still placing their orders. Miss Indecisive is really drawing things out. Now she's stressing over which muffin to get—will it be apple cinnamon or blueberry?

*Seriously?*

I glance back at Dani with an exaggerated frown that has her snickering again.

"So, are you a Java Jeans regular?" I can't help asking, because how has she been in Nolan since January and I haven't bumped into her once?

Although, it's possible my brain wasn't expecting to see her, so we could have passed and not noticed each other.

"I wouldn't say a regular. My roommate owns a kick-ass coffee machine, so I usually make something on that, but I wanted to go for a walk this morning and figured I'd reward myself with a coffee afterward."

My eyes skim down her body before I can stop myself.

Damn, she looks good in yoga pants.

I gaze down at her tiny sneakers and am reminded of those times we'd sit on the floor opposite each other and put the soles of our feet together, waging a war on who could force whose legs to bend.

I let her win more times than I can count, but I'm pretty sure she knew that.

My lips twitch, and the curious smile on her face has me wondering what she's thinking.

"Next," the guy behind the counter calls.

I spin and shuffle forward, quickly placing my standard macchiato order before asking Dani what she's having.

"You don't have to buy me coffee."

"I know." I smile at her. "So, what would you like?"

Biting her lips together, she steps forward, hesitating for a moment, then ordering, "A double-shot latte with coconut milk, please."

The man rings up the order, and I pay with my phone.

"Thank you. I'll owe you one." Dani smiles up at me.

"You don't have to owe me anything." Shuffling away from her, I wait by the counter, awkwardly waving goodbye to the two girls who were flirting with me earlier.

Shit, I really hope they don't keep an eye out for me and try to pounce when I'm walking to class.

Wily and I had that once. And when I say pounce, I mean they *literally* pounced on our asses. Wily thought it was hilarious. Me, not so much. I like my women grounded.

"So, they're not your type, huh?" Dani sidles up beside me.

I shake my head, resisting the urge to say anything offensive. It's Dani, so I can probably say anything. But... I haven't seen her in years, and who knows how much she's changed in that time.

"Do you have a girlfriend or...?" Her eyebrows rise, and I have to shake my head.

"Nah. Still single."

"I take it from the look on your face that you don't love that idea. Have you come through a painful breakup or something?"

I can shake my head with gratitude this time. I've been through lots of little breakups. Nothing too major, because I seem incapable of going out with a girl for more than a few weeks before getting "cold feet" and bailing.

"Just haven't found the right one yet," I mumble. "And

with graduation just around the corner..." I shrug. "Not sure it's a good time, you know?"

"Oh, come on." She nudges me with her elbow. "Any time's a good time to fall in love."

My eyebrows shoot up. "You speaking from experience?"

Her entire face crumples, lines quickly forming on her forehead as her shoulders deflate. "Only ever been in love once."

"Yeah, I know." I brush my hand down her arm, trying to comfort her. "Think you'll ever let yourself go there again?"

"I want to." She nods, her voice cracking. "I'm really trying. I know it's time."

"Yeah," I whisper, dipping my chin and not wanting to look at her. Damn, I can feel her sadness as if it's my own.

I know the pain she's been through. I mean, I experienced a version of it. Atlas was like my other half. Going about my days, knowing he's not on this planet anymore? Yeah, it sucks.

"Ty. 'Sup, man?" Grady walks into view, and I raise my chin at him.

"Hey, man."

"You ordered already?"

"Yeah, I'll be heading off to class in a minute."

"Wait for me. I'll walk with you." Grady does a double take, obviously sensing Dani's curious gaze. "Oh, hey. You work at Offside."

"I do." She smiles and sticks out her hand. "Dani Hill."

"Nice to meet you. I'm Grady." He shakes her hand while pointing at me. "You know our boy, here?"

"Yeah." She nods. "Tyrell and I go way back."

"Nice." He studies her face while obviously trying not to ask a million questions.

"Flash, let's go," Carson barks from his place in the line. "I'm not paying for your ass again."

"Get me a double shot!" Zander calls from the door, holding up two fingers before going back to his phone call.

"See you around, Dani." Grady gives her a light pat on the shoulder before falling into line next to Carson, and I feel obliged to explain who all of these people are.

"Cap." I point to the door. "His real name's Zander. Quarterback. Carson and Grady."

She glances at each one before smiling back at me. "Roommates?"

"Yeah, we live at a house right near Greek Row."

"Nice." She keeps nodding.

"How about you?"

"I'm living with Tobin Evans. Do you remember him? He was my neighbor growing up."

I scour my brain but have to shake my head.

"That's okay. Anyway, I live with him and his boyfriend, Jed, and we have another roomie, Nix. She's a sophomore this year. I don't know if you'll know her, but she's a real pocket rocket, that's for sure." She starts to laugh, and I'm glad she's living with good people.

"Sounds like a cool place to be."

"It is. I love our apartment. It's got a great vibe." Her voice trails off, a sad frown sweeping over her face.

"What is it?"

Her shoulder hitches, her nose wrinkling. "I just found out last night that Tobin and Jed are moving to

New York. Jed's been offered a great job, and Tobin's been accepted to a college in Manhattan, so he's all buzzing. I'm really happy for them both, but I'm kinda sad that things will be changing soon. I feel like I've only just arrived, and I'm not ready to say goodbye to this awesome living situation, you know?"

"Yeah," I murmur, totally getting it. I'm gonna miss Football Frat big-time after I graduate.

Shit, it's just around the corner, and I'm so not ready.

"Here you go, guys." A young woman with a bright smile places our coffees on the counter.

"Thanks," I murmur, passing Dani her cup and wondering when I'm gonna see her again.

I'll probably notice her all the time now that my brain knows she's in Nolan.

But it feels weird to just walk away from her, and I did promise Atlas last night that I'd keep an eye out, right?

Talking to her just now hasn't been soaked in sadness.

If anything, there's been a comfortable nostalgia floating around us. It hasn't been all bad.

"Well, thanks for the coffee." She lifts her take-out cup and looks ready to walk out the door.

"Hey, um…" I pull my phone out of my pocket. "Should we swap numbers? You know, just in case you need anything. I mean, I know you have your roommates and you've been getting on just fine without me. I just… Is your old number still the same? I have you in my contacts list, and I—"

"No, I've changed my number." She holds out her hand, and I hesitate for just a second before unlocking my screen and passing her my phone.

"You'll probably never need to use it, but… you know."

Her lips twitch, her thumb shaking a little as she enters her number. "It's a good idea." Handing the phone back, she pulls hers out from the side pocket of her yoga pants. "Text me so I can have your number too."

I send a lame thumbs-up emoji because I don't know what else to do.

"Perfect." She smiles at her screen, not looking up until just before she turns. "Thanks, Ty."

"Bye, Dani," I whisper to her back, staring after her until my Football Frat brothers surround me, blocking my view of Atlas's girl.

# CHAPTER 7
## DANI

Tyrell bought me coffee.

That was so sweet of him.

To be honest, when I noticed he was standing in front of me this morning, I nearly bailed. I wasn't sure I could handle bumping into him twice in less than twenty-four hours, but then those girls were flirting and he got all shy, and it brought back all these sweet memories of him in high school.

He was *always* being chased by the girls, and he never knew what to do with them. It was hilarious. Atlas and I would watch him squirming. Occasionally, he'd manage to flirt back, and he did date a few girls in high school, but never for long. He'd always find something wrong with them and bail before things got too serious.

I wonder if he's ever had a girlfriend for more than a month or two.

I wonder if I should ask him.

I wonder if I'll ever bump into him again.

*You have his number now. You could call him. Text him. Meet up?*

The thought makes my stomach clench and I blink, focusing back on the guy opposite me.

Yeah, I really should not be letting my mind wander off to Tyrell Territory when I'm on a date with someone else.

Whoops.

Resting my elbow on the table, I prop my chin in my hand and try to focus on Sutton.

He looks really good. I caught an Uber to the restaurant, in case I felt like a drink, and when I arrived, he was waiting outside for me, looking like a cover model in his dark jeans, pale blue Henley shirt, and a brown jacket. His hair is styled, sweeping across his forehead, and I like his blue eyes. They're like *so* blue. Quite stunning, really.

My gaze drops to his lips as he continues talking.

He's been going on for a while now, telling me all about his college experience, what he's studying, what he hopes to do after graduation. He's managed to arrange a summer internship with some investment company, and man, is he proud of himself.

Giving him a weak smile, I nod, trying to focus on what he's saying while my mind starts to wander again.

It's safe to say I'm a little bored. Which is a shame, because this is my first date since Atlas passed away, and I was really hoping for something awesome. But from the moment we sat down, all Sutton has done is talk about himself.

It's like we're in a freaking job interview and he's trying to sell me on all the reasons why I should like him.

*Sorry to tell you, Sutton, but it ain't workin'. You're boring me to tears.*

It's impossible not to think of Atlas as Sutton starts laughing and launches into a new story about how his mother thinks he's going to be a multimillionaire by the age of thirty.

Whoop-de-do.

Atlas never cared too much about money.

He was all about the music.

And me.

Damn, he cared a lot about me.

I will never forget our first date. We were nearly fifteen years old, and he took me out for ice cream. It was all he could afford. He bought us a caramel sundae to share, and we sat opposite each other in a booth. I was so nervous I wasn't sure I could eat a bite, but Atlas started asking me questions. He got me talking, and before I knew it, we were discovering our shared love of music, denim jackets, and fried chicken. I told him all about my family and he opened up about his dad leaving and how horrible it was. His mom wouldn't stop crying, and I couldn't believe how deep and heavy we'd gotten on our first date.

I held his hand, and he rubbed his thumb over my knuckle. Then he looked at me across the table with his glassy eyes... and I knew I was going to love him for the rest of my life.

I'm not feeling that way about Sutton, and it's stealing my appetite.

The chicken enchiladas I ordered arrive and smell delicious, but I'm suddenly not hungry.

All I can think about is ice cream melting down the

side of the bowl, a betrayed boy who'd just lost his father, and the home he was quickly erecting in my heart.

We were pretty much inseparable after that.

He spent hours at my house—he fell in love with my family. He'd come over all the time, Tyrell often trailing after him, if he wasn't at football practice.

We'd sit on my bed, Atlas playing his guitar and me singing along. We'd find harmonies, he'd write lyrics, and I'd imagine a future together. I wanted to see him succeed and had grand plans of becoming his agent or manager or whatever they called it. I'd find him gigs and make sure the world knew just how talented he was.

My heart starts pulsing a dull, aching beat, and I snatch up my cutlery, forcing myself to focus on my food... and whatever Sutton is saying about the stock market.

"People are idiots." He laughs. "They have no idea how to manage money, which is why it's so important that jobs like the one I'm going to secure exist. I'm helping humanity by looking after the funds they have. I'm going to make people rich and myself even richer." He laughs again, and the sound is grating.

I nod and force myself to say, "Sounds like a good plan."

"It is, right? I've got it all mapped out."

I raise my eyebrows, spearing a mouthful of enchilada and adding a dollop of sour cream. "That can be dangerous."

"What?" He looks confused as he scoops rice and beans onto his fork.

"Mapping out your life like that." I shrug. "You never know what's going to happen."

"Yes, I do. I have a plan. I'm sticking to it. I'm in charge of my own destiny."

"Yeah, but... life can sometimes throw you curveballs. I'm not saying you shouldn't have a plan, but you seriously never know what's gonna get you out of the blue. Sometimes you can dream and imagine your future, and the universe will have other ideas."

He chews his Mexican chicken and rice, studying me while he finishes his mouthful. I shift uncomfortably in my seat, wondering why I wanted his number in the first place. This date does not feel right. He's about to say something I'm not going to like.

"I think that's bullshit. Life can try to throw me off course, but I'll just find another way back onto it. I hate it when people use 'the universe' as an excuse for everything, you know? We're our own bosses, and we have to take responsibility for our own actions. I'm not gonna just sit back and let life happen to me. I'm gonna happen to life." He grins, and I don't know what to say.

Part of me wants to spit out the raw, ugly truth.

*Oh yeah, just you wait, buddy. One day, you think you've got it all figured out, and the next thing you know, you're holding your dying boyfriend in your arms.*

But this date is taking a shitty turn, and I don't want to make it worse.

So I just nod and fill my mouth with food so I don't have to say anything.

And Sutton just goes ahead and keeps on talking.

By the time the waiter clears our plates, I know all about his five-year plan and how brilliant his life is going to be.

"Would you like to see the dessert menu?" the waiter asks.

"No thank you," I quickly reply before Sutton can.

He gives me a bemused look, then skims his eyes down my body. "You one of those girls who doesn't eat sugar? My mom's like that. Counts every calorie. It's painful."

"Uh... no." I shake my head. *I just want to wrap up this damn date so I can get out of here!* "I'm just full after my meal."

"But you didn't even finish it."

I give him an awkward smile and pat my stomach. "I have a small appetite."

"Huh." He nods, wiping his mouth with the napkin. "Well, do you want to just grab the check and go, then?"

*Yes!!!*

"Sure." I bob my head, forcing a smile.

Sutton raises his hand, clicking his fingers to get the waiter's attention.

Irritations sizzles through me, and I can't even explain why.

"Check, please." Sutton points at our table, and the waiter nods.

And once again, I'm transported back seven years to that little ice cream parlor in Colorado Springs. To a sweet boy who had to scrape pennies together in order to buy us a sundae. We sat for over two hours in that booth, laughing and talking and drinking water, because we couldn't afford anything more than the ice cream.

He sang me little ditties. It felt like everything I said sparked a song lyric, and I loved every second of it.

Unlike this painful monstrosity.

Seriously.

Why the hell did I ask for Sutton's number?

*Because you didn't realize that he was a self-absorbed money man. You interacted with him for like five minutes.*

"Here you go, sir." The waiter hands the check to Sutton.

"Thank you." He grins up at him, then scans the bill before glancing at me. "So, do you want to split this, or are you paying… you know, since you asked me out."

My lips part, this weird sinking sensation coursing through my body, pulling my stomach down to my knees and lodging my heart in my intestines.

*What the fuck?*

"Uh…" I blink, trying to get my head around this shit. He's just sat there telling me how good he is with his money. How rich he is. How his investments are all doing so well. And he can't even fork out for dinner?

On a first date?

Not to be old-fashioned, but seriously?

I guess I am the kind of girl who wants a little chivalry in her life. The kind of girl who wants to go out with a man who will fucking pay for dinner! Or at least *offer* to pay!

Snatching the check off him, I rise from the table and murmur, "I'll pay."

I should be saying we should split the bill, but I'm so desperate to get out of this that I don't want to take the time to work out the math.

I'll just pay.

I'll use up what's left of this week's paycheck on this shitty date, and then I never have to see Sutton "I'm the king of my own fucking universe" again.

"Did you enjoy your meal?" the lovely lady behind the counter asks as I swipe my debit card.

"The food was delicious, thank you." I smile at her.

Sutton appears behind me, pulling on his jacket and grabbing a mint out of the glass on the counter.

"Enjoy your evening." The lady smiles.

"Thank you," I squeak, heading for the door at a fast clip.

Unfortunately, Sutton catches up to me easily. "So, you just gonna head home now, or did you want to do something else?"

"I think I'm gonna go." I point over my shoulder.

"Where do you live?"

*Like I'm going to tell you!*

I smile at him, knowing I should be thanking him for the date. But I can't. I cannot make those words come out of my mouth!

"You seem in a hurry."

"I…" Giving him an edgy smile, I keep walking backward away from him, needing to create as much distance as possible. "I… just need to get home."

"Okay, well…" He flicks his hand in the air. "I guess I'll see you around?"

"Yeah, maybe." I nod and spin away, riled beyond belief.

He didn't even thank me for dinner.

What a putz!

Clipping down the sidewalk, I wrap my arms around myself, hunching my shoulders against the cool breeze. It's April now, but the wind still has a brisk edge to it at this time of night.

I really shouldn't be walking home by myself in the dark, but I just need a minute.

I'll order an Uber soon... once I'm a good block away from Sutton.

Ugh!

That date was the worst!

Sudden tears blind me, and I stutter to a stop, blinking in surprise.

"I am not going to cry over that asshole!" I growl.

*That's not why you're crying.*

I sniff, blinking at my stupid tears and letting the sorrow I've been holding at bay flood me.

I'm supposed to be moving on with my life—letting Atlas go.

It took so much courage to go on that date, and it was a complete fail!

Swiping a tear off my cheek, I try to swallow past the swelling in my throat. I don't want to cry. I want to be strong. Brave.

But I just miss him so much.

Everything was so easy with Atlas.

*Not always. It got hard in those last couple of years.*

I snap my eyes shut, not wanting to think about those tumultuous times. I just want to focus on the good stuff— our first date, our first kiss, our first time. I want to remember the hours of singing and laughter and play. I want to relive those times we'd lie on my bed, our fingers intertwined as we dreamed about our future together.

We had it all mapped out.

And then he went and died.

I curl in on myself, the ache inside me turning to a

sharp pain that makes me feel like I've been stabbed through the heart.

My knees buckle and I sink down, crouching on the sidewalk in a little ball and no doubt looking ridiculous.

But I can't move right now.

I can barely breathe.

I should call Tobin or Jed. They can come and get me.

*And mop up your tears yet again? Don't put them through that. Besides, they never really get it anyway.*

"Tyrell would," I whisper, staring down at the dirty concrete beneath me before slowly rising back up.

Tyrell would get it.

And I have his number now.

Pulling out my phone, I unlock it and find his name, gazing at the numbers until they start to blur.

*Just call. He won't mind. He'll understand.*

My thumb hovers over the green circle, and I know I'm right.

He's the only one who will get just how damn hard it is to move on from a guy like Atlas.

# CHAPTER 8
## TYRELL

If you'd asked me when I first got to Nolan U if I'd be sitting in the living room of Football Frat watching a nearly three-year-old perform her version of ballet in a pink fairy costume, I would have told you, "You're crazy, man."

But here I am, with my ass stuck in this chair, smiling like this is the cutest damn thing in the world.

Because it is.

She's just started singing too, and her sweet little voice—pitchy and off-key—is hilarious.

Grady starts to quiver beside me, biting his lips together and trying not to laugh out loud as Zoey's voice crescendos into the room.

I have no idea what the words mean. I think she's just making this up on the spot.

She finishes with an enthusiastic twirl that makes her fall over, then jumps up, raising her arms in the air and saying, "Thank you, everybody. Thank you." Then she bows, letting us know it's time to clap.

And we deliver.

Zander and Wily are the loudest of the lot as we cheer on our little girl.

Damn, I'm gonna miss her when I leave, but the ones to feel the biggest hole will be Carson and Grady. Carson complains about living with a toddler, but I glance at his face now, and that adoring way he looks at her... yeah, he's gonna be a wreck when she goes.

We still have no idea where Zander and his little family are gonna end up. The draft can't come fast enough.

"Okay, we're out. Good job, Zoey Bird." Carson raises his thumb, and she waves excitedly while he wraps his arm around Nylah's waist and leads her from the room.

"Time for bed, lil' missy." Zander stands and is rewarded with instant protests from his daughter.

"I'm not tired!"

"Fairies need their sleep." He picks her up. "Especially dancing fairies who can sing as well as you can. If you don't sleep, your body doesn't have time to get its energy back, and then you won't be able to dance and sing at all."

Her eyes bulge, her soft gasp damn adorable as she rests her head on Zander's shoulder. "Zoey sleep now."

"Good idea." Zander rests his cheek on her head, sharing a smile with Sienna before walking out of the room to the converted garage out back.

Sienna jumps up to follow them, and I move to the couch, knowing I should be getting my ass upstairs to study but really not loving that idea.

Finals are mere weeks away, and I should get my ass

in gear, but my brain's foggy after an intense day, and I just don't feel like it.

What I need is the perfect excuse to get out of it, but I doubt I'll get any from this lot.

Wily and Satch are already moving to the dining table for a study session. They've had to start working downstairs because they get too "distracted" in his room, and Satch is worried that Wily won't be prepared enough for his final exams.

"I'm gonna go get the dishes done." Blake stands up.

"Bee, you've been cleaning all day." Grady tries to snag her hand and stop her.

"I know, but you have studying to do, and I don't want to get in your way."

"But—"

"The sooner you get that done, the sooner we can..." She gives him a heated smile, and he bolts off the couch, racing for the stairs while Blake laughs and smacks his ass when he passes her.

Okay, living in Love City is seriously starting to get old.

Rising from the couch with a soft growl, I traipse up to my room and force my tired brain to concentrate on engineering shit. It's an effort, and I end up doing that thing where I review my notes from today's classes in ten-minute bursts before getting distracted or doodling shit on the paper I'm supposed to be writing on.

Thank God my phone rings an hour later to end my misery.

Lifting it out of the charging cradle, I glance at the screen, then do a double take.

It's Dani.

She's calling me.

Why is she calling me?

My gut twists into a pretzel as my thumb hovers over the screen.

*Slide to answer, brah. Slide to answer!*

Clearing my throat, I hesitantly answer the call just before it cuts off. "Hey, Dani. What's up?"

She sniffs, and for a second, I think she's crying. *What the fuck?*

"Dani?"

"Hey, Ty."

Oh shit, she *is* crying!

"Dani? What's wrong?"

"I just…" She sucks in a breath. "I'm sorry to call you like this I… I've just had a really bad date, and I didn't know who else to talk to. It's my first one since Atlas, and it took so much courage to go, you know? And it was… it was a total shit show." Her voice breaks and she starts sniffing again while my stomach pretzel turns into a rock.

"What happened? Was he a sleaze or something? He didn't touch you when you didn't want him to, did he?" Anger fires through me, hot and fast.

"No, he was just… ugh! I can't even. It was a horrible date, and now I'm walking home in the dark and I—"

"What?" I bark, heading for the door. "You're walking in the dark? Where?"

"Um… I can't see the street sign from here, and I still don't know Nolan well enough to tell you. I know I should get an Uber, but…" She sighs. "I needed a minute to gather myself before walking in the door and getting questioned by my roommates. They'll no doubt be desperate to know how it went, and they'll take one look at my face and..." Her soft whimper makes my chest hurt.

"I'm coming to get you." I thunder down the stairs, plucking my keys out of the bowl and shoving my shoes on.

"You good, man?" Wily calls from the dining room.

"Gotta go out" is the only answer I can manage before bolting out the door. "You got me a street name yet?" I say to Dani.

"Ty, you don't have to come get me. I'm sure you have better things to do with your time."

"I'm comin'. I hate the idea of you wandering around at night by yourself."

"I have pepper spray in my bag."

"That's not the point. I'm sure you can defend yourself just fine." I hop into my SUV and start the engine. The phone changes to car audio as I reverse out of the driveway.

From memory, Dani had some definite fight about her. I remember her scrapping with a girl in high school once. We were at a party, and this chick made a play for Atlas, even though she knew the guy was taken. Dani was furious and tried to get her to back off. The girl got handsy, and Dani staked her claim like a freaking ninja.

Atlas just stood there in awe while I waded into the fight and broke the girls apart before someone lost a chunk of hair. Girls fight mean. They don't seem to have the same unspoken rules as guys do. They just go for it.

Dani came away with scratches on her face, and the other girl was sporting a bloody nose and a fat lip.

Now *that* was a shit show.

I'm really curious to find out what tonight's shit show

looked like. It better not have been anything like that, because if that asshole laid a hand on her, he's gonna have to pay the price.

"I've just reached the corner of Tenth and Cedar," Dani cuts into my thoughts. "Do you know where that is?"

"Yeah." I turn left from my street and head her way, probably going a little too fast, but there's this urgency to reach her quickly.

She's crying.

It's dark.

She's all alone.

*I'll take care of her, Atlas. I promise.*

She sniffs again and I cringe, hating that she's so upset.

"So... he wasn't sleazy. I'm hoping like hell he wasn't handsy."

"No." Dani calms my nerves. "He didn't even kiss me goodbye. Not that I would have wanted him to." She makes a noise, and I can picture her shuddering. "He was just... Look, some girls might like having dinner with a guy who talks nonstop about himself and how great he is, but it's definitely not my thing. We didn't have a conversation. He spoke, and I was forced to listen. And then..." She huffs.

"Then what?"

"He didn't offer to pay for dinner. He handed me the check and asked if I wanted to split it or if I was going to pay the whole thing since I asked him out."

"Aw, hell no," I bark. "He did not fuckin' do that."

"He did."

"Please tell me you split it."

"No," she whines. "I paid the whole thing because I was so pissed off, and I just wanted to get out of there and away from his clueless ass. I'm not being old-fashioned expecting the guy to pay, am I?"

"No. He should have at least offered, and then it's up to *you* to say if you want to split or pay or whatever."

She lets out a sigh, and I press the accelerator a little harder. "It was made so much worse by the fact that he'd spent the whole dinner talking about investments and how well he was already doing and how he's gonna be a multimillionaire by the age of thirty." She scoffs. "Then he doesn't offer to pay for dinner? He's probably got way more money than I do."

"Yeah, because he makes the girls he dates pay for his fucking meals!" I growl, slowing to negotiate the corner, then picking up my pace again and gunning it to Dani.

I arrive less than a minute later, my heart hurting the second I spot her.

She looks so small and vulnerable, standing on the corner with her arm wrapped around her waist and the phone pressed to her ear.

The second she hears me coming, she spins and hangs up the call.

"Hey, Ty." She gives me a watery smile as she slips into the car.

"Hey." I rest my hand lightly on the wheel, taking her in with a gentle smile. "You okay?"

"I feel better already." She sucks in a breath. "Thanks for coming to get me."

"Anytime. Where do you want to go now?"

"Can we just sit for a minute? Then I'll get you to take me home."

"Sure thing." I cut the engine and settle back in my seat, angling my body to face her.

She brushes a tear off her cheek before digging a tissue out of her purse and blowing her nose. I let silence reign for a minute while she cleans herself up, dabbing her eyes and cheeks before finally looking at me.

"Am I pathetic?"

"No." I shake my head. "You're brave. For putting yourself out there. First date since Atlas. That's huge."

And surprising, to be honest. Atlas died years ago now. I figured she would have found her feet and moved on.

But she got stuck.

And now she's trying to get out... and her first date was shit.

Damn, that's so fucking unfair.

"I really wanted it to go well." Her voice is croaky. "He seemed so nice when I met him at the bar last night. My expectations were obviously way too high. I just wanted this to be easy. But it's not." She shakes her head, her eyebrows wrinkling. "It's not gonna be easy at all, and it's tempting to crawl back into my cave and forget it."

I brush my fingers lightly down her arm, trying to comfort her but having no idea what to say.

"But if I do that... I'm gonna die an old, lonely cat lady."

A soft snicker punches out of me. "That is not gonna happen to you. You don't even like cats, do you?"

She sniffs and nods, her eyes glassing over as she lets out a whimpering laugh. "Yeah. I mean, they're not all bad, but cats can be assholes."

I nod because they can, although my Rook is an

angel, if you ask me. If you ask my mom, she's a demon from the underworld.

"I guess I'll die surrounded by parakeets or something. I don't know." Dani's voice cracks.

"That's not gonna happen to you," I repeat. "You'll meet someone, you'll fall in love again, and it'll be great."

"You don't sound like you believe that," she murmurs.

I lean forward, hoping my expression is emphatic enough. "I do. You're a great girl, Dani. Any guy would be lucky to have you."

Her smile is sad, her brown gaze aching. "I only ever wanted him. I mean, I wasn't even looking. I was fourteen... nearly fifteen. He came into my orbit and took over my entire world. And that's exactly the way I wanted it. I loved him. I loved him with all I had." She lets out a shuddering breath. "And then he was gone, and for the last couple of years, I've just been floating out in space, you know? Tethered to nothing. No one. And..." She shakes her head. "I don't want to live like that anymore. I miss him." Pressing the back of her hand to her mouth, she fights tears for a minute, and I just sit there, once again having no idea what to say.

Shit.

I wish I was better at this stuff.

Atlas always had the words. He was the mouth, and I was the silent partner, the guy who had his back.

*Until you didn't.*

I snap my eyes shut, hating myself. Hating that I wasn't there to stop it. Hating that it's hurt way more than Atlas. Dani is suffering too, and I can't help but take the blame.

"It's more than that, though," she whispers, and my

eyes pop open. "I miss being someone's partner. I miss having a special person. A man who makes me feel like I'm the most important. Like I'm their one and they're mine and..." She threads her fingers together, shaking her hands in the air. "I want that again. I pine for it... but I have no idea how to find it."

*Aw man, me too.*

Although there's no *again* for me. I've never found a girl to make me feel all of those things. But I want it. Seeing all my friends get it has only intensified this feeling for me.

"Am I being a romantic sap or—"

"No, of course not." I wrap my hand around her inter-laced fingers and give them a soft squeeze. "I want that too. I get it. And it's not just about romance. It's about partnership. There's nothing wrong with wanting that."

She looks right at me, the streetlight coming in through the windshield making her face glow. "So, how do I get it? How do I find that again?"

I sigh, about to tell her that I have no idea... until a thought hits me.

Holding my breath while I quickly run it through in my head, I finally let out a rush of air, then tell her, "I'll help you."

"What do you mean?"

"I'm gonna find you the perfect guy." I grin. "I've been here for four years. I know plenty of people in Nolan, and all of them are better than that jackass you went out with tonight. Let me hook you up with a decent date."

She gapes at me for a second, then starts to laugh. "Are you serious?"

"Yeah." I nod. "Let me have a think about who's worthy of a date with you, and I'll set something up."

Her expression crumples into an uncertain frown.

I grin at her. "Come on, Dee. You trust me, right?"

"Yes." She nods without hesitation, then bites her lips together.

"What?"

"I don't know. It's just... scary? Or... something."

"Hey." Leaning toward her, I rest my fingers lightly on her shoulder. "It's gonna be okay. I won't set you up with anyone who's gonna treat you bad, I swear."

"I know." She nods. "I know you'd never do that to me."

I smile at her, shifting away and nestling my shoulder into my seat, trying to think of who I could ask.

There are plenty of guys on the team who are pretty decent. But are any of them good enough for Dani?

# CHAPTER 9
## DANI

Tyrell drives me back to my apartment, Whitney Houston playing softly in the background. Oh, that's right. I remember now. Tyrell's mom adores Whitney Houston... and he does too. Atlas used to hassle the shit out of him for that, but Tyrell refused to say one bad thing about the woman with the best damn voice in the world.

It is pretty good.

I go quiet so I can listen. He's got it playing softly, unlike Atlas, who blasted everything. He had one volume for his car stereo—maximum. You could hear him coming from three blocks away.

Biting my lips together, I let myself remember the way my eardrums used to ring on a permanent basis. But damn, I loved driving around with Atlas and singing. I didn't even care what the music was—it was always punk rock of some kind.

I hardly ever listen to music now.

I don't even know what I like anymore. Atlas pulled me into *his* music sphere, and I didn't mind. Punk rock's cool. I love that kind of music. But is it the only music I like?

Because I'm kind of digging on this Whitney number right now—"Higher Love."

Tyrell is bobbing his head to the beat, his eyes darting my way when he senses me gazing at him.

"You good?"

"Yeah." I smile. "Thanks again for coming to get me."

"Of course. Anytime."

And I know he means it, which is why I invite him up after he's found a parking space a few down from my apartment building.

He hesitates for a second before unbuckling his seat belt. "Sure. I'll walk you up."

I give him an edgy smile, wondering why the hell I want him to meet my roommates.

*What are you doing?*

*Why did you invite this boy up?*

*Girl, you're crazy.*

Ugh, Jed was a swooning mess, drooling over him at the bar, and Tobin will be even worse. Even though they're completely in love with each other, they still check out hot guys all the time—and there is no denying that Tyrell Jackson is a hottie.

He's so tall and obviously strong. I can feel his overwhelming presence behind me as we take the stairs.

Why I'm taking the stairs I don't know. It's just a habit now, I guess.

Tyrell doesn't seem to mind, but the guy has always been unflappable, so I guess it makes sense.

He just quietly gets on and does. No complaining. No fuss.

Atlas used to love that about him. In all the chaos he threw himself into, he always knew that Tyrell would have his back. He could be reckless, because Tyrell would always be there to save him.

Until he wasn't.

Until I wasn't.

I wince, grateful Tyrell can't see my face as I try to ward off the guilt and regret that lives permanently inside me. I never should have stormed away after our fight. I should have stuck around and made sure he didn't take those drugs.

"So, the elevator broken or something?" Tyrell eventually asks me as we hit the last flight of stairs.

"No." I laugh and smile over my shoulder. "Jed and Tobin always take the stairs, so I got into the habit, and now I don't even think to use the elevator."

"It's a good habit," he murmurs.

"Thanks." I pull my key out of my purse and squeeze it in my fingers.

My heart has started racing, and it's not the standard *I've been exercising* racing. More of a nervous racing, my body tensing as I slip the key into the lock and open the door.

Tobin and Jed are on the couch, watching *Heartstopper*. They are so addicted to that show. I have no idea how many times they've watched it, but they're suckers for high school romance.

I get it. High school romance is the best. I lived the perfect love story in high school, and what I wouldn't give to turn back time and do it all over again.

"Hey, guys." I tuck my keys away before placing my purse down on the kitchen counter. "How's it going?"

"Yeah, good, we're just—" Tobin's voice cuts off as he glances back at me, then spots Tyrell in the doorway. His lips part, his eyes bulging in awe and... yep, there's the appreciation. "Hi there." He greets Tyrell in a breathy voice, following it up with a giggle before spinning to have a silent conversation with Jed.

Jed nods, his eyes rounding, and I can almost hear him saying, *"I know! I told you. Didn't I tell you!"*

Clearing his throat, Tobin spins back around, resting his forearm on the back of the couch before perching his chin on top of it. "I'm Tobin. And you are...?" He eyes Tyrell up like he's a tasty treat, and I internally groan.

"Uh... hi." Tyrell's voice is so deep compared to Tobin's. He rumbles out an awkward hello, waving at the couple on the couch who look about ready to ask him if he's open to a threesome.

Seriously!

Stepping in front of Tyrell, I try to create a protective shield, which is kind of a joke considering how tall he is. The top of my head reaches to only just above his shoulders, and he's such a broad, imposing unit that I basically fit within his outline. But I can still hide the middle part, right?

"So, I thought Dani was out with Sutton tonight." Jed taps his boyfriend on the shoulder. "Why is she coming home with Tyrell here?"

I roll my eyes, dipping my chin and muttering to the floor, "Sutton was a bust."

"What?" Jed pops off the couch, straightening his shirt as he moves around to me. "What happened?"

I'm in his arms before I know what's happening, and Tobin vaults off the couch too. I'm soon cocooned between my roommates as they ask me multiple questions about the date, and I mumble out my answers.

"Ugh. What a putz!" Tobin's the first to break away from the hug, resting his hands on his hips and frowning at Jed. "Why did you recommend him?"

"I didn't!" Jed tries to defend himself. "She asked me if he was safe, and I said yes. I didn't know he was an arrogant douchebag. Of course I wouldn't have told her to go for it if I'd known that." He rolls his eyes, letting me go, but still hovering nearby. "Girl, why didn't you call us?"

"I don't know," I grumble, crossing my arms and glancing at Tyrell.

He gives me one of his gentle smiles, and I immediately do know.

I called him because he's Black Jack. The quiet guy Atlas could always rely on. The one who came when he called, who listened when he ranted, who calmed things down when tensions got too high.

"Well, I'm... gonna take off." He points over his shoulder.

"Are you sure?" Tobin's sweet face drops with disappointment. "You're welcome to stay. We're probably going to crack open the ice cream and have sympathy sundaes."

Tyrell grins. "In that case, I should definitely go." He pats his rock-hard abs. "Ice cream's a weakness for me. Better leave and avoid temptation."

I smile back at him when he catches my eye, then mouth, "Thank you."

"Anytime." His deep voice is husky. "I'll text you, okay?"

"Okay." I nod, this warm sensation buzzing through

my chest as I wave goodbye and watch him walk out the door.

The second he's gone, both Jed and Tobin start swooning, gushing about how hot he is and how sweet it was that he dropped everything to come get me when I called.

"I don't even know why I called," I say, opening the container of ice cream Tobin hands me.

Cookie dough with caramel ripple. Yum!

I'm not sure I'm ready to admit that I didn't think they'd understand. I don't want to hurt their feelings.

Pulling me to the couch, which is shaped like an L, I'm shoved into the corner pocket while they sit on either side of me and make me rehash the date. I don't spare a detail while they make all the supportive, appropriate noises only true friends can make.

"What an asshat," Jed grumbles. "I'm spitting in his next beer."

Tobin grins. "I love you, baby."

Jed's lips twitch, and they share a gooey smile while I focus on the ice cream. I've eaten half the container already and am starting to feel sick, but I can't seem to stop scooping out little spoonfuls to suck on.

"But let's stop talking about Spunktrumpet Sutton and start—"

"Spunktrumpet?" I laugh. "What does that even mean?"

Tobin smirks. "It's a UK term that I recently discovered, and it means an obnoxious person who can't *shut up*. Hence the trumpet part."

Jed tips his head back, howling with laughter. "Babe, how did you discover that word?"

"I was getting over using fuck nugget as an insult and wanted some fresh material. I love that this one is UK-based, because it makes it rare here, and I can be the sole provider of this insult in Nolan, Colorado." He lifts his chin, looking all triumphant. "It makes me special."

Jed leans across me, grabbing Tobin's face and giving him a deep kiss. "You are special, baby."

Tobin blushes, and I'm about two seconds away from leaving them to it when Jed senses me squirming between them and pings back like he wasn't about to devour his boyfriend right on top of me.

"So, Tyrell's offered to find you the perfect man, huh?"

"Apparently," I mumble, passing my ice cream to Tobin before I start puking up creamy lava. Seriously, I've eaten way too much, and my stomach is hating on me right now.

"I think *he's* the perfect man," Tobin murmurs, placing the ice cream on the coffee table before glancing at Jed. "For Dani. Don't you think? The perfect man for our girl, here?"

"Hells yeah. I said that last night, but she didn't want to hear it." He points a thumb at me like I'm a crazy person.

I shake my head while Tobin bulges his eyes at me. "Why aren't you into it? He's hot, obviously so kind, so why? Why, Dani Hill? Why?"

It's impossible not to laugh at his exasperation, and I lightly palm his face, turning it away from me. "Stop it. I'm not gonna go out with Atlas's best friend. That is too weird. Besides, it's... Tyrell. I mean, I've never looked at him that way. He's just... That will never be an option, okay? He may be good-looking and sweet, but there's...

It's not like that between us. Never has been. Never will be."

Resting my hand on Tobin's shoulder, I use him to pull myself out of the corner and walk around my roommate.

"I'm gonna take a long, hot shower. Try to wash this night off me and then catch myself some sleep." I walk for the bathroom, calling over my shoulder, "Thanks for the ice cream, roomies."

"You're welcome!" Jed replies.

"Still think you're wrong about the Ty-Man!" Tobin hassles me.

I shake my head, ignoring his comment, because seriously...

Tyrell and me?

Yeah, that can never be a thing.

# CHAPTER 10
## TYRELL

I drive back to Football Frat, my mind running through a list of guys I know and wondering which ones will be a good fit for Dani.

Her next date needs to be perfect. He might not be *the guy*, but she needs to walk away with a smile on her face and the belief that moving on is possible.

Shit, the look on her face. Those tears. They sliced me up. Atlas would have been torn to shreds to see her that way. I've got to help her out. For his sake. For hers.

"Would you have taken those pills if you knew, man? If you could have seen into the future? Seen the way she'd suffer?"

I cling to the hope that he wouldn't have. He was drunk, not thinking straight, being reckless, and no one had been around to check him.

*Except he'd been at a crowded party, surrounded by people who supposedly admired him.*

"Fuck." I run a hand through my hair, desperate to

shake off these blues and second-guessing my decision to help Dani.

Being around her is unearthing all this past pain, and I can feel myself getting sucked back into that blackness I had to fight so hard to get out of. There was this constant cloud hanging over me—dark and brooding. It suffocated me, made me want to hide away and...

I pause at the intersection, giving the other car the right of way and noticing that it's Carson and Nylah. Following them home, I park right behind Zander's SUV, which Carson obviously borrowed. He really needs to get himself some wheels, especially since the three people he's been borrowing from will be leaving after graduation.

Apparently, his mom has offered to buy him a new bike, but he wants to get some old thing and do it up. He loves mechanics, so it's gonna be his summer project. I hope it all works out for him. I'm a little worried that I'm not going to be here next year to keep a quiet eye on him. But he has Nylah now, and she's calmed him down a lot. He's not the wild, angry bad boy he was when I first moved into Football Frat.

He'll also have Grady to keep him in check... and whoever else they decide to let move in. I hope they find good guys. I'm assuming they'll ask their teammates. I think Lincoln would work... or maybe Johnson or Rheems. Knowing them, they'll go for guys on the offensive team. That's worked well for us.

Opening the door, I jump out and raise my chin in greeting to Nylah, who's grinning at me. "Where've you been?" she asks.

"Just helping out a friend." I shove my hands into my pockets and follow them across the grass and up the front steps.

"Is he or she okay?" she asks when we reach the front door. "Are we talking moving furniture around help? Or studying help? Or—"

"Kitten, stop being so damn nosy," Carson grumbles as he kicks off his boots.

Nylah laughs. "I'm just asking."

I grin down at her. "She had a bad date. I just gave her a ride home."

"Oh no. How bad? Like dire or scary or the kind you have to rant about?"

"The ranting kind."

"Yikes." She makes a face at me while Carson pulls her into the living room.

Everyone's in there, watching a replay of *The Big Bang Theory*. Grady and Blake are cracking up while Sienna grins at the screen and Zander plays on his phone. He's addicted to some block game.

I pull a chair in from the dining room and watch the last five minutes of the episode while Nylah and Carson get comfy on the beanbag near my feet.

"So, you want to do another episode?" Wily picks up the remote, aiming it at the screen, and I decide to put my foot in it.

"Actually, guys. I need your help."

*What are you doing? Why are you involving them?*

I have no idea, but the TV goes off immediately, and soon every eye in the room is directed at me. Even Zander slips his phone away, and my mouth goes instantly dry.

*Damn, boy, you're a fool.*

"Uh..." I clear my throat, scratching the back of my head and shifting uncomfortably on this chair, which suddenly feels too small. "Well, I... I have this friend, and she just had a really shitty date, so I offered to find a nice guy for her to go out with. She's only just getting back on the horse, you know? And she really needs a good experience."

"Why don't you just take her out?" Grady asks.

"Uh... no."

"Why not?" Blake shifts on the couch, stretching her legs across Grady's lap. Her socked feet end up against Satch's thigh, but Wily's girlfriend doesn't seem to mind. She's too busy looking at me with a sweet smile, like she knows what I'm about to say.

"Well, she's... she used to go out with my best friend. They were endgame, and I can't step on that. Even though he's passed away now, it feels wrong to... entertain that idea. There are rules. A bro code, you know?"

All eyes turn to Grady, and he tips his head back with a groan.

Wily snickers, reaching around Satch to lightly punch his arm. "You getting it now?"

"I got it before," Grady grumbles. "Why do you think I resisted her for so long? It's not like I just dove right in. I fought against this for—"

"Yeah, yeah, we get it," Carson cuts the argument short. "We don't need to keep rehashing that shit. Wily doesn't want to admit it, but he's actually fine with you dating his sister."

"I never said that," Wily growls.

"The fact that he's not breathing through a tube is

proof enough, dude." Carson smirks at the big, blond guard who is trying and failing to maintain his glare.

Wily's lips twitch before he finally gives in to his grin and throws all the attention back on me. "So, you need to find this girl a guy. Any ideas?"

"Yeah, maybe." I scrub a hand over my mouth. "But I don't know if any of them are good enough."

"Who's on the list so far?" Zander asks.

"I was thinking maybe Lincoln. He's single, right?"

"No way," Carson barks. "He's friends with Fleischer. That automatically makes him an asshole."

"He *tolerates* Fleischer." Zander raises his eyebrows. "There's a big difference."

"Not in my book," Carson clips. "Think of someone else."

"Well, there's a guy in my anthropology class who could be a contender," Nylah pipes up. "He's really funny and smart, easy to talk to. And he has these amazing green eyes that are just—"

"Hey!" Carson snaps. "What the fuck?"

Nylah whips a look at him. "What?" She takes one look at his face and starts to laugh. "Aw, baby. Don't be jealous. I only have eyes for you."

"Doesn't sound like it." He scowls. "Green eyes, my ass. What's so great about green eyes anyway?"

Nylah keeps giggling, touching Carson's cheek and forcing him to face her. "I'm trying to talk him up for Dani, not me."

He's still looking kind of salty as she presses her mouth to his. It takes a moment, but he finally relents, giving in to her sweet affection with a soft growl, running his hand behind her neck and kissing her deeply.

I look away, then hear her softly mumble, "Love you, caveman."

Rolling my eyes, I look around the room and try to ignore that soft surge of jealousy rising through me. I don't want to feel that way about any couple in this room.

But damn, it'd be nice to have a girl sitting on my lap, kissing me and telling me I'm her man.

*Stop it. Just focus on Dani and finding her a guy.*

Pulling out my phone, I open up a fresh Note and ignore the fact that Nylah and Carson are still making out.

"What's his name?" I ask her, nudging the beanbag with my toe.

"Oh, um..." Nylah turns to face me while Carson presses a kiss to her neck. "Andy. But I can't remember his last name. I can find out his contact details for you tomorrow, though. We have a class together in the morning."

"Cool." I jot down *Andy (Nylah's anthropology class)*. "Text me when you get his deets."

A soft growl rumbles in Carson's throat, and I look away from his frown while Nylah starts to giggle again.

"Any other ideas?" I ask the room.

There's a beat of silence before Satch speaks up. "There's a really sweet guy in my study group. Super friendly and nice. He's a tutor like me, and he's great at helping people."

"What kind of nice?" Sienna asks. "Ned Flanders or Keanu Reeves?"

Satch's nose wrinkles as she thinks, her teeth sinking into her bottom lip before she admits, "Yeah, he'd definitely say 'Okily-dokily.'"

Carson and Nylah snicker while Grady frowns. "What? Who's Ned Flanders?"

Blake pings away from him like she can't believe he just said that. "From *The Simpsons*. You know, the yellow guys... Homer, Bart, Lisa..." She tips her head, her face crumpling with confusion at Grady's blank expression. "Really? Not even a meme? Come on."

He shrugs, and she pulls out her phone to show him while I ask Satch the guy's name.

"Paul Polaski." She glances up at Wily. "Can you please pass my phone, babe?"

"You have his number?" Wily frowns, reaching for her device.

"He's in my study group. I kind of have to have it."

Wily nods, handing it over, then wrapping his arm around her shoulders while Satch pulls up the number and reads it out to me.

"You think he'd be interested in taking out someone like Dani?" I ask.

"Well, I don't really know her, so I'm not sure what the personality match would be, but Paul's really kind. Even if it wasn't a good fit, he'd still give her a nice evening out, you know?"

"Oh yeah, I have seen these memes before." Grady nods. "And which one's Ned Flanders?"

Blake giggles and finds a clip of him. We all sit there while Grady watches Ned pop up from behind a hedge to greet Homer. "Hi-diddly-ho, neighborino!"

Grady winces while Blake cracks up laughing. "Yeah, that's way too friendly."

I frown down at the digits on my phone, suddenly unsure.

"He is really sweet, though." Satch tries to stand up for her study buddy. "And he wouldn't treat her like crap. Maybe she's into super friendly."

She looks back at me, and I wish I could give her a swift answer, but I'm not sure.

I know the Dani from high school. She's no doubt changed a lot since then.

But if she's looking for a guy like Atlas, a Ned Flanders dude is not gonna work.

"You said you wanted to ease her back into dating." Wily shrugs. "Maybe a super-friendly guy is exactly what she needs. It'll take any romantic pressure off."

"And he'll definitely listen to her and not talk about himself the whole time. I don't think there's an arrogant bone in Paul's body," Satch adds.

"Okay." I nod, sighing as I rest back in my chair. "Well, do you want to see if he can meet up for coffee or something in the morning and we can find out if he's interested?"

"You want to screen the guy first?" Zander grins at me.

"Hell yeah, I do. I'm not recommending someone I haven't even met."

"Good call." Sienna nods. "I'm kind of curious to meet him now too. Can we all go?"

Satch giggles and pauses texting to cringe at Sienna. "That poor man. No, you are not doing that to him. Sitting down with a bunch of massive, intimidating football players and a crew of curious women? I will not put him through that. It's gonna be Tyrell and me only."

Sienna gives her a disappointed pout, then points at Satch. "I want full deets afterward, though. Okay?"

"Yes, ma'am." Satch gives her a mock salute, then

finishes her text while I start to worry if this is the worst idea I've ever come up with.

Seriously, what was I thinking?

Telling Dani I'd find her Mr. Right? I must be out of my damn mind.

# CHAPTER 11
## DANI

"No way, that's crazy!" Charli argues, lightly slapping Nix with the back of her hand. "Girl, *estás loca*!" She rattles off a few more things in Spanish that I don't understand, and Nix rolls her eyes.

Lunches with Nix and her college buddies are always entertaining, that's for sure. We're currently sitting at a table in the sunshine while Nix bickers with Charli—her best friend since freshman year—about Charli's brother, Darian, currently a junior on the Nolan U Cougars basketball team.

"I'm *telling* you. It happened."

"I don't believe you." Charli shakes her head, and I glance at Jolie, who got roped into this friend group at the end of last year. She's sitting across from me, stifling a giggle with her hand. "My brother may be a womanizing pig sometimes, but he's not a full-blown asshole."

Nix scoffs. "A womanizing pig is the *definition* of an asshole."

"He can be sweet sometimes," Jolie murmurs. "He was

really nice to Nylah that night. Do you remember? When he took her to the winter dance?"

"Okay, fine. So he lost his head for one night and behaved like a decent human being, but for the other 364 days of the year, he is all pig with no redeeming qualities."

Charli can't help a short laugh. "Why are you so hard on him?"

"Because he told me I had a monobrow, then attacked me with a pair of tweezers."

"He was joking." Charli snorts. "To be honest, he was probably just using it as an excuse to touch you or something. That boy thinks you're hot."

"That boy can't stand me either," Nix bites back. "And as if I would ever let him put one of those dirty little fingers on me."

Now Charli's the one rolling her eyes. "You know his eyebrow has never grown back the same."

Nix raises her chin, sniffing the air imperiously. "Serves him right for trying to pluck mine."

"Yeah, but did you have to shave the entire thing off?"

"I would have shaved both of them if he hadn't woken up."

Jolie giggles. "And found you straddling him. He must have thought he'd woken up in heaven."

"Until he figured out what she did, and all hell broke loose." Charli winces.

Nix puffs out her chest with a triumphant grin. "I mean, I know he's told me I'm not allowed to come within three feet of him again, but I swear it was worth it."

I grin, glancing around the table and almost wishing I was part of this shared history. Nix and Charli are both sophomores now, and Jolie came along when she started dating one of Charli's roommates. He plays basketball too, and I think his name is... Ben? That sounds right.

A lot of names get thrown around when I meet up with these girls, and it's hard to keep track of them all.

All I do know is that Nix hates Charli's brother, which is a shame, because Charli and Darian are obviously tight. It must be really awkward for Charli being caught in the middle like that. Though now that Nix is all loved-up with a new boyfriend, she's not hanging out with Charli as much, so I think it's relieved some of the tension.

Darian obviously doesn't hold any warm feelings toward Nix either, and I can only imagine the intensity of their angst if they ever cross paths.

"Anyway, let's talk about something else." Charli picks up the other half of her chicken salad wrap and glances at me. "Heard your date bombed last night."

My mouth pops open, and I throw Nix an accusing frown.

The little pixie raises her hands but doesn't actually look that apologetic. "I'm sorry. She asked, and I spilled."

"Why did you even tell her I was going out in the first place?"

"She's my bestie." Nix reaches across the table and grabs Charli's wrist. "I tell her everything."

"She does." Charli nods, talking with her mouth full. "And she loves to spill the tea on her roommates, so... watch out."

I narrow my eyes at Nix, who once again tries to justify her gossipy ways. "In fairness, your tea hasn't been all that tasty until last night, so I mostly talk about Tobs and Jeddy."

"I'm sure they would love to hear that."

"Oh, they know." Nix flicks her fingers through the air. "They don't mind. And Charli's super happy for them over the whole New York thing."

"It sounds amazing." Jolie's eyes bulge. "Moving to the big city like that. Wow." Her smile is pure excitement.

"See?" Nix points across the table. "I make people smile with my awesome news. Look how happy our Jo-Jo is, and she's not even the one going."

"Maybe one day." Jolie grins. "Living in an apartment in Manhattan, maybe working for some high-flying paper or magazine company. Ben could play for the Knicks. It'd be amazing."

Charli smiles at her. "Girl, you got it all planned. I'm vibing off this big-time. Just make sure you have a spare room in your apartment so I can come visit."

"And me!" Nix raises her hand, and I can't help teasing her.

"She can fly in on her fairy wings." I laugh, knowing that's exactly what Tobin would say.

Nix gives me a playful growl and lightly pinches my arm.

I grab her hand and laugh at her... until my phone buzzes with a text.

Flipping it over, I check the screen and can't help an audible gasp.

"What is it?" Charli wipes her mouth with a paper napkin.

"Is everything okay?" Jolie leans forward, her blue eyes bright with concern.

"Uh... yeah. It's just... um..." Huffing out a nervous breath, I unlock my screen and read the message again. "Tyrell said he's found me a guy to go out with. Am I keen?"

"Really? Did he send a picture?" Jolie holds out her hand for the phone.

"No." I shake my head while Charli frowns at her friend.

"Why would she need to see a picture? Looks shouldn't matter. What's he like as a *person*?"

I shrug, reading the next text. "Tyrell says he's a super-friendly, nice guy who is a tutor... and he's in Elizabeth Satchwell's study group." My nose wrinkles. "Do any of you guys know Elizabeth Satchwell?"

"Oh yeah. She's a sweetheart." Jolie bobs her head. "She's dating Wily Wilson, who lives at Football Frat along with my roommate's boyfriend, Carson."

"Okay." My forehead wrinkles. "So, do you think we can trust her opinion?"

Jolie keeps nodding as Nix reminds me, "You trust Tyrell. You told me that this morning, and if you trust him, then you have to believe that he wouldn't set you up with a douchey guy."

"She's right." Charli balls the napkin in her fist and shoots for the trash can on the edge of the courtyard. It goes in perfectly. "I don't really know Tyrell, but he's pretty respected at this school. You can trust him."

"Yeah, I know." I nod, a smile breaking over my face as another text comes through.

.  .  .

*Black Jack: If you want, I can sit at another table in the restaurant. I've got your back, Dee. Always.*

"What?" Nix nudges me. "Why're you smiling?"

"He said he'll sit at another table. Keep an eye on me throughout the date. If I want him too."

"Awwww," Jolie gushes. "That is so sweet and protective."

"Ew. Or totally creepy." Nix's face wrinkles in disgust. "Stalker vibes!"

"No, it's not." Charli laughs at her friend. "It'll be like having a bodyguard." She starts jumping in her seat, getting all excited. "You'll be like a celebrity."

I hiss and rub my forehead. "I don't know, you guys. Do I even want to do this?"

"Yes," Nix says emphatically. "You want to put yourself out there again. You know you do. And sure, it's scary, but if you want to avoid the whole gray hair, parakeet situation you were telling me about this morning, then you need to say yes to that text. Here." Grabbing the phone before I can stop her, Nix replies for me.

I cringe but don't try snatching the phone back.

"There you go." She grins, passing my device back. I check the screen to make sure she hasn't been too embarrassing.

*Me: Thanks, Ty. That's so sweet of you. Okay, I'll do it. Let me know the details.*

. . .

He responds before I even set my phone back down, and my insides sizzle. "The guy's name is Paul, and he's free on Saturday." I glance up at my tablemates. "Should I do it?"

"Yes!" all three girls say in unison.

"But make it a lunch." Charli points at me. "Lunches seem more low pressure."

"True." Jolie nods, and then her phone alarm starts beeping. "Grrr. I have to get to my next class. But say yes to the offer of him watching over you. It's not creepy, it's sweet." She gives Nix a pointed look.

Nix pokes out her tongue in disgust, then starts grinning at me. "I guess it is a sweet offer. If things go bad, he can step in or call you with an 'emergency' of some kind." Her air quotes are cute, and I smile at her, picking up my phone again.

*Me: And thanks for the offer of watching out for me, Black Jack. I'll take you up on that too. Let Paul know I'm free for lunch on Saturday. I have an evening shift at Offside, so it's the only meal I can do. It's weird to go on a breakfast date, right?*

*Black Jack: Lunch it is. I'll send you the time and place soon.*

I send him back a thumbs-up emoji because I'm not sure how else to respond.

My nerves have suddenly gone into chaos, my jittery stomach making it impossible to finish my nachos.

"It could be great," Nix murmurs, her smile kind.

"It's going to be amazing." Jolie tinkles her fingers through the air as she walks away. "Catch you guys later!"

"Byeee," Charli calls after her, then checks the time. "I should head off in a minute too. I've got a study session in the library."

Nix snorts. "You mean a make-out session with your *boyfriend.*"

Charli doesn't say anything, but her bronze cheeks heat with color as she ignores the comment and glances at her. "You walking that way?"

"No, I'm going to enjoy this sunshine for a bit longer. I'll see you later."

"'Kay. *Chao, chicas.*"

"Bye." I wave.

"Later, Chuck," Nix calls after her.

Charli frowns and gives her the finger, making Nix laugh and throw one right back.

I grin and shake my head. "You two are funny."

"What can I say, I adore that girl. She feels like the closest thing I'll ever have to a sister."

"Do you have any siblings?" I ask, suddenly realizing that I don't know. I haven't really spoken to her about her family before.

Nix clenches her jaw, sniffing and shaking her head before quickly changing the topic. "So, not to be overly girlish, but... what are you gonna wear for your date?"

I groan, dipping my chin and confessing, "I have no idea."

# CHAPTER 12
## TYRELL

Nolan's a big enough town that there are a variety of places to choose from for lunch. So why the hell Paul chose The Hungry House is beyond me. It's on the far side of town, near the hospital. Its decor is jarringly bright. We're talking orange and green, like a monster came in and puked everywhere, and the owners were like, "Yeah, I'm diggin' it."

I shift on the shiny vinyl booth seat, my pants making a fart noise that grabs the attention of the table beside me. The little girl spins in her chair, bulging her eyes, then covering her mouth and giggling.

"Kee-Kee. Turn yourself back around. Don't be rude," her mother quips before giving me an apologetic smile.

"It was the…" I point at the booth seat, then give up, brushing my fingers through the air.

The mother's lips twitch as she concentrates back on her kids.

I turn my attention to the couple I'm spying on.

Paul doesn't actually know I'm here. I figured it would

freak the poor guy out, so I followed them like a secret agent tracking a target and slipped in around five minutes after they did. I directed the waitress to seat me at a table out of view, and thankfully I was able to sneak in unnoticed.

I'm feeling like a bit of a creeper, leaning around the edge of the wall to check on Dani's date. She spotted me about half an hour ago, and her quiet smile was adorable. She's happy I'm here, which is the only thing stopping me from bailing.

My eyes narrow as Paul's hand snakes across the table. He brushes his fingers over the top of Dani's knuckles, and I watch him like a hawk. But after a comment that makes Dani grin, he's pulling his hand back and digging into his loaded fries again.

Damn, he's a slow eater. That boy got his food over twenty minutes ago, and he's only half done. I demolished my burger in about five flat. At least the food here is good.

Dani's picking at the last of her salad. She finished her chicken tenders pretty fast. They must have been delicious... or she was nervous and eating to cover it.

I study her face, her shoulders, her fingers, looking for signs of distress, but she seems fine. Satch is right about Paul being a nice guy. He's got a grin wider than Wily's, which he's using on the regular.

There seems to be a sincerity about him.

When I first met with him and Satch for coffee, I kept my guard up, testing him out with gruff comments and questions, but he stayed calm and kind, laughing off my "grumpy mode" until I finally relaxed and told him why I'd been acting that way.

He was pretty good about it and seemed happy to take Dani out, be the perfect gentleman, and help her ease back into the dating scene.

Dani says something and Paul tips his head back, his laughter booming across the restaurant. Dani winces, then bites her lips together when he looks at her again. Forcing a smile, she grabs her basically empty glass and sips out the last of the melted ice cubes.

I don't think she's feeling this date.

But she's not unhappy, which is good.

This right here was all about her experiencing a one-on-one with another guy. This is just a baby step toward her new life.

An ache blooms in my chest. I slump back in my seat, staring down at my plate, the last few crispy fries scattered around the edges. I pick one up and draw patterns with my ketchup, trying not to dwell on how wrong it is that Dani's trying to find another guy.

I mean, it's not wrong. She deserves to be happy.

But she was.

With Atlas.

She was so fucking happy. They both were.

No awkward dates. Ever.

He told me all about the first time he took her out for ice cream, and it sounded perfect. From day one, they just clicked. They were soulmates, and it's a fucking travesty that he's not here anymore.

How the hell is anyone supposed to move on from their soulmate?

Glancing around the edge of the booth again, I notice Dani collecting her bag and standing up.

It's over already?

I glance at my watch. Just over an hour. So, not a total disaster but hardly the "I'm so into you, I've lost track of time" date.

Tapping my fingers on the table, I wait for them to finish paying, and my phone starts to ding with texts from Wily.

*Wily: How's the date going? Satch is making me ask.*

*Me: It's wrapping up already, but everyone was smiling throughout.*

*Wily: Over already? That was fast. Are you sure it wasn't all fake smiles?*

*Me: They could be going off to do something else. I'll follow in a second... which makes me feel like a stalker. Should I be bailing?*

*Wily: You told her you'd have her back. If they're shifting locations, you need to be there for her.*

He's right. Of course he's right.

Standing up with a sigh, I check the coast is clear before paying for my meal and heading out the door.

I don't spot Dani at first and wonder if I'm gonna have

to call her for a check-in, but then I hear Paul's loud laughter again and turn in time to see him pull Dani into a hug.

He lifts her off the ground, and I quickly duck back into the restaurant before he spots me.

Leaning against the wall, I watch them through the window, my insides coiling as I wait to see what this hug will become.

Nothing.

It becomes nothing.

Thank fuck for that.

Paul pats her on the back before letting her go, then grins down at her. Another pat on the arm and he's waving goodbye.

What the hell? Why isn't he driving her home?

Dani stays on the curb, smiling and waving while he drives off. As soon as it's clear, I jump out of the restaurant and hurry toward her.

"What gives?" I stretch my arms wide. "Why isn't he driving you home?"

She grins up at my indignation like it's amusing.

"What?" I frown down at her.

"He's off to visit one of his tutoring students at the hospital. He offered to let me come, but I declined." Her eyebrows rise, wrinkling her forehead. "He then offered to drive me home first, but I didn't want him having to ping-pong all over town for me, so I told him I'd grab an Uber—which he offered to arrange and pay for, by the way."

Now my eyebrows are rising. Not bad.

Her smile grows a little wider. "He also paid for lunch and was the perfect gentleman. He felt bad about having to leave early, but his student isn't well, and he promised to check on him today."

"Is everything okay?"

"Yeah, I think so. Just a really shocking stomach bug or something. He's severely dehydrated and had to be admitted last night. Paul wants to check in. Be a friendly face, you know."

"That's really nice of him."

"Well..." Dani steps up beside me, threading her arm around mine. "He *is* a really nice guy."

I nod, not understanding this weird pull in my chest. Like a resistance.

Am I really okay with her moving on from Atlas?

What the hell? Of course I am! She deserves happiness.

*Dude, shut the fuck up and just listen to her.*

"But I don't think we'll be doing the date thing again. I'll happily catch up as a friend, but..." She shakes her head. "There was nothing romantic about that date. I don't think he was feeling it either." She looks up and cringes. "At least I hope he wasn't."

Relief pulses through me.

Why?

I have no idea, but I smile down at her as we stroll along the street toward my SUV.

I parked two blocks away, not wanting to get spotted. Probably overcompensated a bit there, but the sun is shining, and Dani's not due at work for another two hours, so we're good. We can stroll.

"There was just... no chemistry, you know?"

I nod, and she sighs.

"Do you think I'll ever find that again? That easy *don't*

*even have to think about it* chemistry. That feeling in your gut where you just *know* this person is yours to keep, to cherish... to love."

My mouth goes dry, my throat swelling as I lamely shrug and give her a helpless frown.

Her smile is sad when she shakes her head. We go quiet, and I try and fill this space.

Anything to make her feel better.

Anything to fix this for her.

"Uh..." I clear my throat as we near my SUV, stopping her on the sidewalk and turning her to face me. My hands look huge on her small shoulders, so I hold her extra lightly and try to lighten the mood. "Let's play a game."

Her eyebrow arches while her lips quirk into a lopsided smile that's just too damn cute. "A game?"

"Yeah, let's pretend that I'm the host of a dating show or something, and you're describing your perfect man to me."

She laughs, then sinks her teeth into her bottom lip, and I hold my breath, wondering if she'll play along.

# CHAPTER 13
## DANI

Tyrell is too cute, working overtime to make me feel better.

For a second, I contemplate telling him that he really doesn't have to do that and asking if he can just take me home.

But I don't want to hurt his feelings, and the idea of lightening the mood is kind of appealing. I don't want every conversation we have to be this somber "I miss Atlas" ordeal.

So, I blink, look up at him again, and whisper, "Okay. Let's play."

"Alrighty then." He puts on a presenter's voice that has me giggling.

Unlocking his car, he holds open the passenger door for me while stumbling through a dating show introduction.

"Welcome to the Dani Dating Show. This afternoon, we're going to find out what Miss Hill is looking for in a man. On a quest for a fresh new start, our lovely lady here is braving the world of romance. Can she describe her dreamboat guy?"

He closes the door, and I buckle up while he runs around to the driver's side. He's so tall, it only takes him three strides before he's getting behind the wheel, glancing to check on me before starting up the engine.

"So, Miss Hill, what are you looking for in a man? Let's start with his personality." He's still using the presenter voice, and it's cracking me up.

"Um..." I laugh, then brush my teeth over my bottom lip as I think about it. "He needs to be sweet, considerate of other people, and care about his family. The kind of guy who would do anything for them. Not in that *being walked all over* kind of way, but in that *you're important to me, so I'll make time for you* kind of way."

"Like your dad," Tyrell murmurs, and my smile is instant.

"Yeah. Like my dad."

"That's good. What else?"

"Okay, uh..." I'm doing my best not to list off all of Atlas's best traits. And if I'm completely honest, much to my sadness, I'm struggling to remember all of the intricate details that made him who he was. It's been so long since I spent time with him. I can still see his face in my head, hear his laughter, see him singing onstage, but he's fading.

And I need to figure out what I want. As an adult woman. What kind of guy do I want? Is it different from what I had?

"You need some ideas?" Tyrell glances at me.

"No, I... was just thinking." I swallow and scan the

street as we drive back to the other side of town. "He needs to be easy to talk to. Like I can tell him anything and not worry that he'll be judging me."

"Yeah, definitely. Me too," Tyrell's voice rumbles. I really do love how deep it is. I always have. When I first met him, he'd hit puberty earlier than Atlas, and it was kind of hilarious. These two best friends, one towering over the other. This big bulk of Black muscle next to his skinny white friend. Tyrell's voice was deep while Atlas had a softer, gentler sound, still cracking occasionally. He was all blond scruff with these haunted gray eyes, so different from the calm, brown gaze Tyrell would study me with.

"And what else?" I ask myself. "I want him to be chill, calm in a crisis. Smart, can think things through rather than just throwing himself into the fray."

*Huh. That's interesting. You're basically describing the opposite of Atlas. You realize that, right?*

I stiffen, shaking my head and wrapping up the personality thing. Without being asked to, I shift to likes and dislikes.

"He needs to love music, not mind it playing all the time. He needs to enjoy dancing. He doesn't have to love it, but he has to like it enough that if I'm in the mood to get down on the dance floor, I won't be boogieing alone."

Tyrell chuckles, tapping his thumb on the wheel as we slow at the set of traffic lights.

"He needs to want to travel. See the world with me."

Tyrell whips his head to give me a surprised smile. "You want to travel?"

"Oh yeah." I give him an excited grin. "I've been

saving for years. I just haven't found the guts to head off on my own."

"Where do you want to go?"

"Anywhere. Everywhere."

"Come on, girl. Give me specific places. Are we talking Paris or Prague? Morocco or Thailand? What parts of the world do you really want to experience?"

"Okay..." An excited buzz travels through me as I shift in my seat. "Well, I want to see all of that. And the Pyramids of Giza and Petra. And I want to walk the streets of Pompeii and stand in the Colosseum in Rome. I want to paddleboard over crystal-clear waters in the Maldives, and even though I can't ski or snowboard, I want to learn on the Swiss Alps."

His lips curl into a smile as I talk, his head bobbing along like he totally understands my excitement.

"I want to swim with sharks in the Caribbean, and I want to hike the forests of New Zealand. I want to see the Taj Mahal with my own eyes, and I want to experience all the different cultures around the world. So, yeah... I really need someone who's got the travel bug."

"Wow." Tyrell laughs. "I had no idea. Have you always been like this?" He glances at me, and I hitch my shoulder.

"I mean, I always loved finding out things about the world as a kid. And Atlas and I used to daydream about him becoming a famous rock star and touring the world. Oh! Iceland. I forgot to say I want to check out Scandinavia. Those countries look amazing. Such rugged terrain."

He nods. "So, you and Atlas used to dream about tripping around the world, huh?"

"Well, it was mostly me, but Atlas loved the idea of touring with his band." My voice trails off, that familiar sadness swamping me until Tyrell throws out a metaphorical hand and pulls me out of the mire.

"I want to travel too. Strap on a pack, get on plane, and... go see the world."

"Really?" I look at him. "Since when?"

"I don't know." He tips his head, steering the car left and heading down Main Street. "I always thought football would be my everything, but after Atlas died... I don't know what happened, but I just kind of lost my fire for it. I still love playing, and I'm glad I never bailed on my team. It's just the pro life... all the attention, the cameras, the interviews. The intensity of it all." He makes a clicking noise with his tongue. "I don't want that shit. I want to be anonymous... And you know, you watch all these movies and documentaries in different parts of the world, and it just looks so awesome. I want to see those places with my own eyes."

My insides warm, a soft glow spreading through me as I recognize that excitement in his voice. He gets it. And I get it. There's so much more outside of this country, and I can't believe I never knew he wanted to experience it as much as I did.

We sit in silence for a moment, and I watch the foot traffic ambling down the street. Saturdays are always busier. I glance at my watch, checking how much time I have before my shift starts.

I'm still good, so I relax back into my seat and hope Tyrell doesn't drive too fast. I'm enjoying this ride.

"So, we need to find you a man who's into travel and what else?"

"Um..." My lips twitch as I try to come up with more. "It'd be great if he could cook. I mean, I can, I just don't love it." I stick out my tongue and Tyrell laughs, shaking his head.

"Oh man, I know, right? I need to find me a woman who can cook." He makes a face. "And that makes me sound like some 1950s sexist asshole, but I don't love being in the kitchen either."

"You're not sexist." I giggle, brushing my hand down his arm. "And while I'm over here listing all the things I want, what about you? What do you want in a girlfriend?"

His cheeks puff out like a chipmunk's before he blows out a breath and starts creating his own list. "She needs to be kind, understanding. Nonjudgmental. She needs to know how to handle people with special needs."

"Cyrus," I murmur.

"That's right." Tyrell nods, his expression serious. "I can't date a girl who won't give everything to try and communicate and connect with my brother."

I watch his jaw clench and wonder if he's dated a girl who *hasn't* been that way, and he's determined never to make that mistake again.

"Is he the reason why you haven't started traveling yet?" I quietly ask.

Tyrell grips the wheel, his entire arm tensing. I watch those muscles clench, unable to help admiring his obvious strength. "College has kept me here, but... I sometimes worry that it'll stop me from going. My parents really need the support right now. Dad's recovering from an injury and I spent spring break in Texas, trying to persuade Cyrus that letting Letitia drive him places was a safe option."

"Who's Letitia?"

"She's one of the tutors at the college Cyrus attends. She's been assigned to look after him and two other students with Down syndrome. Because my dad's been around with flexible work hours, he's been driving his boy all over the place, but with a broken clavicle, he's had to give that role to someone else. And Cyrus always takes time to adjust to new things."

"Was he okay by the time you left?"

"Yeah. It took four trips of me sitting with him in the back while Letitia drove, but he eventually warmed to the idea." Tyrell's face dips into a frown. "He cried when I left. Does it every damn time, and it kills me." Scrubbing a hand down his face, he lets out a frustrated sigh. "Makes me worry that if I go off to explore the world... how's my family gonna cope, you know? Mom's been dropping hints for over a year now that after graduation, it'd be great if I could move back home or set up a place of my own in Dallas."

He glances at me, and I give him a sympathetic smile. "That must be tough."

I shrug. "I shouldn't complain. I come from an amazing family. We all love and support one another."

"So, maybe if they knew how much you wanted to travel, they'd support that too."

Pulling up to the curb outside my apartment, Tyrell cuts the engine and turns to face me. "What if telling them breaks their hearts?"

Poor guy. He looks so tortured by that idea.

"They love you, Ty. They'll want you to chase your dreams. And it's not like you'll be gone forever, right?"

"Yeah," he mumbles, then cringes. "Why has this

conversation turned itself around and landed on me? Girl, we're supposed to be finding you a man."

I grin. "And finding you a woman."

He tips his head, looking a little wistful, and...

You know what?

Springing up straight, I reach for his arm, squeezing his wrist as an idea hits me. "I'm gonna find you a girl."

"What?" He frowns.

"Yes! If you're looking for a guy for me, then I'm going to set you up too. We can go on double dates, have each other's backs." I grin. "Yes! I'm loving this."

"I don't know." Tyrell winces. "I'm not... You don't have to..."

"I *want* to. And besides, it takes the heat off me. If we're doing this together, then I won't feel so much pressure."

"Ooookay. How you gonna find me a girl?" He narrows his eyes. "You only just moved here a few months ago."

"I work at Offside. I see a lot of girls come through my door. Plus, my roommates can help me. Don't you worry, Mr. Jackson. I'm gonna get you the nicest girl on campus."

A reluctant smile slowly grows on his face, and he looks away from me, shaking his head like he's so not into this idea, but he's pretty sure he can't fight me on it either.

Eventually he clears his throat with a nod and promises the same. "And I'm gonna get you a music-loving traveling man who can cook and has the sweetest heart in town."

"That's it." I giggle, thanking him for dropping me home before jumping out of his SUV.

Spinning with a grin, I wave goodbye as he pulls away, then run upstairs to get changed for my shift at work.

I don't understand why, but I have these happy little bubbles popping in my chest. I think it's just nice to have a mission that's not centered around me moving on with my life. For once, I can think about somebody else and finding them the perfect partner.

# CHAPTER 14
## TYRELL

Instant regret.

The second I pulled away from Dani's apartment, I was swamped with it.

Why the hell did I agree to her finding me some girl?

Probably because she seemed relieved by the idea of doing this together, of not being the sole focus around this whole dating thing.

Okay, so the idea of a double date is kind of fun. It definitely makes things less intense.

Which is why I chose Lincoln to come with me.

Yes, Carson had a little hissy fit, but he doesn't have to hang out with the guy, and Carson needs to get over his hate for Fleischer... and all people associated with him. Lincoln is one of those guys who is friends with everyone.

I think Dani's gonna like him.

I checked, and he plays piano (sort of—his mom made him learn as a kid), but his taste in music is good. I queried him on that too, and he reminded me that we've roomed together before, and we're both eclectic in our taste.

He comes from a good family—three younger sisters, who all adore him, which proves he knows how to treat girls right.

He says he can cook, although I haven't tasted the evidence, so who knows.

He's a junior, so a little younger than Dani, but it means he'll be kicking around Nolan for another year at least. If there's a spark, they'll have plenty of time to do something about it.

I haven't had a chance to ask him about travel yet, because my interrogation got interrupted by Coach. Right now, we're driving to the restaurant, and I don't have time to quiz him on all the places he wants to travel to.

Not when I'm busy grilling him on treating Dani right.

"Seriously, man?" He gives me a skeptical frown, and I point my finger at him.

"Don't give me that look."

"I'm not sitting here while you lecture me on how to treat a first date... or any woman. I know girls, man. I've grown up surrounded by them, and my mama didn't let me get away with anything. She slapped me up the side of the head if I put a toe out of line, so you better believe me when I tell you, I know how to be a gentleman. I didn't have a choice."

I throw him a side-eye. "But you wanna treat girls right, though. Right?"

"Of course I do. I'm not an asshole." He flicks my arm with the back of his hand. "Boy, why'd you even ask me to do this if you're doubting me?"

"I just..." I huff out a breath and have to apologize. "I'm sorry. I just want to make sure she has a good night. Dani's lost big, you know? She's trying to put herself back out there, and she's vulnerable right now, so you need to play this right. That's all I'm saying."

"I will, brother. Trust me. And I know you'll kick my ass if I don't." He bulges his dark brown eyes at me, and I can't help a soft snort.

"I will, but I'm not gonna have to. Sorry, brah. I don't know why I'm so nervous."

"Because she's setting you up with some chick you've never met before?" He laughs at me. "Maybe that's it."

"Yeah," I have to admit. I've been on plenty of dates at Nolan U. Why should this one be so much more nerve-racking?

"Do you even know her name?"

"Chastity. I think."

"And how does Dani know her?"

"She lives on the second floor of Dani's building. They go walking together sometimes."

"Is she a student?"

"Yeah. She's a senior. Dani said she's studying engineering. Thought it might be a good fit, you know? We'll have something in common. Something to talk about."

"Okay." Lincoln nods. "And if not? If things don't go as smoothly as you hope, do you want like a safe word or something?"

"A safe word?" I whip my head to look at him just before pulling into the small parking lot behind the restaurant.

"Yeah, you know, just some phrase we can say to each other if we want to bail early."

*Why would he want to bail early on Dani?*

I nearly tell him he's crazy, but he keeps talking before I get the chance.

"How about I start talking about finals week and how it's only one month away." He grins. "And then you'll be like, 'Damn, man. I'm behind on my studying.'"

I give him a skeptical frown.

"And then I'll start going on about busy schedules, and you'll regretfully say that as much fun as we're having, we really need to get our asses home and hit the books."

"That sounds completely lame," I murmur.

"Yeah, I know." He laughs. "But what else have you got?"

I think for a moment and come up with nothing. Checking my watch, I see we've only got a minute before we're due in there, so I just have to flick my hands up and admit, "I don't have anything better."

"Okay." Lincoln claps his hands together. "So, we probably won't have to use it, but if we do, we pull out the study excuse, and even if you're having the best time, you have to bail. And I'll do the same for you."

I reluctantly agree, although the chances of him needing to bail are slim to none. It's Dani. He's not gonna want to leave her for studying.

Me, on the other hand... who knows?

"You sure you're okay bailing early if you have to?" I double-check with him.

"Yeah, man. I've got your back. And you've got mine." He winks. "It's only fair."

With an agreed nod, we open our doors and walk

around the building to the front entrance of the restaurant.

I spot Dani first. She's decked out in a pair of black pants that hug her legs and butt. Damn, she's got nice curves. Always has. Her denim jacket hides the top half of her body, but I know. Atlas couldn't get enough of her shape, and I'd hear all about it. It was impossible not to look, especially over those summer months when she'd run around in cutoff denim shorts and that orange bikini top she loved.

She hasn't changed all that much.

"Is that her?" Lincoln nudges me, looking through the window. "The denim jacket and hoop earrings?"

"Yeah, man."

"Damn, boy. Thank you."

"Hey." I grab his arm before he can walk inside. "Treat her—"

"*Good.* I know, I know." Lincoln rolls his eyes, shaking me off and striding into the restaurant.

I shuffle up behind him, nerves racing through me like wildfire as I pause behind him and check out Chastity.

She's taller than Dani. Long and lean with bronze skin and almond-shaped eyes. Her smile is sweet, kind of shy, and I try to settle her obvious nerves with a smile of my own.

I'm just starting to worry that this is the worst idea in the history of man when Dani spins around, spots us walking toward them, and beams me a brilliant grin that settles my insides.

*She's gonna be here,* I remind myself.

And that one thought calms those nerves and turns my smile genuine as I walk toward her and make the introductions.

# CHAPTER 15
## DANI

So, Lincoln's a hottie. It's hard to resist a Black man with a strong jawline like his. I could immediately tell he was an athlete the second he walked into the restaurant. And I could also tell he was a gentleman when Tyrell introduced us.

It helped me relax.

Actually, having Tyrell here helps me relax.

It's weird how I haven't seen him in so long, yet it hasn't taken much to fall back into the easy friendship we had as teenagers.

Which is why I can't help reminding him about the time we smuggled all of that candy into the movie theater.

Tyrell's smile is instant. "And that old guy behind us got all shitty because the movie was boring as hell and we started a Skittles war."

I snort, covering my mouth and giggling as I'm sent back in time to that obscure little theater. I don't know what possessed us to go there. It was one of those artsy places that only showed foreign films. I think we were just bored and happened to be on that side of town. I can't even remember why, but...

"I feel kind of sorry for him now." I cringe. "At the time, I thought it was hilarious, but now I look back and feel so bad. He was just trying to enjoy his film, and we were laughing hyenas, making trouble behind him."

"Sounds like you two got up to some mischief." Chastity directs her comment to Tyrell.

Her smile is broad and flirty, and my insides shrink. But why? They shouldn't. She's so obviously into Tyrell, and that's a good thing.

Focusing my attention back on Lincoln, I try to think of something to say. Conversation hasn't exactly flowed since we sat down.

He's sweet and all, but he's obviously obsessed with football.

Giving him an awkward smile, I straighten my cutlery as I wait for my food to arrive and force out a question. "So, what else do you enjoy doing... other than football?"

He lets out a short laugh. "What else is there? Between that and keeping up with my homework, I basically have no life."

I nod, wincing at his plight. Has college been like that for Tyrell too? I sneak a quick look at him. He's nodding.

"Yeah, being a college athlete is a busy job," he agrees with his teammate. "But we can still squeeze in a little fun. Like now." He winks at me, then grins at Chastity. She blushes, and I straighten my fork again.

"Okay, so let's pretend you had some spare time. What would you do with it?" I direct the question to

Lincoln, because that's who I'm supposed to be here for, although I'd love to know Tyrell's answer as well.

Lincoln shrugs, his face pinching like the question is annoying.

I swallow and take a sip from my water glass.

"Uh... I guess I like to run?"

"Oh come on. That's still a sports thing. Is that all you're about?" Chastity challenges him.

"Pretty much."

My eyebrows wrinkle and I glance at Tyrell, who's frowning at him. "You told me you played piano as a kid. You like music, don't you?"

"Yeah, I guess," Lincoln murmurs, and I jump all over it.

"What kind of music do you like? I played piano when I was a kid, and I definitely went through a jazz phase." I grin. "But then I hit my teen years, and it became all about punk rock and..." My voice trails off, the mildly bored expression on Lincoln's face deflating me.

"I'll listen to pretty much anything, and I don't play piano anymore."

"You been to any good concerts lately?" I cling to anything that might ignite a decent spark of conversation between us.

"Uh..." He scratches his forehead. "No, but I did get to the Basketball All-Star game recently. That was awesome."

*Great. More sports.*

"I got to see Pink last year," Chastity tells us, and I perk up, throwing my attention her way.

"Oh my gosh, I love her so much."

"I know, right? She kicks ass! Her concert was so amazing. Like seriously, the best I've ever been to."

I grin. "I'd love to see her live. Who else have you been to?"

This sparks a conversation that lasts until the food arrives. Thank goodness! Even Lincoln pitches in, finally admitting that he went to see Dua Lipa with his little sisters.

"Just to play bodyguard, you know?" He's trying to play it off all cool, but I bet he loved it.

Part of me wonders if I should tease him, but... we're not there yet.

Tyrell, on the other hand...

"Yeah, I took Lacey to see Ariana Grande a couple of years ago. We could only afford two tickets, and my mama's not into that kind of music, so I drew the short straw."

"Yeah, right." I nudge him with my elbow. "I bet you loved every second of it."

His lips twitch, and I crack up laughing.

"You did! You totally got into it. I bet you were singing louder than anybody by the end of the concert."

"Maybe," he mumbles, scratching his forehead and making me laugh while he fumbles with his cutlery and attacks the steak he ordered.

I smile across the table, but Lincoln's not looking at me. He's too busy devouring his Alfredo pasta.

Staring down at my chicken parmigiana, I say a quick grace in my head—a lifelong habit—then dig in.

The food is delicious, and I savor each bite while Chastity launches into a long engineering-related story that has Tyrell grinning.

"He is a hard-ass, but he's a smart guy, so I don't mind him so much."

They're talking about professors and throwing out names that mean nothing to me, and possibly Lincoln. He's looking mildly bored again.

He's wolfed down his food and is now just sitting there, staring at an empty plate. So I try to engage again.

"How long have you been playing football?" I'm not actually that interested in sports, but my parents always taught me to ask questions about others in order to spark conversation, and it's clear that football is king in this guy's life.

He shuffles in his seat, telling me about how he started playing when he was five.

"Wow. And you still love it?"

"Even more than I did back then." His lips rise into a half smile. "I'd love to go pro, and I've got myself an agent already, but who knows. He's already warned me how hard it is to get selected, so all I can do is keep playing my best and hoping."

"What would you do if you didn't get in?"

"Who the fuck knows." His expression bunches with obvious stress.

"Well, what are you studying? I mean, is there an avenue there you can pursue?"

"I'm majoring in sports management, but I don't enjoy studying that much. I'd rather be on the field, you know?"

"Yeah, well, you must love studying the game, though, right? I bet you have that playbook memorized from cover to cover."

His lips curl into a slow smile, and he nods. "Yeah, pretty much."

"I don't know if I've ever been that passionate about anything, you know?" *Except Atlas, but I don't want to bring him into this right now.* "Maybe music. Or… traveling? I'd love to see the world."

"Really?" Lincoln seems confused by this answer.

"Yeah. Don't you ever want to go overseas?"

He doesn't seem too excited by the idea, and then he goes and kills it completely. "We live in the best country on the planet. Why would I want to leave it?"

My gut twists as I try to keep my voice light and amiable. "I don't know… to experience other cultures. To enrich your life."

"I've got everything I want." He smiles, and now I'm scrambling to think of something else to talk about.

Tyrell is answering one of Chastity's questions, and I try to tune in to what he's saying.

"…and that about sums it up, I guess."

"Wow." Chastity smiles at him across the table. "You're amazing."

"No." Tyrell shakes his head. "I'm nothin' special." When he sees me looking, he says, "I was just explaining how growing up with a brother who has special needs is… well, it's been challenging, but ultimately made us better versions of ourselves, you know? You can't be selfish when there's someone who needs you like that."

"That *does* make you amazing, whether you want to accept it or not." Chastity's smile is dreamy, and I get it.

Tyrell has always been a great guy. A protector, yet so humble about it.

"Yeah, he's great." Lincoln lifts his chin to his buddy.

"Good brother, great football player, and an awesome study partner." He grins. "Actually, how are you all feeling about finals week only being a month away?" Glancing at his watch, he sits up a little higher in his seat. "Time's just ticking by, and I feel like I'm having to snatch every free second of studying that I can, you know?"

Tyrell's eyebrows dip into a deep frown as he stares across the table. I can't quite read his expression. Is he pissed off or confused? Why is he reacting this way to Lincoln's comments about studying?

He was always pretty studious at school. Does he not want to—

"I don't want to be rude or anything." Lincoln clears his throat. "But I've got a study schedule I'm really trying to stick to. You girls don't mind if Tyrell and I wrap this up and hit the books, do you?"

"Oh." Chastity blinks, checking her phone screen. "Yeah, actually that's not a totally heinous idea, but..." Glancing up, she drinks Tyrell in. "Can we do this again sometime?"

"Uh..." He swallows and so obviously forces himself to nod.

Yikes.

Poor Chastity. She picks up his hesitation immediately, and the way her expression drops...

Oh shit.

"Sorry. I mean, I was just..." He closes his eyes, cringing, and I quickly jump in with a save.

"I'm guessing your mind has already shifted to the books. Are you worried about an upcoming exam?" I touch his arm, and he turns to give me a grateful smile. It doesn't reach his lips, but I can see his eyes warm with relief.

"Yeah, I have one doozy that's been keeping me up at night."

"Oh really? Exam worry? Yeah, I get that." Chastity laughs, but the sound is fake.

Lincoln rises from his chair. "I'll go track down that bill, and then we can get out of here."

"I'll help you pay." Tyrell jumps up, following him to the counter while Chastity and I gather our things.

"Well, that was going well until he made it blatantly obvious that I'm more into him than he is to me." Chastity rolls her eyes.

"I don't think that—"

"Dani." She gives me a look that tells me to stop bullshitting her.

All I can do is sigh. "I'm sorry."

"That's okay." She huffs. "I don't think Lincoln's that into you either."

"Yeah, well, no huge loss there. I wasn't feeling it myself. He was so friendly and bubbly when he first walked in here, but then he started droning on about football, and I think he saw my eyes glazing over. There was no going back after that."

"Ugh!" Chastity rises from her seat, brushing a hand down her dress to straighten it. "Why does dating have to suck so badly?"

"I know, right?" I give her a sympathetic smile, surprised by how not bummed out I feel.

But I really don't.

If anything, I'm feeling nothing. Or just... neutral.

This date wasn't a winner, but it was fun hanging out with Tyrell and Chastity for a while.

Holding out my hand, I wait for her to reach for mine, then give it a squeeze. "You know the best part of this night for me?"

"What?"

"Getting to know you better." I smile up at her, and she grins right back.

"Girl, yes. Thank you." Pulling me into a hug, she laughs against my ear, squeezing me tight before kissing my cheek.

"All paid up." Tyrell returns, looking between us and obviously trying to figure out what we were just talking about.

"Thanks for that." I smile at him, then nod at Lincoln. "It was nice to meet you."

"Yeah, you too." He extends his hand, and I give it an awkward shake while Tyrell gives him another quizzical frown.

Shaking his head, he follows Lincoln out of the restaurant before walking us to Chastity's car.

"Thanks for a great evening." He raises his hand in farewell.

Chastity scoffs, opening her car door and slipping inside while I wince at Tyrell.

"I'm sorry," he mumbles. "I didn't mean to be rude. She just caught me off guard."

"Don't worry about it. You obviously weren't feeling it."

"But she's really nice. I just..." He cringes, and I squeeze his arm to reassure him.

"It's okay, Ty. I'll find you a winner next time."

"Should there be a next time?" He scratches the back of his neck.

"Hey, Jackson, let's go, man!" Lincoln calls from beside Tyrell's SUV.

"Comin'!" Ty lifts his hand before looking back to me and asking again, "Should there be a next time?"

I bite my lips together and force myself to nod. "We can't give up so quickly. Good things take time, right? I'm in if you are."

He studies me for a long beat, and I squirm in my heels until he finally nods, his voice all soft and rumbly. "Okay. I'll, uh... try to find you a better match too."

It's impossible not to grin. Although this date wasn't a winner, it was fun, and I'm up for it again... as long as he's there to be my wingman.

"I look forward to it, Black Jack."

His smile grows as he starts ambling backward, giving me a final wave before spinning around and jogging to his SUV.

I have to force myself to turn away from him and slip into Chastity's car. She already has Pink playing and cranks up the volume on "Just Like A Pill" as we drive out of the parking lot.

I start humming along, then belt out the lyrics when we get to the chorus.

She lets out a half-hearted laugh before joining me, and we sing that tune at the top of our lungs as we drive back to our apartment building, both still very much single.

# APRIL 21ST

*Black Jack: Still feeling bad about Chastity. Was she okay by the time you got back to the apartment?*

*Dani Girl: Yeah, she was fine. She gets that dating is hard. I think she was really into you. I'm sorry you didn't feel the same way. Awkward!*

*Black Jack: Shit, I'm sorry too. I didn't mean to come across like a douche. I'm sorry about Lincoln. All he could talk about was football, and then it was like drawing blood from a stone.*

*Dani Girl: Yeah, a little obsessed with the game. I'm glad you're not like that. I couldn't handle double dates with you if that's all you ever talked about.*

*Black Jack: There's more to life.*

*Dani Girl: So, what's next? You got someone else lined up, or are you going to have to look around?*

*Black Jack: There's a guy in Nylah's anthropology class. Andy. You cool with that?*

*Dani Girl: Sure. Nylah's Carson's girlfriend, right? I had lunch with her roommate the other day.*

*Black Jack: Oh yeah? How do you know Jolie?*

*Dani Girl: She's friends with Charli, who is best friends with my roommate, Nix.*

*Black Jack: Small world.*

*Dani Girl: Nolan feels like a very small world.*

*Black Jack: It's not that much smaller than Colorado Springs.*

*Dani Girl: Colorado Springs is a very small world too!*

*Black Jack: True. So, which city is first on your travel list?*

*Dani Girl: Either London or Rome. How about you?"*

*Black Jack: Yeah, London sounds cool. So does Rome.*

*Dani Girl: But what city is on your list? Not mine.*

*Black Jack: I'd have to say Dubai. That place looks insane.*

*Dani Girl: I know, right? That's definitely on my list too. Hey, I better let you get on with your studying. I'll catch up with you again soon.*

*Black Jack: Sounds good. I'll get in touch with this Andy guy. Let me know when you're free for another double date.*

# APRIL 24TH

*Dani Girl: How's the draft party going? Thanks for the invite. Sorry I have to work. It's up on the TV at Offside, so I'll keep an eye on it.*

*Black Jack: You probably don't want to be here anyway. It's pretty tense. I'll keep you updated, though.*

# APRIL 27TH

*Dani Girl: Yay!! Tell him congratulations!!!*

*Black Jack: I'm not sure he's ever going to stop celebrating.*

# APRIL 28TH

*Dani Girl: So, a lunch date in the park was a fun idea. Thanks for that. It was cool throwing a ball around after we ate.*

*Black Jack: Yeah, I really liked that part. Do you think Lola did?*

*Dani Girl: I think so? Although, she did seem kind of afraid of the ball... and maybe for good reason.*

*Black Jack: Poor thing. I thought I'd passed it really gently, but the way she howled...*

*Dani Girl: You DID pass it gently. She was being overly dramatic. Her nose didn't even bleed.*

*Black Jack: I thought she saw it coming.*

*Dani Girl: It's not your fault she can't catch a ball.*

*Black Jack: She was nice enough about it, though. Once she stopped crying.*

*Dani Girl: Yeah. She was sweet, but... I'm not sure she's right for you. You're an athlete. You can't fall for a girl who can't play catch.*

*Black Jack: Athletes can date non-sporty people.*

*Dani Girl: So you really liked her, then? Do you think you'll go out again?*

*Black Jack: Not sure. What did you think of Andy?*

*Dani Girl: Yeah, nice guy. Amazing eyes. Never seen green like it. Nice smile too. He's cute, and super smart.*

*Black Jack: Yeah, definitely. Had a bit of a strange laugh, though, right? And his fascination with rats was kind of weird too.*

*Dani Girl: His laugh was... Okay, you're right, it was like nothing I've ever heard before. A barking chuckle thing that sounded like he was choking. And I didn't mind the rat conversation so much. I had no idea rats could laugh.*

*Black Jack: Yeah, I didn't know how smart they were. Or maybe I did, but I'd never really thought about it.*

*Dani Girl: Super smart. And their social behaviors... wow. I had no idea.*

*Black Jack: And now we're talking about rats.*

*Dani Girl: LOL! So, what do you want to talk about, then?*

*Black Jack: The way you snorted at Lola.*

*Dani Girl: I couldn't help it! "All I Want for Christmas" is NOT a Whitney Houston song. She was trying to impress you by pretending to know Whitney, and it ended up just being embarrassing. And then she had the audacity to say that Whitney and Mariah are basically the same person.*

*Black Jack: Yeah, that one was like a punch to the chest.*
*Dani Girl: !!!*

*Black Jack: You just snorted again, didn't you?*

*Dani Girl: Maybe.*

*Black Jack: You totally did. Girl, I can hear it in my head.*

*Dani Girl: I swear I'll do better next time. Lola came across as so sweet in the coffee shop.*

*Black Jack: She was sweet, but she doesn't know Whitney, and I'm not sure I can date a girl like that. You're right. She's not the one for me... And you're snorting again.*

*Dani Girl: You make it impossible not to!*

*Black Jack: So, are you gonna go out with Andy again?*

*Dani Girl: Think I'd rather do another double date with you. Got someone else lined up for me?*

*Black Jack: You bet I do. A guy from my team's been asking— Cole. He's second-string and not football obsessed. Did a one-year student exchange to Denmark when he was in high school, so at least we know he loves to travel. You want me to set something up?*

*Dani Girl: Sure. Tobin's gunning for me to set you up with his yoga instructor. What do you think?*

*Black Jack: Sounds flexible. Let's green-light that one.*

# APRIL 30TH

*Black Jack: Just heard a busker murder "I Will Always Love You." I think my ears are bleeding.*

*Dani Girl: Oh no! Here's a comforting cyber hug. You better listen to the Whitney version now. Blast that shit until your ears feel better.*

*Black Jack: Good call. See you for date night tomorrow.*

*Dani Girl: Sounds good. Ms. Yoga and I will meet you at the restaurant.*

# MAY 1ST

*Black Jack: For such a flexible person, I've never met someone so intolerant of... everything.*

*Dani Girl: OMG, I know! What was Tobin thinking? I'm seriously going to have to kick his ass. Cole was nice, though. His travel stories were fun.*

*Black Jack: Until they were interrupted by the vegan eco-freak. Sorry. That's harsh. I'm just still riled that she accused me of being a murderer for enjoying a hamburger. And then we had to sit through a 13-minute (I timed it!) diatribe about how the colonists decimated the bison. I get it. If anyone understands white oppression and stupidity, it's us. But she sat there with her white ass perched in her chair, talking at us like we didn't understand just how bad the colonists were. We fucking get it!*

*Dani Girl: I know. I had to resist the urge to slap a hand over her mouth, but I was worried she might snarl and bite me or something.*

*Black Jack: She seemed too zen for that, but she probably would have lectured you on freedom of speech or some shit.*

*Dani Girl: I seriously think Tobin was pranking us. He didn't warn me at all about the eating thing. If he had, I would have chosen a place with more than one vegan option on the menu. I felt so bad for the waiter. She made like twenty adjustments to her order.*

*Black Jack: I feel sorry for the chef too.*

*Dani Girl: Ugh! Nightmare. I swear the next girl I set you up with will be the tits.*

*Black Jack: The tits?*

*Dani Girl: Yes, Tobin taught it to me. He's going through a British slang phase. It means excellent or great.*

*Black Jack: The tits. Okay then.*

*Dani Girl: I know. So funny, right?*

*Black Jack: Let's hope our next date is a winner.*

*Dani Girl: Fingers crossed!*

# MAY 2ND

*Dani Girl: Tobin's ass has been kicked. Nix helped. He has lost all date suggestion privileges.*

# CHAPTER 16
## TYRELL

Between practices, cramming for finals, and three double dates with Dani, life has been manic. I still can't believe Lincoln bailed early on our first one. He must be out of his damn mind. I questioned him hard on the drive back to his place, but he told me that as pretty as Dani was, he just wasn't feeling it.

What the actual fuck? How could he not be feeling it with a girl like her?

I guess I should be grateful she wasn't feeling it with him either.

Or any of the guys she's gone out with so far.

Maybe tonight will be a winner. Who knows. My insides buzz like I've swallowed a cup full of bees. I don't get why. I'm working hard to find her the perfect guy, but after each failed date, I can't help feeling a sense of relief. I don't understand it.

"Come on, Mr. NFL!" Nylah claps. "Throw the ball like you mean it!"

Carson laughs at her teasing taunts, and my mind jumps away from the field we're messing around on to the Football Frat living room last weekend.

Man, that draft party was... the tits.

I still can't stop grinning at Dani's new slang. And I'm not sure I'll ever stop feeling happy about the results of this year's NFL draft picks...

Sienna, Zander, Zoey, and their families went live to the draft announcement, while Wily, Satch, and his family stayed behind. He didn't want to be limping around on a bum leg.

Blake had her camera at the ready, ever hopeful that his name would be announced at some point during the three days.

She decided to go all out and invited the entire team around to Football Frat so we could support Wily together. Of course, they couldn't all make it, but people dribbled in and out between classes and training. The house felt like Grand Central Station for a few days.

We were all rooting for Zander too, and on Friday afternoon, when his name was announced, the roar that rose through the house was deafening.

"With the forty-fifth pick for this year's NFL draft, the Los Angeles Chargers select Zander Donohue, quarterback, Nolan University."

Holy shit. He did it. He fucking did it!

We all knew he would, but it was epic to watch him celebrating on TV. His dad was jumping around like a crazy person, but Zander only had eyes for Sienna, who was smiling at him, fighting tears and hugging Zoey to her chest as she reached for Zander to kiss him.

"Looks like we're moving to LA." At least I think that was what she said.

He grinned, bobbing his head and laughing as he swooped her off her feet, spinning her and Zoey around.

Damn. Los Angeles. Not bad.

"We'll have to find an excuse to visit," Blake said to Grady, then grinned at her brother. "Your name will be coming up soon, shithead. I refuse to believe anything else."

Wily put on a brave smile, which he desperately tried to keep in place.

But it faded a little more each day, and the closer we got to the sixth-round picks, the tenser things became. Wily's dad was a ball of nerves, and his anxiety was permeating the entire house. His mother wasn't much better, and Blake started getting really shitty with them, her snarky barbs turning my muscles into iron and giving me a headache.

A bunch of the team still showed up on that third afternoon. Even Coach Jones made an exception and popped in to sit with us for a while. I was grateful. We were onto the final day. If Wily's name wasn't announced by tonight, it'd be no-go-pro for our boy, and we were all feeling it.

Wily hadn't said a word all day, and the silence that fell over the room when the sixth-round picks came to a finish was fucking depressing.

"Let's get drinks before the final round." Blake jumped up, yanking her mother, who was on the verge of bawling, out of the room. "Pull yourself together," she hissed. "Wily doesn't need the pressure of your tears."

I trailed after the pair and helped them carry cans of beers and soda, distributing them among the team while we waited.

"Okay, it's starting!" someone finally shouted, and we all crowded into the room.

"No one's called," Wily mumbled. "This is over."

"Don't say that yet," Grady told him, then whipped his head away from the TV when Wily's phone started ringing.

Satch let out a soft gasp while Wily's eyes bulged. He gaped at the device on the coffee table.

"Well, answer it!" Blake screeched.

Wily looked to Satch, who gave him a calm smile. "It's gonna be okay." Reaching for his phone, she swiped her thumb across the screen, then handed it to him.

"Hello," he croaked, and we all held our breath until he closed his eyes with a relieved shudder. "Thank you, sir."

And that's when he started crying. Not sobs, just these quiet tears that trickled down his face as he smiled and nodded.

"That means a lot. Thank you... Yeah... Yeah, I'll work hard for you, Coach. You can count on it... Thank you." A broad smile crossed his face. "Yes, sir."

With a thick swallow, he hung up the phone. We were all gaping at him, desperate for news, but all he did was point at the TV screen.

"And for the two-hundred-and-twenty-seventh pick for this year's NFL draft, the Arizona Cardinals select Wily Wilson, left guard, Nolan University."

I'm pretty sure our cheering for this injured man was louder and longer than anything we'd heard before. Blake recorded the whole thing while we jumped around, jostling him and shouting like maniacs. His face popped up on-screen, along with a bunch of us as we congratulated our teammate on a well-deserved selection.

If he hadn't gotten injured, he would have been way higher up in the draft, but the point was... he got picked! And I was so incredibly stoked for him.

Satch squeezed Wily tight when he hugged her, laughing and crying along with the rest of his family.

"So proud of you, shithead." Blake climbed over Grady to get to her brother, and it was group hugs all around.

I glanced across the room, sharing a quick look with Carson, who was definitely smiling, but it wasn't reaching his eyes.

Damn, he and Grady were really gonna feel it.

I was gonna miss my brothers too.



Raising my hands, I catch the ball Zander throws at me, then start running down the field toward the playground. Zoey is on my tail along with Grady, who is catching up fast.

I laugh, dodging left when Wily comes at me. He's being extra careful with his knee, and we're all avoiding tackling him, but it's good to be out of the house on this sunny day, hanging with my Football Frat family.

Changes are definitely afoot for us, but at least we're not being sent all over the place. Arizona's not that far from Texas, and LA's just a skip and a jump on from there. We'll keep in touch, right?

We have to.

I may want to travel the world, but I need my roots to remain solid back in the USA. And these guys... this family we've created in Nolan, they're part of my roots, and I never want to lose what I've got with them.

# CHAPTER 17
## DANI

The sun is shining again, and I can smell that awesome spring freshness in the air. Yes! Bring on summer, baby. This blue sky and those blossoms peeking out of the tree we just passed are putting me in a good mood, although there's a strong chance it's about to sour.

"What?" My steps fumble as I glance at Nix jogging beside me.

"Yeah, we talked about it last night, and after the summer break, Ricky and I are gonna move in together." Her gleeful smile quickly dips into a look of remorse. "Sorry. I know that screws you over."

"No." I shake my head, sharing a silent look with Tobin, who's running on the other side of her.

He winces, his lips pulling into a pout before he blows out a breath and slows his pace to a walk. "Jed and I were hoping to sign the lease over to both of you, but Nix, if you're leaving..."

She stutters to a stop and lets out a huff. "I'm sorry, you guys. I'm not trying to be a pain in the ass, but things are going really well for Ricky and me. I'm ready for this next step."

"Depending on how your summer goes," Tobin quips.

I can't help a soft snort, and Nix is forced to agree with us, even though I can tell she really doesn't want to.

"Okay, fine. If the summer turns into a shit show, I won't be moving my stuff to his place."

"But we need to make a decision before then," I remind her. "And I can't take that lease on for the summer. I don't want to use up all my savings on rent."

"We could try to find you some new roommates before then," Tobin says hopefully.

"Three? With summer on our doorstep? Yeah, I can't see that happening," I mumble, scuffing the ground with my sneaker.

Tobin reaches behind Nix to rub my shoulder. "Aw, Dani Girl. What are you gonna do?"

"I don't know." I shrug, not wanting to think about how depressing Nolan's going to be without Tobin and Jed. And now Nix is moving in with Mr. Ricky, and I'm... I don't know what I am.

I need to get myself a fella.

If only one of these dates would work out.

I've been having a blast going out with Tyrell. Although, our last double date was a disaster thanks to the yoga queen. But it was fun debriefing afterward. Tyrell was so riled, which I'm not used to seeing, and it ended up making me giggle.

Tyrell Jackson all flustered and indignant that way is kinda cute.

I managed to get my game face on by the time I spoke

to Tobin about it. He let out this horrified gasp as I recalled every ugly detail of the date.

Then he started laughing. "Did she really do that?"

"Yes!" I gave him an exasperated frown, and Nix, who had overheard the whole thing, backed me up.

Tobin swore he wasn't pranking Tyrell and me, but I still revoked his privileges.

He pouted at me, then eventually sighed, "Fair enough. I was just trying to help you guys out."

He then shared a look with Nix that I didn't understand, his lips fighting a grin as he sauntered out of the room.

"What was that about?" I questioned Nix before she could take off too.

She shrugged. "Not sure."

But the way she quickly hurried to her bedroom had my suspicions firing.

Shit, I hope this date tonight goes better. Thankfully, Tobin had nothing to do with the selection process.

I wonder what this new guy is going to be like for me.

Cole was nice enough, but thanks to the yoga queen, I didn't really get a decent read on him.

But even if I had, would I be into him?

He seemed like a sweet guy, but he just wasn't...

*Atlas?*

I wince, wishing that thought didn't pop into my head after every damn date. Atlas isn't here anymore. Do I really have to be haunted by him for the rest of my life? I love that man. I always will, but surely he'd want me to move on and be happy.

*The right man is out there. You just have to be patient.*

*And a decent boyfriend has nothing to do with your housing situation, so would you focus, please?*

I sigh and get back into the conversation with my jogging buddies. "I'll start looking for a new apartment. Either a small studio I can afford on my own, or maybe I'll find some other people who have a spot open."

"Football Frat will have a few spaces." Nix winks at me, her grin wicked and playful.

I laugh. "Football Frat is for football players."

She makes a "Mmm" sound in her throat. "But wouldn't it be delicious living there?"

Wiggling her eyebrows, she teases me some more, and once again I have to remind her that one, Tyrell is not an option, and two, he won't even be there.

"He's graduating soon, and then he'll be moving back to Texas, so just stop already."

"Okay, okay. But I still argue that he's the hottest guy on the team, and the fact that he's not even an *option* is insane to me." Nix pouts, her expression so cute that I have to nudge her with my elbow and laugh again.

Seriously. How many times do I have to explain the situation to these guys?

"Where are you going tonight?" Tobin glides into a redirect, and I can't decide if I'm grateful or not.

My housing problem is getting me down, and talking double dates with Tyrell is a definite pick-me-up, but... are they just going to hassle me all over again?

"I think we're heading for that diner with the awesome milkshakes?"

"Oh yes! I love that place. Eat Your Faves." Nix smacks her lips together. "Get the loaded fries. They are the best!"

Tobin, on the other hand, wrinkles his nose like one of us has just dropped a stinky fart. "Why are you going there? It'll be full of college students."

"Uh, news flash." Nix looks up at him. "Three of them *are* college students."

"Yeah, but it's so unromantic. You go to that diner for study purposes or an unhealthy sugar kick. You don't go there for a date."

"Plenty of people go there for dates," Nix argues. "And for a *first* date, I say it's perfect. Pressure-free and fun."

Tobin still looks unimpressed. Thank God Nix is here so I don't have to try and justify this choice on my own. It was actually my suggestion. I keep hearing people talk about these milkshakes, and I felt like french fries and milkshakes sounded like a good, safe, fun option for a double date.

Tyrell has never met the girl I'm bringing. She's a friend of a friend of Nix's, and apparently she's really nice.

I haven't met the guy Tyrell has lined up either, but he's promised me he's not an athlete and is big into music. The guy plays guitar and is one of his teammate's younger brothers or something.

I hope tonight goes well.

Although, even if it doesn't, it'll still be fun to hang with Tyrell again.

*And speak of the devil.*

My lips quirk as I glance across the field we're walking beside and notice him running. He's chasing a little toddler with blonde curls who's holding a football and laughing so hard she can barely stay on her feet.

Probably because Tyrell is not the only one trying to catch her.

She lets out a squeal as he makes a dive, so obviously missing her on purpose. He rolls on the grass and she runs around his head, still giggling away while another guy with messy hair growls and tries to catch her.

"Go, Zoey Bird. Go!" a Black girl shouts, beckoning the cute blonde toward her.

Oh wait, that's Nylah Jones. Tyrell and Jolie have told me all about her.

Actually, Tyrell's told me about every person on this field. I'm sure of it.

As my ambling steps fizzle to a complete stop, I stare across the grass at what has to be the Football Frat family.

Wow. No wonder Tyrell loves these guys so much. You can immediately feel how tight they all are, watching the way they laugh together while these big, tough players try to simultaneously entertain and shield Zoey.

It's freaking adorable.

"Oh, my poor heart." Tobin lays a hand over his chest. "She has got to be the cutest thing I have ever seen."

"I know, right? And I'm not even into kids." Nix watches the girls celebrate as Zoey crosses the line, slamming the ball down and doing a little dance.

I laugh at her antics, catching the attention of... well, that has to be Grady Newman. He lightly slaps Tyrell on the arm to get his attention, and my insides hitch as Black Jack turns to spot me.

His smile is instant. I end up reciprocating it and walking toward him before I can stop myself.

"Hey." He goes to give me a hug, then steps back when he realizes how sweaty he is.

Crossing my arms, I grin up at him, then acknowledge the curious gazes all studying me and my friends.

"Hi, everyone." I raise my hand. "I'm Dani."

"Hey, Dani" is called in various ways from the group in front of me.

"And these are my roommates Nix and Tobin."

My friends wave while Nylah nudges herself forward. "Hey, Nixie. Nice to see you again."

"You too." She points at her. "Although you missed our last lunch. What was up with that?"

"Finals are on our doorstep." Nylah laughs. "I was studying in the library."

"With your boyfriend?" Nix gives her a skeptical frown. "In other words, you were getting hot and heavy in the stacks when you should have been chowing down with me, Jolie, and Chuck."

Nylah winces, then starts laughing. "Sorry, not sorry?" Her soft giggle turns into a belly laugh when Carson comes up behind her, wrapping his arm around her waist and plucking her off the ground.

"So, congratulations." I smile at Zander and Wily, recognizing both of them from the article in the most recent *Nolan U Sports Digest*. Nix brought it home with her, and I read it over breakfast this morning.

"Thanks." They both grin at me, looking proud as punch.

"Daddy, Lahlay Charger," Zoey tells me in her cute little voice, pointing up at her father.

"LA Charger," Tyrell softly murmurs when he glances at me.

I nod, thanking him with a wink.

I grin down at her. "That's pretty cool. You're gonna be

moving to Los Angeles. Wow. You know, that's the city of angels."

Zoey's eyes round, her lips parting. "I'm gonna meet an angel?"

"Lil' bug, you *are* an angel, so we're going to the right place." Sienna smiles down at her, and I love the way she's brushing her fingers through her daughter's hair.

This is just cuteness overload.

It makes me wonder if I'll ever have kids of my own.

If they're as cute as this little one, then it's gonna have to be a yes.

Zoey grins up at her mother before looking at me, then holding out the ball. "You play?"

"Oh, um..."

"Great idea." Tyrell grins, lightly tapping my shoulder and checking with my friends. "You guys in too?"

"Oh, I don't do... football." Tobin waves his hand in the air.

"Aw, come on, Tobs. You love balls." Nix winks at him, her wicked grin back in place as he glares at her.

I can't help a quick, snorting laugh.

Slapping my hand over my mouth, I spin away before Tobin can see me, then find Zoey right at my feet.

"You play my team."

"Okay." Taking her hand, I let her lead me across the grass and quickly find out that this is not really football.

This is... get the ball and try to reach the other end of the field without anyone catching you.

Nix manages to coax Tobin into the game after some heavy-duty hassling, and soon all three of us are as sweaty as the rest of them.

Out of breath, I rest my hands on my knees and suck

in some lungfuls of air after my reckless sprint down the field. Like I was ever gonna catch Tyrell with his big, long strides.

It was nice to hearing him laughing as I chased him, though.

He really does have a great laugh.

"You good?" He stops beside me, resting his large hand on my back.

"Yeah," I puff, sucking in another breath before standing tall.

His hand slips away, and I'm surprised by the rush of disappointment that flitters through me.

I have no idea what that's about, and I step to the side, disconcerted by whatever the hell is happening in my stomach right now.

Out of habit, I glance at my watch, then have to remind myself that I swapped shifts at work so I could go on this date tonight. I don't have to rush off anywhere, but for some reason, I'm suddenly desperate to leave.

"Well, we should head out." I catch Tobin's eye, and after a micro-moment of confusion, he picks up my silent SOS signal and backs me up like the true friend he is.

"Okay, well, that's enough sweat for me for one day."

"But not enough balls," Nix murmurs, then laughs when Tobin tries to punch her in the arm. "What? Did you not just tell me before that you have a date with your boyfriend tonight?" Her laugh is gleeful as she jumps away from Tobin. He starts chasing her toward the play-ground, and I jog backward, waving goodbye to the Foot-ball Frat crew.

"Thanks for letting us play." I point to Zoey.

She grins back at me, hugging the ball to her chest

and waving goodbye. Wily has her in his arms, and she looks like a happy girl as she blows me kisses and shouts, "Byeeeeee!"

"See you tonight." Tyrell raises his hand, calling after me. "I'll pick you up at seven."

And there goes that weird hitch in my chest again.

"Yeah, I'll, uh... I'll be ready."

Spinning before he can see my smile slip away, I race after my two crazy roommates and try to shake off this feeling.

I don't even know what this feeling is!

Man, I really hope this guy Tyrell's lined up for me is a winner, because I'm not sure how many more of these double dates is healthy for me. I love spending time with Tyrell... but am I enjoying it a little too much?

# CHAPTER 18
## TYRELL

I show up just before seven o'clock, the way my mama taught me to.

*"Never be late, Tyrell. You respect other people's time, you hear me?"*

I always heard her. Mama made sure of it.

My lips twitch as I climb the stairs to the fourth floor, not even thinking to use the elevator until I'm on the second-to-last landing.

Shaking my head with a rueful grin, I make it to the top, surprised by the spray of nerves ricocheting inside my chest. This is the fourth double date Dani and I have been on. I shouldn't be nervous at all.

Although, this is the first one I've picked her up for.

I don't even know why we arranged it this way, but here I am, knocking on her door like she's *my* date tonight.

*I wish she was.*

The thought jolts me, and I shake my head, instantly pushing it back.

No, I don't.

I'm here to meet that friend of a friend, and she's gonna be great and...

Well, to be honest, I've barely been paying any attention to these girls Dani has been finding for me. I only said yes to take the pressure off her. I didn't want her feeling like she was under a spotlight. This double-dating thing has been a casual, safer way of doing this "find her a man" plan, and I'm pretty sure it's helped her relax. So I'm gonna keep on doing it, but how can I possibly entertain any serious notions with the girls she's introducing me to when I'll be leaving soon?

No, this whole thing has to be about Dani and finding her the right guy.

I'm surprised by how hard it's been, but none of them are quite right. She's either not feeling it or they're not feeling it. I haven't seen bright, powerful sparks flying around yet. Not the way they did with Atlas.

"Hey." Tobin answers the door, grinning up at me like I'm a lollipop he wants to lick.

I guess I should take it as a compliment, but his open hunger is a little disconcerting, especially because he has a boyfriend... who is also eyeing me up the exact same way.

"Hi, Jed." I wave at him, and he shakes his head in these slow swipes back and forth.

"It's a travesty you're not gay."

I clear my throat and give him an awkward smile. "Your boyfriend's right there, man."

"Oh, and he adores me." Tobin pats his chest. "But we just think you're a full-blown hottie, and if you were gay, well, maybe we'd ask you to join the team, you know?"

He winks at me, and my smile gets a little tighter and more superficial.

Each to their own, you know? I'm not judging. I just know for myself that I'm a one-girl-at-a-time kinda guy. And if I was gay, I'm pretty sure I'd only have eyes for my man.

But I don't think I'll ever be gay.

And that is made abundantly clear to me the second Dani walks into the open living area and I'm struck dumb by the sight of her.

This hot flush travels through my body, an electric pulse that shorts out my brain.

All I can do is stare at her for a second, drink her in, because damn...

She's wearing a blue dress tonight, like the color of the sky on a clear day. The straps are thin over her shoulders, and holy shit, she's not wearing a bra. Her luscious boobs are tucked inside the gathered fabric, and then it comes in at the waist before flaring out to her knees.

She's barely wearing any makeup, as far as I can tell, but she doesn't need it. This girl glows without even trying, and I'm—

"Ty, are you okay?" Dani frowns at me, obviously worried.

"Uh..." I blink and clear my throat. "Yeah. I'm... I... Good. I'm good." I give her a thumbs-up, then internally cringe. *A thumbs-up, really?*

If she was my girl, I'd be dropping to my knees and telling her how damn sexy she looks. I'd be begging her not to go out, lifting her into my arms and taking her back into her bedroom so I could strip that dress off her body and—

"Are you sure you're okay?"

"Yeah." I bob my head, nodding like a maniac while I try to get my logical brain back online. "You look great," I manage to squeeze out.

"Doesn't she?" Tobin smiles at her, walking over to straighten the left shoulder strap. "You look divine, Dani Girl. See, aren't you glad I persuaded Vicky to change the venue? If you'd just gone to that diner, you wouldn't have had an excuse to put on a pretty dress. Now you get to eat fancy food and look super sexy doing it."

She runs a hand down the skirt part, a nervous habit she's had the whole time I've known her. "Yep. Thanks for that."

I'm not sure how grateful she really is. I don't care where we eat. Sure, I was looking forward to loaded fries and a shake, but fancy-ass food can be good too. And this Vicky chick's uncle owns the restaurant or something, so the food will be affordable with the discount she'll get.

"The shoes comfortable enough?" Jed asks, staring at her like he's assessing a piece of art.

"Yeah, they'll work." Dani tips on the heels, then looks at me. "These belong to Nix and they're a size too small, but I can always slip them off under the table, right?"

"No," Tobin tells her at the exact same time I say, "Of course you can."

She grins at me, then gives Tobin a pointed look.

"Oh, what does he know." Tobin flicks his hand at me, then spins to eye me up and tut. "Okay, fine, so the man can dress himself. But promise me that if you slip those shoes off, you remember to put them back on and don't walk out of the restaurant holding them."

"I won't, Dad." She laughs, patting his arm.

Tobin rolls his eyes, then pulls her into a hug. "You look gorgeous."

"Thanks for helping me pick out the dress."

"Anytime. I love shopping with you. Wait until you visit me in New York. We're gonna shop 'til we drop."

Jed groans. "You're gonna make me broke, baby."

Tobin laughs. "Oh, you love me."

Jed's smile turns soft and mushy as he gazes at his boyfriend, and it's clear to everyone that yes, he is very much in love.

I wonder what it must be like to feel that. Skimming my eyes over Dani once more, I get a hint and then have to give myself a sharp kick in the ass, because I shouldn't be feeling anything but platonic friendship for this stunning, kind, interesting woman.

"Shall we go?" I rush out the words, suddenly desperate to get out of here and to the restaurant.

She can meet Rhys, who Peters assures me is the nicest guy and sounds like a really good match for Dani. Man, I hope so.

I think that while my insides surge with rebellion.

Clenching my jaw, I walk to the elevator, figuring Dani's not gonna wanna use the stairs in those heels.

"You read my mind," she murmurs, straightening her jacket. "Thank you."

"Of course." I smile down at her. "You really do look great."

She snorts. "Yeah, I don't know. As much as I love this dress, a big part of me would feel a million times more comfortable in my cargo pants and combat boots, you know?"

"Yeah, well, you'd look awesome in that getup too." I laugh, then run my eyes down her body as the elevator doors ping open. "But, girl, that dress."

"I know, right?" She laughs. "I'm not even wearing a bra." She winces, resting a hand over her chest while my insides go nuts all over again. "Just promise me that if something slips out, you'll let me know."

Shit. The imagery in my head right now is threatening an immediate hard-on. I swallow and nod, croaking out, "Yeah, of course. I've got your back."

*And her front, apparently.*

Fuck.

Letting her step ahead of me, I lightly rest my hand on her lower back before reminding myself that she's not my date.

I quickly tuck my hand into my pocket and lean against the elevator wall, trying to create some distance between us.

Seriously, I should not be this attracted to a woman I'm trying to set up with someone else.

*Shit, Atlas, I'm sorry. I wish you were here so you could see how damn hot she looks tonight. You'd be speechless, man.*

Keeping my best friend in the forefront of my mind, I don't touch Dani again as we walk out of her building. I do open the door for her, then help her make sure the skirt part of her dress doesn't get caught when she slips into my SUV.

As I walk around to the driver's side, I start up a quick mantra.

*She's not mine. She's not mine. She's not mine.*

I desperately try to remind myself that we're meeting

up with other people tonight. People we're supposed to be interested in. But when I glance at Dani one more time, I can't help worrying that I'm gonna be losing the battle big-time.

# CHAPTER 19
## DANI

"So, Rhys Peters."

"That's right." Tyrell nods, clenching his jaw as he drives us to the restaurant.

It's weird. He's been clenching his jaw a lot since leaving my apartment, and I kind of want to ask what's bugging him, but I also don't want to pry. Maybe he's nervous about meeting Vicky. I've only met her once, but Jolie assures me she's really cool and fun, and she works at the paper with her. She does the graphic design or something, so she's creative, which is cool, and she's really smart as well, which will be a great match for Ty.

Plus, she's a stunner.

Legs that go on forever, tall and elegant with this friendly smile and bright eyes. I think her father's Puerto Rican and her mother is Scottish or something. Anyway, she looks like a supermodel.

My insides squirm, wondering what Tyrell will think. Wondering how well they'll hit it off.

Oh shit, if it goes well, will he sleep with her?

*So what if he does?*

Now I'm the one clenching my jaw.

He's been polite to all the girls I've invited so far, but I haven't noticed any real spark. Maybe tonight will be the one. He's definitely going to find her attractive—that's a given.

Biting my lips together, I ignore the weird tension in my stomach and focus on the road ahead.

Rhys Peters.

Plays guitar.

An art major.

Two years younger than me, but according to Tyrell, his brother says he's mature for his age. Like an old man on young shoulders.

*"He's more of a grown-up than I'll ever be."* That's what Peters said, apparently.

"What's Peters's first name?"

"Oh, uh…" Tyrell has to think about it.

I can't help laughing. "Come on, you must know."

"Yeah, I do. I'm just so used to calling him Peters that I—" He clicks his fingers. "Marcus."

"Marcus," I repeat. "Marcus and Rhys."

"That's right."

"Cool. Do they seem close?"

Tyrell shrugs. "They must be a little close if he's setting up a blind date for his brother, but I think they're pretty different. One's obsessed with sports, the other with music."

"Kinda like you and Atlas," I say without thinking.

Holding my breath, I wait for the inevitable sadness that follows any mention of his name, but Tyrell just smiles and nods. "Yeah. Like that."

Slowing to a stop, Tyrell maneuvers the car into a parallel parking space, his strong arm coming around the back of my seat while he makes parking an SUV look like the easiest thing in the world. This car doesn't have one of those fancy screens to guide him into the spot; he's going old-school, and this might sound weird, but it's super sexy.

A thrill races down my body, so I clutch my purse, reminding myself that I'm here for Rhys. Tyrell and I can never be a thing. I wouldn't do that to Atlas.

*Atlas isn't here!*

But he is. Somehow he always will be, and I just can't shake that.

Opening the door, I carefully step out, ensuring I don't twist my ankle when my foot hits the concrete. These shoes are too small, and my feet are already killing me. I can't wait to sit down so I can take the damn things off.

"You good?" Tyrell's hand shoots out to steady me, his fingers curling around my elbow.

I smile him a thank-you, appreciating his warmth beside me as we walk down the block to the restaurant. It's a French one. We wouldn't normally go this fancy, but Victoria's aunt and uncle own the place, and she gets a table here whenever she wants. I don't know why she didn't suggest it initially. I think I suggested Eat Your Faves and she just went with it. Until she got a call from Jolie, who had gotten a call from Tobin. I was kind of pissed off for his interfering at first, but I'm over it now.

French food, while no loaded fries, will be delicious.

I think she gets half-price meals too, which is convenient because all of this dating is starting to add up.

Tyrell and the guy always offer to pay, and sometimes I've taken them up on that. But to keep things fair, I've insisted on paying a few times as well. I don't want Tyrell out of pocket because of me. It's not like he has a job right now, and this is probably eating into his savings.

"Tonight's on me," I tell him as he opens the door.

His eyebrows dip and I can sense the protest he's about to make, but I hold up my hand to stop him.

"It's my turn, so just let me do it, okay?"

His lips purse as we stand there in the open doorway. I refuse to go in until he agrees with me.

After a short sigh, he finally nods. "But at least let me offer first, okay?"

"Of course." I smile, then wink at him. "Gotta make you look good for the lady, right?"

"What's her name again?" he whispers as he follows me into the restaurant.

"Victoria. But I think she prefers Vicky."

"Got it." He puts on a smile as the hostess leads us to a table near the back.

Vicky and Rhys are already there and...

Oooo! He is cuuuute!

My lips twitch as I drink in this gorgeous man with bronze skin and eyes that match my dress. He looks like a musician, not a rock star. He has more of an indie vibe with his linen shirt and necklaces. I bet he listens to bands like The 1975 and loves Vampire Weekend. His hair is dark and curly, tied back in a stubby ponytail, and I feel an instant kick of desire as he stands up to greet us.

"Hey there." He smiles at me, drinking me in like I'm important.

"Hi." Oh my gosh, what is my mouth doing right now? I bet I look like an excited groupie. Ugh!

Slipping my jacket off, I hang it over the back of my chair, stealing a quick glance at Tyrell, who's shaking Vicky's hand and so obviously admiring her too.

See? I knew he'd be into her.

She is so freaking beautiful!

Pulling out the chair for her, Tyrell waits until she's settled before taking his own seat.

I catch his eye and am rewarded with a little eye bulge. I bite my lips together to hide my grin. Oh yeah, he thinks she's hot. Intimidatingly so, I'm guessing, by the way he's twitching like he doesn't know what to do with his hands.

Resting one palm over his knuckles, he leans his elbows on the table, then springs back like his mama's here and she's quipped, "Boy, get your elbows off the table."

"So, Dani, I hear you work at Offside." Rhys smiles at me.

"I do." I lift my glass when he picks up the water jug to fill it. "Thank you."

He smiles, and oh my gosh, look at that smile! He's so beautiful.

"Have you ever played there? Tyrell tells me you're a musician."

"I am, and I'd love to. There's a pretty long list, and I'm on it, just waiting for my turn. Although, my sets would be pretty chill compared to some of the music that's played there."

"We get everything," I assure him. "Last week, we had a country band, and they got some line dancing going.

People really got into it. And then this weekend, we've got a punk rock band doing their thing. I'm sure a chill indie set would be perfect for one of our quieter nights."

"How do you know I play chill indie?" His lips rise into a lopsided smirk.

I grin, playing with the little cross emblem around my neck. My parents gave it to me for my twelfth birthday, and I've worn it ever since. "You have that look about you. Tyrell told me you play guitar. I guess I just look at you and picture a man with his guitar, strumming and singing songs with a Jason Mraz vibe or maybe a Hozier feel?"

"Oh man, nailed it." He laughs. "That is absolutely me. I write my own stuff, but I definitely draw inspiration from those types of genres. I love a blend of alternative rock with like a folk, reggae edge. That probably sounds like a really weird combination."

"No, I love that." I smile. "Anyone willing to experiment with their creativity is on the right path if you ask me. Fusing different styles of music is a great way to play and have fun. And then you end up with a sound that's just yours, you know? I'd love to hear your stuff sometime."

His sweet smile tells me I've just made his day.

"Maybe you can bump him up the list," Vicky suggests. "I'd come hear you play at Offside."

"Thanks." He smiles at her, and I take that moment to wiggle my eyebrows at Tyrell. This date is going great. Maybe our best one yet!

Surely Ty's getting the sense too, right?

So why isn't he smiling?

Why is he studying the menu like the only thing on there is snails soaked in vinegar?

## CHAPTER 20
# TYRELL

So, Rhys is fucking perfect.

And it's annoying the hell out of me.

I should be happy that he and Dani are clicking so easily. Of course they were going to. He's ticking all the boxes, right?

Musical.

Sexy, in that long-hair, artsy kind of way.

Of course she's into that. The guy is just like Atlas.

Except that he's not. Atlas had an edge to him. A toughness that I don't sense in Rhys. Particularly when he launched into his story about the first time he met his puppy.

"The second I laid eyes on Arthur, I just got this sense, you know? He was staring up at me with those big brown eyes and..." He shook his head, a smile tugging at his lips. "I knew he was the one."

Both girls swooned, and I sat here clenching my jaw.

I'm still clenching it while we wait for dessert to

arrive. I don't even feel like anything sweet, but I ordered because everyone else did and...

Dammit! What the hell is wrong with me?

Rhys is a really nice guy. Dani deserves nice. She deserves fucking epic, and I should be so happy right now. I did it! I found her Mr. Right.

*Atlas, brother, what are you thinking?*

*You like him?*

As always, I sit here waiting for an answer that will never come. As much as I talk to my best friend, he never talks back.

Which is possibly why I haven't been thinking about him as much in the last year. Until Dani walked back into my life. Now he's front and center all over again.

Actually, *she's* kind of been front and center lately. And I'm about to lose her to perfect Mr. Rhys Peters.

Shit!

Dani laughs, resting her fingers on Rhys's arm while he tells a story about how he's been trying to teach Arthur how to play the piano.

"I've got a video."

"Let's see it!" Vicky wiggles her fingers when he pulls out his phone.

I lean back in my chair, hating the way Dani leans in to watch this video of a dog whacking piano keys. Shit, Cyrus would love it. He's got such a thing about animals. My parents bought each of us a kitten one Christmas, and Cyrus cried. He was so freaking happy. He named his little girl Peaches because she was orange. I named my cat Rook, and Lacey named hers Samson. They were all from the same litter and played and fought like siblings.

Unfortunately, Samson died about two years ago—hit

by a car. Lacey cried for two days, and Cyrus cried for a solid week. I'm so grateful Peaches is still going strong. She's nearly thirteen now, and I don't know what we're gonna do when she passes on. Maybe we should think about getting another kitten now, so Cyrus will never be without.

I think about my old boy, Rook, and hope he's doing okay. Cyrus promised to take care of him for me and sends me updates on the regular. Although, I really don't need to know the consistency of his shits and that he's finishing his food each day, but Cyrus is a man of details when it comes to our pets.

Routine is everything for him.

Glancing at my watch, I note the time. He'll be texting in thirty-four minutes, and as much as I hate to pull out my phone on a date, I will always make an exception for my brother.

"He's the cutest. And I love Arthur for a name. That's so adorable."

"Yeah, he's just got a kingly kind of vibe, don't you think?" Rhys turns the phone so I can see a picture of his golden retriever.

I nod and mutter, "Cute."

"Yeah, he's awesome. I really miss him, but he makes me feel so loved every time I walk through the front door that it makes up for being away. Gonna get to spend the whole summer with him soon." He grins, then leans his arms on the table. "So, what are you ladies up to for the summer?"

I notice that he's stopped trying to pull me into the conversation. Probably because I'm being a grumpy dick.

Shit, I'm not trying to be. It's just that every time

Dani's hand lands on his arm or she laughs at something he says, my skin starts to crawl or I get this sharp, pinching sensation in my chest.

I don't know what the fuck it's about, but—

*Yes, you do. You know exactly what this is about.*

Scratching my jawline, I try to deny the voice in my head, but what is the fucking point?

The truth is, I'm hating this because it's the first double date Dani and I have been on where she hasn't been touching *my* arm and laughing with *me*. This is the first date where her attention has been captured by the other guy.

And it's fucking killing me.

Which means...

Shit.

I've done the one thing I was trying to avoid.

I've gone and caught feelings for my best friend's girl.

# CHAPTER 21
## DANI

Grrrrr. What is up with Tyrell tonight?

He's gotten so quiet, and it's infuriating me, but I can't let any of that show, which is why I'm staying so focused on Rhys.

It's not hard.

He's smooth and charming, but also seems genuine. I love his hair. I love the way his face lights with a smile so easily. He's a great guy, and the way he talks about his dog makes my heart melt.

I want to hear him play guitar.

I will definitely be seeing if I can bump his name up the list at Offside. We have got to get this man onstage.

And I'm sure Tyrell would agree with me on that.

Why is he still looking so sour? This date has gone so well!

Although, he's barely been a part of it. Are the others picking up his angsty vibes too? I wonder if they're assuming he's just a quiet, reserved guy. Happy to watch from the sidelines.

I mean, he is that.

Black Jack.

The Silent Knight.

My lips quirk as I think about that label. That journalist was spot-on. Ty *is* a silent knight.

But it's annoying the hell out of me that he's being a silent *grumpy* knight right now.

Eyeing him across the table, I bulge my eyes at him, but he looks away before we can have any kind of silent conversation like we've had on other dates.

Balling my hands into little fists under the table, I resist the urge to kick him and focus back on Vicky, who's telling us a story about this cathedral she went to in Germany.

"It's absolutely massive, and the architecture is just stunning. If you think about when it was constructed, it's mind-blowing." This look of awe lifts her face into a smile. "The engineering is so impressive."

Vicky turns to Tyrell, who I *know* will be interested in this kind of thing. It's a historic building in Europe, so of course he'll be into it.

"Yeah." He kind of sighs. "Sounds impressive."

Seriously? Could he look more disinterested right now?

What the hell is his problem?

"I bet the acoustics in there are next-level." Rhys sits forward with a grin, and I turn my attention to him because he's gorgeous and nice and not being a grumpy turd right now.

"Oh yeah. I spent two hours in there just walking around, then sitting in a pew, soaking it all in."

"I'd love to play my guitar in a place like that. Do a

show in an old church with a high ceiling. That would be so cool." Rhys grins.

"So, you like to travel?" I ask, resting my fingers on his arm again. I can't help it. He's got great arms, and he doesn't seem to mind me touching him.

He smiles at me. "I've only been to Hawaii so far, but that was fun. I'd definitely love to get to Europe at some point."

"You should." Vicky nods, smiling at the waiter as he approaches with our desserts.

Yes! Chocolate mousse!

"Here you go." He sets down our desserts, and I smile at my chocolate decadence before casting a quick glance across the table.

Tyrell is frowning down at his slice of cheesecake like he might be sick.

Oh shit, is he not feeling well?

Is that why he's being so quiet and unenthusiastic?

Sudden guilt hits me. Shit, I've been stewing over his grumpy ass while he's possibly sitting there trying not to throw up.

I nudge his leg under the table, and he glances at me.

"You okay?" I mouth while Vicky tells Rhys all about the other places she visited on her whirlwind trip through Europe last summer.

Tyrell nods, frowning like he's confused by my query.

"Sore tummy?" I touch my hand to my stomach.

His eyebrows dip even closer together as he shakes his head.

"What's wrong?" I mouth.

He shakes his head again, grabbing his dessert fork

and shoveling a large mouthful of cheesecake into his piehole.

Okay, fine. So he's not feeling sick, then.

Now I'm back to being annoyed with his cranky ass.

My chocolate mousse doesn't taste as sweet as I'm expecting it to, but I don't think it's the chef's fault. I think it's the sour notes Tyrell is flinging across the table. I'm almost relieved when dinner is over.

"Can I drive you home?" Rhys asks as we rise from the table.

Tyrell's head whips to look at the man helping me into my jacket.

"Uh…"

"With no expectations of coming in or anything." Rhys smiles when I turn to face him, and I can see that he means it.

Wow. A real gentleman. This guy really is perfect.

I glance at Tyrell, whose nostrils are flaring, his mouth set in a straight line, and… you know what?

"Yes." I look away from my friend and smile at Rhys. "That'd be lovely. Thank you."

Tyrell makes a soft growl in his throat, which makes us all turn to him with varying looks of surprise.

He tries to disguise it by clearing his throat, but we all heard that growl, and I have to gape at him, because seriously, what the fuck is his problem?

Clenching his jaw for what must be the three hundredth time tonight, he turns to Vicky with a scowl. "You need a ride?"

"No." She pulls her jacket a little tighter around herself. "I'm gonna head out back and hang with my aunt and uncle for a while." With a polite nod, she steps away from him, then gives me a hug and thanks Rhys for a wonderful evening. Tyrell gets nothing else from her, and he doesn't freaking deserve it.

I can't hide my angst when I give him a final glare. "I'll see you later."

"Yep." He pops the *P*, his jaw working to the side as he stays put by the table, watching Rhys lead me out of the restaurant.

I can't believe him!

This is the first good connection I've had throughout all these dates, and he has to go and ruin it.

"You okay?" Rhys asks as he walks beside me to his car.

"Oh, yeah." I force a smile, praying he won't ask me about Tyrell. Did he notice how grumpy the guy was?

Grrr!

*Just stop thinking about him. Focus on Rhys.*

"So, when are you performing again? Got any gigs coming up?" I force out.

Thankfully, he responds with an easy smile, and conversation is soon focused on street performances and collecting dimes in his guitar case.

He keeps me thoroughly entertained as he drives me back to my apartment.

When he pulls up to the curb, my insides flail for just a second. What's the expectation here?

This is the first date that's gone well. The first time I've gotten a ride home from the actual guy instead of Tyrell.

*Wait, is that why Tyrell growled? Was he annoyed that someone else was driving me home? But why? Shouldn't he be happy about that?*

*Maybe he was annoyed because things were going great for me and Rhys but not him and Vicky.*

*Shit. I need to talk to him. Make sure he's okay.*

"Uh... Dani?"

"Sorry, what?" I blink, only just registering that Rhys has been talking to me this whole time.

He lets out a soft laugh. "I just asked if you wanted to get together again sometime."

"Oh, um..." I nod. "Yeah, sure."

He smiles. "I had a really fun time with you tonight."

I nod. "Me too."

"Great." I drink in his gorgeous smile. "Well, I'll... see you around, then?"

"Sure."

"Did you want to exchange numbers or...?"

"Oh, yeah." I dig out my phone, my breath evaporating when I spot a text I didn't hear come through.

*Black Jack: I'm sorry for being a dick. Hope you're having a good time with Rhys. If you're up for a date debrief, give me a call.*

"Dani?" Rhys asks again. "Everything okay?"

"Yeah, I just... um..." I lift my phone with an awkward laugh. "My friend texted me, and I..." I let out a soft breath, unsure why I can't finish that sentence.

"You know what?" Rhys grips the wheel and looks out the windshield. "Why don't you deal with that tonight, and I'll grab your number another time. I can sense you're distracted. I'll just give Tyrell a text, and he can send me your number. Is that cool?"

"Yeah." I nod, confused by this weird feeling in my chest. I don't even know what it is, but all I can think about is talking to Tyrell.

I want to see him.

Find out what his problem is.

"Hey, thanks again for a great evening. I really enjoyed it." Rhys smiles at me, and I force myself to slip the phone back into my purse and look at him.

He really is beautiful.

Surprising myself, I reach out and cup his cheek, softly whispering, "Thank you."

He gazes at me, silently asking permission to kiss me good night. He doesn't have to say anything, and although my heart has launched itself into my throat, I lean forward anyway.

This is all part of moving on with my life, right?

Kissing another guy.

Letting Atlas go and...

*This is the first guy you will have kissed since him. Do you even remember how to?*

Ignoring the panicked taunts in my head, I lean a little closer... and a little closer... until Rhys's lips are pressed against mine.

Closing my eyes, I sink into it, really trying to feel that thing. That spark. You know? The one that came so easily for Atlas and me. The one that curls your toes and sends a current jolting through your body. The one that makes your insides want to dance and rave and...

*Nothing.*

*Wait, maybe I just need to deepen it.*

Threading my fingers around Rhys's neck, I brush my tongue across his lips and he responds, opening his mouth to me. Our tongues glide together for just a moment, but...

*Nope. Nothing.*

We try for just another second, but I'm starting to get the sense that maybe there's no spark for him either.

Seriously?

But he's so perfect!

My insides are wailing as I ease away from him and we share an awkward smile.

Clearing his throat, he nods and murmurs, "Thanks again for a great date."

"Yeah, you... you too." My laughter is wispy and insincere, so I push the door open and make a quick escape.

The wind catches my dress as I walk around the back of his car, and I quickly snatch it down, holding it against my thigh as Rhys sticks his hand out the window and waves goodbye.

I frown after his car, disappointment searing me as I watch him drive away.

No spark.

Shit. I'm never gonna find myself a man.

With a soft huff, I shake my head and wrench my phone out of my purse.

Reading Tyrell's text again, I send back a quick reply.

*I'm ready for a debrief now. But I don't want to do it over the phone. Meet me at that park a block from my place. You know the one with the red bench seat?*

. . .

Why I want to see him, I'm not even sure, but as I wrap my arms around myself and stomp toward the playground, I start running through scenarios.

Maybe I want to be able to slap him for being a douche.

Or maybe I want to cry on his shoulder because I thought Rhys was so great, yet when I kissed him...

My shoulders slump and I pause on the sidewalk to take off Nix's shoes. They've been torturing my feet ever since I slipped them back on.

Padding along in my bare feet, I try not to think about how dirty the concrete is and instead focus on why I feel so compelled to see Tyrell "Grumpy Ass" Jackson.

Maybe I just want to sit on a bench beside him and shoot the breeze like we've done after other dates.

Or maybe I just want the comfort of being with someone who's known me since I was fourteen. Someone who knows Atlas.

Shit. I have no idea which reason is making me plunk my butt down on this cold red bench.

The emotions inside me are a torrent—a hurricane—of angst, and I don't know whether to feel relief, agitation, or this weird pulse of something I don't want to identify when Tyrell jumps out of his SUV and starts striding toward me.

# CHAPTER 22
## TYRELL

She pops to her feet as soon as she sees me coming, and I'm relieved she's taken those heels off. I could tell they were hurting her feet when she reluctantly slipped them back on under the table.

Shit. She looks pissed.

And I deserve it.

I was a total dick tonight. But how do I explain my behavior?

The idea of trying to justify myself forms a quick rock in my throat. It's impossible to swallow down, and my steps slow the closer I get to her.

Shit, this is bad.

Do I play it cool?

Pretend like nothing was off tonight?

"Hey." I try to smile at her the second I'm within range and figure that yeah, playing it cool is definitely the safest option.

"Hey." She spits out the word, all short and clipped and...

*Shit, shit, shit.*

I messed up tonight.

*So fix it!*

"Rhys seems like a nice guy." Those idiot words are out of my mouth before I can stop them, and it's instant regret.

Her eyebrows pucker, her frown deepening and...

*Oh fuck. Please don't cry.*

"I'm sorry," I quickly blurt. "I didn't mean to be a douche. I don't even know why I was acting like a grumpy asshole."

*Yes, you do. Just tell her!*

I clear my throat. "And—"

"Shut up." She shakes her head, crossing her arms and sniffing. "I don't get it."

I'm not sure exactly what she means, so I bite my lips together and wait her out.

"I mean, we're going on all of these stupid dates to try and find me the right guy, and then we find one who's actually amazing, and you act like..." She flicks her eyes at me, her gaze searing the flesh off my bones. "You act like a cantankerous old man."

"I didn't mean to—"

"Poor Vicky! Who knows what she's saying to her aunt and uncle right now."

I cringe, rubbing the back of my hair.

"I just don't know if I can do this anymore."

It's like a punch to the gut... and I can't keep denying why that is.

My heart starts to race, pounding through my body like an army marching to its doom.

After a heavy sigh, she mumbles, "I'm wondering if we should just... drop this whole thing."

"Don't say that," I croak. "I'm gonna find you the right guy."

"Atlas was the right guy!" she snaps. "And he's dead."

The words slash through me, and I'm a wounded warrior, swaying on my feet as I watch her nostrils flare, her expression buckling for a second before she pulls it back into line.

"And Rhys was nice. He was awesome." She clears her throat, her arms tightening around herself like she's not telling me something.

My insides revolt, but I force myself to keep it locked down. She deserves better than me complaining about her finding a decent guy.

I'm such an asshole.

Gritting my teeth, I look away from her, squeezing the back of my neck and reprimanding myself for not being a better friend.

*Stop acting like a dick!*

"So, you gonna go out with him again?" I shove my hands into my pockets and tip back on my heels, my heart now marching right down to my knees.

"Yeah, maybe," she mutters, then flicks her arms in the air while this acidic cloud of smoke fills my chest. "I just don't get it, you know?"

I don't actually know but decide that giving her the space to rant is the best option, so I don't try to work it out.

"I mean, did you not like Rhys? Was there something wrong with him?"

That cloud turns to a toxic gas, and breathing

becomes nearly impossible. All I can manage is a short shake of my head.

"Is something else going on with you? Is that why you tried to screw up this date?"

I wince and shake my head again but still can't find the words I need.

She tuts, rolling her eyes. "This is useless. If you're not gonna talk to me, then this debrief is a waste of fucking time!" she growls. "Just forget it. I can work this shit out on my own!"

With a huff, she flicks her arms up, then goes to storm away.

*Don't let her leave! Tell her the truth!*

Panic clutches me, and I snatch her wrist before she can go.

"He wasn't me," I whisper.

"What?" she snaps, turning to frown at me.

My heart's now jumped up into my throat, pulsing right next to that boulder that's stealing all of my volume.

But I've said it now, and I'm gonna have to say it again.

Turning to face her properly, I rub my thumb across her smooth skin and admit once more, "He wasn't me. That's what was wrong with him. That's what's wrong with all the guys you've been dating." I give her a pained frown and say it one more time, so there's no way she won't get it. "None of them are me."

Her lips part, her eyes going wide like she's on the verge of freaking out.

I don't know what to do.

I've said it.

This secret I didn't even fully realize I was harboring is out there, and I better fucking do something with it.

Letting go of her arm, I reach for her face instead, tracing the shocked lines of her expression, my thumb skimming her lower lip as I fight the urge to kiss her.

Would she even want me to?

This is Atlas's girl.

*Atlas is dead! He's not here anymore.* You *are!*

But would she want me?

I'm nothing like him. How could she be in love with a guy like Atlas and then want a guy like me?

I can't stop touching her, though. Now that the pads of my fingers are tracing her delicate skin, I never want to stop. I love the shape of her face, those big, beautiful eyes, those luscious lips.

I... I want to kiss them. To taste her. To...

She still hasn't said anything.

But she hasn't moved away either.

She's just gazing up at me like she can't believe what I said.

But it's true.

Now that it's out there, I know it's true. I'm going ahead and falling for this woman. I didn't mean to. It happened before I even realized, and now that I'm finally acknowledging it, I better fucking make it count.

As I gaze down at her mouth, my heart starts to thunder between my ears.

*Do it, man. Just do it!*

I lean in, slowly inching my way into her space. The tip of my nose reaches her first, and I brush it against the side of her cheek, moving to the straight line of her nose.

Her breath fans across my skin.

I'm going slow, giving her every chance to reject me. But she's not.

Whether it's curiosity or desire, I'm not sure, but her lips are right there.

Another shaky breath punches out of her, and I wonder if I should pull away, but there's no stopping this now.

My lips skim over hers, a delicate, tentative touch.

She sucks in a quick breath before I apply a little more pressure.

Our lips meet... and stay connected.

I hold my position, giving her every chance in the world to pull away...

But she doesn't.

So I lean a little closer, shuffling forward one step and threading my arm around her waist.

Tipping my head, I hold that kiss, and then something magical happens.

Her trembling fingers touch my neck, her thumb skimming my earlobe before she parts her lips and deepens the kiss.

My tongue acts of its own accord, brushing against hers with a gentle swipe. I can't be demanding about this. Part of me wants to grab the back of her head, bury my fingers in those spiral curls, and take what my body is craving.

But I don't want to scare her off, so I force myself to keep playing it slow, drawing out this tender kiss, a thrill racing through my body when her tongue slides against mine once more—a slow, easy exploration that's sending my insides into chaos.

Fuck, she feels good.

I can't help a soft moan as I pull her a little tighter

against me, my fingers curling into the skirt part of this sexy dress.

She rises up to her tiptoes, her tongue lashing mine again, like she's about to let go and throw herself into a make-out session...

But then she pulls back, pausing like she's trying to decide something, before shaking her head and then lurching back even more.

Pushing her hand into my shoulder, she holds me at arm's length yet curls her fingers into my jacket.

It's like she can't decide if she wants to pull me in or push me away.

I search her face, silently asking what she wants. Half of her is cast in shadow, the light over the park not enough to highlight her full reaction, so I hold my breath and try to figure out what to say.

But she speaks before I can. "I have to go."

"Dani," I croak.

"No." She shakes her head, wrenching out of my arms. "I have to..." Her steps falter as she walks away.

"Please, can I at least... walk you home?"

"No." She shakes her head again, picking up her pace. "I just... I have to..." With a soft whimper, she snatches her heels off the park bench and starts running.

I watch her go, tracking her movements until I can see her safely on the other side of the road. Her apartment is just around the corner. I'm confident she'll make it there without a problem, especially at the pace she's running.

"Fuck," I mutter, gripping the top of my head, suddenly swamped by guilt.

I can feel Atlas's presence all around me, like a shroud covering me from head to toe.

"I'm sorry, man," I murmur.

As usual, I don't hear any audible answer, just a feeling.

He's pissed. He's pissed with me because I kissed his girl.

"I'm sorry," I say, a little louder this time. "I couldn't help it. I just... I hate the idea of her falling for someone else, you know? And I swear, I didn't even know I felt this way. And I definitely didn't feel it when you guys were together. I swear, okay? I promise you, I never went after your girl. But... hanging out with her lately has been..." I glance up, wincing at the night sky. "I didn't mean to do it. But she's awesome. I get why you were so hung up on her. I mean, I think I got it then, but I *really* get it now." I sigh, palming the back of my head and staring down at the ground. "What should I do?"

I don't expect an answer, yet still feel disappointed when one doesn't come.

Why do I keep talking to him?

Why do I keep trying to have these one-sided conversations?

Why do I feel so damn guilty when he's not actually here!

The idea hurts, like someone's poking this festering wound with the tip of their sword.

"Why am I even stressing?" I mutter, kicking the grass with my shoe. "She doesn't want me anyway."

I spin with a heavy sigh, my mind watching her run away from me over and over again as I shuffle to my car and thump into the driver's seat.

Why waste my time on guilt when nothing's going to happen between us?

"Shit!" I thump the wheel.

I promised Atlas I'd look out for her, but I've gone and fucked it up.

Tipping my head back, I let out a frustrated groan that turns into a full-blown yell that bounces off the windows of my car and right back to me.

I don't know what the fuck I'm supposed to do now.

Should I try and see Dani again?

Is there even any point?

She's probably gonna start hanging with Rhys, and I'll be leaving soon anyway.

"Just fucking drive home and forget about this whole damn thing."

I start the engine with a growl and squeal away from the curb, my insides filled with buzzing, irritated bees... and I have no fucking idea how I'm supposed to eradicate them.

# CHAPTER 23
## DANI

Tyrell kissed me.

He kissed me, and it was…

Aw man, it felt amazing!

His lips on mine were just…

And the way he croaked out his confession, all soft and husky and…

*"He's not me."*

Those words traveled right through me, igniting parts of my soul that I didn't even know were dormant. But the second those whispered words registered, I felt this ping in my chest.

I mean, sure, I was shocked.

I never expected to hear something like that from Atlas's best friend.

How long has he felt that way? Always, or is this a new development?

I've spent the past twenty-four hours obsessing over it, trying to recall every interaction from high school and read into it. Did those shy smiles he used to give me mean more? Was he harboring these secret feelings all these years?

*Does he feel as guilty over the kiss as I do?*

"You shouldn't feel guilty," Jed replies.

*Oh shit, did I just say that out loud?*

I bulge my eyes at him, and he smirks. "You know I'm right. I don't want to be cruel or anything, but Atlas isn't here anymore." Lightly touching my shoulder, he ignores the guy at the bar, waving to get our attention, and softly whispers, "He's dead... and Tyrell is very much alive."

I frown, muttering, "I wish I hadn't told you," before moving around to plaster on a smile and serve the man impatiently waiting for a drinks order.

I didn't mean to spill my guts to my roommates, but they happened to be walking into the apartment as I came running toward it. I must have looked like a wreck, because they bundled me between them, walked me up the stairs, and made me confess every detail of the date.

And like the weakling I am, I spilled everything... from how perfect Rhys was to how imperfect our kiss was to... to Tyrell blowing my mind with his mouth and tongue and body and sweet, sweet confession.

*"He's not me."*

Ugh, those words are going to ring through me forever. The way he said them. His husky, deep voice, so vulnerable.

"Thank you," the man clips, taking the two beers and turning back to his table.

I watch him go, jumping when Jed appears behind me like a stealth ninja and whispers, "I still don't get why you ran away. That kiss sounded perfect. And it's Tyrell. I mean, come on, girl. He's—"

"Atlas's best friend," I grit out.

"That's not it. And you can't keep bringing a dead guy into the equation."

I give him an appalled frown.

"I'm sorry if that sounds harsh. I'm not trying to hurt you, but you need to face up to reality."

"What do you think I've been trying to do!" I hiss, forcing another smile when a customer walks past the bar. "Can I get you anything?"

"No, I'm good for now. Thanks." She smiles at me, throws Jed an appreciative look, then walks down to her friends at the other end of the bar.

"You want to know what I think?"

"No." I snatch the towel off his shoulder and start wiping down the already clean bar.

"I think you've been desperately trying to move on, and nothing's really resonated with you until last night. That kiss hit you right in the feels, and now you're scared shitless because for the first time since losing Atlas, falling for someone else is a very real possibility."

I go still, my entire body frozen by his confronting words.

"Dani," he whispers. "Girl, you know I love you. And I want to see you happy. This is what this big move was all about. And happiness is now within your grasp. Snatch that shit and skip into your sunset."

"What if it doesn't work out?"

Jed lets out a soft sigh, and I turn to see him shake his head. "Life is all about uncertainties. I can't tell you if it's going to work out or not. But I can tell you that you'll regret it if you curl into a ball and spend the rest of your life trying to protect yourself from pain. Because all that's gonna cause you is a different kind of pain. A lonely, miserable pain, and I don't want that for you."

My stomach churns, my fingers digging into the dish towel.

"Do you want that for you?"

"Of course not," I rasp. "I just…"

"Need to stop thinking so hard." He squeezes my shoulder, his booming voice rising with a bright cheerfulness. "Hey, what can I get you tonight?"

I shuffle away from him while he servers another customer and am kind of relieved when two giggling girls skip up to the counter and put in a drinks order. They're underage, and that uses up my time—a great distraction from my Tyrell problem.

Tyrell.

He passed on my number to Rhys. I got a text from the guy this afternoon, asking when I'd like to catch up again. I told him I was really busy for the next few days and needed to check my schedule at work. I told him I'd let him know… and I still haven't.

Because Tyrell passed on my number, which means he totally accepted my rejection last night and… Dammit! Why does that sit so ugly in my chest?

I don't want to catch up with Rhys again.

I want to spend more time with Ty.

Except I don't, because Jed's right—it's freaking terrifying.

But as hard as I try not to think about him, I can't stop. He dances through my brain for the rest of my shift, and I'm exhausted by the time closing rolls around. We always close up earlier on Sunday nights, and it's just after ten as Jed and I walk to his car.

Thankfully, he hasn't mentioned another word about Tyrell. All I want to do right now is go home, have a really long, hot shower, then curl up in bed and sleep so I don't have to think anymore.

*Curl up into a little ball and try not to feel, you mean?*

I scowl at the irritating taunts in my brain and glare out the windshield.

Jed still hasn't started the engine, and after a long beat, I turn to him and snip, "Can we go, please?"

"Are you sure you want to go home?"

"Yes!" I give him an emphatic look.

He snickers, starting the engine and teasing me. "You're not gonna be able to sleep."

My reply is a threatening growl, but unfortunately, next to this big lug, I'm more like a chihuahua than the threatening bear I want to be.

"He's the one who lights you up, girl."

"Shut up," I warn him.

"He's the one who puts the biggest smile on your face."

"Stop talking."

"He's the one who made you *feel* something when you kissed."

"Jed!" I slap my thigh.

"Look, I know you don't want to hear all this stuff. The truth sucks sometimes, but *this truth* doesn't. This is a good, happy, beautiful truth that you're denying yourself out of fear. No good decision has ever been made out of fear, and I can't sit silently by while you ignore all your feelings."

I cross my arms, slumping back in my seat and clenching my jaw.

"If Tobin was here, he'd be saying exactly the same thing. Except louder. And faster." Jed grins. "And with a lot more sass."

I snort, shaking my head and fighting a soft snicker.

Jed lets out a sigh, and I can't think what to say next.

He's right. Tyrell liking me, wanting to kiss me... being really good at it... those are all beautiful truths, and I can't even understand *why* I'm denying myself.

The fear thing is probably correct too.

Dammit. I had no idea I was so transparent.

My eyes start to burn as I glare out the window, not even paying attention to where Jed's driving until he starts to slow and work his way through a part of town I don't recognize.

"Where are we going?" I whip around to look at him.

He works his jaw to the side, quietly murmuring, "Don't hate me."

"What?"

"I'm doing this because I love you."

"Jed, what the hell?" I snap.

Turning onto a street full of houses, he heads about two-thirds down, then pulls to a stop outside an old Victorian-style villa. There are a bunch of cars parked in the driveway and lights on in four of the windows.

"Where are we?" I grit out.

Jed releases another slow sigh, then points at the house. "That's Football Frat."

My face bunches into a frown while my stomach drops out my ass.

"That's where Tyrell lives, and if he's home right now, I think you should talk to him."

"I'm gonna kill you," I whisper. "You won't see it

coming, and Tobin will totally forgive me when he finds out what you've done."

Jed laughs, the sound low and rumbly. "It was his idea. He texted me just before closing. Told me we have to do our girl this favor."

Whipping back to face him properly, I can feel my throat swell, my nose starting to burn as I clutch his arm and practically beg him, "Take me home. I can't do this."

Cupping my cheek, he gives it a gentle pat. "Yes, you can. You need to. This is eating you alive, and you need to clear the air."

"How?"

"Just tell him how you feel, why you bailed on the kiss. Tell him that you like him and it's scary."

I let out a shuddering breath, the jumping bugs in my stomach starting to settle into a low, vibrating hum that I can feel all the way down my legs.

"You need to do this, Dani. So, get your ass out of my car and go get yourself this man."

Unbuckling my seat belt for me, he pulls it around my arm, then leans across and opens my door for me as well.

"You're really not gonna take me home, are you?"

"I'll wait five minutes in case he's lost his damn mind."

I nod, my breaths kind of punchy.

"You can do it." Jed lightly pushes me out the door.

I land on my feet, giving him one more agonized frown before tugging my sweater down and forcing my legs to move.

Having no idea what I'm gonna say, I start to tremble

as I walk up those front steps, then turn to look back at Jed.

He leans out his window, giving me a big thumbs-up and a cheerful smile. Easy for him. He's in a loving relationship.

*Which is what you want too, right?*

*So go and make it happen for yourself.*

# CHAPTER 24
## TYRELL

"It's really late, brother. You've got to get yourself some sleep." I try to wrap up the call for the fourth time, but Cyrus is not having it.

He's in such a chatty mood after a fun night out with some friends.

They went to the movies, then out for ice cream afterward. He's never usually allowed sugar this late at night, and now I know why Mama is always so strict.

"I can't sleep. I'm too... I'm... I'm pumped up, Ty. That movie made me pumped up."

"You really liked it, huh?" I grin into the phone screen, laughing at my brother's expression.

"I want... I'm gonna be an action star. I want to be an action star."

"You'd be a great movie star." I nod, knowing better than to be practical with the guy. He just wants to dream, and I'm gonna let him. "And those explosions didn't scare you too bad?"

"Nope." He grins, looking all proud of himself. "They

were big, and they just... they're just pretending. It's... Mama says it's called... it's special."

"Yeah, special effects. No one actually gets hurt."

"Mama said." Cyrus nods and repeats himself a few times. "Mama said, Mama said."

He's getting tired. I can sense it. He's got these little tics that give him away. As soon as his left eye starts twitching, I'm wrapping up this call. An overtired Cyrus is hard to deal with, and Dad's still recovering from his accident. They don't need any more pressure.

Faking a big yawn, I stretch my arm wide and tell him, "I'm getting tired. I'm gonna have to go soon. I've got training in the morning."

"You gonna lift weights?"

"Yep."

"Next time you're home, can you... can we... I want to lift weights."

"Yeah, I can take you to the gym with me." I smile. "That'll be fun. You can show me how strong you are."

"I'm strong." He lifts his arm, curling it to show off his bicep. His body is vibrating with the effort, and I grin.

"Brah, you are. Look at that. Bet them girls you went out with tonight love how strong you are."

Cyrus starts giggling. "Nah. They're my friends, Ty."

"Yeah, but you like Gwen, though, right? She's pretty."

His laughter increases, getting loud and adorably childlike. "She is pretty. She's—"

"Hey, big man!" Grady calls up the stairs. "You got a visitor."

I pop off my pillows, sitting up with a confused frown.

"Right now?" I shout.

"What is it?" Cyrus asks.

Looking at my phone screen, I pull a funny face. "I've got a visitor. I better go."

"No, wait. Can I... can I see? I want to see. Let me... let me see."

"Uh..." I stand up, tugging the waistband of my sweats as I walk to the door with the phone still in my hand.

"Is it... is it a girl?" My brother starts grinning. "Are you gonna have all the..." His voice drops to a whisper. "Are you gonna have all the sex?"

"Cyrus," I reprimand him, and he starts to giggle.

Rolling my eyes, I fight my own laughter. "Okay, bud. Let's go see who it is." Trotting down the stairs, I glance up from my phone and come to a stop halfway down the stairwell.

Dani.

What's she doing here?

And why does she have to be so gorgeous?

I mean, she's always been beautiful, but she's been getting prettier by the day. And then I kissed her, and she turned into the most stunning creature on the planet.

Now I can't take my eyes off her as she inches to the bottom of the stairs and waves up at me. "Hey, Ty." Her smile is sweet and kind of nervous. It tugs me down the stairs, but I'm still looking for my voice.

"Who is it?" Cyrus asks.

I blink, glancing at my phone while Dani's face lights with a smile.

"Are you talking to Cyrus?"

"Who is it? Who is it?" My brother starts bouncing, making the phone jiggle in his hand.

"It's, um..." I lick my lips. "It's Dani. Do you remember Dani?"

"Let me see!" Cyrus practically wails.

Dani laughs, her face lighting as I spin the phone so she can talk to my brother. "Hi, Cy-Cy."

Damn, Atlas always used to call him that.

"You might not remember me, but I met you a few times. In high school."

"Hi, Dani." He gives her the sweetest smile, and I'm pretty sure he doesn't remember her, but... the way she's interacting with him right now is making my heart do weird shit.

"...went to the movies."

"Wow. That's awesome." She smiles. "Did you have a good time?"

"Yeah. I did. And it's really late now, and I'm not... I'm not asleep yet."

"That's because you're a young man now." Dani nods. "A college student, right?"

"Yeah, I go to college. That's what... that's what I was doing. Tonight. I was... I was with my *college* friends." He sounds so proud, and I can't help smiling as I try to catch Dani's eye.

"I'm really happy for you." She grins, finally looking at me with that brown gaze that...

Yeah, I'm in trouble.

I wonder why she's here. What she's come to say.

Clearing my throat, I spin the phone back to face me. "Hey, brother, I better go, okay? It's time for me to hang out with Dani now."

"Are you gonna have... will you be doing all the sex?"

"Cyrus." I bulge my eyes at my brother, but he starts

giggling, which makes Dani snort, and all I can do is shake my head at this super-awkward situation. "Okay, I'm hanging up. Go to sleep."

"Night-night, Dani."

"Good night, Cyrus."

"I love you," I tell him, just before ending the call.

"Love you!" he yells, and I hang up before he can say anything else that is completely inappropriate.

"Sorry about that." I cringe, tucking the phone into my back pocket.

Dani lets out an awkward giggle, then waves her hand through the air. "That's okay. It's nice to see he's so happy."

"Yeah, he's doing really well." I reach for the banister, needing something to hold on to. Having spent the day obsessing over last night's kiss, my head is spinning with her standing only a few steps down from me.

I've been trying so hard not to feel like shit about what went down. I even passed on her details when Rhys texted me to get them. It fucking slayed me, but I did it, knowing Dani's happiness is more important than my own.

She's seriously the last person I expected to see here tonight.

Maybe she thinks we need to talk about what happened. That's obviously why she's here, but... what the hell is she gonna say?

Am I about to see her for the last time?

Or is this the start of something I desperately want but I'm not sure how to handle?

# CHAPTER 25
## DANI

"So, um…" I lick my lips, not sure how to start. My nerves are seizing up, turning into sharp spikes that are massacring my insides.

Letting out an edgy laugh, I scratch the back of my curls and stare down at his feet. They're so big. Long and broad and… He's got handsome toes.

Can toes be handsome?

These ones are.

They're a beautiful shape and all the right lengths. My second toe is longer than my big toe, but not Tyrell's. The height order is just so, giving his toes a perfect curve from his big to his pinkie and…

*Why the fuck are you focusing on handsome toes right now? He's waiting!*

Clearing my throat, I snap my gaze back up to his and drink in his expression. He's usually got this cool, quiet, calm about him, but when his lips curl into a smile that doesn't reach his eyes, I realize he's just as nervous as me.

And he's *still* waiting for me to say something.

"I wasn't happy with how we left things... and I guess I just wanted to make sure we're okay." The words tumble out of me in a jumble, and I'm not sure he even heard them.

He takes a beat to decipher my drivel and then nods, his smile turning sad as he slips his hand into the pocket of his sweats. They're hanging low on his hips, and I can picture the muscles underneath his T-shirt. He had a six-pack in high school that the girls constantly drooled over. I bet it's still there.

*And it could be all yours if you just get over yourself!*

Closing my eyes, I swallow, those spiky nerves digging into my stomach, my chest, my throat.

"Yeah. I mean, of course we're okay." His voice rumbles. "I'll always be there for you."

I open my eyes in time to see his stoic smile.

And my heart turns to liquid, melting into a puddle of soft affection as I take in that gentle gaze of his.

My rejection last night hurt him. It's so freaking obvious, but he's still got that stoic smile at the ready. He's still willing to set aside all his feelings for me. To be there for me and what I need.

But what about what *he* needs?

*What about what you both obviously want?*

I can barely breathe as I climb the stairs, moving right past him so I can spin two steps above where he's standing and be eye level with him.

Studying his face, my lips twitch into a smile as I reach for his hand and curl my fingers around it. His large fingers envelop mine, his long thumb brushing over my skin with a tenderness that makes my liquid heart pulse with a fresh beat. One I haven't felt in years.

Sucking in a shaky breath, I softly whisper, "I'm scared."

His gaze jumps to meet mine. His eyes are a rich, dark brown. So beautiful. All I can do is stare into them as his deep voice goes all soft and husky. "Me too. For probably all the same reasons you are."

I nod, letting out a shaky laugh as tears burn the back of my throat.

Are we doing this?

Are we really stepping into this new territory together?

"We don't have to do anything you don't want to." His tender expression can't hide the edge of disappointment.

Oh, he wants me. He wants to be my man. And when he raises our joined hands to his lips and kisses my knuckle, I realize that I'd be a fool to keep denying myself.

Yes, Tyrell is the last guy I thought I'd catch feelings for, but the truth is... I have. I didn't even realize until he pointed out how he felt about me. But it's like a switch clicked in my brain, and suddenly it was so obvious.

And although this leap is terrifying, in this moment right here...

A smile curls my lips as I rest my forehead against his. He closes his eyes, his lips still pressed against my fingers.

The talons that have been clutching my stomach start to release, a warm buzz firing into the space. It feels good, safe... exciting. A giddy sensation bubbles up my throat, and I press a kiss to his cheek. His head pops up, his eyes snapping open, and he catches my smile just before I move my lips to his mouth.

Those luscious, warm lips of his are tentative at first,

but it doesn't take long for him to realize that I am invested in this kiss. His hands slip out of mine, resting on my waist before wrapping around my body.

I lean into him, deepening the kiss and smiling at the moan reverberating in his throat. He grins too, our smiles pressed together before I sweep my tongue into his mouth and wrap my arms around his neck. We're glued together now, our bodies pressed tight, my insides electrifying as he glides that luscious tongue across mine and makes my eyes roll back with pleasure. A pleasure I haven't felt in a really, really long time.

*I'm kissing Tyrell Jackson! This is so weird and good and—*

*Don't think about it, just melt into this kiss, girl. Enjoy it!*

And I am. I'm relishing every second of this. Every sensation. His hands are so big, splaying across my back, traveling up my spine to grip the back of my neck before traveling back down to my tailbone.

I cup the back of his head, letting out a soft moan of my own when he tips his head to change the angle and—

"If you are gonna have *all the sex*, can you not to do it on the staircase?" someone shouts from the living room.

I wrench my mouth off Tyrell's, my eyes bulging with embarrassment. He dips his chin with a soft growl as a different voice calls out.

"It's a house rule, you know? No sex in shared spaces."

"I know the rules!" Tyrell bites back. "I'm the one who has to remind your horny asses constantly!"

I can't help a giggle. Tyrell's exasperated indignation is adorable.

"And I'm not dragging her up to my room for *all the sex*, okay? This is only our second kiss!"

Surprising disappointment mixed with a bucketload of swoon swirls through me. The idea of being dragged up to his room for *all the sex* has my body in a frenzy. I wasn't expecting that, but my body obviously wants it. But my heart... oh my heart. *"It's only our second kiss."* How sweet is he?

"Oooo." Two women pop into view, looking all excited. I recognize Nylah immediately, and the blonde one is familiar too. Blake? That's her name.

"Are you guys together-together now?" she asks, her blue eyes sparkling with excitement.

"Uh..." Tyrell spins back to look at me, his querying frown enough to melt my heart all over again.

It's a valid question. A slightly terrifying one, but...

I look into those brown eyes and start to nod.

I do want to try this thing with him. That's why I'm here, right?

That's why I'm kissing him.

That's why...

Touching his face, my lips rise into a smile as I lean toward him again and answer their question with an open-mouth kiss that has me melting against him once more.

Tyrell Jackson.

I never would have thought this was an option.

But here I am.

And when his tongue slides against mine with so much hope, so much promise, I know I'll regret it forever if I don't dive into this thing.

I'm ready to move on.

I just didn't realize I'd be doing it with Atlas's best friend.

# CHAPTER 26
## TYRELL

Since Dani and I have officially started dating, it's been a flurry of text messages and phone calls as we try to squeeze in every second of time we can between her job, my classes, homework, football training, and gym work-outs. Thankfully, football isn't too intense. The coaches are just keeping the team fit and steady until the season begins and training intensifies. I won't even be playing, but I'm still turning up to every practice and giving it my all.

I can't wait for today's to be over, because Dani is waiting for me. She's not working tonight, so we'll be going on our first official date. Well, not our first date. We've done a bunch of doubles, but this will be the first one just the two of us.

Exam prep can wait. Everything can wait.

All that matters tonight is my girl.

Wow, feels weird saying that, but that's what she is, right?

My girl.

This sensation I'm still getting used to whistles through my chest. I scratch between my pecs, not entirely sure how to manage it. This thing with her is different from anything I've felt before.

I've booked us into an Italian place on the outskirts of town. I want to take her somewhere away from campus, so there's less chance of prying eyes and nosy neighbors near our table.

"Jackson! Let's go!" Coach yells, and I throw myself into the drill, making sure the freshman practice squad I'm working with is getting the most benefit out of our session.

We work on blocking, and then Coach pulls a few of us aside to focus on his "snap-punch" move. I demonstrate the technique I've been using all season, and the guys follow me easily. They're gonna be good. These young ones are fast and aren't afraid of the defensive line. Hopefully they'll move up to second-string over the next year and get some field time.

I work with each of them, perfecting their ability to snap the ball, then quickly be ready to block.

"Nice." I nod. "Now, next time, bring your foot forward and really punch out with your hand. It's a springing movement, not a swipe." I show them what I mean, and one by one they settle into position, snapping the ball, then punching out with their hands.

They all know this stuff. They've been playing ball for years. We're just getting down to the finer details, working on their moves until they're perfect. It only takes a second to make or break a game.

"Good work, good work." Coach Jones claps as he walks past, checking in on each of the drills.

A sadness I don't even understand sweeps through me when I realize that I'm not gonna be on this field for much longer. The coaches aren't gonna be talking to me, yelling at me, encouraging me, berating sloppy play. There'll be no team around me, no men to lead into battle.

Shit. My days of football are nearly over.

Standing tall, I rest my hands on my hips, grateful when Coach blows the whistle to bring us all in.

"Good work, gentlemen." He stands on his usual box so he can see us all, and I stare up at him, not really listening as my mind wanders forward to the future.

Where will I be?

Probably Dallas. Mama's really putting the pressure on to come home. She needs the support, and they've been missing me. We're a tight family, and Cyrus in particular really needs me around.

It's my duty to be there for him, right?

*But what about Dani?* The thought is like a punch to the stomach.

Am I seriously going to be leaving her in a few short weeks? We're just getting started with this thing. Is that a good idea?

Maybe I should be making plans to stay in Nolan.

*Isn't that jumping the gun? You're about to go on your first date, not propose freaking marriage.*

Fuck. I close my eyes, praying that I don't fall into my three-date trap like I always do.

I get so far, and then it comes to that moment where it could go one way or the other... and I've always bailed.

I don't get why.

Shit, that better not happen with Dani.

Maybe I should be stepping back.

I don't want to lead her on and hurt her.

*You've never felt this way about anyone before. You are NOT bailing on this date.*

"All right." Coach Jones claps his hands together. "Have a good night."

I glance up in dazed confusion, and Carson snickers at me before muttering, "He's called off practice for tomorrow and Thursday. Wants us to focus on studying for finals. What is up with you, man?"

"He's got his first date tonight," Zander singsongs, then starts laughing.

"Although, it's not really, right? You've been going out with this girl on doubles. Tonight shouldn't be intimidating." Grady throws the ball up, then catches it with one hand.

"It's different," I argue. "There's a lot more pressure."

"True, but you seem into this girl, and you were friends first, so it should be easy, right?" Carson slaps me on the shoulder. "Just chill, man."

"Yeah, thanks," I mutter, shaking my head and trailing them into the locker room.

As usual, conversation shifts to the future, which does nothing to ease my already frayed nerves.

Zander's talking about packing boxes and moving companies. The Chargers have a full relocation service that will help with all of this. Sienna has been looking at listings with a real estate agent the team has connected her with. She wants a little bungalow near the arena but has also been researching good schools and communities nearby. I think they might be aiming for Torrance, which is just outside of Inglewood. I don't know. I've heard a few suburbs batted around as they quickly make plans for their future. She's also been looking into preschools and playgroups for Zoey. Our little girl needs to socialize with kids her own age.

Damn, I'm gonna miss her.

I need to start planning a trip to Los Angeles.

And Arizona. Wily's gonna be based in Glendale, I think. I don't even know where that is, but I'm gonna have to plan a road trip or start saving for flights, because I want to get to some of their games, that's for sure. Although, who knows when Wily will get any field time. But he made an NFL team, and that's his foot in the door. He'll be working his ass off to prove himself. I'm excited to see him do it.

*But you won't see it.*

Damn, I'm gonna miss my boys.

Graduation is coming at me like a bullet train, and I'm not prepared.

Getting out of the shower, I towel myself off and notice my phone screen lighting up.

*Dani Girl: I'm so sorry, but I have to work tonight. They're in a bind and can't find someone else to cover. Tobin's sick and Jed's looking after him, and there's no one else. This sucks. I was really looking forward to tonight.*

My insides deflate, but I force a smile and quickly reply.

. . .

*Me: No stress. Why don't I come hang out at the bar? I can talk to you in sound bites when you get a minute between pulling beers.*

She sends back a laughing emoji, a thumbs-up, and then a heart.

I smile down at her message, making a mental note to cancel my reservation for tonight... and come up with a really awesome alternative first date for us... whenever it happens.

Maybe this cancellation is a sign from the universe that I should be coming up with something better than an Italian restaurant.

Shoving my things into my bag, I follow my crew out of the locker room, my mind churning with ideas of what Dani might like to do.

Shit, I've never put so much thought and effort into a date before.

*Because she's special. You know she is. Don't waste this chance, man.*

# CHAPTER 27
## DANI

Offside has a more relaxed vibe tonight. With finals on everyone's doorstep, the usual hotspots aren't as crowded. Students have got their heads down, desperately preparing for these major exams. It puts me in a salty mood. I don't know why Harrison insisted I come in. One bartender would have been plenty with this traffic, and I could have been out on a date with Tyrell.

A shimmer moves through me. I can't decide if it's nerves or desire, but when I glance up in time to see the door open... and he walks through it...

Yeah, that's desire. As primal and carnal as it can get.

My body wants that man.

From the second his lips touched mine I've known it. I couldn't accept it that first night, and if I'm honest, I'm still struggling to get my head around the fact that... I like Tyrell Jackson. The shy, quiet boy from high school. Atlas's right-hand man.

How is it possible?

The shift doesn't make sense, but...

He notices me, his lips curling into a smile that makes my heart jiggle.

Ever since I turned up at his house, letting him know with a kiss (or a few dozen kisses) that I'm willing to try this thing with him, I haven't been able to stop thinking about us.

I haven't felt this way since Atlas and I first got together. That simmering anticipation, the way my breath catches when my phone buzzes with a fresh text from him.

It's ridiculous and childlike, and I need to get over myself.

Which is why I clear my throat and try to play it cool when Tyrell slips onto a stool at the end of the bar.

"Evening, sir. What can I get you?" I wink at him, and that smile grows into something big and beautiful.

Shit, I'm so done.

I keep thinking it's way too fast, and my roommates keep reminding me that it's not, because Tyrell and I have been double-dating for weeks, then having our debriefs, hanging out, interacting, subconsciously opening our hearts without meaning to.

"What can you recommend?"

Licks of delicious pleasure whisper over my skin at the sound of his deep voice.

I have always loved his voice.

Even when I was with Atlas, I used to tease Tyrell that football was wasted on him. He should be a narrator. He'd always give me that headshake, a smile rising on his lips, but it was edged with panic at the idea of trying to read a book out loud or something. Trying to act out a scene or character. The thought probably gave him hives.

Resting my arms on the bar, I lean in close, brushing my finger over his knuckle. "Depends. How drunk do you want to get?"

And there's that smile again, his brown eyes warm with affection. "I don't need to get drunk. In fact, I'd rather stay sober so I don't lose sight of this very fine view."

Oooo... the boy's got moves.

I can't help a soft giggle, brushing my teeth over my bottom lip as I pull up a glass and pour him a water. "There you go, then."

He laughs, downing half of it as if to prove a point.

"But seriously. Can I get you something?"

"You know..." He looks down at the glass in his hand. "Water's fine for now. I'm just here to hang with you in between orders."

I glance down the bar, my insides skipping when I notice that no one needs anything. Leaning back down, I rest my chin in my hand and ask him, "So, where were we going to be right now?"

"Well..." Skimming his fingers lightly up my forearm, he hopefully doesn't notice what a huge effect such a simple gesture has on me. I love the pads of his fingers. I love how delicate his touch is. "I was gonna take you to an Italian place."

"Oooo. Italian. I love me some Italian."

"Right? Pasta is the masta."

I laugh. "Where did you hear that?"

He snickers. "My sister said it constantly when she was going through her *I want to be a chef* phase. She was obsessed with pasta. I swear I gained like twenty pounds that summer."

Stretching over the counter, I make a show of checking out his body, then give him an impish grin. "Doesn't look like it."

He laughs, patting his flat belly. "I had to work my ass off when I got back. Literally." His eyebrows rise and I laugh again, resisting the urge to tell him it paid off, because damn... he looks good.

That thrill of desire races through me again and I have to stand straight, create some distance between us before my panties get wet.

Seriously. What is wrong with me?

*How about the fact that you haven't had sex in nearly three years?*

*Or maybe it's the fact that Tyrell is crazy stupid fine, and if you were gonna have sex with anyone, then you'd want it to be him.*

But the fact that he's a full-blown hottie is not the only reason why... and that's even scarier than sleeping with a random stranger.

My insides crinkle at the thought, my mind racing as I try to figure it all out.

*Sex with Tyrell will actually mean something.*

That's the scary part.

"Hey, you okay?" Tyrell's fingers skim my arm again, and I force a smile, nodding.

*What am I supposed to say? "I'm horny as hell and can't stop thinking about you boning me"?*

We haven't even been on a proper date yet. I should not be feeling this way. It's new. We should take things slow and easy. A few kisses can't mean an instant lust-fest.

Shaking my head, I back away from the bar a little further.

"Hey, what's wrong?" Tyrell's sweet concern is making my heart buckle now.

"Um..." I point down the bar. "I just need to go... and... restock."

It's lame and pathetic, and the way his eyebrows dip with worry has guilt lashing me as I scurry down to the other end of the bar.

*What are you doing?*

*You should be hanging out with him! You're together now.*

This is weird.

Is Tyrell Jackson my boyfriend?

Am I—

"Excuse me. Can I grab two Coors Lights, please?" A man with a genial smile holds up two fingers, and I fulfill his order, glancing down the bar as he's tapping his card.

Tyrell is sitting there, drawing circles with his finger and looking a little dejected. Shit. I need to do some damage control.

Restocking, my ass. We all know that was a lie. He's not stupid. In fact, he's always been one of the smartest guys I know. He was consistently one of the top students in the class. Seriously. The guy could do no wrong, and I'm freaking out, *missing* out, by coming up with restocking excuses.

*Grow up and get your butt back over there!*

The thought hits me up the side of the head at the exact moment a girl appears behind Tyrell. She's pretty and has a bright smile... aimed directly at him as she walks around to position herself right in front of him.

She leans against the counter, her body language loud enough for the entire place to hear. She wants him... and she's not hiding it or scuttling away.

When she touches his arm and lightly runs her fingers down what I *know* is a beautifully sculpted bicep, this primal instinct grabs a hold of me.

*Get your hands off my man.*

I bite my lips together to stop myself from shouting at her, instead forcing myself to casually walk back down the bar and stake my claim with a smile on my face.

"You sure you don't want anything to drink, baby? It'll be on the house." I wink at him.

He turns to look at me, his twitching lips telling me he knows exactly what I'm playing at, and he's into it.

"Thanks, bae." He smiles, and the girl beside him gives me a slightly sour frown before pasting on a bright grin.

"I'll have a Corona, please." She bounces on her toes, and I have to ask.

"ID?"

"Yep." She pulls out her wallet, and I scan it carefully, making sure it's not a fake. I even rub my thumb over the birth date, but it looks legit, so I have to serve her.

"One Corona." I pop the top and place it on the counter.

"Thanks. Is this one on the house too?" She laughs.

My laugh sounds forced and plastic compared to hers. It cuts off quickly, probably too quickly, but I've got to stake my claim, right? "Only for my man here."

I point at Tyrell and then go the extra mile, curling my fingers around his.

His big thumb brushes my knuckles, and those licks of pleasure are only getting stronger.

"Okay." The girl manages to keep her smile in place as

she looks between us, then gives me a polite nod. "I'm just gonna go and catch up with my girls."

"Great idea."

*Oh man, I am being such a bitch right now.*

She looks at Tyrell. "I'll see you around."

"Yeah." He tips his chin, and we both watch her walk away, moving around tables and homing in on a guy about to start a round of darts.

"She's on the hunt," Tyrell murmurs, lifting my hand to his lips and pressing a kiss to my knuckles. "Thank God I've got myself a woman."

I can't help an instant smile, my lips quivering when he turns to gaze at me like I'm special.

"Thank God it's you."

A breath whistles out between my lips, and I don't know what to say.

I'm his woman.

He's my man.

Is it really that simple?

*It can be. If you'll just let it.*

"Dani, let's go," someone whisper-barks behind me. "There are people waiting."

With a soft gasp, I glance down the bar and notice two groups who have just come in. I was oblivious, too busy wrapped up in the burning look Tyrell Jackson was giving me.

"Sorry." I wince at my boss, then turn to wince at Ty.

"Don't worry about it. We'll get out of here as soon as your shift is done." He kisses my hand one more time before letting me go.

Get out of here. That sounds good to me.

My body continues to burn with anticipation as I

hurry through my tasks. Every time there's a lull, I head back down the bar and offer Tyrell another drink, but he seems happy with water.

With only thirty minutes left until my shift ends, I'm on the cusp of losing my mind. I seriously have no idea what's come over me, but the thought of getting out of here to go and... do what? Make out with Tyrell Jackson?... has whipped me into a frenzy.

I nearly dropped one full glass of beer and only just caught it, wedging the slippery cup between my thigh and the counter. I had to pull a new one for the customer, which Harrison will be pissed about, but he'll just have to get over it.

I have twenty-seven minutes until I can walk out—

"Dani, I need you to close up tonight. I just got a call, and my missus is puking her guts out. I have to leave and take care of the baby."

My lips part, and I can't even be annoyed with him for dumping this on me because his reasons are so damn valid.

"Okay," I squeak, my insides pinching with disappointment.

I gaze down the bar. Tyrell is still patiently waiting for me, sipping on his water and... dammit!

With a sad huff, I shuffle over to him. "I have to close up tonight. I'm really sorry. Don't feel like you have to stay. I know it's getting really late. You should just go and—"

"I'm staying." His husky whisper runs all the way through me.

"You don't have to."

"I know." I love the way his lips curl up at the corners. His smile is so soft. So sweet. So calm.

I want to kiss it. Feel it. Taste it.

Sinking my teeth into my bottom lip, I let some of my desire show, and the look of heat he gives right back to me is enough to make my lady parts sing.

I am in so much trouble.

Maybe it's a good thing I'm closing. Maybe it'll force me to slow the hell down and not jump this man like my body is begging me to.

How is this happening to me?

Last week, sure, I was aware of Tyrell and how gorgeous he is—he's always been gorgeous! But then one confession later, one leap of faith, and I'm a hungry lioness. It's insane.

*Your poor, dormant body is probably desperate for release.*

But I can't be the only reason. I don't want my first time with Tyrell to just be some primal, meaningless thing.

And it's too soon.

We haven't even been on our first official date.

I will not be throwing my body at this man after closing tonight.

I have more damn control than that.

At least I think I do...

# CHAPTER 28
## TYRELL

Dani seems tense tonight.

I don't know exactly why. Maybe she's nervous about us being a couple now or something. I'm not sure. But when the lock clicks on that front door after the last person has left, she gives me an edgy smile before heading for the first set of chairs to start stacking them.

"What can I do to help?" I stand on the other side of the room, watching her carefully. Wondering what I've done to put her so on edge.

"Stack chairs with me?" she squeaks. "Or maybe sweep the floor?"

"Where's the broom at?"

She tells me about the cleaning closet out back, and I dig out the broom, running it around the room while she finishes stacking chairs and wiping down the bar. Walking through the kitchen, she makes sure that everything is switched off and safe while I close the shutters on the far side of the room.

The last thing to go is the lights.

They snap off, plunging the room into darkness. Other than a soft glow from behind the bar, Offside is shut up for the night.

I can't even see the stage from here.

"You want me to get the music?" I ask, inching around the tables in a bid to find the sound system.

She doesn't say anything, and I pause in the middle of the dance space, my lips twitching as a Whitney Houston number comes on. Did she somehow line this one up or something?

Damn, Whitney can sing.

"Dani?" I peer through the darkness, watching her shadowy body move toward me until she's close enough that I can reach her.

She's still not talking as "I Wanna Dance with Somebody" floats around us. I forget about the sound system because I love this damn song. Reaching for her arm, I trail my fingers across the smooth skin of her forearm before capturing her hand and pulling her against me.

I don't know what powers are at play right now, but when she comes willingly, her perfect tits squishing against my chest, I don't fight it.

I wanna dance with Dani Hill. I want to feel the heat with this girl.

The looks she's been throwing me tonight have made it clear that she's wanting the same thing, so I nestle her against my body and start to sway to the beat. It's a fast, upbeat song, but we're treating it like a slow dance.

Her fingers trail up my shoulders, then around the back of my neck as she nuzzles her forehead into my neck. She's so delicate and small against me. My hands feel massive, my clumsy feet too big as I shuffle them around the wooden floor.

The music swells and I close my eyes, concentrating on the feel of her against me. Every point that our bodies are touching seems to radiate with heat—hot spots of energy that burn with this heightened anticipation.

When I arrived here tonight, I had zero intention of doing anything more with her than hanging out... maybe getting a kiss good night. But there's something going on here. I can feel it. The desire pulsing out of her, the heated looks. She wants me.

Is there a chance I'll be sleeping with Dani tonight?

*Shit, Atlas, please don't hate me, man.*

Squeezing my eyes tighter, I wrestle with a wave of guilt, especially when Dani's lips caress my neck, then my chin. She's seeking out my mouth. She wants my lips on hers and... and I can't resist her.

Maybe I should.

I don't know.

All I'm certain of is that I can't deny her a kiss. I can't deny her fucking anything.

When her lips connect with mine, I tighten my hold around her, lifting her off her feet so our heads are aligned.

She sweeps her tongue into my mouth, her hunger so raw and plain and obvious.

She doesn't have to say, "I want you." I can feel the desire within her. I can taste it.

And fuck if that doesn't make me hard as a steel pole.

The erection grows in my pants, complaining about the confines of these trousers. Thankfully, it's angled the right way, allowing it to grow without me having to adjust anything. But it still wants out.

*"Let me play!"* I can practically hear it begging.

But Dani's my focus right now. She has to lead this thing. I'm not crossing any lines she doesn't want to.

What we've got going here is too precious—too fragile —to mess with.

My heart is beating louder and faster with every swipe of her tongue, and I can feel myself caving, the instinct telling me to just take her right here and now.

The song has shifted. I can't remember the title, but I know it. I know these lyrics. The band is singing about sweet touches and intoxicating kisses. They're telling me to pleasure this woman. To make her come.

"Mmmm." I moan, trailing my hand down her body and gripping her ass. Pulling away, I try to gauge her reaction. Does she want my hand here? Am I reading these signals right?

It's not like I'm a playboy. Sure, I've slept with a few girls in my time, but I'm hardly Casanova. Those girls were begging me. Dani hasn't said a damn thing.

"Is this okay?" I whisper. "To put my hand here?"

"Uh-huh." Her voice is breathy as she lunges for my mouth again.

I drink from her, slashing my tongue against hers and running my hand down her leg, hooking my fingers under her knee so she can wrap herself around me.

She moves with me, her hips bucking when she obviously notices my erection.

Her whimper is exquisite, popping into my mouth before she wrenches her lips off mine and blows a shaky breath across my cheek.

"Do you want this?"

"Yes?" She says it like a question, and I have to pull back to check her face.

With the darkness, it's basically impossible to read her. All we've got is words and touch, and I have to know.

"Dani, it's okay to change your mind. We can stop right now if you want to."

"I don't."

"Are you sure?" I resist the urge to kiss her when she tries to seek out my mouth again. "Dani. You've got to be sure."

She pauses and my heart stutters in my chest, threatening cardiac arrest as I wait her out.

"It's okay," I whisper, when all she gives me is a few panting breaths against my cheek.

I'm about to put her down when her legs squeeze around me tighter, her sweet pussy rubbing against my desperate cock.

"My body wants you so bad I can barely contain myself," she rasps.

"I understand that feeling," I croak back, my voice all rough and rugged, my hips connecting with hers, grinding against her with enough pressure to make her whimper again. "But what do *you* want? Because if you're not ready, I'm gonna need to put you down and step back."

She tips her hips again, gyrating against my body in a move that nearly blinds me.

Fuck. She's so hot.

"I can't stop," she whispers, her voice taking on an urgent edge. "Please don't stop. I want this." Her breath hits my cheek, her fingers digging into the back of my neck. "I want you."

And then her lips are on me again, claiming my mouth. Her tongue dominates me, taking out every one of my senses.

She's all that matters.

Pleasuring her.

Making her come.

I'm still not sure if she's ready for all of me, but I can make this count.

Walking her toward the stage, I fumble through the dark until we're bumping into the wood.

Glancing toward the door and windows, I check that no one can see us, but it's so dark in here, I doubt they can.

Behind the bar is lit up, but this stage area is cloaked in darkness and I take advantage, perching her sweet ass on the edge of the stage so my hands can roam more freely.

The first thing to go is her shirt. She whips that off for me, her chest heaving as I press my lips against the curve of her breast.

She tips her head back, groaning when I lick between them. Within seconds, she's unclasping her bra and throwing it onto the stage before clawing my shirt off as well.

I can't see her pert tits in all their glory, but I can feel them. They fit into my hands perfectly, and I palm them both, loving the way her nipples respond to my touch, puckering in obvious anticipation.

I don't make her wait. Her needy desperation is a turn-on and makes it easy to deliver, sucking each nipple in turn before nibbling kisses back up to her neck. The cross necklace she always wears sticks to her skin as I lick a line past it. She grips my shoulders, her short nails digging into me when I slide my tongue back into her mouth.

She feels so fucking good, and I'm lost to her mouth, her body. My hands continue to roam, to massage her boobs until they start walking south. Gliding down her salacious curves, I round her ass, giving those perfect cheeks a squeeze while she whimpers against my lips.

"Yes," she whispers, tipping her head back when I trail my tongue down her body, between her boobs, drawing a line toward her pussy. I dip the tip of my tongue into her belly button before reaching her jeans and slowly releasing the button.

Her breath hitches, and I pause to check once more.

"And you're sure you wan—"

"Yes!" she groans, her back arching. "Please stop asking stupid questions."

I snicker, popping the button and slowly lowering the zipper.

She helps me, wiggling them off her hips, and I take those panties as well, my insides jolting with pleasure when I notice how wet they are.

Fuck, this woman is going to undo me.

The second that delicate fabric hits the floor, she spreads her legs, hooking her knee over my shoulder and quietly demanding something I am more than happy to give.

I brush my lips across her quivering inner thigh, then work my way up to her pussy. She lets out a mewling whimper and my dick twitches, wanting in on the action too. But it's just gonna have to fucking wait.

Dani's breath catches when I press my tongue against her clit. Her husky moan is all things sexy as I drag the tip down to her opening, and the way her fingers scrape across my scalp when I flatten my tongue against her tells me everything I need to know.

She's loving this right now, and it's an honor to deliver for her.

Her heel digs into my back as I continue to work her clit with my tongue. She's on fire—she *is* fucking fire—and I'm scorched by the time I slip my fingers into her warm, soft oasis.

Holy shit, she's perfect.

Her insides clench around me as I glide my fingers back and forth, trying to work her G-spot. Shit, I hope I have the right place. I keep licking her clit, covering all my bases while she writhes on the stage, her sweet pants and groans blending with the music. Her body is a symphony, and I will play this tune all fucking night if I can.

"Ahhhh." Her cry crescendos over us, morphing into a new kind of moan she hasn't made before.

She's coming. I can sense the shift in her body. The urgent energy. The way her legs are starting to vibrate.

Another sweet sound punches out of her, and I thrust my fingers deeper, curling them inside her as I work her clit until she starts to buck her hips and weep all over my digits. She's a hot, slippery mess, and it's the sexiest thing I've ever felt.

"Ahhhh!" she cries again, arching her back and

surrendering completely to the orgasm ripping through her.

I wish the lights were on so I could see this in all its beauty.

She's so fucking hot.

And making her come was incredible.

My body wants more, is begging for a taste of her sweet, wet pussy, but I refuse to demand what she's not ready to give.

Slipping my fingers out of her, I kiss my way back up her body, my knees nearly buckling when she rasps, "Please tell me you've got a rubber in your wallet."

# CHAPTER 29
## DANI

"I don't." His hoarse response ends me.

It's impossible to hide my disappointment as I sit up on my elbows and practically yell at him, "Are you serious?"

"It's our first date. I didn't expect this. I'd never demand anything of you."

"But you want it, right?" My voice suddenly sounds so unsure. So... vulnerable.

He didn't just blow my mind with that orgasm because he felt obliged, did he?

He spent all this time checking to see if I wanted him, but I never asked if he wanted me back!

Shit, what if him going down on me was just a way to satisfy me, and then he can be on his way and—

"Of course I do." He brushes his lips across my neck. "Of course I want you."

"Then why didn't you bring a condom?" I whine, my needy body turning me into a petulant child.

He sighs against my cheek, then rests his forehead on my shoulder. "Because I'm an idiot?"

I cup the back of his head, having to concede that the fact that he came here tonight with zero expectations is kind of sweet. He's a gentleman, and it's one of the things I love about him. So I can't go complaining.

My body is just on fire right now, and I know I won't be fully sated until I feel his—

"The bathroom," I suddenly croak. "There'll be some in there."

His head pings off my shoulder, his muscles tensing beneath me. I run my hands across his powerful shoulders, down those arms that are so fucking glorious I want to spend the rest of the night memorizing their shape.

"I'll be right back." He chokes out the words before taking off at a sprint... and stubbing his toe, I think.

I hear a few gruff curses after a stumble.

"You okay?" I call through the darkness, and he mutters something before I hear more rushed banging.

His urgency is a compliment.

But as I wait on the stage, the idea of what we're about to do... what we've already done... starts to hit me.

He's my first since Atlas.

Actually, he'll only be the second man I've ever slept with, and I'm suddenly hyperaware of what's about to happen.

Resting my fingers on my thighs, I curl them into loose fists, really letting that thought sink in. Tyrell just went down on me. The only other lips to ever do that were Atlas's. The only other fingers to ever touch my most intimate parts were Atlas's. And now a brand-new cock is about to enter that space.

"Do I really want this?" I whisper, my stomach jittering, then jumping into my throat as I hear the bathroom door swing open.

I hold my breath, listening to Tyrell rush back across the floor.

He slows before he reaches me, his last few measured steps settling my heart into a beat that's manageable.

When he gets close enough to make out properly, I reach for his face, cupping his cheek and wondering how he'll react if I suddenly change my mind.

Turning his head, he presses a kiss to my palm, and it's so sweet, so tender.

My heart starts to liquefy once again, and I know this has to be the moment. I can't go chickening out now.

I have to move on from my first love.

Atlas will always be that for me. But now he's gone, and I deserve this second chance. Don't I?

That's still up for debate. That old familiar guilt niggles me, reminding me of how I left him that night. How I abandoned him. How I could have saved his life if I'd only been there.

My stomach plummets from my throat right down to my feet and—

"Hey," Tyrell whispers against my ear. "It's okay. It's okay for you to change your mind."

And that one little assurance is enough to wash away my trepidation.

His breath on my skin, his powerful body leaning into mine—it ignites something inside me again. That hunger comes back with a vengeance, and I know if I don't do this now, I'll regret it all night long.

I need this man.

I *want* this man.

I have to make this moment count. This is my chance to finally step into this new life I've been trying to make happen for myself.

Having sex with Tyrell isn't just about the physical pleasure. It's a symbol of my willingness to honestly start fresh.

"I'm not changing my mind." My voice trembles as I skim my fingers down his chest.

His nipples respond to my touch, hardening as I trace my fingers around them. Leaning forward, I press a kiss to his shoulder, then curl my arms around his body, pulling him flush against me.

The second his jean-clad erection skims between my legs, that spark turns my simmering fire into a hot inferno.

I need this.

I want this.

I'm doing it.

Scrambling for his pants, I quickly unbutton them, yanking down the fly, then pushing them off his hips.

His cock, finally freed from its confines, twitches in the air between us. I skim my fingers over its head, impressed and maybe just a little intimidated by the length and girth of him.

Holy shit.

Tyrell Jackson is all man.

A big, beautiful giant, and I'm about to take him inside me.

My pussy starts weeping all over again, my heart thundering as I reach for the condom packet and open it.

I may not have done this in a while, but it's all so familiar... yet new at the same time.

I roll the condom on, skimming my fingers back down his length and enjoying his soft moan when I lightly squeeze him.

He's so hard, so long... so powerful.

Yet I know he won't use that power against me.

He may be as big as a bouncer, but he's a gentle giant. I know this. I've seen this.

And that thought has my body scrambling back on the stage. He crawls up after me, and I wish I could see him, moving like a panther in the night.

As soon as he's within reach, I rest my hands on his shoulders, loving the way his muscles flex beneath my touch.

"You're so beautiful, Dani," he whispers against my skin, kissing my shoulder, my neck, my jaw... my lips.

I cup the back of his head, pulling him deeper into the kiss, drowning beneath him as our tongues lash together.

He nestles between my parted legs, and my stomach is now back in its place, hitching in anticipation when I feel him shift, putting his weight on one elbow so he can reach down and line himself up.

"You ready?" he asks in a featherlight voice that sends tendrils of sweet pleasure skipping though me.

"Yes," I whisper back, biting my bottom lip when he nudges inside me.

It's just an exploratory nudge. He pauses, checking my reaction, and I reach around him, squeezing his back and silently telling him to keep going.

So he does.

With one smooth thrust, he stretches me wide open, and I can't contain my cry. It's a mix of shock and pleasure. He's big and intrusive, but in all the right ways.

I dig my fingers into him, my body working to adjust in record time because I want this.

"You okay? I'm not hurting you, am I?"

"No," I squeak, and I can sense him going to move, to retreat. "Don't you dare." I grip his back. "I want you in here."

"But you're so tight. So small. I don't want to hurt you."

"Just let me adjust for a second," I rasp, my fingers clenching his taut muscles, silently begging for him not to bail.

Resting his cheek against mine, he holds his position. I can feel his muscles trembling with the effort, and I run my hands down his back, smooth, reassuring lines until I'm able to whisper, "I'm ready."

"You sure?" He presses a kiss to my cheek.

"Get your ass moving, Black Jack."

He snickers into my ear, the sound making me smile until he starts to move and my mouth pops open, my eyes bulging as his first thrust causes a jolt of pleasure to spear right through my center.

Holy shit, he feels good!

A breath punches out of me, my chest starting to heave when he thrusts into me again—a slow, smooth plunge that is all things erotic. I'd forgotten how mind-blowing sex could be. I'd forgotten how much I love the feeling of being pierced this way. Of having a body covering me, moving inside me.

Splaying my hand on his back, I rise and fall with

him, starting to meet each of his plunging thrusts so he can go that much deeper. Be that much closer to me.

The way he moves. It's so smooth, so calm. I cling to him, loving every second of this ride. The burning in my belly starts to spread, pleasure near blinding me as we rise and fall together.

Up and down.

Closer and closer.

He moans against my ear, pressing another kiss to my cheek before rising up to cover my mouth with his. I can barely concentrate on our lashing tongues, every nerve in my body catching fire. It's a white heat. No, a blue heat. No, a scorching red flame!

My body starts to splinter, shattering from the inside out until I'm coming all over again, gasping breaths punching out of me as I buck my hips and drink from this man.

My parched soul is refreshed until it's bubbling over, water running through me, sweet bliss gushing over him until his own hips start to buck.

He's coming.

I can feel that urgent swell of power.

Power he's barely able to control.

I want to tell him to unleash it, to take me hard and fast and—

A choking groan comes out of him as he thrusts deep one last time, quivering inside me, over me... all around me.

I pull him down on top of me, his weight a heavy blanket. I wrap my legs around him and dig my heels into that taut butt of his.

Damn, he is so fine.

Every inch of him is marble. Granite muscles, yet soft and warm to the touch.

I can't help a heady groan as he finally relaxes over me.

Our bodies are rubber and my limbs fall apart, my arms flopping down onto the stage with a loud smack.

"You good?" Tyrell's still catching his breath, his heart thundering against my chest.

"Yeah," I murmur, trailing my fingers lightly up his back. "That was... It was..." I can't even find the words.

Tyrell's lips curl into a smile; I can feel it forming against my cheek. Then he rises up, and although I can't see his face that clearly, I can picture his soft gaze when he whispers, "I know, right?"

# CHAPTER 30
## TYRELL

Guilt.

It's eating me up.

And I can't whisper a word of what I'm feeling to Dani because I don't want *her* feeling bad about hooking up on that stage.

It was fucking epic.

I haven't felt that way... ever.

And it kills me that I've just had the best sex of my life... with someone else's woman.

*She doesn't belong to Atlas! He's dead. Gone. Buried.*

Logically, I know all of this stuff, but as I drive Dani home, my fingers wrapped around the wheel, all I can feel is guilt. Fucking guilt.

Because if it weren't for me, Atlas would have been the one making love to her on that stage.

I don't deserve mind-blowing sex with this woman, yet I took it anyway. And as her sweet scent wafts over to me and I glance her way... I know without a doubt that I want to have her again. Take her and enjoy her and pleasure her. I want to hear those moans and wails. I want to watch her writhe in ecstasy. I want to make her feel good, because that's what she deserves.

But do I deserve her in return?

No.

*Shit, Atlas, man. I'm sorry.*

*I get why you couldn't get enough of her. Why you always talked about her like she was the sun, the moon, the stars. I thought it was overly romantic bullshit, but I see it now. Dani Hill is the kind of woman you learn poetry for.*

"Well..." She breathes out the word, then kind of laughs when I pull to a stop outside her apartment. "Thanks for a good night." I can sense her blushing and skim my thumb over her cheek as she reaches for the door handle.

"Wait." I jump out before she can get out of the car.

I might be swamped with guilt right now, but she doesn't need to know that. And I'm not some douche who's just gonna watch her get out of my car and walk away.

Her door is already open by the time I get around the SUV, and I close it for her, boxing her against it before she can disappear into her apartment.

"You're amazing," I whisper, running the tip of my nose across her cheek. "You know that, right?"

She lets out a soft giggle, resting her hands on either side of my waist. "I could ask you the same question."

I smile, wishing I could say, *"Yes, I'm amazing, and us together is fucking amazing."* But how can I?

With a soft swallow, I tip her chin, pressing my lips to hers and enjoying the way she responds to me, rising on her toes, pulling me in. I relax into the kiss, tasting her with my tongue, loving the way her body melds against mine when I wrap my arm around her waist.

I lift her off her feet for a brief moment, then force myself to put her down. As much as I want to spend the night with her wrapped in my arms, I need some space for a second. I need to process this war raging inside me. What I want versus what I deserve.

"Do you... do you want to come up?"

*Yes! I want to hold you all damn night.*

"I better not." I sigh. "I have an early workout in the morning, and it's your day off tomorrow. I want you to be able to sleep in."

She smiles up at me, the streetlight above us illuminating her pretty face. "You're sweet."

"You're gorgeous." I drink her in, loving her smile and the way her face just lit up at my honest assessment.

"Good night, Black Jack."

"Good night, Dani Girl."

Rising on her tiptoes one more time, she pecks my lips, then ducks under my arm and walks toward the door.

I spin, leaning against my car and watching her until she's disappeared inside. She gives me one more wave through the glass before taking the stairs... and I can finally slump with a huff and mutter a string of curses.

"Fuck. Shit. I know. I'm scum. I'm sorry, Atlas. I'm sorry."

I say it the whole way home, totally ruining my night and forgetting to dwell on how perfect it was sitting there at the end of the bar, watching Dani work, then getting to dance with her, kiss her, pleasure her. Shit, she was fucking amazing. Being inside her was better than anything I've had before. She moved with me. Our rhythm was so in sync.

"So..." I shake my head and, for a horrible second, picture what it must have been like for Dani and Atlas. "Fuck!" I squeeze my eyes shut, begging my brain not to go there. He was always very protective of their relationship, and although he told me about how they lost their virginity together, he tended to keep their private times private, and I respected that. Even though I was hella curious about sex, I didn't push him. They were like sixteen, I think. They'd been dating for a year when they finally crossed that line, and it brought them even closer together.

And tonight has brought me and Dani closer together too. I can feel it in my core.

Which is why I've got to shake this guilt, or it's going to destroy us. But how do I do that?

It should have been Atlas tonight.

"He should still be here," I mutter to myself as I close the front door of Football Frat and lean my forehead against it.

"You okay, man?" Grady's voice is a soft rumble, but it still gives me an electric jolt. I spin around to find him standing at the bottom of the stairs with a glass of water in his hand.

"Uh..." I nod, but obviously look anything but good, because he changes trajectory, tipping his head in the direction of the living room.

I should tell him, *"Nah, I'm good. I'm just gonna go to bed."* But instead, I follow him, plunking onto the opposite end of the couch and staring at him. He stares right back, patiently waiting the way he always does.

Grady's a good guy to talk to. I like the way he doesn't try to coax and cajole. There's a lot of space with him, which is why after only a short minute, I end up spilling...

"I slept with Dani tonight."

His eyebrows rise, his lips twitching with a smile.

"I didn't plan it that way. She was closing up, and when the lights went off, the music was still playing. We danced and... one thing led to another."

"Nice, man. I know how much she means to you."

"Yeah." I tap the back of the couch, staring at the blank TV screen and internally gasping for air. The guilt is a thick swamp, taking me under, trying to choke me out.

"So, what's the problem? You not into her anymore? Did you not feel it when—"

"Of course I'm into her." I bulge my eyes at him. "She's fucking perfect, and the sex was..." I bite my lips together before I spill too much. I doubt Dani wants me talking about her glorious tits or the way she felt wrapped around me.

Grady watches me carefully, like he's trying to read my mind, and I can tell the moment it dawns on him.

And if anyone in this house gets it, it's him.

"She's your best friend's girl. Or at least, she used to be."

My throat swells, and all I can do is nod.

"I know that you already know this," he starts, his tone measured. "And you probably don't need me to say it out loud, but the look on your face right now is forcing the words out of me." Grady shuffles on the couch, angling his body toward mine. "Atlas is dead, man. It's okay to move on. He'd want that for her. For you."

"But would he want us together?" I fire out the question. "She was his woman. He loved her, more than anything else."

"Then why was he so reckless? Why'd he end his life?"

"He didn't commit suicide," I bite back, refusing to believe that. "And if I'd been there, he wouldn't have taken those pills. I would have been keeping an eye on him."

"That wasn't your responsibility," Grady reminds me softly. "You carry so much guilt around not being there for him that night... but you never seem to acknowledge his part in all this. You didn't force those drugs down his throat. He took them. He messed up. And don't even get me started on all the other people who would have been around him that night, who could have checked him but didn't. And who gave him those pills, huh? It wasn't you." His voice is so emphatic. "None of that's on you, brother."

I clench my jaw, wishing I could believe that, logically knowing there's a grain of truth to what he's saying.

But maybe if I'd been there, he wouldn't have been tempted to do it. He was probably pissed off, wounded, because I hadn't showed. Just like his father never showed. His best friend had let him down, and he wanted to numb that feeling. So he drank too much and mixed his drugs... and ended his life.

*"That wasn't your responsibility."*

The thought takes me out, slamming into me like a smack around the ears. My head rings with those four words, because I've never let myself think them before. I didn't want to blame my dead friend, so I took it all on myself. And I've never really sat with the idea that Atlas had a part to play.

"Falling in love with his woman... that's nothing to feel guilty about either." Grady's words catch me off guard, and I spin to face him, blinking as I try to process what he said.

*Falling in love.*

Is that what I'm doing?

The way I felt tonight sure makes me wonder, because this is something new. Something I've never experienced. Dani has never been more precious to me.

Shit, maybe I am falling in love with her!

"You're giving each other a fresh start, and that's a good thing. Don't go fucking it up by drowning yourself in remorse." Again, Grady's words slap me hard.

I blink, staring at him until he becomes a blurry blob on the couch.

"Tyrell?" He waves his hand in front of my face, pulling himself back into focus. "You hearing me, man?"

"Yeah," I croak, then force myself to nod. "Yeah, I'm hearing you."

His compassionate smile makes my insides buckle.

"Look, I know this is a journey, and maybe it's not my place to say all of that to you, but I love you, man. And I want to see you happy. You've definitely been lighter since you started this double-date thing. And... you asked God to find you a woman, remember?"

I snicker, shaking my head. "And he found me my best friend's girl?"

Grady winces. "Yeah, the Big G's got a sick sense of

humor. I'm sure he was laughing his ass off when he put me and Blake together."

My snicker turns into a genuine laugh.

"I tried to fight so hard against everything I was feeling for her." Grady shakes his head. "And it made me fucking miserable. All because I didn't want to hurt Wily. In the end, it made everything worse. I should have just owned it right from the start, talked to him about how I was feeling."

I go still, his words sinking into me.

"And I shouldn't have fought so hard. I ended up hurting Blake by rejecting her, and what a fucking waste. Thankfully, we got through it pretty quickly, but still... all that angst when I should have just been honest."

Now I'm nodding, although I still can't say anything.

"Don't let your guilt over something that happened three years ago ruin what could be an amazing, beautiful thing. You and Dani both deserve to be happy. You're two good people. And good people should be together, you know?"

My lips curl into a grateful smile, and I manage to rasp a soft "Thanks, man."

He holds out his hand, and I give it a quick slide before snapping my fingers and watching him walk up the stairs... to his bed... where Blake is no doubt waiting for him.

Pulling out my phone, I brush my thumb over the screen and send Dani a quick text.

*Me: Thanks for the best date I've ever had.*

. . .

*Dani Girl: That wasn't a date. That was you watching me work.*

*Me: The ending was pretty date-like.*

*Dani Girl: The ending was perfect.*

I smile at her words, clutching the phone in my hand before sending her a string of emojis and a quick good night. She returns the favor, and I head up to my room, begging myself to believe that what happened between us was meant to be... and that Atlas, wherever he is in the afterlife, will forgive me for taking something that meant so much to him.

# CHAPTER 31
## DANI

Tonight was perfect.

But I still can't shake the feeling that maybe it wasn't supposed to happen.

After nearly three years of no sex, experiencing that again was so freaking good! And to have Tyrell be the one to pleasure me... well, it wasn't as awkward as I thought it would be. If anything, it felt like the most natural thing in the world. Which is probably why I'm freaking out.

Because Atlas has always been my one and only.

But that's not the case anymore, and shouldn't it feel weirder than this?

But it really was perfect.

If I could play that scenario out any other way, I couldn't find a better version. Doing it with Tyrell on that stage was sexy and sweet and erotic and...

I flop back down on my bed with a sigh, my arms splaying wide as I grin up at the ceiling, only to have that uncertainty butt into me again.

My smile fades, my stomach twisting as I pull my phone close and reread my texts with Tyrell.

He is a sweetheart.

And I didn't plan on sleeping with him tonight.

That worry that I've moved too fast skitters through me again. Why can't I just revel in what happened? Why can't I just enjoy it?

*Because you have a ghost sitting on your shoulder, hovering behind you, around you.*

Snapping my eyes shut, I squeeze them tight and try to shake those thoughts from my brain. But I can't.

Atlas has been with me for so long now.

I've clung to him, loving the idea of his ghost keeping me company. But now it's just weird.

What if he was watching Tyrell and me on that stage?

I jolt up into a sitting position, fisting my curls and shaking my head. "No, please. Don't go there, brain. Please."

Did I hurt his feelings?

*He's gone! He has no feelings!*

Logic is begging me to listen to reason, but my heart and chest hurt so bad right now.

I press the heel of my hand between my boobs and quickly stand up, pacing the small space from my bed to my chest of drawers and back.

Gripping my phone, I wonder about calling my sister. I need to hash this out, but...

I glance at the time. It's way too late. She has kids now. All of my siblings do. But Shante's twins are only five, and life is so hectic for her. She's back working full-time, and sleep is a precious commodity. I can't go calling her at 1:04 a.m. She'll kill me.

"Go get some tea." I order myself out of my room, desperate for anything to quiet this restless itch in my chest.

I try to work in stealth mode, not wanting to disturb anyone else in the house. Tobin woke up sick this morning, which is why Jed wouldn't cover my shift at work tonight. He wanted to stay home and look after him. And who knows where Nix is. She might be at her boyfriend's place for all I know.

Filling a mug with water, I wince when the microwave door opens with a loud *pop!* I bite my lip and gently place the mug inside before pressing the buttons, which all sound like alarms at this time of night.

*How badly do you really need tea?*

Glancing over my shoulder at Nix's bedroom door, which is shut up tight, I press Start on the microwave. I need tea. I'll just stop the microwave when there's only one second left so it doesn't do that loud beeping thing.

It whirs in the quiet room, and I tiptoe across the tiles, pulling out a chamomile teabag and teaspoon.

Watching the countdown on the microwave, I open the door just before the time is up and nearly spill hot water all over myself when Nix's bedroom door flings open and she strolls out in a pair of boxer shorts and a tank top with shoe-string straps that's way too small for her. Her belly button is on full display, and I glance at the glinting stud she got herself for Christmas. I would never get my belly button pierced, but it really suits her.

"Hey." She raises her chin at me.

I cringe. "I didn't wake you, did I?"

"Nope. I was watching a movie on my laptop."

"Oh yeah? Which one?"

She shrugs. "I'm just working my way through my annual Batman binge."

"Which version?"

Her eyebrows wrinkle like I'm insane for even asking that question. "The Christopher Nolan ones. They are the *only* ones worth watching."

I snicker. "I'm sure some people might disagree with you on that—"

"Well, they'd be idiots. *The Dark Knight* trilogy is by far the best. It's classy, it's dark. It's all the things Batman should be."

"Okay." I nod, not really wanting to get into it with her. I don't watch a lot of movies. I'm more of a doco girl, but Nix will never let me hear the end of it if I admit that I'd rather watch an hour and a half of real-life facts about ancient Egypt than sit through two hours of some guy in a cape beating up deranged bad guys and... whatever else he does. "So, no boyfriend tonight?" I dunk my teabag a few more times before squeezing it against the side of my mug.

"Nah. He's getting all stressed about exams and wants a few days to focus on studying." She pouts, but her lips quickly rise into a grin. "He's promised to be free this weekend so we can hang out."

"Nice." I nod. "How's your studying going?"

"Yeah, pretty good. I think." Her little pixie nose wrinkles. "Kind of hate studying, so it's probably a case of me needing to do a shit ton more but hoping I can just wing it during finals week."

I raise my eyebrows. "Well, that's, uh... one strategy."

She grins, her cheeks flushing red before she narrows her eyes at me.

"What?"

"I don't know." She tips her head, studying me closely, like she's a sniffer dog at the airport and senses something is off.

I ping up straight, scratching my collarbone and trying to look unaffected by her assessment. "Okay, well, I'm gonna—"

"Wait." She points at me. "Something's different."

"Nope," I lie, grabbing my mug and spilling hot tea over the side of it. I hiss, quickly wiping my hand.

"Run it under cold water," Nix tells me.

"No, I'm good."

"What is up with you?"

"Nothing."

"Something is definitely up." She turns on the tap and starts muttering, "Making tea at one in the morning and trying to distract me, asking about studying and—" She gasps, her eyes bulging as she grabs my hand and shoves it under the cold water. "Did something happen with you and Ty tonight? Oh my gosh, it was good, wasn't it? You've got this glow about you. Oh shit! Did you have sex with him?" She practically yells the last part, and of course within a second, Jed and Tobin's door is popping open, and I'm soon surrounded by curious roommates.

I glare down at the girl who is still holding my hand under the cold spray. She gives me an unapologetic smile until I nudge her away from me and claim my hand back. Drying it off, I let out a sigh when Jed leans his elbows on the kitchen counter with a bemused smirk and Tobin gives me a red-nosed smile.

"You should be back in bed," I mumble, hanging the

dish towel back up. "We can discuss my love life in the morning."

"Your love life?" Nix's laughter is sparkly and filled with delight. "You totally slept with him!" She gives me a friendly slap on the butt.

"We need details." Tobin sniffs, taking a seat next to Jed and letting out an involuntary groan.

Jed steadies him and Tobin sighs, resting his head on Jed's shoulder.

"Seriously, dude. This germ-fest of yours should not be in the kitchen." Nix wrinkles her nose. "Take your snot back to your own room."

"Hey." Jed gives her a sharp look. "Leave him alone. He just needs to get out of the space for a minute. I'll take him back to bed soon."

"What, so you can get sick too?" Her disgusted look remains firmly intact.

Jed gives her a deadpan stare. "I'll sleep on the couch tonight."

"Whatever, dude. You've been hanging out in the germ zone all freaking day. You're gonna get sick."

"He is not." Tobin's blocked nose and croaky throat make him sound funny. "My man is as strong as an ox. He hasn't been sick once since we got together. As long as you don't count the food poisoning incident, which I still blame my mother for. That woman should not be allowed to cook Thanksgiving meals."

"She was trying to be nice."

"She was trying to impress you, and it was an epic backfire," Tobin argues.

Jed laughs. "She's a sweetheart."

"Yeah, well, the fact that you forgave her won you

some major brownie points. I think she likes you more than me now."

"No way. You're her precious boy." Jed kisses Tobin's forehead, then turns back to me.

A rush of heat floods my body as I carefully pick up my mug and wrap my fingers around it. Blowing on the hot tea, I take a sip and wonder if I can just walk to my room without confessing anything.

"Not a chance." Jed reads my mind, his lips rising into a smirk. "Spill, girl."

I huff, throwing a side-eye at Nix before getting it over with. "Fine. Tyrell and I had sex."

"Was it good?" Nix bounces on her toes. "I bet it was fucking amazing! He is so hot."

"He *is* hot," I have to admit, my body buzzing just thinking about how divine he felt inside me.

"Bet he's sporting himself a freaking Excalibur in those pants of his," Tobin croaks.

"Guys," I quickly reprimand them. "I am not talking to you about Tyrell's penis!"

Tobin lets out a hoarse laugh that quickly turns into a coughing fit. He splutters into his elbow while Jed rubs his back with a wince.

"You good, baby?" he softly checks once Tobin's done.

Nix is now on the opposite side of the room, staying as far away from Tobin's bugs as possible.

"So, it was good, though?" she calls from armchair by the window.

I sip my tea, giving myself another minute before answering them. I have to. I need someone to talk to, and since I can't wake my sister, I should probably just tell these guys everything.

Chewing my lip for a second, I finally let out a sigh and say, "It was amazing. I haven't had sex in a really long time, and I didn't plan on it tonight. But I'd just locked up, and we started dancing, and I just couldn't resist him."

"Wait." Jed holds up his hand. "You did it at Offside?"

I blush.

"Where?"

Biting my lips together, I bulge my eyes at him before blurting, "On the stage."

"Oh shit!" Nix jumps up, springing to her feet with a laugh and forgetting all about Tobin's cold as she bounds back into the kitchen. "Your bare ass has been on the stage at Offside?" She laughs the words, and I quickly grab her arm.

"Do *not* tell anyone that." I look around the room. "You guys all have to swear."

"We swear, we swear," Jed assures me before his lips rise into a smirk. "Damn, girl."

"Oh, shut up." I squeeze my eyes shut, letting out a soft wail. "I didn't mean for it to happen!"

"But..." Nix reaches for my arm, giving it a little rub. "You wanted it, though, right? I mean, you really like this guy."

"Yeah, of course I do! And I wanted it, like... *a lot*. But..." I sigh, my shoulders deflating as I stare into my mug of tea.

"But what?" Tobin sniffs. "What's the problem?"

"We haven't even been on a proper date yet. It feels..." I shake my head.

"Too fast?"

"Like you're being a slut?"

"Intense."

They all throw out their answers, and I frown at Tobin's slut comment.

"Sorry," he mumbles, pointing at his head. "I'm sick. My filter's not working properly. I don't think you're a slut. Far from it."

Jed snickers, giving him another kiss on the forehead before looking at me. "Intense," he repeats. "Like emotionally, right?"

"Well, yeah. I mean..." My right shoulder hitches. "I've never slept with anyone but Atlas, and that was like three years ago. I've been on all these dates, and I've barely kissed any of the guys I've gone out with, and then I kiss Tyrell like twice and he's going down on me after closing tonight!"

"He went down on you as well?" Nix's glee at my exploits is starting to grate.

I grit my teeth and refuse to reply to her comments. I probably should be celebrating with her. That was one hell of an orgasm.

But I'm trying to process shit here!

"Hey." Jed taps the counter, grabbing my attention.

I reluctantly look at him, but my insides settle the second I catch that sweet expression on his face.

"Girl, I get that this is scary for you. Moving on is a big deal."

Nix calms down, nodding along with him. "He's right. But when you think about it, it's not that fast. I mean, you've been on all those double dates with him. You were probably flirting with him more than the guy you were supposed to be with. You just didn't realize it."

My cheeks heat as I take another sip of tea.

She's probably right.

Tyrell and I have had a blast on all those double dates. Except for the yoga one, although that was kind of funny, and then the last one when Tyrell got all shitty because he could see how well it was going.

Crap. I really hope Rhys doesn't reach out and try to connect anymore. He was the last to text, and I haven't started up another conversation with him. I don't want to give him the wrong idea.

He's a good guy, and he deserves a woman who is totally into him. Maybe it would have been easier for me to pursue something with him, but when we kissed it was just... lackluster.

And when I kiss Tyrell it... sets my body on fire.

And sleeping with him...

I close my eyes, tipping my head back until it hits the cupboard behind me.

Nix gives my arm a squeeze. "Hey, it's okay. Tyrell's a good guy. You should be celebrating this."

"I know," I whisper. "I guess I just... feel bad."

"Why?" Jed's voice is deep with obvious concern.

"Because..." I purse my lips to the side, fighting a sudden swelling in my throat. "Atlas isn't my one and only anymore. And I've been talking for weeks... *months*... about moving on, and now it's finally happening, and I... I don't know how to feel about it."

My eyes are still closed, but I hear the scraping of a stool and then two strong arms wrap around me. Jed pulls me to his chest, cradling my head against his shoulder.

Nix comes in from the other side, wrapping her little arms around me until I'm sandwiched between them.

"I'm hugging you in spirit," Tobin calls from his perch on the other side of the counter. "And I know I didn't know Atlas super well, but I do know that he loved you and he'd want you to be happy."

*Would he?*

After the way we left things... our final conversation, all terse words and biting anger... I don't know what he'd want for me.

But I can guarantee me falling for his best friend would be a really hard pill for him to swallow.

"At the end of the day, it's up to you and what feels right." Jed gives me a final squeeze before letting go and stepping back so he can look me in the eye. "But don't regret tonight, okay? Whether it turns into something more, something permanent in your life, or just becomes a distant memory, don't regret it. You had epic sex on the stage at Offside. That's hot, girl." He grins.

"It is pretty freaking hot," Nix agrees. She hugs my waist one last time before jumping away from me with a spirited laugh.

I glance between my roommates and can't help smiling along with them.

They're right.

It was so hot.

And I really can't go regretting it.

# CHAPTER 32
## TYRELL

After a restless sleep, my alarm wakes me with a jolt.

It's a freaking foghorn, and I reach for my phone, accidentally slapping it onto the floor in my bid to shut the thing up.

"Fuck," I growl, leaping out of bed, my foot catching in the damn sheet.

I thump onto the floor, grappling to pick up my phone and shut it up.

"Ahh!" I punch my finger onto the screen until the damn thing goes quiet.

Lying down, I rest my head on the hard floor and gaze up at the ceiling. It's still dark. Five in the fucking morning, and the last thing I feel like doing is a workout at the gym.

Maybe I could just skip today.

I'm seconds away from crawling back into bed when there's a soft knock on my door.

"Ty, let's go, man."

It's Grady. I hate how fucking chipper he is in the mornings.

*No, you don't. You're just being a grumpy ass.*

Forcing myself up, I quickly get changed, pulling on my shorts just as my door pops open.

"Brah, you ready or what?" Grady whisper-barks.

"I'm ready," I growl, throwing on a T-shirt and grabbing my hoodie.

I trundle after him and meet up with Carson, who's already at the front door, taking off for Coach's house. They go for a run together most mornings. I can't believe they're still doing that, but Carson seems to get a kick out of impressing his girlfriend's father, so he goes, almost every morning.

Shoving on my shoes, I grumble my way out the door, Wily behind me. He's way too chipper in the mornings as well, and I'm grateful when Zander appears out of his garage and offers to drive.

I jump in the front passenger seat and let the two morning larks sit in the back.

Seriously.

My head is pounding with tension. I really did not get enough sleep last night. You'd think my body would be relaxed and sated after what went down at Offside, but my brain just wouldn't switch off.

I should be reveling in the fact that I got to experience Dani's luscious body.

But the experience is being marred by this... guilt.

Grady's comments from last night whistle through me as I tune out their voices and force my mind back to the night Atlas died.

It was so fucking hideous.

Walking into that party. Hearing Dani's screams. Seeing Atlas's pale face, his open eyes staring at nothing because he was dead. OD'd.

*On pills you didn't force down his throat.*

*I should have been there to stop him.*

*He wasn't your responsibility. He was a grown-ass man who chose to mix his drugs. That shouldn't be on you.*

*If anyone's to blame, it's the guy who gave Atlas those pills.*

We never did find that out. The police investigation into the whole thing was useless. They put it down to reckless partying and did barely any follow-up. We were all too shell-shocked and devastated to push for anything, and it all got swept under the carpet.

It seems too late to action anything now, and what good will it do? It won't bring Atlas back.

*But it might stop the person from giving drugs to someone else?*

I frown, rubbing my forehead.

I never usually let myself sit in these kinds of thoughts. I don't want to tarnish Atlas in any way. He's my best friend. He—

Glancing left, I look at Zander, smiling at something Wily just said, then laughing when Grady adds a witty one-liner. I'm only tuning in now, so I don't really know what they're talking about.

But these guys right here... they're my best friends now.

Because Atlas OD'd.

Atlas was reckless.

Atlas left Dani and me.

A hot rush of anger fires through me. I never usually let it. I've been clamping down that emotion for years, throwing it on myself instead. Hating myself for not being there for him. But what about *him*? He wouldn't have been thinking about me and Dani, the consequences of his actions as he downed more drinks and swallowed those drugs.

He may not have meant to kill himself, but he did.

He left us.

"I have the right to move on." The words pop out of me, and it's not until Zander glances my way and says, "What?" that I realize I even said them aloud.

"Huh?" I turn to him.

"What are you talking about?" His eyebrows wrinkle. "What do you mean, you're moving on?"

I blow out a breath, then feel Grady's fingers grip my shoulder. "You do have a right to move on. To be happy. It's okay to fall for Dani, you know?"

"Oooo." Wily laughs. "You getting hardcore feels for Dani? When did this happen?"

"They've been going on all those dates. It was bound to happen." Zander grins. "I'm happy for you, man."

"Yeah." I nod, letting myself smile. "She's awesome."

"She's hot," Wily agrees.

I throw a frown over my shoulder.

"What? She is!" He looks to Grady for backup. "I'm not saying she's as pretty as my Satch."

"She's definitely not as gorgeous Blake," Grady mumbles.

"Hey!" I snap. "She's a fucking queen." Scowling into the back seat, I point between them. "And she's stunning. Every inch of her."

Zander snickers, pulling into the stadium parking lot. "All of our women are beautiful. We don't need to be getting into an argument about this." Braking, he cuts the engine and eyeballs me. "Now, what's this about 'every inch of her'? Did you two get it on last night?"

"Maybe," I murmur.

Wily whoops. "They totally did! Is she still up in your room?"

"No." I frown. "I dropped her home after. She's got a day off, and she deserves to sleep in."

"Where did you do it?" Zander asks.

I wince and softly mumble, "At Offside. After closing. On the stage."

"What?" Grady laughs. "You didn't tell me that part."

Pinching the bridge of my nose, I softly warn them, "Tell anyone and I will slay you all."

Zander gives my arm a good-natured slap. "You know your secret's safe with us, man."

"Yeah." I sigh, pushing my door open and stepping out into the crisp morning air.

"So..." Wily hitches his bag onto his shoulder and limps around the car. "Considering you had hot sex last night, you seem kinda down this morning. Are you bummed out that you couldn't spend the night with her after or something? I didn't peg you for being that much of a sap."

"It's not sappy to want to sleep beside your woman after you've had sex with her." Zander frowns at Wily.

"No, I know that. I just..." Wily shakes his head, wisely shutting up.

Grady jumps in. "It's the fact that Dani used to be Atlas's girl."

"Oh." Zander and Wily nod in unison.

"That makes sense." Zander shoots me a kind smile.

"But... it is okay for you to move on. And if she's the one, then don't let shitty reasons stop you from being together."

I can tell he's speaking from experience. His entire being resonates with it, plus we all know that he will forever regret breaking up with Sienna in high school and then screwing up so badly in his first year of college. His actions nearly cost him Sienna and Zoey forever. He had to do some major work to win his woman back, and now he's playing happy family. I know for a fact that he's been looking at diamond rings. It wouldn't surprise me if he proposes when they get to LA, or maybe even before they leave.

"Yeah, man," Wily agrees. "Life's too short to hesitate. You need to go for it with this girl."

"I think he kind of already has." Grady smirks. "Maybe you should think about taking her out on a date next."

Zander laughs while Grady winks at me, and I shake my head. I seriously have no response to that, because yep, Dani and I definitely jumped the gun last night.

But damn if it didn't feel right at the time.

Our bodies were working of their own accord, and I've got a feeling they'll want to do the exact same thing next time we're together.

But I can't just turn what we have into a sex-fest. I want more than that. I want a relationship with her. And I've been building one of those every time we've gone on a double date together.

It's time to treat her like the queen she is.

Dumping my hoodie on the floor beside the weights

area, I jump onto a treadmill to warm up and figure I may as well ask the fucking room.

"Everyone, give me your favorite date scenarios. I'm taking out the best girl I know, and I want to make it special."

Every guy in the gym pauses, like I've just lost my fucking mind, before cracking up and hassling the shit out of me.

I frown, giving them all the finger as they laugh at me before upping the pace on my machine. I'm just breaking into a slow jog when one of them calls from across the room.

"Mini golf is always a winner for me."

"I'd go for an outdoor movie. There's usually one playing at this time of year."

"There's a cool night market in Fledgling every second Saturday of the month. That's coming up this weekend. Take her there. Buy her some cotton candy or a piece of handmade jewelry," Wily tells me.

I glance at him and grin.

"Yes, Satch told me about it, and yes, I'm planning on taking her there before I move to Arizona." His smile drops away, his eyebrows dipping.

Yeah, the thought of leaving her is killing him.

"Maybe she'll transfer."

He sighs, resting his hand on my machine. "I don't want her doing anything she doesn't want to do. If she moves, it's gotta be for her, not me."

"Maybe she'll love Arizona State."

"Yeah, I mean, she's already looking into it." Wily glances at me. "I didn't ask her to, but she got online the same night I was selected." His lips twitch with a grin. "Think she's gonna apply."

"She'll definitely get in."

"Yeah, I'm pretty sure they'll take her. I just... She's never been that far from her parents before."

I slow my pace, my muscles nice and warm to start lifting weights. "She can handle it, man. And you'll be there. Plus, she'll be away from those bitchy girls."

"What if new bitchy girls crop up in Arizona? What if I'm out of town? Who's gonna protect her?"

"What if she makes amazing friends in Arizona? What if she copes just fine while you're away? What if she can protect herself?"

He growls as I fire the questions right back at him, but he knows I'm right. Satch is growing in confidence every day, and she hasn't had one incident with those bullies since she stood up for herself that night.

"Look..." I stop the machine and step down, standing beside Wily as I reassure him. "The truth is, she'll probably be just fine if she stays in Nolan, and she'll be just fine if she moves to Glendale with you."

"Agreed." Zander steps up to join the conversation. "At the end of the day, the decision comes down to which place she'll feel happier in. And my guess is that moving in with you is what she wants the most. She loves you, man."

Wily's lips curl into a grin. "I know that's the option I want. It'll definitely make *me* a happy man if she comes with me. I just want what's best for her. She needs to make this decision for herself, not for me."

"She will," I try to assure him, but I don't honestly know. I haven't exactly spent hours with Satch. She seems sweet, and I can imagine her making decisions that are in Wily's best interest. But he's busy making decisions that are in *her* best interest, so maybe between the two of them, they can figure out what they both want and make it work.

*They'll make it work.*

Every couple in Football Frat seems to have an endgame vibe. Which is why I was seeking my own.

*And maybe you've found it.*

My chest hitches at the idea, a smile creeping over my lips.

"Go with the market idea." Wily gives me a nudge as I walk to the chest press and he heads over to the mat for some resistance training.

"Need a spotter?" Zander comes up behind me, and I nod, lying down and getting comfy under the bar while he smiles at me and starts to tell me all about his first date with Sienna.

The guy made envelopes with little riddles she had to work out.

Talk about a romantic.

"She loved it." He grins, his expression turning nostalgic as he obviously relives his high school romance... and my brain starts ticking over with date ideas.

I want to give Dani the perfect night.

I want to show her that I'm in on this thing. All the way.

# CHAPTER 33

## DANI

Without me knowing, Tyrell arranged for my Saturday night shift to be covered so that he could finally take me out on a date.

It was the sweetest thing and the nicest surprise.

I got a text from him on Saturday morning, letting me know that I was all his for the night.

A thrill skipped through me. And Tobin, who had bounced back from his cold, went into full fashionista mode. He dragged me out shopping, and we argued over dresses and a freaking sparkly pink onesie thing that no one on the planet should ever actually wear in public.

Finally, I found a top that paired perfectly with the jeans I was already wearing, and he relented and let me settle on just that one item, plus a pair of heels.

I swear, that man is going to make me broke.

But he does make me look good.

And when Tyrell arrives and his eyes rove over me like I'm a supermodel, it makes me grateful for Tobin's help.

He gives me a wink and mouths, "I told you!" just before I walk out the door, tucking up against Tyrell's side.

I love how tall he is.

How strong he is.

How safe I feel when I'm beside him.

We drive toward Denver, and I keep asking him where we're going, but he seems set on surprising me.

And he does.

We start with a super-fun escape room that has us working together beautifully. I swear, his brain is awesome, and we totally nailed the puzzles, getting out of there in forty-three minutes and making it onto the leaderboard. We celebrated with gelato ice creams, and then he took me to an obscure secondhand bookstore he'd researched online. It was so cool! We spent ages in there roaming the shelves. I ended up buying some picture books for my nephews, a chapter book for my seven-year-old niece, and a baby book for the latest addition to the family.

Kiara is one, and she's the cutest thing on the planet.

I tell Tyrell all about my growing family, showing him photos.

"I bet you're their favorite aunt."

I blush, knowing he's right but not wanting to say it. Those kids adore me, and it shows every time I walk in one of their front doors.

My older brother, Jesse, had his little Elsa when he was only eighteen. His girlfriend moved in with us while she was pregnant, and the entire family stepped up to support them so they could still graduate from high school and attend college. I was on babysitting duty a lot, and Elsa and I are really close now.

She's an avid reader and top of her class, so finding books that are advanced enough for her, yet still cover appropriate topics for a seven-year-old, can be challenging. But she's mad about horses, and she'll love this one.

I read the back again, excited to give it to her and wondering when I'll make it back to Colorado Springs.

Man, what will my family say when they know I'm dating Tyrell Jackson? I still haven't told them I've been dating anyone yet. They saw me fall apart after Atlas died, and I bet some of them think I'll be single forever.

I really should give them a heads-up that my move to Nolan has been a real gamechanger, but I just want to see how things play out with Tyrell first. I don't want to jump the gun.

*Oh, you mean like you did on Tuesday night?*

I blush, biting my lips together to hide my smile. A shiver races down my body, pooling between my legs as I wonder if I'll get to experience the wonder that is Tyrell Jackson all over again tonight.

I glance at him, my lips twitching as I try to guess where we're off to next. It's been an epic date, and we've had so much fun together.

"You hungry?" He looks at me and I nod, feeling my body swell with a different kind of hunger as he turns onto a new street and I watch his bicep curl, study the muscles in his forearm, and relive those large hands skimming over my body, cupping my breasts, my butt...

And I'm getting wet again.

Part of me wants to blurt, *"Forget food! Just feed my insatiable hunger for you!"*

But I hold my tongue and force myself to sit in the restaurant, order off the menu, and engage in civilized conversation.

Actually, it's pretty important conversation. Tyrell's trying to figure out what he wants to do after graduation. His family is really putting the pressure on, and I remind him that Cyrus has been coping just fine without him for four years. And although it's good to be there for your family, you also need to weigh up the cost of living your best life.

"I'll probably head back for the summer, make sure everyone is really settled, and then..." He shrugs.

"Get a job?" I tease.

"Yeah. Of course. Dad's already got a potential interview lined up with me for the civil engineering company he works for. I'd be starting at the bottom, but that's how these things work. I just..." He tuts.

"What?"

"Well... ultimately, I just want to save my pennies so I can head off and see the world. I'm happy to live on a dime to do it, so maybe just a year of hard work and then I can be off."

"Sounds amazing."

He stares at me, and for a second, I wonder if he's about to ask me if I'd like to join him.

Eeeep! Too soon! Too fast! Too high of a risk that I'll say yes, because the idea of traveling the world with Black Jack sounds pretty perfect to me.

The fact that I'm even thinking that makes my belly quake, but I keep it locked down, focusing instead on asking him where he'd go first.

We talk about Dubai, and then our meals are served

as we daydream our way through Asia. By the time we're done eating, we're over in Europe, scoping out the sights and sounds of Austria and Switzerland, Belgium and Germany.

We drive back to my apartment, working our way down through Morocco and all the way to a safari in South Africa.

We're both giddy as I walk him up to my apartment, sneaking into my room and stripping off each other's clothes while we catch a cruise from Durban to Perth... and our imaginings of touring Australia are soon lost to exquisite kisses and hungry tongues.

I grip the back of Tyrell's neck as he lifts me off the floor and walks me to my bed. His naked torso is pressed against mine, his hot kisses sending spikes of pleasure all the way through me.

When he kneels on the edge of the bed and gently lowers me down on the mattress, I bring him with me, loving his weight squishing me into the bed.

He nibbles a path along my jawline, lifting my arms above my head and locking my wrists in place with his hands. I tip my head back with a groan, relishing his attentive tongue, which is licking every spot and crevice.

My hips thrust upward, grinding into his erection as our underwear rubs together.

I moan, my eyes rolling back in my head when he gets to my breasts and savors each one—licking, sucking, teasing, igniting.

My body is a hub of pleasure as he takes his sweet time tasting me and sending my nerves into a frenzy.

"Ty, please...," I whisper, a moan overriding my words when his fingers inch inside my underwear and quickly find my clit. I lift my hips, scrambling to pull the fabric away as his digits start to dance. He plays a sweet tune on my body, slipping his fingers inside me and working my G-spot like a pro.

"Holy shit," I murmur, feeling the orgasm building with a force I wasn't counting on.

It's too quick! Too soon!

I want this to last all night, but my weak body gives in with only a few more strokes. His mouth suctioned over my nipple isn't helping either, and I'm soon falling apart, shattering with a series of mewling whimpers.

He smiles against my skin, his fingers still inside me while I buck and strain.

"You like that, Dani Girl?"

"It's the tits," I groan, and he starts to laugh, his warm breath hitting my skin.

I snort and giggle with him as he kisses a trail up my body, lightly sucking my neck before capturing my laughter in his mouth. I drink from him, lashing my tongue against his and gripping the back of his shoulders.

His body is covering mine once more, his rock-hard dick resting against me, and the fire I'm feeling for this man is next-level.

My body yearns and pines, my hands shaking with desire and anticipation as I yank his boxer briefs down, just far enough so I can wrap my fingers around his glorious cock and start pumping.

He groans, pressing a kiss to the curve of my breast and quickly losing his breath as I tease and coax his... Excalibur. I grin, loving how big he is. Brushing my thumb over his head, I wipe the bead off, circling the moisture around his cock and drinking him in when he reaches up to kiss me again.

His lips claim mine, owning them with a heady passion as he once again grabs my arms and lifts them over my head. Nestling between my thighs, he nudges the tip of his cock against me.

"I want you," he mumbles between kisses. "I want you so fucking bad."

"Then take me." I kiss him back.

He pulls away, glancing down at me. "You got protection?"

I smile up at him, and he grins back when I direct him to the top drawer of my nightstand.

Sitting up on my elbows, I watch him with hooded eyes as he suits up. Biting my bottom lip, I can't fight my smile when he lies back over me, grabbing my arms for the third time tonight and locking my wrists in place.

It's so fucking sexy, I'm weeping for him by the time he nudges inside me.

That first thrust is exquisite, and I can't help a lusty cry as he once again owns me, just like he did on that stage.

Our bodies gyrate together, finding a heady rhythm that suits us. I work with him, meeting each of his plunging thrusts and threading my fingers between his when he releases my wrists and glides his palms over mine.

Opening his eyes, he stares down at me, his brown gaze filled with such tender affection... and maybe a touch of wonder. I smile up at him, lost in that gaze before he hits a sweet spot that has my eyes snapping shut in ecstasy.

"That's it, baby," he croons, repeating the move, his slow, deep thrust taking out my senses once more.

I squeeze his hands, gasping breaths punching out of me when he picks up his pace and starts a deep hammering that is all... things... right.

Each thrust is magic, our bodies slapping together like a drumbeat.

He feels so good I think I might explode.

This is so intense.

So...

It's so...

"Ah!" I cry out, a flood of pleasure rippling through my body as he keeps plunging into me. I arch my back and he rises to his knees, grabbing my hips and supporting me as I'm taken out by a second orgasm.

He doesn't let up, pistoning into me with short jerks that send me over the edge completely. At this new angle, I can't control that next sob of passion that pops out of my mouth, my hands scrambling to squeeze his arm as I struggle to navigate this erotic minefield.

"Yes, baby. Yes." He grips my hips, tucking my legs around him as I tip my head back and arch a little higher.

Panting and slick with sweat, I take each of his short thrusts, smiling in wonder at how fucking good this feels!

I drop down to my back and he covers me again, his movements turning slow and deep as he continues to ride me.

My pussy is a weeping mess, electrified and aching, wondering how much more it can take when his breaths turn deep and heavy. I can feel the shift, a groan rising in his throat as he presses his cheek against mine and starts to pick up his pace again.

His hips jerk with deep, fast movements just before he lets out a strangled groan and releases inside me. I wrap my arms and legs around him, holding him close as he orgasms on top of me.

He feels divine, his muscles quaking, his heart hammering.

*Thump. Thump. Thump.*

I close my eyes, reveling in his heartbeat, kissing his shoulder and clinging to him.

"I'm not sure I'll ever be able to move again." His voice softly rumbles in my ear, and I can't help giggling in reply.

He pushes into me, grinding our hips together so I can't laugh him right out of me.

I shift my body to accommodate him and open my eyes, smiling when I notice him gazing down at me again. As he gently traces my hairline with the tip of his finger, I notice this blooming sensation stirring in my chest.

I've felt it before.

But not for him.

I felt it for the first boy to steal my heart, the man I thought I was going to marry, the ghost who seems to linger still.

Before I can stop them, my eyes glass with tears.

"What is it?" Tyrell whispers, shifting off me. "Am I hurting you? Did I hurt you?"

"No," I whisper, shifting my butt back and pulling my knees to my chest. "That was amazing. Even better than the first time, and that's saying a lot."

My smile is fleeting, which means Tyrell doesn't even smile at all.

He's now perched on the edge of the bed like he's

seconds away from getting dressed, from bolting out the door if I tell him this is too much and I'm not ready.

But that's not the truth.

I sniff, swiping a finger under my nose.

"What is it?" Tyrell reaches for me, curling his large hand over my knee. "Did I do something wrong?"

"No." I shake my head again and smile at him, resting my hand over his and tracing the length of his fingers. "It's not that. I just..." Brushing my teeth over my bottom lip, I wonder how to word this or if I should even be saying it at all.

"Dani," he softly begs. "Please, talk to me."

I swallow, plucking up my flailing courage and whispering, "Are we doing the right thing?"

"What do you mean?" Tyrell eyes me cautiously.

And I force the words out. "By Atlas. Do you think he'd mind us... being together?"

He glances at the rumpled bedsheets, his fingers trailing down my leg and covering my foot before he lets out a soft sigh and asks, "Where's this coming from?"

I shrug, not even sure, really. Why am I once again letting epic sex be ruined by these thoughts?

"You're the only other man I've ever been with," I finally say. "I guess I really am moving on, and I... I don't know why I'm struggling with it."

Tyrell's eyebrows dip together, his expression downright wounded as he tries to accept what I just said.

Shit. I don't want to hurt him.

Gliding his hand off my foot and across the mattress, I feel the loss instantly and have to fight the urge to beg him to touch me again.

"But, um..." He clears his throat. "That's what you wanted, though, right? To move on?"

"Yes." I wrap my arms tighter around my legs. "I really want to let go and move forward, but..." I bite my lips together, a shudder rolling through me before I find the courage to say, "He should be here, Ty. If it weren't for me, he'd still be alive."

# CHAPTER 34
## TYRELL

Her soft statement slams into me like a sledgehammer.

What the fuck did she just say?

I gape at her for a second, trying to process it.

She's blaming herself for his death?

Nah, that ain't right.

I was the one who should have been there to protect him. I'm Black Jack.

She shouldn't be carrying this shit.

Unless she...

No way.

I shake my head, answering the question for her before I even ask it. "You gave him the drugs?"

"No, of course not!" She looks horrified that I'd even think it.

"Then why are you blaming yourself? You didn't do anything wrong."

Her chin bunches, tears lining her lashes as her face buckles with pain. "I did, Ty. I..." She sniffs, and my stomach clenches into a ball so tight, it hurts. "We got into a big fight, and I stormed off. I left him there. And he was drunk and not thinking straight. If I'd been by his side, I never would have let him take those pills."

*They got in a fight?*

I didn't know about that part.

I sigh, hating that she's holding herself responsible. Atlas could be an asshole when he'd had too much to drink.

*I should have been there.*

*This wouldn't have happened if I'd just fucking been there!*

Dipping my chin, I softly murmur, "That's not on you. I was the one who should have showed up. I told him I'd be there. And I wasn't. I let him down." My voice starts to shake, then break. "Dani, I let you down too. I'm sorry. I'm so fucking sorry."

"No, hey... don't say that. I was his girlfriend. I shouldn't have stormed off like that. *I* was the one who let him down." Her voice cracks, and I look up in time to watch her slash a tear off her cheek—an angry, bitter swipe.

Shit, she hates herself for what she did, and I can't... tolerate that. Because it's not right. I'll carry this burden. This guilt. But I don't want her to bear an ounce of it, because...

She didn't force those drugs down his throat.

*Just like you didn't.*

Grady's words swirl through my brain, and I suddenly get why he was trying to push so hard to make me see it.

Watching Dani wrestle with this remorse is killing me.

"Dani," I whisper, shifting on the bed so I can reach

her, touch her, rest my hand on her leg and beg her to understand.

"Don't." She shakes her head and holds up her hand. "I don't deserve it. You weren't there, Ty. You didn't see. You didn't hear what I said to him." She whimpers, resting her forehead on her knees. "It was the last thing I said to him."

I swallow, hating this, but wondering if she needs to confess before we'll have any chance of moving on. Licking my lips, I reluctantly ask, "What did you say?"

She sniffs, her body shuddering, her voice muffled because she won't look up. "I told him to go to hell." She shudders again, and this heartbreaking sob punches out of her. "He was drunk and acting like an idiot. I was begging him to stop, but he was in one of his wild moods. You know how he could get sometimes."

*Yeah, I did. That's why I was so good at playing bodyguard.*

When his father just left like that... something inside him broke. It sparked this wild recklessness within him. He'd always been somebody who liked to push things, dance along that line and sometimes fling himself right over it. But after his dad left, that line became a transparent blur, and I had to step into its place. I had to be his line.

Until I moved to Nolan.

Until I got caught up with football.

Until I let him down by not showing up when I said I would.

Cupping the back of my head, I dig my fingers into my scalp and mumble, "I should have been there. You should be blaming me."

"You didn't do anything wrong." She looks up, her glassy eyes so haunted.

I stare her right in the eye and tell her with certainty, "Neither did you."

"But..." She shakes her head, biting her bottom lip as her chest heaves.

With a soft sigh, I try to get a clearer picture of what went down that night. "He must have done something to make you say that to him and then feel like you had to leave."

Her expression crumples, her head shake turning into a nod. "He was really rude to me, in front of everybody. He told me I was a killjoy, then accused me of being a fucking princess, demanding too much of him, weighing him down." She sniffs. "Shit, Ty, I thought he was about to break up with me, in front of his band and all those stupid people who claimed to be his friend but didn't give a flying fuck about him." Her words are sharp with bitterness. I stay quiet, letting her get them all out. "So, I went on the defensive. I told him to stop acting like such a dick. Told him the drinking was making him crazy and I didn't want to be around him."

I tense, waiting for the next part, not wanting to hear it but also desperate to know.

I'm so riled at Atlas for talking to her that way. She was his fucking sun! And he treated her like that?

My voice is a low rumble when I have to coax Dani to keep going. "How'd he respond?"

"He told me to fuck off." Her eyebrows bunch as fresh tears stream down her face. "I knew he didn't mean it. Not really. He was drunk. Not thinking straight. But I was so hurt and humiliated that I told him to go to hell, and then I stormed out of there." She punches out a dry, broken laugh. "I made it two whole blocks before I calmed down enough to start thinking logically, and then I ran back to make sure he was okay." She sniffs, her voice turning into a soft squeak. "I couldn't find him. None of his friends would tell me anything. Just vague *not sures* and *maybe that ways*. I didn't know what to think. I bounced from wondering if he'd chased after me and we'd missed each other to him screwing a groupie in the back room." She shudders. "I was a mess. And when I finally found him in that bathroom..." Fresh tears spill from her eyes. "He wasn't okay, Ty. I should have stayed. I should have dragged him out of there. If I'd stayed, he—"

"He might have said more mean shit to you. He might have escalated to... who knows what," I growl, so pissed off that he could treat her that way. She was his champion. Stood by him through everything. For him to treat her like that is making me see red. If I'd been there, I would have hauled his ass outside and forced him home... into a fucking cold shower. That idiot!

My shoulders slump, my hold on Dani's knee tightening as I listen to her cry.

Shit. So much blame. We're both carrying so much blame.

But...

"We didn't make him take those drugs, Dani."

She sucks in a shuddering breath, then goes completely still.

She heard me, but she hasn't acknowledged it yet, so I try again.

"We didn't make him take those drugs."

Looking up at me, I'm forced to soak in her wrecked

expression, those haunted eyes filled with tears, the trembling of her lips.

"It's okay to be pissed off with him about that. It's okay to be angry at him for treating you that way."

"I don't want to hate him."

"You never could. But..." I swallow. "You can still love someone and be mad at them. You have a right to be pissed over the way he treated you."

She shakes her head. "I can't turn him into the bad guy."

"Yet you're letting yourself be the villain?"

Her lips part.

"Dani, you were just protecting yourself that night. And you're allowed to do that. He was being a dick, and if I'd been there, there's no way I would have let him treat you like that."

Guilt slams into me again.

*I should have been there. I should have been there!*

I don't know what my face is doing, but when I blink, I notice a softening in her expression. She curls her fingers around mine, squeezing tight and whispering, "If I had a right to protect myself, then you had a right to celebrate your win."

Her soft words curl around me. I drink them in like they mean everything. Because they do. She could have hated on me so hard for not being there, but she doesn't seem to blame me at all. She blames herself, and... I can't stand it.

"Dani..." I shuffle forward, cupping her cheek, scrambling for the right words to say. "I personally don't think there's anything to forgive, because you didn't do anything wrong. But just in case you need to hear it... I forgive you."

She bites her lips together, looking away from me as she obviously fights a fresh wave of tears. After a soft, wispy breath, she rasps, "I forgive you too. Even though I've never once blamed you for getting there late. I didn't. He wasn't paying you to be his bodyguard. You weren't dutybound to stay by his side. He knew that."

"Just like he knew you were only trying to keep him safe. Just like he knew how much you loved him."

"I love him." She nods. "I'll always love him, and I want to keep him perfect in my memory."

My chest hurts as I rasp, "But he wasn't perfect."

"He has to be."

"No, Dani. He doesn't. He was a fuckup sometimes. You know this. That's why we had to work so hard to keep an eye on him. And now we're carrying all this guilt and shame when he's the one who fucked up."

"Don't!" She whips a horrified look at me. "Don't say that about him."

"Dani." My voice is a low rumble. "He fucked up. And we all paid a price for that."

"But he wouldn't overdose!" She pushes my hand off her knee and scrambles off the bed. "He wasn't that reckless!"

"He could be sometimes."

Snatching a sweater off the floor, she throws it over her naked body. "If I hadn't stormed off all angry with him, I would have been there to stop him."

"And I could have been there to stop him too, but he could have stopped *himself*. We don't have to carry the entire blame for this. We didn't force those pills down his throat. He took them by *choice*."

I hate the thought that Atlas did that, and it's always bothered me. It's eaten at me that no one else around him thought to check him. Someone must have offered him those pills, and we've never found out who... so I threw all the blame on myself. I took it all. I have no idea why, but I've been carrying this ever since I heard Dani screaming for him to wake up.

Dani lets out another whimpering sob, slapping a hand over her mouth like she's trying to hold it all in. But then she bends forward, her body buckling.

I leap off the bed, racing around to catch her before she hits the floor.

Gathering her into my arms, I hold her against me while she shrieks, "Why, Atlas! Why did you to this to me!"

Her screams are harrowing, reminding me of the night she found him dead.

It makes me wonder if she's ever let herself say it before. If she's ever let herself be angry with him for leaving her way too soon.

Thumping onto the floor, I rest my back against the wall and cradle her in my lap, letting her cry and yell at Atlas until she's spent. Until all that's left are puffy breaths and a heaving chest.

# CHAPTER 35

## DANI

Tyrell didn't say anything to try and make me feel better.

He just held me.

And that was all I needed him to do.

I have no idea how long we sat on that floor, but eventually he stood up. It was awkward, but he kept me clutched to his torso, lifting me with him and carrying me to the bed.

I couldn't speak, couldn't do anything but act like a limp doll. He laid me down, then nestled in behind me, his strong arms wrapping around me and keeping me close all night.

I'm not sure how much I slept, but as my eyes creep open, I can sense it's the morning. The sun is glowing around the edges of my blinds.

I move my legs, curling them over Tyrell's knees. He's still behind me, his even breaths telling me he's asleep. His arms are around me, though. I'm secure in his embrace.

And for reasons I can't understand... I feel lighter somehow.

There's a calm within me... and this warm pulsing in my chest. It's not hard or erratic. It's a slow, even beat, telling me that I'm okay, whispering that this man holding on to me is good and kind and...

He'd never hurt me the way Atlas did.

As much as I hate to acknowledge it, Atlas *did* hurt me that night. He cut me deep, and we were never able to resolve things. It's eaten away at me, a festering disease masked by guilt and shame.

Maybe it's been wrong of me to try and keep his memory so pure. If his life hadn't ended that night, I probably would have had a massive bitch and moan to my sister, then sat Atlas down and told it to him straight.

But I never did either of those things.

And I never told anyone close to me what really went down that night. I'd told them I'd left because I was tired, not because Atlas told me to fuck off.

Now that I've opened that door again, the memory comes back to me crystal clear. Atlas's glazed, drunken expression. His slurred words. The pain he inflicted when he snarled at me.

I was so *angry* with him.

But deep down, I knew he still cared about me. And that's what hurts. He didn't mean to say those things, and we never got to resolve it.

*Nothing you do will ever change that. It's time to let go.*

Running my fingers lightly down Tyrell's arm, I press my lips against his skin and shift my focus. I close that door in my brain and instead take a mental note of every point my body is touching this man behind me. I relive the date night, the laughter, the fun, the sex. I soak in the knowledge that Tyrell isn't a reckless rock star. He's a good, kind, solid man. And even though he's so different to Atlas, he's gone and found a way into my heart. Not just in that sisterly affectionate way I used to feel for him, but in that giddy romantic way.

Just like his arms are wrapped around me now, he's claiming my heart, wrapping around it and holding it securely.

He won't break it the way Atlas did.

I don't know how I know it; I just do.

I'm safe with him.

My belly trembles as I dare to skip ahead to the future. Should I let myself go there? Do I risk imagining a life on the road with him? A life overseas, exploring different countries and cultures. Do I let myself dream of waking up beside him each morning? Or making him coffee and eating breakfast in bed?

A smile curls my lips, the idea sending a delighted thrill right through me.

I can do this.

I can be with Tyrell and love it.

*It's okay to love it. You're allowed to move on.*

Sucking in a quiet breath, I slowly move Tyrell's arm, desperate not to wake him. Wriggling away from his deliciously warm body, I shuffle to the edge of the bed, then sneak into the kitchen, closing the door behind me.

The space is empty, thank God, so I set about preparing coffee. I wonder if anyone heard me wailing last night. I wince, really hoping that even if they did, they won't say anything about it. I so don't want to go there.

I want to bask in this newfound peace I'm feeling.

I want to revel in these bubbles of joy that keep popping in my chest.

Shit. I'm happy.

Like... really happy.

A soft giggle comes out of me just as Tobin swans into the kitchen.

"Good morning, *ma chérie.*" He kisses my cheek.

"Good morning." I smile at him, pressing coffee grounds into the portafilter basket with the tamper.

"Oooo. You making us all a cup?" Tobin grabs out a mug.

"No," I tell him, locking the basket in place and letting it brew while I sort out steaming the milk. I know Tyrell likes a macchiato, and I've taught myself to make them and really like them myself now.

Tobin tips his head with a pout... until he sees me pulling two small coffee cups from the cupboard. His face lights with a grin. "He stayed the whole night! Yes, girl!" When he raises his hand for a high five, I can't resist the adorable look on his face, so I slap his palm and end up giggling again. "So... how was the date?"

"Fun." I nod. "*So* fun. We did a bunch of stuff and—"

"Ended up in bed together." His excited expression is too cute.

"Yes. That part was fun too." I wink, then hold my breath, just waiting for him to mention my midnight wailing, but he's still not saying anything.

Maybe they weren't home for it.

Or maybe he instinctively knows not to go there.

I watch his expression carefully for a minute and

don't miss his subtle wink before he stands tall and moves to the refrigerator.

"Jed, babe, are you doing coffee this morning?"

"You know it!" he calls from their bedroom, and I wince.

"What?" Tobin frowns at me.

"What's with all the yelling?" I whisper-bark. "My man is still asleep."

"*Your* man?" His face lights with excitement. "What the hell happened in that room last night? You guys definitely made gains. I can feel it! Did he say 'I love you'? Did *you* say it? Holy shit, girl. Tell me everything!" He grabs my shoulders and gives me a little shake.

"No, I just..." I start laughing. "Would you stop? He's my boyfriend, okay? You already know that."

His bottom lip pushes into an exaggerated pout. "So, no 'I love yous'?"

"No." My lips twitch with a smile. I'm not sure why. Maybe it's because those words aren't scaring me as much as I think they should.

I've only ever told one man that I love him.

But the idea of loving Tyrell is... well, it's kind of easy.

Oh man... maybe I really do!

I blink, surprised, yet not that surprised. He's a pretty easy guy to fall for.

And he was so good to me last night.

The way he held me.

I lean against the counter with a sigh that must be swoony, because Tobin nearly loses his shit with excitement. "You are so in love, girl!" he squeals, tugging me into a hug that's so tight, I can barely breathe.

"Okay, okay," I squeak, patting his back, grateful when Jed appears to rescue me.

"Did you hear!" Tobin lets me go and jumps into Jed's arm. His boyfriend gives him a solid kiss, laughing at his excitement.

"Yeah, baby. I heard."

"Love is in the air," Tobin sings, wrapping his arms around Jed's waist and resting his head against his shoulder. "I'm a happy man."

"So am I." Jed squeezes him, then goes in for another kiss.

I leave them to it as I finish up the coffees. I'm about to disappear with them into my bedroom when Tobin quickly stops me.

"Where are you going?"

I spin at his question, smirking at him. "There's an extremely hot, naked man in my bed. I'm going to give him some caffeine." I wiggle my eyebrows. "You know, fuel him up for another round." I'm trying to be playful, but in reality, I'm protecting Tyrell from this lot. If he comes out here, they are going to pounce all over him.

Nix's door swings open just as Jed announces, "I'm gonna make breakfast for everyone, fuel that man up properly."

Tobin points at me. "Then you can go and get your horny ass laid."

"Oooo, who's getting laid?" Nix skips into the room, swamped by an oversized shirt.

I glance across the room and spot her boyfriend trailing out after her. He's shirtless, his sweats hanging low on his hips, and it's hard not to be impressed by the sight. But he has nothing on my giant of a man, and I have to fight a grin.

"Dani is getting laid after we've fueled her and her boyfriend up."

"Oooo. Dani's got a boyfriend?" Nix winks at me, her tongue peeking out the side of her mouth.

I roll my eyes. "You guys, seriously. Can you not—"

My request is cut off when my bedroom door swings open and Black Jack walks out of my room. He's wearing nothing but the pants he had on last night, and hot damn. My insides trill as I drink him in. The way his lips are twitching tells me just what my expression must be doing right now.

He can see how much I want him, and the hungry look he gives me in return nearly has me bailing on breakfast.

"Don't you dare," Tobin quips before grinning at Tyrell. "Good morning, stud muffin."

"No, it's the Silent Knight," Nix corrects him.

Tyrell cringes while Jed laughs. "Shango, baby!"

I hand my poor boyfriend his coffee, groaning at how embarrassing my roommates are.

"Thank you," he whispers, bending down to kiss my cheek, then the side of my neck, before straightening up and greeting everybody.

I introduce him to Nix's boyfriend, Ricky, before he takes a seat at the counter and pulls me against his side.

I lean into him, loving his arm around my waist as I sip my coffee.

Loving how thrilling, yet totally normal, this all feels.

Me drinking morning coffee with Tyrell Jackson.

Yeah, I could definitely get used to this.

# CHAPTER 36
## TYRELL

Dani's roommates are funny. Well, Tobin and Jed are. I like the way they interact with each other. They're obviously so in love, and it's... it's sweet.

Nix and her boyfriend are giving off cute vibes as well.

At least Nix is. She's all chipper and bouncy, like she's snorted a line of love dust and is still riding the high. Ricky can't stop touching her, brushing his fingers down her arm, nuzzling her neck in between mouthfuls of bacon and egg.

I get it. I've got my hip pressed against Dani's. We're all piled around the breakfast bar. There weren't enough stools for everyone, so I offered to stand, but Dani wouldn't let me.

"You're way taller than me. You sit, I'll stand, and it'll be perfect." She winked at me, and I couldn't argue with her.

Tobin's standing as well, and I glance across the counter at him while he continues to tell his story about

New York City. Oh man, those two are buzzing about their big shift.

Dani's gone really quiet beside me, and I try to catch her eye as Tobin laughs. "And I'm gonna be catching the subway to school. Can you believe it? The subway! I've never done that before."

Nix snickers and starts teasing him. "You are going to be so obviously small town. That place is going to eat you alive."

"No, it won't," Jed defends him. "My man can handle anything. He and New York will be besties by the end of the summer."

"When do you head out?" I ask, using my toast to mop up the last of my egg yolk.

"We'll leave just after graduation," Tobin responds. "I want to stick around to support some of my friends who are graduating, and then we'll hit the road."

My eyebrows rise. "You're driving?"

"Yes." Tobin beams. "Jed doesn't want to leave his car behind. He loves his baby, so we'll road-trip!" He sings the last two words and Jed laughs, squeezing the back of his neck and pulling him in for a kiss.

I glance at Dani, who's nibbling a piece of bacon. She flashes me a smile, but it's sad. She's really going to miss these guys.

Shit, I don't want to leave her.

I don't want to drive down to Dallas after graduation, knowing she'll be here all by herself.

*She'll have Nix.*

"We're leaving a couple of days after graduation," Nix murmurs. "I'm gonna hang with Ricky's family for the summer, and then when we get back..." She looks to

Dani, her expression edged with concern or guilt or... something. "I'm going to be moving in with him."

"So, it's official." Dani nods like she knew this was coming, her smile tight and unbelievable. "That's cool. I'm happy for you guys." She tries really hard to make her smile brighter, and I tuck my hand around her hip, pulling her a little closer against me.

Nix bobs her head, obviously trying to play it cool but failing miserably. She is so excited about the idea of spending more time with her man. I check his expression, expecting the same thing, but...

Damn, he's wearing the same smile Dani is.

I glance at Jed and Tobin, who seem oblivious, then check Dani's expression, but she's back to staring at her plate.

When I look at Ricky and Nix again, she's gazing up at him with a dreamy smile, and he's planting a kiss on her forehead, cupping the back of her hair like she's precious. Maybe I just imagined it.

Turning my focus back to Dani, I try to catch her eye, but she's refusing to look at me, lost in her own little bubble of sadness. I'm guessing when she moved in here at the beginning of the year, no one was planning to go anywhere, and now her world is being turned upside-down. All of her people are leaving and...

The thought is killing me.

"Don't worry, Dani Girl. We'll find excuses to see each other again." Jed's voice is soft, sweet with understanding. "You can come visit us in New York."

"Yes!" Tobin claps his hands. "We'll definitely find reasons to hang out together again. Maybe we can pop back for a weekend or something. We're going to make this work." Abandoning what's left of his breakfast, he rushes around the counter and pulls Dani into a hug. "We love you, and we're going to miss you so much."

Dani lets out a soft laugh of appreciation.

Tobin pulls back, holding her shoulders. "And no matter what, we'll always be here for you. We're only ever a video chat away, okay?"

Dani nods. "I know, and I'm really excited for you guys. You're all going to have the best summer."

"And what are you going to do?" Nix gives her a pointed look. "If you tell me you're going to be moping around Nolan, I will have to slap some sense into you."

"I have to." She laughs. "I can't afford to just flit off somewhere. I'll keep working at Offside. There'll be summer school students to hydrate and look after. It'll be fine."

"But where are you going to live?" Jed asks, obviously concerned.

"I'm not sure yet, but I have two weeks to find a place." She glances around at everyone, and I have to fight the urge to blurt, "Come to Texas with me!"

I doubt she wants me asking her that in front of everyone, so I swallow the words down and let her finish.

"The lease doesn't run out on this place for another two weeks, right? Worst-case scenario, I'll move into a motel until I find something."

Jed frowns and shakes his head.

"It'll be fine," she assures him. "I can do this. It'll be good for me." Her voice is so strained it's hard to believe her.

Everyone's concerned frowns are so skeptical, and I don't know what to say right now.

She's so obviously feeling the awkward tension, and when she lets out this high-pitched kind of laugh, shaking her head, my insides buckle.

"Would you all stop looking at me like that?" She huffs, then points at Jed and Tobin. "You two, go start packing. You've only got two weeks. And you..." She points to Nix. "You go do the same." Then her finger lands on me. "And you, I want you naked in my bed, ASAP."

Nix cracks up laughing as Dani snatches my hand, dragging me off the stool and pulling me toward her bedroom door.

"Have fun, you two!" Tobin calls after us, and all I can do is follow this woman the way she needs me to.

She can't distract herself from this problem with sex, but I get the feeling she's not ready to talk about it, so I go with her, kicking the door shut with my foot and catching her in my arms when she launches herself at me.

Her kisses are hungry, intense, and part of me wants to tell her to slow down, take a breath. But I don't want her thinking I'm not into this.

When her legs wrap around me, I palm her ass, giving both cheeks a squeeze as I walk back toward the bed. Dropping her down on the mattress, I enjoy her giggle, then catch my breath when she scrambles to the edge, keeping her gaze firmly on mine as she unbuttons my pants and lowers the fly.

I cup her head, my fingers squishing her spiral curls as she lowers my pants, setting my rock-hard dick free. It twitches in anticipation, and I suck in a sharp breath when she wraps her fingers around it and pumps a couple of times before licking a line from the base to the tip. When she draws it into her mouth, black dots dance in front of my eyes.

Holy shit.

I haven't had a blow job in a while, and I forgot how epically good they are.

Squeezing the base, she sucks and licks, teasing my body into a frenzy. Lightly cupping the back of her head, I groan, my knees threatening to buckle. I squeeze my ass cheeks and choke out, "I'm gonna blow."

Her lips pop off my dick. "Not yet," she whispers. "I want you inside me again."

Scrambling to take her sweater off, she exposes her glorious body to me, and I gaze down at her. She's all beautiful curves and smooth skin. When she flops back on the mattress, rolling over to reach into her nightstand, I rest my hand on her hip, curving it around her perfect ass and squeezing again.

She giggles. "Tobin bought me this box of condoms as a sort of joke when I went on my first date. He told me I had to save them for Mr. Right, though, and thank God I did." She peeks a look over her shoulder, her smile playful and sweet.

And all I can think is that she just called me Mr. Right.

Fuck, those words will ring in my head all damn day.

I go to move, kneeling on the edge of the bed.

"No, wait." She pushes me back up. "I want standing."

Wiggling her eyebrows, she takes full control of this situation, wrapping my dick before lying back down and spreading her legs for me.

Her arms splay wide on the bed, her feet rising in the

air, and I can see her beautiful pussy, ready and waiting for me.

Licking my fingers, I reach down for her, checking to see how wet she is. I don't want to hurt her.

"You sure?" I check again.

"Yes," she breathes, her body twitching when I brush her clit. "Get inside me, Ty. Please."

I do as she commands, bending my knees so I can line us up. She groans when my head parts her folds, and then her back arches when I slowly push my way inside her.

Fuck, she's fire.

Her sweet pussy wrapping my cock is the best feeling in the word. I've worried that I'm too big for her. She's so tight, and I'm definitely stretching her every time I glide into this warm oasis, but she doesn't seem to mind.

Leaning forward, I suck her tits, circling her dark nipples and loving the sounds I'm getting out of her. Those soft little pants and mewling whimpers. Damn, it's hot.

Her hips rise, grinding against me, demanding friction, so I pull back before sinking into her again. Her moan is divine, so I do it again, keeping things slow and smooth.

When her hips start to thrust back, silently demanding more, I rest my knee on the edge of the bed and move deeper inside her.

She whimpers, lifting her knees to her tits and fisting the bedsheets on either side of her.

She's feeling good, and I take that as a sign to go deeper still.

Pushing into her, I thrust until my dick can't go any farther, then pull back and thrust again.

"Yes," she moans. "Yes!"

Smoothing my hands down her legs, I capture her thighs, pushing her knees into her chest, and plunge into her again, my hips starting to work like a piston as I deliver the way she wants me to.

My pace picks up as her moans of pleasure increase in volume. For a second, I wonder if I should tell her to be a little quieter. All of her roommates are home. But she's having too much fun, and who gives a fuck, right? They all know what we're doing in here. They might as well know how much she's enjoying it.

Gliding into her again, I feel those flames build and burn, my limbs starting to sizzle as this familiar heat rises within me.

Fuck. Yes! It feels so good.

"Mmmm." Dani groans again, her teeth sinking into her bottom lip. So sexy. So fucking sexy.

"That's my girl," I pant, changing my thrusts to short, sharp hits that jiggle her tits.

"Oh!" She tips her head back, fisting the sheets even tighter before she lets out another wail and covers her face. "Oh shit, oh shit! Yes! Yes! Yeeeesss." The last word comes out as a low groan, her body tensing and trembling before a warm sensation hits my tip and her pussy clutches me.

Fuck.

I start to pump, hard and fast. Long, deep thrusts. I can't help myself. I'm so fucking turned on right now, I think I'm gonna explode.

Her mewling whimpers return, falling into time with my thrusts until I start groaning myself.

Squeezing her thighs, I feel that fire flood my veins and let out a strangled moan as the inevitable explosion hits me. Thrusting deep, my ass cheeks squeeze tight as I bury myself inside her, not sure how I'm ever gonna leave. I pull back and thrust again. Then again... and one more time as she drains me dry, her perfect pussy destroying me.

She lets out a sigh, tipping her head back as a soft, awe-filled laugh pops out of her. She pulls her legs down so she can wrap them around me, and I lean over her, finding her mouth and kissing her deep. I glide my tongue against hers, loving the way her arms move around my neck. She clings to me, locking her ankles, and I scoop her against my body and crawl us up the bed until I can lie on top of her.

Her head sinks into the pillow, and I rest my weight on my elbows, still catching my breath as I trace the edge of her pretty face.

"You're so beautiful," I murmur, kissing her again before she can respond.

She tells me with her tongue that she's grateful... that she's into me and...

And I have to ask.

It might be an idiotic thing to say, but I will regret it forever if I don't at least try.

With my heart hammering in my chest, I lean back and gaze down at her, my throat swelling with nerves as I softly whisper, "Move to Dallas with me?"

# CHAPTER 37
## DANI

What did he just say?

It might be my post-sex brain that's cloudy, but I'm sure he just said, "Move to Dallas with me."

He said it like a question, but it's really a statement, right?

Move to Dallas with me.

Holy shit.

He's serious.

I study his expression. His brown eyes are rich with vulnerability, his lips dipping with this sweet concern, like he's cautiously anticipating my reaction.

Oh shit. What do I say?

It's pretty fast, right?

*Really? He's lying naked on top of you right now.*

But there's a big difference between having sex with someone and moving to another state with them!

Do I want that?

Do I want to shift my life again?

What's in Dallas for me?

*Tyrell! Tyrell Jackson will be in Dallas.*

I can't move my entire life for one human being.

*You moved for Tobin when he invited you and you didn't know anyone in Nolan. That's worked out great.*

Yeah, but this is different.

Dallas.

I don't even know if I'll like Dallas.

"Uh…" Tyrell lets out a disappointed sigh. "Sorry, it's too fast, right? Too soon." He rolls off me, staring up at the ceiling, and I curl into his side, resting my hand on his chest and trying to figure out what to say.

I don't want to reject him.

But…

"Why are you asking me?"

"Huh?" He turns his head on the pillow, obviously surprised by the question.

I swallow and splutter, "I mean… why? Is it because you don't think I can handle Nolan on my own? You want to protect me?"

"No." He shuffles around on the bed so we're lying face-to-face on our sides. Taking my hand in his, he plays with my fingers, kissing the tip of my index before turning my heart to putty. "I'm asking because the thought of leaving you is killing me. Maybe it's selfish, I don't know." He sighs. "But I've been wanting to find a woman for a long time, and I can never seem to get past a second or third date."

"We've only been on one official one." I frown.

He snickers, his smile so beautiful it knocks the breath of me.

"We've been hanging out for weeks, and I've been falling. I just didn't know I was. And now I'm here. With you.

Like this." He lifts my fingers to his lips again, gently kissing them. "And I don't want to be anywhere else but with you. And I'd offer to stay, but my family really needs me right now, and so my next best solution is to take you with me." His eyes fill with that sweet vulnerability again. "If you want to."

I open my mouth, part of me desperate to scream *Yes!*

But another part of me is just not sure.

Where would we live?

Would we move in with his family?

I don't know if I want that.

*But you want him. You can't deny that.*

I do.

Yet the idea of moving everything for a guy is a lot.

I made my entire world about Atlas, and when he died, I was completely lost. I'm still trying to figure out what I want to be. What makes me happy.

I don't know if I want to rearrange my life for someone else. Even though I'm confident Tyrell would never OD on any kind of substance, what if something else happened to him?

And what if we moved in together and it didn't work out?

This all feels too much.

My heart starts to race as my mouth continues to goldfish.

"It's okay," he whispers, leaning in to kiss my forehead before rolling onto his back and tucking me against his side. I rest my head on his shoulder, splaying my hand over his hard pec and feeling kind of bad.

I think I've hurt his feelings.

"You don't have to decide anything right now, and if

you don't want to come, it's okay. I'll, uh, just... I'll make sure I come up here on the regular, and we can do long-distance, right? Unless..." His words trail off, and I have to move onto my elbow so I can see his face.

Oh shit, he looks gutted. "Unless what?"

"Unless this was just a... short-term thing for you." He swallows, and my heart starts to crack.

"I didn't know what this was going to be. I've been trying really hard not to plan my life out too far, you know?" I draw a circle on his chest with the tip of my index finger. "I used to have such massive dreams, and I've learned the hard way that life often has other plans. You just have to live one day at a time."

He nods, his lips pursing as he obviously wrestles with disappointment.

Shit.

"I... I really like being with you." I haphazardly stick a Band-Aid over this conversation, trying to soothe the obvious wound I'm creating. "And I'll think about Dallas, okay? I really will."

He turns to me, and I'm wondering if he's about to say, *"Don't worry about it."*

Will he rescind that offer? Have I just made an idiot move?

But instead, his lips curl into a smile. "Only say yes if you want to, okay?"

"Okay." I nod, appreciating the freedom he's giving me, but still hating the underlying disappointment of my lackluster response.

"Hey." Pressing a kiss to his cheek, I rest my nose against the side of his face and promise him. "I will seriously think about it. I really enjoy being with you. And...

I think I'm falling too, which is a little terrifying, you know?"

He turns to me, his eyes lighting with soft hope as his lips curl up at the edges. "I know."

Cupping his face, I brush my thumb over his lips before kissing him and hoping I'll have an obvious "feel good" answer sooner rather than later. These past few days... weeks... with Tyrell have been uplifting for my soul, and I don't want to lose what I've got going with him.

But uprooting my life to move to Texas?

Taking our relationship to this next level so fast?

I'm just not sure.

# CHAPTER 38
## TYRELL

She's not sure.

Fuck. I shouldn't have asked.

I knew I shouldn't have, but the words just came out of me.

Because I don't want to lose her.

Which is why I didn't let that burning disappointment take me from her bed last weekend. I stayed. Spent the whole day there. Even helped her pack a few boxes. She doesn't actually have that much stuff, so she can just put her clothes in a suitcase and leave.

I hate the idea of her moving into a motel, so I offered to help her look for some places in Nolan.

She seemed surprised by my offer, but I just mumbled, "You want all your options open, right?"

I think she was grateful that I'm not making her feel bad over not jumping on my offer.

Shit, she didn't jump.

She hesitated. And fuck, that stings.

I ended up leaving on Sunday evening, returning to Football Frat with my tail between my legs.

And the rest of this week, I've had my head down as I survive finals week. Graduation is only a few days away, and I've only caught moments with Dani. We've had two more dates, and she spent the night at Football Frat on Friday, which was awesome. We were all celebrating the end of exams. It was a low-key event, just the original crew and our women. Everyone was nice to Dani, and I think she could feel the warmth of the place.

She seemed to really connect with Satch, which was cool. They sat next to each other for ages, talking about who knows what, but I loved seeing it. Satch is shy and sweet, and it can take some effort to draw her out, but Dani seemed to do it within minutes.

Standing tall, I gaze around Wily's room. It's looking sparse and empty as he finishes packing up the last of his shit.

"Damn, I'm gonna miss this place," I mutter.

Wily glances at me, running a hand through his blond hair. "Yeah, me too, man." He gives me a sad, resigned smile. "It's been an epic few years here."

"Yeah." I bite my lips together, trying to squash down my sadness. The thought of moving to Dallas just isn't sitting right.

Not without Dani.

Damn, how do I convince her to come with me?

It's taken maximum effort not to keep raising the issue, asking if she's made a decision yet.

She still hasn't found an apartment, as far as I'm aware, and I don't know what she's gonna do. It's driving me crazy.

"But we'll still see each other again. You're coming to visit us in Glendale, right?"

"Us?" My head pops up.

"Oh shit, didn't I tell you?" His smile gets all big and cheesy. "Satch got into Arizona State. She's coming with me."

My lips part, a smile rising as I take in his excitement. I refuse to be jealous, even though a small part of me is. His woman's following him. Supporting him.

Because she's totally in love with him.

And that's what's eating at me. I don't know how Dani feels. She makes love to me. She kisses me. Her eyes sometimes tell me she's fallen as deep as I have. But she's never actually said it. And she hasn't told me she's coming to Dallas. So what the hell am I supposed to think?

Does she love me? Or not?

"Stoked for you, man." I raise my chin at him.

"Thanks, bro." He lets out this euphoric kind of giggle. "Couldn't believe it when she told me she was moving her entire life for me. I was never gonna demand that of her, you know? She's tight with her family, and I didn't think she'd want to move so far away from them, but they're encouraging her to go." He opens another empty box and starts throwing books and magazines into it. "I've told her I'll pay for her to fly back on the regular so she can do weekends with them, and I've offered to have her parents come to us as well." His smile just keeps getting bigger. "I'm relieved, to be honest. I knew Grady and Carson were happy to keep an eye on her, but the thought of her staying in this school with those bitches still roaming campus just didn't sit right with me."

"Yeah, I get it, man." And I do. The thought of leaving Dani here without Jed or Tobin or Nix to have her back? It's eating me alive.

I know she's an independent woman who can take care of herself.

But I want to take care of her too... if only she'd let me.

My phone starts to ring and I pull it out of my back pocket, my insides tensing when I see Mama's name on my screen.

"I better take this, man." I head for Wily's door.

"Yep, cool." He waves at me. "Thanks for your help."

"No problem." I swipe my thumb across the screen and head for my room. "Hey, Mama."

"Hey. How's my boy doin'?"

"Yeah, good. Just helping Wily pack up his room."

"Oof. That's a job right there."

"Don't I know it. The guy has so much junk and doesn't want to get rid of any of it."

She laughs. "And how's your packing going?"

"Yeah, I'm getting there." I walk into my room, staring at the pile of neatly stacked boxes by my closet. My walls are clear, all the posters taken down, and I can't get over this impending sadness weighing on me.

I thought I'd be more ready than this.

"We're so looking forward to having you with us again." I can hear the smile in Mama's voice, and I don't want to squash it, so I force out all the right answers.

"Yeah, it's gonna be great."

"And I agree that having a few weeks off before looking for a job is a great idea. You're never gonna get that opportunity again. But when you're ready, Dad's already got that contact lined up for you. I can't see why he wouldn't want to take you on, but if he's gone and lost his damn mind, there'll probably be some jobs available at the factory. Also, one of my girls at work has got a friend in the landscaping business, and then we have that other connection with the building company I told you about a while back."

"Yeah." I nod, hating the way they're mapping out my life for me.

"You can earn some pennies while you look for the job you really want."

*I don't want some boring nine-to-five. I want to travel. See the world. But how do I tell you that?*

With a thick swallow, I keep bobbing my head and making appropriate murmurs of agreement until she changes topic.

"Now, graduation. We'll be arriving on Friday morning. And the ceremony is at three, right?"

"Yep. Do you need me to come pick you guys up?"

"No, you'll be busy getting yourself ready, so we've rented a car. We should be there by one, at the latest. We were going to come on the Thursday originally, but your dad still isn't great, and I don't want to put more pressure on him. I don't think he should be coming at all, but he's insisting that he wants to see his boy graduate."

"Tell him I appreciate that, but if he can't make it, I understand."

"Of course he's gonna be there. If I can't stop him, you sure as hell can't."

I snicker. That's true. Mama's a powerful force in our house, which means Dad must be really digging his heels in.

"He's proud of you."

I nod, appreciation making my throat swell.

Shit. They need me right now. I can't be traveling the world or staying in Nolan. I have to go back to Dallas, no matter where my heart is.

"I'll make sure he's well taken care of while he's here."

"I know you will." Mama's voice gets all soft. "You're a good boy, Tyrell. I'm proud of you too."

"Thanks, Mama."

"And we're really looking forward to seeing Dani again. It's been such a long time."

"Yeah." I nod, hoping it'll go well. I really want my parents to like my girl. When I mentioned that I was dating her, they were initially surprised.

"Atlas's girl?" Dad couldn't hide his shock, but Mama nudged him with her elbow and started asking questions. By the end of the call, they were both happy for me... and Dad ended up grinning.

"She's Tyrell's girl now."

*Oh man, I hope she is. I hope she stays that way forever.*

*Please, baby. Move to Dallas with me!*

"Okay, well, we'll be seeing you in a few days, then." Her voice gets bright with excitement.

"Cool. Love you."

"Love you too, boy. Love you too."

I hang up, glancing at the time on my phone screen before sinking onto my bed with a sigh.

It's all coming to an end.

This college journey... and maybe my time with Dani.

"Shit," I mumble, cupping the back of my head. "Please don't let that end. Please."

The idea of leaving her is only making my feelings

that much clearer. I've fallen in love with this woman. I never meant to, but it's gone and happened, and I can't stop it.

I don't *want* to stop it.

So even if she doesn't want to move to Dallas with me, I need to find ways of making sure I can see her again. We can do long-distance while she figures out what she wants to do. I'm open to that.

I'll miss her like crazy. But I'll do whatever it takes not to lose her for good.

# CHAPTER 39
## DANI

Tyrell picked me up from work last night. I still haven't given him a decision, and it's definitely lurking there between us, but he's not demanding anything from me, and so I've stayed quiet. Mulling it over as my apartment, that I love so much, gets packed up.

He drove me back there, and when I confessed that my feet were aching after a long shift, he took me into my room and massaged them for me. His fingers are strong, his smooth strokes making my eyes roll to the back of my head. Making it impossible not to love him.

He is an amazing man.

Why haven't I said yes yet?

I close my eyes, remembering the way he made love to me, the foot rub turning into sensual kisses to my ankles. He worked his way up my body, peeling off my clothes and taking great care to make sure every inch of me was attended to. I came with his tongue in my mouth, his fingers rubbing my clit into a frenzy. Then I came again when he was inside me, my nails digging into his back as he kissed my chin, then paused to drink me in.

I smiled up at him, feeling him all the way inside me, around me, covering me.

Clutching his shoulders, I felt my heart swell with affection, and I nearly said, *nearly whispered*, "I love you." But then he started moving again, gently thrusting in and out of me with slow, quiet strokes.

We stared at each other until the heat between us got too intense and I had to tip my head back, had to revel in the feel of his lips sucking my neck, my shoulder. His tongue glided back up to my mouth, his lips covering mine as he jerked and shuddered inside me, his butt cheeks clenching as he thrust deep and hard.

I clung to him, kissing him as if it was our last.

But it won't be.

It can't be.

He's not flying back to Dallas until after the weekend.

I still have time to decide. I still have time.

"There he... there he is!" Cyrus points, getting all excited as he watches his brother walk up onto the stage.

Tyrell's family were nice enough to invite me to sit next to them for the graduation ceremony. They scored an extra ticket—I'm not even sure how—so I'm here, sitting at the back of the large auditorium and gazing down at a sea of blue gowns as the university celebrates their graduates.

I've spent the majority of the ceremony tuning out while different speeches were made, but now I blink, forcing my head back into the moment as I watch Tyrell, all handsome in his gown and cap, accepting his degree.

"Yes! My boy!" His mama rises to her feet, cheering loudly while his sister snaps photos on her phone. His father struggles to his feet as well, whooping and cheering.

"Yay, Tyrell!" Cyrus laughs, giggling in his sweet way and clapping loudly. "Yay! That's my brother. That's my brother!" he yells to everyone around us.

The crowd laughs, joining in the celebration and glancing at Cyrus.

"Good boy." Mrs. Jackson takes his hand and makes him sit back down again. "That was good, cheering for Tyrell, baby."

"He's my brother." Cyrus keeps grinning, turning his smile on me and whispering, "Tyrell graduated."

"I know. He did so good."

"Yeah." Cyrus nods, giving me an adorable grin before turning back to see who's going next.

The rest of the ceremony runs smoothly, pockets of families rising to cheer as their son, daughter, sibling, or grandchild goes up to get their diplomas.

I glance over my shoulder, taking in the row associated with Football Frat. They're loud and playful, cheering on their housemates, but it's impossible to miss the frown on Carson's face and the sad wrinkle between Grady's eyebrows. They're going to miss their friends.

I turn back to face the front, making myself think ahead for once, imagining what it's going to be like here without Jed and Tobin. Nix will still be around, but we won't be living together anymore.

And Tyrell will be gone.

Now that I see how long his father's recovery is taking

and how much his mother is carrying, I get why he feels he needs to go home.

Nolan won't be the same without him.

Yes, I didn't know he was here for the first few months, so I was living quite happily without him.

Well, not happily, but I was getting by just fine.

But since we've started spending time together, he's become a really important aspect of this place, and when he leaves, I'm going to feel it.

I'm gonna feel it big.

*So why don't you just go with him?*

My heart picks up as I try to imagine what that might look like. Driving down to Dallas with him, moving in with his family. His sweet, kind family who gave me hugs the second they saw me. They remember me. They asked me how I was doing, and they seem thrilled that I'm dating Tyrell.

He didn't call me his girlfriend, and his mama told him off for not saying it.

"You're dating the girl, ain't you? Call her yours, boy."

His smile fled and he murmured, "We're just seeing how things go. We don't need the pressure of labels."

And I wanted to correct him, to wipe that look off his face.

*You can't move for him. You have to move for you!*

Atlas skips through my mind, surprising me with his sudden presence. He's been fading lately. I don't think about him every day the way I used to. I don't obsess about him, and it's been a nice relief.

But here he is, floating through my brain. Is he trying to tell me something?

My heart buckles the way it always does, this heavy

pulse of yearning bursting through me, but it fades with surprising speed.

Because I'm not lost without him anymore.

I'm making something of my life. Sure, I haven't figured out a career path yet, but I love tending bar. I love living with friends. I love... being with Tyrell. I haven't been this content and happy in a really long time.

I'm moving on, and every decision isn't soaked in my dead boyfriend's memory or my mourning.

Like a soft whisper traveling through me, I feel it. This knowledge. This hope.

I can do this.

I can do this because I want to.

A loud cheer goes up. I blink, suddenly coming to as a wave of blue graduation caps fire into the air. My hands automatically start clapping, and I smile as Cyrus cheers and jumps beside me.

"Okay, let's go find your brother and get some photos." Mrs. Jackson takes Cyrus's hand and orders Lacey to get off her damn phone before she takes it off her, then pauses to make sure her husband is okay shuffling down the row of seats.

I stand and wander after Tyrell's family. With the human traffic jam, it's a slow trek back outside, but we eventually make it. I'm grateful for the cloudless blue sky as I watch them hug and celebrate with him. He lifts Lacey off her feet and spins her around, then wraps Cyrus in a strong hug. His brother is so excited, and Tyrell grins at him.

He's such a good man.

I love the way he interacts with his family, carefully hugging his father and then kissing his mama's cheek.

He searches me out then, and I step forward, wrapping my arms around him and knowing.

I can do this.

I can do this because I want to.

Before he can let me go, I squeeze him a little tighter and whisper in his ear, "I'm coming to Texas with you."

# CHAPTER 40
## TYRELL

Holy shit.

I tip my head back so I can look at her face, make sure I heard her right.

She smiles at me, nodding, then laughing when I let out a whoop and spin her around.

"You serious?"

"Yes." She laughs. "Yes. Let's spend the summer together and see how things go."

I'll take it. Summer together sounds perfect.

"Thank you," I whisper, gazing at her beautiful smile and having to kiss it.

"Oooo! Kissing!" Cyrus starts laughing. "Mama, they're kissing."

"Yes, I can see that, baby." Her bemused tone has me grinning against Dani's lips, and she giggles into my mouth.

I reluctantly put her down, then stand for a billion photos.

It takes forever by the time my parents photograph

me with them, then my siblings, then all my friends, then Dani, then everyone.

I'm so done by the time they finally let us go.

"So, you've got that party tonight?" Mama asks as we amble to the parking lot.

"Yes, ma'am."

"Okay, well, you enjoy that now. We'll see you in the morning. We have time for breakfast together before we drive back to the airport." She pulls me down so she can kiss my cheek, and I give her a sideways hug, not wanting to release Dani's hand.

"You two have fun." Dad waves at me, then carefully steps off the curb and walks to the car, holding Cyrus's hand. My brother is waving and smiling at people, being his friendly self, while Lacey is glued to her phone.

I watch my family go, then turn to smile down at Dani. "We've got a couple of hours before the party. What do you want to do?"

She thinks for a second, and then her lips rise into a playful smirk. I start to laugh, lifting her off her feet and running for my car. She giggles against my shoulder, her body jostling as we head back to her place and rush into her room.

It's all frantic kisses and passionate licks as we tug off each other's clothes and "celebrate" my graduation. I lift her naked body off the floor, her legs coming around me as she clings to my shoulders.

I slip inside her, tucking my hands under her butt and bouncing us together.

She feels so fucking good, her tits bumping up and down against my chest as I set a rapid pace that feels so amazing.

Like so much better than anything I've—

"Oh fuck, I forgot to wrap." I walk us toward her bed.

She whimpers, sinking onto me with a groan. "It doesn't matter, just pull out."

"It does matter," I argue, my voice strained as I kneel on the bed and reluctantly pull out of her.

She whimpers again, pouting at me before rolling over and reaching into her nightstand drawer.

"Eeep. There's only one left."

I curve my hand over her perfect ass with a smile. "Then we better make it count."

She looks over her shoulder, her gaze hot and hooded as she tears the condom wrapper open with her teeth.

Holy fuck.

My insides tremble when she spins around, rolling the condom over my dick with her eyes trained on my face. The intensity between us is so hot, the air is practically sparking with electricity.

She's coming with me to Dallas.

I cup her cheek, brushing my thumb across her skin and silently thanking her.

She leans back with a smile, sinking her teeth into her bottom lip before laughing and flipping onto her stomach.

"Really?" I double-check, smiling when she glances over her shoulder with a sexy wink, then shoves her ass in the air toward me.

I kneel on the edge of her bed, gently pulling her cheeks apart and leaning down to lick her opening.

She moans, thrusting her butt back toward my face, so I do it again, licking and teasing until she's a trembling mess, wailing into her pillow, her chest heaving.

"Good girl," I purr. "I love it when you come." Gliding my hands up her inner thighs, I then line myself up.

Taking my time, I gently guide myself into her, loving every groan and squeak that pops out of her sexy little mouth.

Fuck, it feels amazing being inside her like this.

Thrusting my hips, I bury myself, her warm, wet center pulling me in.

"You feel good, baby." My voice is a rough, husky mess. "You feel so fucking good." And before I can stop myself, the words pop out. "I love you."

She goes still, whipping her head back to look at me.

And I freeze inside her.

This is so not the moment to confess my love for the first time. Shit! What the hell was I thinking?

Her eyes round, her lips parting, and I don't know what to do.

Does she want me out?

Or do I keep going?

"I..." I lick my lips, holding her hips.

"Do you mean it?" she whispers.

"Of course I do." I swallow, then wince. "I'm sorry I'm being so fucking unromantic about this. It just..." I lick my lips *again* and look her right in the eye. "I mean it."

Her lips curl at the edges, her eyes taking on a teasing glint. "So, what's so unromantic, then? You're taking me from behind and confessing your love."

I cringe, groaning and about to pull out of her.

"Don't you dare," she warns me.

I still, resting my hands back on her hips and wondering what I'm supposed to do here.

"You take me, boy. And you make us come. And the

whole time you're doing it, I'll be hearing those three words in my head." She grins, thrusting her butt back and taking all of me.

I ease back a little, not wanting to hurt her, then slowly gyrate my hips.

"Yes," she moans, fisting the duvet cover and rocking with me when I move again.

Picking up my pace, I squeeze her hips and listen out for her different moans. I'm starting to understand them, knowing when she wants me to go fast, slow, hard, soft. I do my best to deliver, and when I'm close to coming, I know that I have to make this count, so I quickly pull out of her and spin her over.

She lands on her back, and I press a kiss to her stomach, working my way up her body and suckling each nipple before lying over her and pressing my nose into the side of her cheek.

"I love you," I whisper, sucking her earlobe into my mouth.

She hasn't said it back, but the way she squeezes my shoulders, then presses a kiss against my skin makes me wonder if she's feeling it but just can't find the courage to say it.

That's okay. I'm not pressuring her into anything.

Slipping back inside her, I bring her home with short, sweet strokes that work her G-spot. As soon as she's shuddering and jerking beneath me, I push myself deep inside her, thrusting smooth and long until her clenching pussy undoes me.

"Ahhhh," I groan into her ear. "I love you. Fuck, I love you."

Waves of pleasure roll through me, and I stay buried

inside her while I ride them out, my heart thundering, my soft pants hitting the side of her face.

She hooks her legs around me, digging her heels into my ass and holding me against her like she can't let go.

Wriggling my fingers under her back, I suction her against me, rolling us onto our sides so we can keep puffing and panting against each other's cheeks and just revel in our awesome session.

"We're good together," I murmur, kissing her shoulder. "We're fucking awesome at the sex thing."

She giggles, her tits jiggling. "Damn right we are."

Sucking my neck, she leaves a sweet little hickey just above my collarbone, and I hold her tight, loving her with every ounce of me.

# CHAPTER 41
## DANI

He loves me.

Tyrell Jackson loves me.

And my heart hasn't stopped singing since he whispered the words. At first, it was a shock. And he so obviously didn't mean to say it then, but the second and third time... I felt those words all the way to my core.

When he's inside me like that, filling me body, mind, and soul, it's hard to think straight.

He's really good at the sex thing, and the fact that I get to enjoy his body the way I do is a privilege.

And now he loves me as well.

Which is like... wow.

*So why haven't you said it back?*

I'm not sure. Maybe because the *I love you too* thing can sound kind of weak sometimes, like I'm only saying it because he did. Or maybe it's because I've only ever said those words to one man before, and saying them to Tyrell will shift out relationship in a really big way.

*You're moving to Dallas with him!* my brain argues.

*Only for the summer!*

I snap my eyes shut, begging the two sides of my brain to be quiet.

He loves me. Why can't I just focus on that... and how good it felt when he flipped me over, looked me right in the eye, and said those words like he meant them.

*Because he* does *mean them!*

I go still, staring at my reflection in the bedroom mirror as I smooth down my dress. Tobin picked it out for me, spewing clothes all over my bed as he tried to find the perfect thing to wear for this graduation party I'm going to with Tyrell and all his friends. It's at some massive house off campus, and I think I want to go, but I'm not really sure.

Atlas and I used to go to parties all the time, but I was put off them after his OD nightmare.

This will be my first party like that since then, and I will be glued to Tyrell's side. Of this, I am sure.

*He loves me.*

The words swirl through me again, and I smile at myself.

He's a safe bet.

No, more than that... he's a grand prize.

He's sweet and sexy, and kind and good.

"He's so good," I whisper. And I'm lucky to have his love.

Which is why, after the party tonight, I'm going to invite him back here, and as we drift off to sleep in each other's arms, I'm going to tell him.

Because I do love Tyrell Jackson.

I probably always have. First in a sisterly, "you're my boyfriend's bestie" kind of way... but it's shifted now.

I love that man or I wouldn't be going to Dallas, would I?

Pausing, I stare at myself and test it out. "I love you, Tyrell."

My eyes instantly glass, the ghost of Atlas wilting beside me.

"I'm sorry," I whisper. "I'm sorry it ended up this way, but you left me." I sniff. "I asked you to walk away, and you wouldn't. You told me to fuck off."

Slashing a tear off my cheek, I keep gazing at my reflection.

"Tyrell would never do that to me. And I'm sorry that you're not here anymore, but he is. And he loves me." I swallow, this feeling blooming in my chest when I whisper. "And I love him."

And holy shit, I mean it.

I do.

I love him.

A smile crests my lips, this buzz illuminating the room around me as I finally let go and take a giant leap into my future.

"I love him." My smile grows a little wider, excitement racing through me when I hear a knock at the door.

Tyrell only left an hour ago. He needed to go home and change for the party, and I wanted to shower up and make myself pretty.

"You're always pretty," he assured me before kissing my lips and trailing his fingers across my stomach.

I watched his very fine ass walk out my door before jumping into a hot shower.

Now I'm ready to go, and as I step out of my room and watch him appear behind Jed, my insides trill again.

*I love you.* It's tempting to blurt it right now, but I want it to be special. So I'm saving up those three little words until the timing is right.

I'll be cocooned in his embrace, and then they'll slip out of me. He can drift off to sleep knowing how much I mean it. In the morning, we'll wake up together, drink coffee, and both be buzzing as we open this next chapter of our new lives.

"Hey." I smile up at him.

"Hey, beautiful," he murmurs against my lips.

"Okay, before you guys go." Tobin pulls us apart with his bright voice. "Ooo0! Tinker Bell! You fine, girl."

Nix swans out of her bedroom door, doing a little spin in her dress.

She does look fine.

Wow.

That thing must be painted on.

She dips her knees, then adjusts the barely-there straps and blushes red.

She obviously has no idea what to do with compliments, and Tobin snickers at her expression.

"What time is Ricky picking you up?" Jed asks.

"Oh, he's meeting me there. He had some stuff he had to do."

"We'll take you." I point between Tyrell and me.

"I was counting on it." She winks at us, and I grin, leaning into Tyrell's side when he tucks his arm around my waist.

"Okay, okay, but before you go, we have something special for you." Tobin's grin is pure excitement, and Jed's deep laugher rumbles through the room as he pulls an envelope from his back pocket and hands it to his boyfriend.

"We're really serious about the whole keeping-in-touch, still-seeing-you-guys thing, so…" Tobin draws out the word.

"So…" Nix spins her hand in the air, urging him to hurry up.

"We bought you concert tickets!" he sings, struggling to open the envelope.

Jed laughs and gently takes it off him, handing us each a ticket for Electric Reverence.

"Oh my gosh!" My eyes bulge. "I love these guys."

"Right?" Tobin dances on his toes. "And you want to know the best part?"

"It's in Nolan!" Nix's head pops up in surprise.

"Yes! The concert is here."

"Why?" Tyrell asks, peering at the small print on his ticket.

"Because two of the founding members used to go here, and they wanted to do something nostalgic, so they're performing here at the end of the summer, just before school goes back, and we all have to go. We even paid extra to attend the after-party."

"No way!" Nix squeals. "We'll get to meet the band?"

"Yes!" Tobin laughs. "We've already booked our flights back from New York, and everyone has to swear they're going to be there."

"Of course we will!" Nix laughs, tipping her head back and squealing. "This is so exciting! Thank you so much!" Skipping across the room, she jumps into Tobin's arms, wrapping her legs around his waist and flashing us her skimpy underwear as her dress rides up. Tyrell blinks and quickly looks away while I try not to laugh as Tobin spins her in a circle.

"Thank you." I get in on the celebrations too, going on my tiptoes to hug Jed.

He wraps his arms around me with a deep laugh. "Of course. We had to find an excuse to see you again."

"This is going to be so fun!" Nix jumps out of Tobin's arms and runs over to Jed. "I can't wait to tell Ricky. He'll be stoked. Thanks for buying him a ticket too. And after-party passes! You guys are legends."

"Of course we are." Jed grins, then kisses the top of her head. "We love you guys and wanted to have something really special to look forward to. We can't wait for this reunion. It's going to be epic."

"So epic!" Nix raises her tickets in the air, darting across the room to obviously put them someplace safe because she returns empty-handed, humming an Electric Reverence song under her breath.

I smile at her, feeling that buzz as Tyrell hands me his ticket and I go tuck them into my nightstand drawer.

Amazing.

And so fun.

I don't usually like planning ahead, but the idea of reuniting for this concert is such a good one. The band is performing in the football stadium, there's going to be a massive crowd, and... we're going to the after-party too. We'll get to meet the band! So freaking amazing.

These tickets must have cost a ton.

I should seriously offer to pay some money, but they'll no doubt tell me it's a gift and refuse my offer.

Those two. I will love them forever.

*And I love Ty.*

My insides trill as I walk back out to the living room and take my boyfriend's hand. He holds it all the way down the stairs, then on the drive to the party. I love the way he plays with my fingers, then lifts them to his lips to kiss the tips and my knuckles.

We end up having to park a block away, but I don't mind the walk. The night air is fresh, the sky clear. Nix is chattering away, her guard completely down as we walk into the house, which is already pumping.

The house is palatial, a three-story monstrosity with odd angles and a mid-century edge. It was so obviously designed by an architect and must have been the talk of the town when it was first constructed. Now it looks kind of old and beat-up, probably turned into unofficial student housing years ago. I wonder how many rooms it has. At least six or seven, surely.

I gaze up at the plethora of lit windows, my lips parting as I drink it in, then walk down the path and into the equivalent of a human beehive. Between the music, chatter, and cacophony of bodies, this place is buzzing.

"You good?" Tyrell murmurs, kissing the tip of my nose before literally getting dragged away from me.

"Ty, buddy, help me out here." Two big guys who are obviously from the football team sandwich him between them, and he's pulled into some discussion/argument over two people I have never heard of before. I'm assuming their NFL players by the way they're talking.

I linger behind him, checking out the crowd as I wait for him to wrap this up.

He looks over his shoulder, throwing me an apologetic wince.

I brush my hand through the air, telling him not to worry about it. "I'll go find us some drinks."

Moving away before he can stop me, I head into the throes, steeling myself against bad memories. That's not going to happen tonight. Tyrell won't get drunk. And besides, this party has a different vibe. I think. There's not the same dark edge in this place, and people seem happy-drunk, not dangerous-drunk. There's a big difference.

Turning sideways, I inch past a group of girls as I head toward the kitchen, but I'm stopped short by a sight I wasn't expecting.

Nix is storming down the hallway, shoving people aside. Tears are blurring her vision, and she looks about ready to fall apart.

"Nix?" I dash over to her, grabbing her arm to slow her down.

"Let me go!" She wrenches herself out of my grasp, then freezes when she sees it's me.

"What's the matter?" I whisper.

"It's over," she growls.

"What's over?"

"He's cheating on me!"

# CHAPTER 42

## DANI

A sob punches out of her as she covers her mouth. "I just saw him with his pants around his ankles. Fuck!" Holding a hand on either side of her head, she tries to draw in a breath, but she can't.

Oh no. Poor Nix.

How can this be happening?

She's supposed to be spending the summer with Ricky. She's supposed to be moving in with him!

I gape down at her, not even sure what to say.

He's cheating on her?

Here? At the party?

What the actual fuck!

I have to get her out of here.

"Come on, let's go." I reach out my hand, but she backs away.

"No. I..." Shaking her head, she holds up her hand. "Just... I need some space. I... I don't want you to come with me. I need to be on my own." Before I can argue, she spins on her heel and runs out of the house.

My chest deflates, sorrow for my friend taking me out, followed swiftly by a healthy dose of fury.

That asshole!

Turning with a growl, I stalk back through the party, opening and closing doors as I go. I know I'm not supposed to be looking into rooms like this, but I don't care.

Ricky needs his ass kicked!

Turning the handle of door number five, I open it with a scowl, eyeing up the room and growling again when I spot Ricky pulling up his pants. He's just zipping his fly when he turns to spot me, his face going pale when he sees who I am. He glances over his shoulder to look at the girl who is pulling her dress back into place.

"It's not what you think." He turns to look at me, his tone slightly slurred.

Okay, so he's drunk, but not so drunk that he can't get it up, and not so drunk that he can't lamely try and defend himself.

He knows he's in the wrong. His guilty expression is a dead giveaway. Oh yeah, and the fact that he's doing up his pants while the tall, sex-on-a-stick model-looking chick on the other side of the bed readjusts her boobs.

"You asshole!" I stalk across the room, slapping his cheek before I can even think about it.

"Hey!" the girl yells at me. "What the hell are you doing?"

I ignore her, snarling up at Ricky. "You just broke Nix's heart!"

He winces and frowns. "You don't have to tell her."

"She knows!" I hiss. "She saw you in here with her!" I point an accusing finger at the woman whose face buckles with confusion. "And now she's running down the street in tears! How the fuck could you do that to her!"

"What?" The woman stalks around the bed, her blue eyes flashing. "You told me you were single! We've been dating for three weeks! Who's Nix?" Her face puckers in disgust.

"Nix is my roommate," I snap at the woman. "She's been dating Ricky for a few *months* now, and they have big plans. *Had* big plans," I correct myself before turning my anger back on Ricky the Douchebag! "What the fuck is wrong with you? Did you want to get caught? Is that why you screwed your bit on the side at this party?"

"Hey!" the woman complains.

"She seduced me!" Ricky tries to justify himself. "I wasn't planning on it, but I arrived and Nix wasn't here yet, and, baby..." He looks to the irate blonde. "You look so hot tonight, and when you asked if I wanted to go somewhere private... how was I supposed to say no to that? I thought I had time before Nix got here. I thought—"

"You asshole!" the woman growls, slapping him. "Don't blame me for this, you two-timing piece of shit!"

Ricky ducks her next attack, quickly jumping a step back and banging into the bookshelf behind him. It rattles, two books toppling over as he winces and rubs his shoulder.

"You're supposed to be spending the summer together," I seethe, stalking toward him. "She's moving into your place when you guys get back!"

He sighs, squeezing his temple. "Yeah, I was going to talk to her about that."

"Ugh. You're despicable!" I slap him again, my fingers stinging when I point up at him. "You stay away from her!"

"And me!" the girl barks, spitting on his bare chest before storming out of the room, her dress strap slipping off her shoulder when she yanks the door open.

Ricky's shoulders slump, and he nurses his cheek. I glare at him one last time before stalking out of the room, my blood close to boiling.

Pulling the phone out of my purse, I send Tobin a quick SOS, then send a text to Nix as well, hoping she's okay. She doesn't respond, but within moments I get a *We'll find her* from my roommates and instantly feel better.

Shit, that was unsettling.

I can't believe the guy Nix was so blissfully in love with could turn on her like that. She had no idea he was a scumbag. None of us did.

But he's been dating another woman for *three weeks*, obviously *sleeping* with her, and dumb enough to do it at a party that he knew Nix would be coming to? What a fucking moron!

She deserves so much better, and it's a good thing that she found out about his cheating ways before she moved in with him. But I'm heartbroken for her.

It makes me want to get out of here. How can I possibly party and celebrate when my roommate is going through this? I need to be there for her.

I'm gonna find Tyrell and see how badly he wants to stay. If I explain the situation to him, I'm sure he'll be happy to bail early.

I just have to find him.

Easing my way down the hallway, I rise on my tiptoes to try and spot him. He's not where he was standing before, which means he's probably looking for me. Spinning back around without looking properly, I manage to turn straight into a guy holding two overflowing Solo cups.

"Oh shit!" I gasp as the cold brew splashes over me, covering my dress and trickling between my breasts.

"Fuck, sorry," the guy slurs, throwing the now-empty cup onto the ground. "You good?" He gives me a blurry-eyed blink, and I can't believe he's already wasted. I've been at this party for all of forty minutes. Admittedly, we arrived late, but still.

Pulling the saturated dress away from my body, I put finding Tyrell on hold and start opening doors in search of the bathroom.

I finally find one, three doors down, and shoulder it open, flicking on the light and snatching a towel off the railing.

That's when I spot him.

On the ground, face down, completely out of it.

"Tyrell," I whisper, flashbacks of finding Atlas exactly the same way making me stumble backward. I hit the edge of the bathtub, my knees buckling as I let out a gut-wrenching scream. "Tyrell!"

# CHAPTER 43
## TYRELL

"Tyrell!" someone screams.

I pause in the kitchen, frowning as I go still, trying to figure out where that shouting is coming from.

"What was that?" The girl beside me goes pale as she obviously hears it too. She looks at her friend, who shrugs, then flinches when another scream rents the air.

This one is nameless, just an outright cry of agony or terror. I'm not sure. But I move to investigate. And I'm not the only one doing that.

People start crowding out the hallway, and I keep an eye out for Dani as I go. She disappeared on me when I got caught in that fucking football conversation that had zero value, because in the end they agreed to disagree over who the best player was. Who gives a shit.

As soon as I noticed she was gone, I started looking for her. She said she was going to find drinks, so I headed to the kitchen. When I couldn't find her there, my stomach sank. I figured we'd probably end up playing a game of "search the party," and I really didn't want to miss her.

I was seconds away from stepping into the hallway when I heard that scream.

Another one fills the air, followed by a sobbing wail, and the closer I get to the source, the more this uneasy feeling in my chest starts to grow. Flashbacks to a party three years ago torture me, and as this unrest blooms inside of me... a thought finally hits.

*Shit, that's not Dani, is it?*

"Excuse me!" I start pushing people out of my way, straining to get to the bathroom.

"Is she okay?"

"What's wrong with her?"

"Did that guy try to attack her?"

"He's passed out cold!"

"Shit, what did she do to him?"

Thankfully, I'm tall enough to see over the bulk of the crowd, and I spot Dani's curls through the gap.

"Dani!" I shout. "Let me through! Move!"

"Hey!" Wily shouts over top of the chatter. "Move aside! His girl's in there!"

People quickly do as they're told, Wily ushering a frightened-looking Satch to the edge of the living room while I bolt through the door.

"Dani!" I kneel in front of her, grabbing her face and moving her to look at me. "Baby, I'm here. It's okay, I'm here."

She blinks, her screams drying up as she takes me in. She's slow to register that it's me, but after a beat, she sucks in a breath and squeaks my name. "Ty."

"Yeah, I'm here. Are you okay?"

She's a shaking mess, of course she's not okay! Her eyes dart past me to the guy on the floor, her lips trembling as she stares at him.

Grady's already behind me, checking on the man, who has obviously had too much to drink.

"He's out cold," he murmurs. "Hey, buddy! Wake up, man."

"Is he breathing?" Dani whispers, her voice a breathy mess.

I take in my friend and the prone guy on the floor... and suddenly it hits me like a sledgehammer.

Holy shit.

Atlas.

I whip back around to check on Dani, and I see it in the glazed look on her face. She's back there, relieving every awful moment of finding Atlas on the bathroom floor and trying to wake him.

Grady manages to rouse a groan from the guy, and I brush my thumbs across her cheeks. "He's fine. He's gonna be okay."

"We still need to get him to a hospital," Grady murmurs. "Hey, Zander! You out there?"

"Yeah, man." Zander's head appears. "What do you need?"

"This guy needs checking out. We either need to call an ambulance or take him to the hospital."

"Ben's already calling 9-1-1," someone shouts from behind Zander, and then a tall guy with shaggy spiral curls appears. I recognize him from the basketball team. "An ambulance is on its way."

Zander disappears from view to no doubt double-check on that phone call, so I focus back on Dani.

"Hey," I whisper, rubbing her cheeks again. "Come back to me. It's okay. No one's dead. Everything's fine."

She lets out a shaky breath, her body shuddering. I need to get her the fuck out of here.

"Come on." I stand up, taking her hand and pulling her to her feet.

Wrapping my arm securely around her, I try to shield her from view as I walk her out of the party. Bug-eyed stares and whispers follow us, but Wily and Zander soon create a barricade.

"She okay?" a concerned voice asks, and I glance up to see Asher Bensen and Liam Carlisle join the line, walking us out of the party like our personal bodyguards.

"Yeah, she's gonna be fine," I answer, hoping with everything I've got that it's true.

As soon as we get outside, our human shield disperses and I walk Dani down to my car, only just remembering Nix.

"We need to let Nix know that we're leaving."

"She's gone already," Dani rasps. She's still shaking, so I hold her a little tighter, slowing my pace to match her shuffle.

"What do you mean, she's gone?" I ask as calmly as I can.

"She left. Ricky's cheating on her. She saw it, and she bailed."

"Holy shit." I blink. "That asshole."

"That's what I said." Dani closes her eyes. "And then I slapped him. Twice."

"Really?" I can't help my instant smile. Squeezing her a little closer, I kiss the top of her head, relieved that she's starting to talk coherently. She's coming back. This nightmare can be over, and we can move on. We can put this behind us and—

"I can't do this." She jolts to a stop, flicking my arm off her shoulder.

A dark sense of foreboding settles in the pit of my stomach, but I try to shake it off, seeking clarification with a soft "Can't do what?"

"This." She points between us.

Fuck. No!

*Don't do this, please, Dani.*

Keeping my emotions in check is an effort, but I clamp down the flood of panic that's threatening to blind me and force myself to say, "I know tonight shook you, but everything's going to be fine."

"No, it's not." Her voice is wooden, her eyes staring past me like she's outside of her body or something. "I thought it was you. On that floor. I thought it was you."

"Me?"

"Yes." She looks up at me then, her eyes all wide and panicked. "I can't put myself through this again."

"It wasn't me, though. I'm here. I'm safe. I would never drink too much. I've never done drugs. Not even one puff of pot. I'm here, baby, and I'm not leaving you."

"You don't know that," she whispers.

"Y-yes, I do," I try to argue as gently as I can. "I wouldn't do that to my body."

"No, you don't know that you're not leaving me. You don't have control!" Her voice rises. "You might not OD, but you could still die. You could get sick or hit by a car or... or shot by some psycho!"

"Dani." I reach for her, but she flicks me away.

"I can't," she sobs, covering her face and speaking into

her hands. "I can't lose someone else. It's too much. My heart can't take it!" She ends up screaming the last part, lowering her hands and staring up at me like she's begging me to get this.

But I can't. I don't want to buy into this thinking.

I don't want to lose her!

"Dani," I practically beg. "Please don't do this. I know that life is uncertain and unpredictable, but don't push me away out of fear. I love you, okay? I love you, and I want to be with you."

"It doesn't matter what you want. It doesn't matter what I want! I can't... I can't do this! I'm not ready for a relationship. I thought I was, but I'm not, okay? It's too much. It's too soon. I'm not strong enough to take a risk with someone."

"Please," I whisper.

She shakes her head, closing her eyes and crossing her arms. "Take me home. Please, just... take me home."

# CHAPTER 44
## DANI

I can tell he doesn't want to, but Tyrell gives in after a long beat. With a heavy sigh, he murmurs, "Come on," and I open my eyes as he's pulling the keys from his pocket.

Trailing after him, I keep my arms crossed tight over my chest, feeling weak and vulnerable. I know I'm hurting him, and I hate that. I'm hurting me too, but I can't tell him that because he might try and convince me to change my mind.

And I can't change my mind right now.

I thought I could do this, but I'm not ready.

My reaction to that guy on the floor is proof enough.

I thought it was Tyrell, and I started screaming like a crazy person. I'm not over Atlas's death. I'm still traumatized by it, and I can't put Tyrell through that. It's not fair to him or me.

I don't know what the hell I want; I just know I have to get away from this strong, beautiful man. I can't explain myself. It's just a gut feeling, a warning that I'm not ready for this. For him. For what being with him actually means.

Ricky cheating on Nix.

Seeing that guy dead on the bathroom floor.

Well, he's not dead. I know that, but I *thought* he was! And I lost it.

I can't risk losing Tyrell. I won't do that to myself.

We don't say anything as he drives me back to my apartment. There happens to be a spot right outside the door, which never happens, so Tyrell pulls into it and turns off the engine.

I want to bolt out the door, but I can feel his pain as he sits there quietly staring at the wheel, his jaw clenching and unclenching.

"I'm sorry," I finally murmur. "I don't want to hurt you."

He shakes his head, his lips curling just a little at the corners. Turning to me with a pained smile, he whispers in a broken voice, "Is there anything I can say to change your mind?"

My nose tingles, tears threatening to take me out.

I hold them in, my body shaking with the effort as I choke out, "No."

Reaching for the door handle before I completely lose my shit, I pop it open and pause just before jumping out of the car.

"I'm always here for you if you need me," he rumbles. "And I know you can't love me right now, but if you change your mind…" His voice cracks, and he stops speaking.

Shit, he's so wounded.

For a fleeting second, I wonder if I should take it all back.

But I can't.

I need to go.

"Goodbye, Ty. You take care in Texas, okay?"

He sniffs, glancing away from me, and oh shit, I think he's crying. "Yeah." He nods. "Yeah, you take care too."

I close the door, sobs pulsing through me as I run for the apartment and quickly punch in the code. My body starts to fold the second I'm inside. Tyrell's still sitting in his car, staring out the windshield like he doesn't know what to do with himself.

"I'm sorry," I whimper, covering my mouth and running for the stairs.

By the time I make it up to our floor, I'm a wreck. And then I can't get my stupid key into the stupid lock, which only makes me cry harder. After my second failed attempt, the door pops open and Jed appears, his face dropping with shock when he gets a look at me.

"What happened?"

I shake my head, walking straight into his chest and clinging to his shirt. "I couldn't do it."

His arms wrap around me immediately, his hand rubbing circles on my back as he pulls me into the apartment and walks me to the couch.

Lifting me into his arms, he takes a seat, snuggling me against him while Nix sits on Tobin's lap, softly crying into his shoulder.

Well, aren't we a fun bunch.

I can sense Tobin and Jed sharing a shocked, devastated look over the tops of our heads, and all I can do is close my eyes and mourn.

Mourn for the man I thought I'd marry.

Mourn for the man I thought I'd move to Texas for.

And maybe I'm mourning a little for the girl who feels like she's stuck in the bottom of a dark well and has no idea how she's going to climb out of it.

# CHAPTER 45
## TYRELL

I wake the next morning with such a deep sense of sadness that I'm not even sure I can get out of bed.

Coming back home last night, all by myself, was so fucking painful.

Splaying my hand over the mattress, I run my palm across the sheet. Dani should be in that spot.

But it's too fast.

Too soon.

She was fucking traumatized last night, in no state to see reason, and part of me wants to grab my phone and start texting her a thread of pleas to reconsider.

*Don't break up with me!*

*I love you.*

. . .

*Please, don't end us. We've only just begun.*

*We can make it work.*

*I'll be whatever you need me to be.*

Each thought is getting lamer than the last.

I can't text her.

She asked me to leave her alone, and I have to respect that. She's got my number. She'll reach out to me when she's ready.

*What if she's never ready?*

The ache in my chest blooms, but I clench my jaw and grit out, "Then you move the fuck on."

Flinging the covers back, I sit up and groan.

My head is pounding, and I didn't even drink anything last night. I'm feeling hungover... wasted on the sadness of heartache.

Shit, it hurts.

I've been broken up with, and broken it off with, a bunch of different girls, but none of it ever felt like this. Because I never loved any of them before.

But I love Dani.

I didn't mean to fall so hard, and she was the last person I thought I *could* be in love with, but there it is. Life's cruel twist of fate. I finally let myself fall for my best friend's girl... I finally accepted the fact that he's not here anymore and it's okay to move on... and then she doesn't even want me.

"Fuck," I mutter, standing up and using the bathroom before shuffling back to my room.

I check the time on my phone and feel a little guilty as I text my mom a partial truth.

*Feeling wrecked this morning. Do you mind if we skip breakfast? I'll be back in Dallas by the end of next week.*

I barely have to wait a minute before Mama's calling me to check.

"Hey, boy. Are you okay? You didn't get yourself drunk last night, did you?"

"No, Mama," I mumble.

"Maybe he was having all the sex!" Cyrus yells in the background, making Lacey laugh and Dad growl.

"Cyrus. We don't talk like that."

Mama stifles a laugh, then of course has to ask, "Were you?"

I huff. "No, Mama. I've just got a really bad headache. I think finals week and the intensity of packing up and going is all catching up with me. I'm sorry, okay? But I'll see you guys next week. I'll start driving down on Wednesday or something."

After a reluctant pause, Mama softly agrees. "Okay. I'll make sure your room's all set up for you and Dani."

My face bunches, this ache turning to a sharp pain. I should tell her not to bother, but I can't form the words right now.

"You look after yourself today, and we'll see you soon. Keep me posted on your arrival, okay?"

"Yes, ma'am."

"I love you, boy."

"Love you too, Mama."

"I love you!" Cyrus yells.

I let out a soft snicker and murmur, "Love you too, Cy."

"You take care," Mama says as a final farewell before hanging up.

Dropping the phone on my bed, I hang my head with a weary sigh, resting my hands on my hips and dreading the coming week. Shit, I'm dreading summer and the months beyond that. I'm just... feeling kind of hopeless about my future, and that sucks.

I want to make my dreams come true. Travel the world... with Dani.

But that's not gonna happen.

Dammit, I shouldn't have let myself toy with those ideas. This is why she never wants to live more than a day or two ahead. She knows how life can kick you in the balls, snatch away your joy without warning.

With a soft growl, I spin and head downstairs, figuring I'll grab a quick bite, then... I don't know... finish packing my room or go for a fucking long run!

"Hey, Ty!" Zoey's sweet voice greets me as soon as I walk into the kitchen.

"Hey, lil' bug." I bend down to scoop her into my arms when she runs toward me.

She giggles when I throw her up, then catch her again. Nestling her sticky cheek against my shoulder, I figure I should probably do a load of laundry today as well.

Her little fingers reach up to brush my face, and then

she sits back to look at me. She holds either side of my cheeks, her blue eyes studying me, her lips turning into a pout. "You sad?"

"I'm okay." I force a smile, and she grins back, her worry erased in the blink of an eye.

She's so sweet, so trusting, so innocent.

I press a kiss to the tip of her nose, that ache blooming all over again. But this one is different. When her little arms wrap around my neck to hug me, I palm her back, my hand covering her tiny body as I whisper, "I love you, Zoey Girl."

She giggles and whispers loudly, "I love you!"

Sienna laughs, her face gooey with affection as I pop Zoey back down on the kitchen floor. She pads across the tiles barefoot, her pink-polished toenails so tiny and cute. Jumping up, she climbs into Zander's lap and leans against his chest, trying to steal his toast when he takes a bite.

"Hey," he reprimands her with a mock scowl, and she giggles, Sienna watching on with this loved-up look that's making my insides crumple.

Shit. Am I ever gonna get that look?

For a fleeting moment, Dani looked at me that way. But not anymore.

It's too fast. Too soon.

*Which means there's still hope!*

But is there really?

She was broken last night. And I can't fix whatever she went through. I understand completely why she was triggered, and I wish I could step in and make it all better. But she doesn't want to let me do that. And maybe it's not my place anyway.

You can't heal someone else.

You can help, if they let you, but it's ultimately up to them.

Shit, I wish I could do more.

I want to call her. Check that she's okay. I want to text Jed or Tobin or... shit, I wonder how Nix is doing.

Ricky, that little fucker.

My insides churn as I step around Grady, popping two slices of bread into the toaster.

"It's a crowded house this morning," he murmurs as Nylah and Carson stroll into the kitchen as well.

"Let's move to the dining table." Zander stands with Zoey securely in his arms. Sienna grabs their plates and trots out of the kitchen with Blake and Grady in their wake.

"See you in a second!" Wily calls from his post behind Satch, who's frying up something delicious.

"Is that bacon?" Nylah sniffs the air. "Is there enough to go around?"

"I can put more on." Satch grins. "We're doing scrambled eggs too, if you want in on that. I'll cook them up as soon as the bacon's done."

"Yes, please." Nylah moves to the fridge to grab the carton of eggs. "How many more should I add? Caveman, you having any of this?"

"Yep." He walks out of the pantry with a box of Pop-Tarts and holds them up with a grin. "Dessert."

"Ew." Nylah's face puckers. "That's not even food."

"How did they end up in the house?" Wily takes the box off him, reading the packet. "Dude, these expired over a year ago."

"They're Pop-Tarts." Carson grabs the box back. "This

shit can't expire. There's so much sugar and fake crap in here, it'll probably last a century."

"Then why do you want to put it in your body?" Nylah's expression is pure disgust. "That's so gross."

Carson gives her a dry look and shakes the box in the air. "I don't like wasting food."

"Whatever." Nylah laughs. "Please, just chuck that crap out and find something else. I'll cut you up some fruit for dessert, although we're eating breakfast, which is technically not a meal that requires dessert."

Rolling his eyes, Carson drops the box into the trash can, then scoops Nylah up around the waist when she gets within range. "Maybe I'll have you for dessert instead."

She lets out an adorable squawk when he scrapes his teeth across her exposed shoulder. She's wearing one of those sweaters that's so baggy, it can barely stay on her body.

"You'll be calorie-free," Carson murmurs, and Wily booms with laughter.

"Dude, you'll be burning calories. Win-win!"

Satch giggles as she removes slices of crispy bacon from the frying pan and loads it up with more. She glances at me then, her expression sweet. "Do you want some?"

"Uh... no. I'll just stick with peanut butter toast, thanks."

"Okay." Her expression softens as she takes me in, her head tipping to the side. "Are you all right?"

I bob my head, my jaw working to the side as I try to contain that surge of emotion barreling through me, threatening to give me away.

"Is, uh... Dani up in your room?" Wily rests his hands on Satch's shoulders, giving them a light rub while he stares at me. "Is she doing okay after last night? She looked pretty shook."

"Oh, yeah." Nylah eyes pop wide. "I heard what happened. We arrived just as the ambulance was pulling away."

Now everyone's looking at me, and I don't know what the fuck to say. Thankfully, my toast pops and I spin to deal with that, the room going quiet as the people behind me obviously start to wonder what the hell I'm not saying.

Bacon sizzles in the frying pan. My knife spreads the peanut butter. And finally, I can't stand this awkward silence anymore.

I talk into the void before anyone else can. "I dropped her home."

*After she broke up with me.*

*She's not coming to Texas.*

*I'm single once again.*

*And I'm fucking heartbroken.*

Sniffing, I manage to rasp, "She just needed some space."

"Is she okay, though? She seemed traumatized," Satch softly asks.

I swallow, glancing over my shoulder, then back to the safety of my toast. "She was. She'll need some time to process, I imagine."

"Well, at least she's got you to help her," Nylah murmurs, and I can't contain my dry, bitter snicker.

Shaking my head, I pick up my toast and spin to stare at them. Opening my mouth, I'm about to tell them, but the words dry up. All I can do is shake my head, and as I walk out of the room, I manage to murmur, "No, she doesn't."

"What does that mean?" Carson calls after me, and I silently beg him not to follow, but of course he fucking trails me down the hallway. I'm heading for the stairs. I can't do the dining table with everyone. They're probably all going to be talking about their futures. Their summers.

Zander and Sienna will be taking Zoey to California. They leave in a few days with her parents. They're going to do a road trip, take a week or so to get there.

Wily and Satch are heading to Fledgling for a week to spend time with her parents before driving to Arizona.

I think Nylah and Carson are going to visit her grand-parents, then are heading across to see his mom and have a vacation in San Francisco before returning to Nolan.

And I can't remember what Grady and Blake are doing. I think they're catching up with his parents, then going to some lake house thing with her family before heading into the forest for a few days.

And what am I doing?

I'm driving down to Dallas, all alone, to move in with my family and do... who the fuck knows.

I may as well start looking for a job immediately. What's the point of having a summer break all by myself?

"Did Dani break up with you?" Carson asks, *way too loudly*, just as I'm passing the archway leading into the dining room.

"What?" Blake blinks, her spoon rattling into her cereal bowl. "When?"

I sigh, dipping my chin before throwing a glare at Carson.

He winces but doesn't look that sorry. Wily and Nylah bunch into the hallway with worried frowns while everyone at the dining room table looks on with sad, sympathetic expressions.

Gritting my teeth, I glance at each one of them before quickly muttering the truth. "Yes, she broke up with me. Last night was some kind of trigger, and she's decided she's not ready for a relationship. So we're done."

"Aw, Ty. I'm so sorry," Sienna whispers, looking about ready to cry.

Why's she so sad? She has her happy family. The love of her life is sitting next to her, running his hand across her shoulders and comforting her.

Dani won't let me do that.

And it's fucking killing me.

But I don't want these guys to worry, so I shrug, trying to play it off. "Better now than further down the road, I guess. I'd never want to be with someone who was feeling pressured into a relationship."

"What are you going to do?" Grady asks me.

I shake my head. "Nothing. Plans don't change. I'm still heading down to Dallas. My family needs me right now, and... I guess I'll just be driving down alone."

"Our plans are flexible." Blake looks at Grady, lightly touching his arm. "I mean, right? We could delay seeing your dad and Emma. They won't mind, will they?"

Grady shakes his head. "I don't think so." He turns to me with raised eyebrows. "Do you want us to come with you?"

I swallow, appreciating the kind gesture but shaking

my head. "No. I don't want any of you to change your plans for me. I'll be all right." I nod, trying to sell this shit with a forced smile. "Don't worry about me. You guys need to get on with your lives. Big adventures and all that shi... stuff."

Zoey's staring up at me with her big blue eyes, obviously sensing the tension in the room and worrying about it.

I wink at her, making my smile bigger. "I'm good, you guys. I'm just gonna..." I point up the stairs, the thought of trying to sit and eat breakfast with them way too much. "I've got some more packing to do."

Walking me and my sad pieces of toast up the stairs, I take them two at a time, needing to get away from the happy family vibes in the dining room. They'll probably end up talking about me and lamenting my sad situation. I feel bad for shitting on their post-graduation excitement, but it's not like I asked for this.

As I wander into my room and gaze around the empty space, I can't help feeling like I failed.

Sure, I got my degree.

I played four great years of college football.

I graduated.

And the one thing I had left to do was find myself a woman. Because the thought of leaving this place alone was kind of miserable.

Yet that's exactly what's happened.

Once again, I am a single man, looking ahead at a lonely future, because the only girl who's made me fall doesn't want me. Or can't handle me or... whatever.

We're not together.

And I'm fucking heartbroken.

# CHAPTER 46
## DANI

It's my last shift at Offside.

I didn't plan for it to happen like this, but after that awful night five days ago, I woke up knowing I had to make some immediate changes. I was losing the apartment, Jed and Tobin, Nix, and... I'd lost Tyrell.

*You mean you pushed him away.*

Snapping my eyes shut, I grip the edge of the counter, blocking that horrible memory from my mind. The look on his face when I told him I couldn't do this anymore will haunt me forever. The dejected way he sat in his car, unmoving, after I walked into my apartment building.

Shit, shit, shit!

It's only been five days, and I'm missing him with an ache that's debilitating.

But I can't go back on my resolve.

I'm not ready for a relationship.

And I can't stay in Nolan anymore.

As much as I don't want to, I'm moving back home. Probably just for the summer, I'm not sure. But I need to reset, and what better place to do it than the safety of my old room.

Sure, it's stuffed full of memories and heartache, but my childhood home also pulses with love. And it'll be nice to hang out with my brother and niece again. He and his girlfriend moved into the converted downstairs floor of my parents' house and have been living there since before Elsa was born. I think everyone keeps waiting for them to find their own place, but they just keep lingering.

It drives Dad crazy, but Mom loves it. She gets to see one of her grandbabies every single day. Although Elsa's seven now, so hardly a grand*baby*.

I'll head there for a while and hang out, then maybe hit the road and catch up with my other siblings. I'm even toying with the idea of driving all the way to NYC. Jed and Tobin said I can visit anytime. Their new apartment has a pullout couch that I can use, and I just might take them up on that offer.

I'm pretty sure I'll do anything not to think about what went down with Tyrell... that party... Atlas.

With a sigh, I finish wiping down the counter, trying not to think or feel anything as I pour drinks, uncap bottles, and send food orders to the kitchen.

It's a Wednesday afternoon, and the place is practically empty. Students have emptied out, turning Nolan into a quiet summer town. I mean, there are still the summer school students here, so the place isn't dead, but it'll definitely be quiet for a few months.

Nix is sticking around.

I was really surprised by this. I thought she'd take advantage of the summer break and be off, but she's too upset to make plans right now. She's not depressed-upset.

She's livid, every decision clouded by this raging anger. It's all hidden behind this mask of indifference, but her snarky comments and that look in her eye she gets when she doesn't know we're watching... yeah, she's pissed... and *hurt*. Ricky betrayed her in the most horrible way, and I still wish I'd slapped him harder.

Poor Nix.

Thankfully, she's managed to secure a place to live for the summer.

Her friend Charli lives with a bunch of guys at this house they call Basketball Base. It's kind of a lame title, which she openly admits, and she doesn't even know who started calling it that, but BB has six bedrooms and is about five blocks from campus. It's usually overflowing with six-foot-plus giants, but it's emptying out for the summer, and Charli has offered to let Nix move in while everyone is away.

She packed her stuff last night, and I'm pretty sure she's moving in there right now.

I said my goodbyes to her this morning, as I'm planning on hitting the road as soon as my shift is done tonight. It means I won't get back to Colorado Springs until midnight, but I don't mind driving the dark, quiet roads. I just want to get home.

Jed and Tobin started their drive to New York two days ago, and I left my keys in our empty apartment this morning. My car is packed to the brim with my stuff, so it's official.

My time in Nolan is over.

My insides tremble.

Reaching into my back pocket, I pull out the two concert tickets Jed and Tobin bought us. I seriously don't know if I'll make it back, although they made me promise I would.

I have to send Tyrell his ticket. I didn't have the courage to drop it off at Football Frat. He's leaving today or tomorrow, I think, so I would have had plenty of time, but I just couldn't bring myself to do it.

Seeing him again might end me.

I've been missing him so badly, picking up my phone on countless occasions to call just so I can hear his voice.

But what good will that do?

I don't want to give him false hope.

I don't want to weaken my resolve.

I'm not ready.

I can't put myself in a position like that again.

I can't lose him.

*You have lost him! You pushed him away!*

Closing my eyes, I fight the burning in my nose and throat, forcing the emotions down.

I need to find out what Tyrell's address is in Dallas. I'm not exactly sure how I'll do that yet—although Nix's friend Charli knows Nylah, and Nylah can probably find it out for me and pass it on. I'll get the address somehow, and I'll send this concert ticket to him.

Then we'll have no more ties binding us.

I'll be free.

*And alone.*

But at least on my own I can't get hurt. And I can't hurt anyone either.

Single people don't have anyone to fight with.

They also don't have anyone to make up with, but that's not the point.

Single people don't have relationship angst. They're free to do what they want, when they want.

I need to figure that out—what I really, truly want to do with my life—and I can't do that when I'm attached to someone.

Trying to move on by dating a bunch of people and falling for Tyrell was a stupid idea.

All it did was make me soft and weak and vulnerable.

I never should have moved to Nolan just to find a guy. That was insane.

I need to find *myself* first.

With a huff, I shove the tickets back into my pocket and spin around when I sense the main door opening.

Eyeing it with curiosity, I wonder who I'm about to serve when my insides turn to liquid. A cold panic drenches me, my heart leaping into my throat as Tyrell Jackson walks into Offside.

# CHAPTER 47
## TYRELL

Dani's behind the bar, staring at me like a deer in headlights.

Shit. Maybe I shouldn't have come.

But I just needed to see her one last time.

I want a proper goodbye, and I hope she'll let me do that.

Although, the second my eyes landed on her, all I could feel was this overwhelming urge to pull her into my arms and beg her to reconsider.

I miss her.

It's only been five days, but I ache and pine.

When Shakespeare wrote that line, *I burn, I pine, I perish...* Yeah, I get it now. That's exactly how it feels.

Clearing my throat, I shove my hands into my jean pockets, staring at her for a beat longer before pulling my hands free and walking toward the bar.

She's still staring at me, her look morphing to wary caution.

I raise my hands, letting her know I'm not here to cause trouble.

"I just want to say goodbye." My voice comes out all rough and uneven when I stop by the bar. "I hope that's okay."

Her swallow is thick, her head moving up and down —the smallest nod known to man.

It's not okay.

Shit, I shouldn't have done this.

Yet I'm not leaving.

My feet are planted with only the bar between us.

"You okay?" I have to ask.

"Yeah." She nods again, a bigger movement this time. "I'm, uh…" Licking her lips, she gives me a weak smile. "This is my last shift. I'm heading… home."

My eyebrows rise. I wasn't expecting that. "To Colorado Springs?"

"Yeah." She looks pained saying it. "Thought I'd catch up with my family again. Maybe do a road trip to New York. I don't know."

"I take it Jed and Tobin got away okay."

She smiles, brushing her teeth over her bottom lip. "They looked really happy. Won't be surprised if one of them proposes by the end of the year. They definitely have… permanent energy, you know?" She threads her fingers together, shaking her hands in the air to demonstrate the vibe, and I get it.

"They're a great couple," I agree. "Endgame."

"Definitely," she squeaks, and I quickly change the subject.

"How's Nix doing?"

"She's hurting." Dani whips the dish towel off her

shoulder and starts wiping down the counter. Her movements are fast and erratic, her brows dipped in concentration. "She's moving into a house in Nolan. Spending the summer here."

"You didn't want to go with her?"

"I just need to get out of here," she clips.

I press my lips together, nodding and not saying a damn word.

"Oh! Um..." Reaching into her back pocket, she pulls two tickets out, and I immediately recognize them. "Here's your..." She holds it out for me.

"You can keep it." I shake my head. "I'm sure there's someone you can invite. Maybe your sister. Or one of your brothers."

"No." She winces. "You should take it. They bought it for you."

Reluctantly, I reach for it, my fingers closing over the card Jed and Tobin printed the QR code on. "Are you gonna come back for it?"

She shrugs. "I'm not sure."

"Yeah, me either."

"We promised we would." Her voice is so small it's hard to hear, but I catch what she says, and for some weird reason, a spark of hope ignites within me.

Is she saying she'll be ready by then?

Will August 9 be the day I get her back?

We'll meet up at this Nolan U concert, and everything will be set right again?

*Don't go there, man. Don't cling to something that probably won't happen.*

*Let her go!*

*Let. Her. Go.*

It's like swallowing a jar full of nails, but I clear my throat and shove the ticket into the back pocket of my shorts before forcing out a goodbye. "Well, I'm hitting the road now, so... you're my last stop."

Her brown eyes hit me then, sad with compassionate understanding. "Are you doing okay? Was it hard to say goodbye?"

I let out a dry laugh. "Goodbyes are always hard. But I'll be seeing them all again eventually. So, even though it's been a brutal day... I'm hanging tough."

She nods, her eyes glassing over.

"I'm sorry if I hurt you," she whispers.

I shake my head, but that's a lie. She did hurt me, so in the end, I turn that shake into a shrug.

"I don't have what it takes to be in a relationship. I just didn't realize it until we were together. That part of me died with Atlas, and I'm sorry that you got hurt while I was figuring it out."

My insides pinch with pain. "So, you're just gonna stay single for the rest of your life?"

Her shoulders rise, then lower with a heavy sigh. "Maybe. Yeah, probably." Her nose wrinkles. "You don't have to understand. It's just something I..."

"Yeah, I..." My words trail off because I seriously don't get it.

She's got so much to give to a relationship, and she's cutting herself off because she's afraid of getting hurt.

She's hurting herself to protect herself.

I wish I could make her understand that.

But I don't think I can.

She's resolved. I can see it in her eyes, her stance.

I can't change her mind.

"Well…" I spread my arms wide. "Would it be okay if I gave you one last hug goodbye?"

Her smile is instant and she sniffs, walking around the bar to oblige me.

The second she steps into my space and I get a whiff of her sweet smell, I realize this is a huge mistake. It's going to be that much harder to forget her after this… that much harder to let her go.

Yet I cling to her, wrapping my arms all the way around her and resting my cheek against her head.

"You take care of yourself," I murmur.

"I will." She squeezes my middle, then pulls back, staring up at me with her big brown eyes.

I go still, wishing I could read her mind.

I think I spot a fleeting look of longing and…

Yeah, there it is again.

She's still holding me.

Still not letting go.

And before I can stop myself, I cup the side of her face, brushing my thumb across her lips.

She lets out a shuddering breath but doesn't pull away, so I act on instinct and lower my mouth to hers. I take it slow, pausing just before we connect, letting her make the last move.

And she does.

She rises up to meet me, pressing a firm kiss to my lips.

I automatically deepen it, because that's what my body is screaming at me to do. And she responds, her tongue gliding against mine before she pulls away.

It was a goodbye kiss.

I can sense it the second her heels land back on the floor.

Letting her go, I give her space to move away, to give me a shaky smile and whisper, "Goodbye, Black Jack."

"Goodbye, Dani Girl."

Releasing a shuddering breath, she turns, hurrying around the counter, desperate to put space between us.

My eyes burn as I watch her, and it takes everything in me to walk away.

But I do.

Somehow, my legs make it to the door.

I turn back one last time before leaving, and she's still watching me. Tears are trickling down her face, and I raise my hand, waving my final goodbye.

She slashes the tears off her cheeks and tries to smile at me, but it doesn't work.

Looks like I'm not the only one who's hurting.

And it kills me that she's doing this to herself.

To us.

But I have to let her go.

I know this in my gut.

And even though I want to reject the idea, talk myself out of it... I force my legs through that door. I step out into the sunshine and head for my SUV.

It's time to move to Dallas.

It's time to leave my college life behind and find something new.

# TWO MONTHS LATER...

# CHAPTER 48
## DANI

I got back from my road trip two days ago. It was a fun break. After spending five weeks in Colorado Springs, wallowing in my room, hanging out with Elsa, and finally going to therapy, I found the strength to hit the road.

I started with my siblings, staying two nights with my oldest brother, Remi, and his wife and one-year-old daughter. That was all things precious, and I left feeling better than I had in weeks. I then stopped in to spend four days with Shantee, my sister, and her husband and twin boys. That was chaotic but lots of fun. I was more than happy to hit the road again, though, and made it across the country, staying in motels along the way and finally ending up in NYC.

I parked my car in long-term parking at Newark Airport and caught the train into the city.

It was wild. I'd never been to a place that big before, but Jed and Tobin took the best care of me. The restaurant where Jed's working is so flash. Tobin made me spend the last of my savings on a new dress that sparkles and hugs my body like nothing I've ever owned before. I got hit on a bunch of times throughout the night, and Tobin had to end up pretending to be my boyfriend. All I could think about was Ty and how, if he'd been beside me, I would have had an *actual* boyfriend. One I loved and cared about. One who could make me smile and feel safe and... listen to Whitney Houston with me. Someone I could travel the world with.

"Ahhh," I softly whine to myself as I leave the grocery store. Mom sent me on a shopping run, and I was happy to go because I'm starting to suffocate in my room.

New York was thrilling and exciting and... Colorado Springs is not.

I want to hit the road again, but I'm out of cash. I need to get back to working and earning.

My parents carried me when I first got back here. They could see I needed time to heal. I ended up telling them everything, and they totally remembered Tyrell.

"Oh, he was such a nice boy. I always liked him." Mom had smiled, then looked slightly horrified as I burst into wailing sobs.

I told them about the party and how triggering it was to see that guy on the floor. Dad had me booked into therapy within a few days.

Sitting with that lovely, softly spoken therapist made me realize I should have done this immediately after Atlas's death. I had no idea I'd been carrying around PTSD over the night he died. I'd just mourned and tried to move on.

But therapy has been helping me to really process my grief and trauma.

I'm feeling stronger. Calmer. More capable of dealing with life.

I can do this.

I can travel and be the woman I need to be. And I'm starting to dream again. About how I want to spend my days. Of course, travel is right up there, but it can't be the only thing. I used to love managing Atlas's band, but I'm not about to jump back into the punk rock world.

But... what if I could take the things I loved about managing and the things I love about tending bar and combine them?

What if I could open my own place?

A jazz bar or a sports bar or some cool kind of coffee lounge. I'm not sure yet, but the idea has definitely piqued my interest. I have no idea how I'll make it happen, and with wanting to travel as well... how can I make what little money I have work for me?

I really need to get myself a job, probably for a few years, and save as much money as I can. I'll make that my only focus, and eventually all these dreams that are firing me up will come to fruition.

I'm still pretty set on being single, but as I carry these heavy grocery bags to my car, I can't help imagining Tyrell beside me. He'd be carrying the bags, and I could swan along beside him, unlocking the car and driving us home. He'd probably help me unpack them, then ask me what I want to do.

He was always thinking about me, never demanding anything or putting pressure on me. I could be myself around him. I just didn't realize I could. Or I wasn't aware that I was just being me. And then I got scared and put all these barriers into place.

And now, I'm... I don't know.

"He's probably moved on already," I mutter to myself, hating that idea with a depth that's causing my stomach to hurt. "But he deserves to be happy." I'm still whispering to myself, no doubt looking like a crazy person .

Dallas is probably full of friendly, gorgeous, kind women. Tyrell's no doubt inundated with dates and invites. There's bound to be someone he can fall in love with. His past-the-third-date girl is out there, and I won't be surprised if he's already found her.

"And that's a good thing," I say, then repeat, "I want him to be happy."

I just wish the idea of him with someone else didn't hurt so much.

I want to be single, right? This is what *I want.*

So why don't I feel better?

Unlocking my car, I dump the groceries in the trunk and am about to get behind the wheel when a male voice grabs my attention.

"Dani?" I whip a look behind me, my eyes narrowing until I recognize the long-haired guy loping toward me.

No way.

My body tenses like it always used to, but I hide it behind a smile... like I always used to.

"Reef." I point my keys at him. "It's been a while."

"Yeah." He slows to a stop, eyeing me up like he can't decide if he wants to use up one of his rare smiles on me.

He still looks exactly the same, sporting his long, scraggly locks, ripped jeans, a baggy hoodie, and a beanie that looks like it hasn't been washed—ever.

He was the bass player in the same band as Atlas, and his fashion sense could be described as stoner-skater boy from a 90s teen movie. The only thing he's missing right now is his beat-up board.

I never 100 percent warmed to the guy. He threw off a vibe that was a completely different frequency to mine. I don't think he liked me much either.

In fact, I still don't think he likes me.

I give him an awkward smile, waiting for him to say something.

I never understood why Atlas looked up to him. He was a little in awe of the guy and couldn't shut up about what a talented musician he was. When Reef invited him to join their band when we were still in high school, it was the biggest honor.

"So..." I tip back on my heels, unable to stand this awkward silence anymore. "How are you?"

*Don't ask him that? Why are you drawing out this conversation?*

He moves a step closer to me, and yep, the guy still reeks of weed.

"Yeah, yeah, I'm good." He tucks a lock of hair behind his ear and eyes me up and down. "You?"

"Yeah." I nod, not sure what else to say. I'm not good. But I'm not bad either. I'm just... existing right now.

He nods, his lips rising into a barely-there smile as he looks away from me, obviously thinking something over. After a beat, he lets out this derisive, scoffing laugh that I don't understand before looking back at me. "Thought you'd left town." He sniffs. "That's what I'd heard anyway."

"I moved up to Nolan for a little bit, but I'm back now." I point at myself. "Obviously."

"Nolan." He narrows his eyes at me. "Causing trouble up in Nolan, huh?"

My head tips back as I try to figure out what he means by that. "Uh…"

"I'm heading up there next week," he murmurs, his head bobbing as he scrapes the asphalt with his Converse.

"Okay." I nod, still wondering why he thinks I'm some kind of troublemaker.

"There's a concert up there, and they've asked me to fill in for the bass player. He can't do the final couple shows, so…" He tips his head, his try for humility completely failing. He is so fucking proud right now.

My lips part, my eyebrows rising. "Are you talking about Electric Reverence?"

"Yeah." He frowns, pointing at me. "You know 'em?"

"Doesn't everybody?" I counter. "How do you…? How did you manage to get that gig?"

"I know one of the guys in the band. We used to hang. Atlas knew him."

"Oh, I… I… I didn't know that," I end in a whisper.

"Yeah, he used to party with us on the regular." His eyes narrow on me again. "You probably met him too." He works his jaw to the side, his voice getting gruff. "You always were at those parties. Always by Atlas's side." He sniffs. "Until you weren't."

My blood runs cold. "What's that supposed to mean?"

That scoffing laugh punches out of him again, and he shakes his head. "Doesn't matter."

"He told me to fuck off," I whisper, steeling myself against that guilt the therapist has trained me to let go of. I made my choice that night. Atlas made his. There is no turning back time. There is only acceptance. Forgiveness.

I wish I hadn't said that now. I wish I'd just kept my mouth shut.

Reef's dark look is making my skin crawl. "You know he didn't mean it."

Gritting my teeth, I cross my arms and squeeze out, "It sure felt like it at the time."

Reef's hard stare tells me he's not buying my shit.

But it's not shit.

Atlas's harsh words cut me that night, and so I took off. And sure, I wish I hadn't. But I did, and this man, standing here trying to make me feel guilty for that, is going to undo weeks of therapy.

Which means I need to get the hell away from him.

Right now.

"Well, I guess I'll see you there," I throw out, then instantly regret it.

*Why did you say that?*

I don't even know if I'm definitely going.

*Yes, you are. Jed and Tobin made you promise! And Nix wants to see you.*

She's seemed brighter the few times I've talked to her, and I did say I'd be there.

Shit. Why did I say that?

Maybe I could just fake a sickie or—

*You want to go! You know you do!*

"Guess you will." Reef's scathing look is enough to make me want to bail. My friends will get it. I so don't have to be there.

*But you do. And you know why.*

I haven't let myself admit it yet, but there's that feeling

again, bubbling and brewing... begging on its knees for me to wake up and acknowledge it.

"Later," Reef mutters before turning to walk away.

Yuck. That conversation was... anything but pleasant. Reef couldn't have been more obvious if he tried. He blames me for Atlas's death.

But he was there too. The memory is obviously still pretty fresh for the guy. Why didn't I challenge him on it? I should have asked him why he didn't keep Atlas safe that night, why he didn't check on his friend, who he obviously still misses. He wouldn't be so dark toward me otherwise.

Shit, the guy will be at the after-party.

I shudder, making a mental note to stay as close to Jed and Tobin as I possibly can. Nix is pretty feisty too, so she'll be an asset. I'll just surround myself with them, and everything will be fine.

As I close my car door, I grip the wheel, my mind shifting to Tyrell.

The instinct to pull out my phone and text him about who I just saw is strong. He'd know Reef. He used to hang with Atlas and his band buddies. He was their personal bodyguard. Black Jack.

"Oh shit," I whimper, resting my forehead against the wheel and letting myself feel that aching cavity in my chest.

I spend most of my days trying to ignore it, but right now, I let it grow and pulse and burn.

"I miss you," I whisper.

And a big part of me really hopes he's at that concert, because I want him by my side at that after-party. Watching over me. Keeping me safe.

More than that, though... I just want to see him again. I want to study his smile and listen to his deep voice. I want to lean against his side and enjoy the feeling of his arm enveloping me.

*Are you sure you want to stay single for the rest of your life?*

The question taunts me, and I sit back with a loud sniff, wiping my cheeks as if tears have fallen. But none have. My face is as dry as my heart right now.

Doubts curl through me, winding around my rib cage, crawling into my chest and making it tight and uncomfortable.

The truth is, I can cope on my own. That road trip proved it.

And now the question I have to answer is... do I really want to?

# CHAPTER 49
## TYRELL

"Again. I want... I want to play again." Cyrus grins at me, his smile adorable and... exhausting.

I've been hanging out with my brother for days on end. With the summer break, he's only got a few classes of summer school to keep him entertained, and the rest is up to us.

My dad has started working again, and Mom is continuing her extra shifts, so it all falls to me and Lacey.

Well, mostly me.

Lacey's too busy being a socialite, and she's scored herself a summer boyfriend, which we're all keeping a careful eye on. That girl's got a little wild in her, and who knows what she'll get up to with that putz.

From the moment I met him, I knew he wasn't good enough for her. And last time, because Dad wasn't here, I told him exactly how things would go down if he crossed any lines he shouldn't.

It wasn't my place, and it's not my usual style. Lacey hasn't spoken to me since I did it, but I was pissed off.

How is it that my nearly seventeen-year-old sister is in a relationship and I'm not?

Even Cyrus has a big crush on one of his classmates, and they went out on a little movie date the other night. I went with them to help them buy tickets and stuff. Her parents weren't happy about their sweet girl (who also has Down syndrome) going out with someone, so I offered to chaperone. I know her father from my summer job, and he was cool with me doing that. I tried to take a back seat as much as I could. Cyrus bought the tickets and popcorn like a pro. I was so proud of him. I snapped some pictures and sent them to her parents, which they seemed to appreciate.

I sat a few rows back, so I wasn't encroaching on them. Although, when she reached for his hand in the middle of the movie, he nearly died of excitement and ended up leaving her to come and tell me what she'd done.

"That's awesome, man. Now get back there so you can keep holding her hand," I whispered.

"Okay." He grinned at me before rushing back down to sit beside her again.

After we dropped her home, I had to spend what felt like three hours dissecting every detail of the date.

And now he's sitting here texting her, telling Abigail all about how he just beat his big brother at a game of Uno.

"Tell her you destroyed me, brah."

Cyrus giggles. "O-okay." Pressing the little microphone icon, he speaks into the phone, "Hi, Abigail. I just... I was playing Ty at cards, and I won. I de—"

"Destroyed," I whisper.

"I destroyed him." He laughs. "I destroyed him, and I'm gonna play again. And I miss you. And I hope... are you...? Is your day good?"

He glances at me, and I nod in approval, giving him a smile.

"Okay. I'm gonna go. But you can text me back." He goes to click the microphone icon again, then changes his mind and keeps going. "If you want to. You can text me back if you want to. I'm... I'm here. I'll text you back if you text me back."

I spin my finger, encouraging him to wrap it up. "Finish strong."

"O-okay. I... bye. Bye, Abigail!" He raises his voice to an enthusiastic yell before pressing Send.

"Did you read it first?" I lean forward.

"Oh, uh... no."

"Probably a good idea to do that next time. Speech to text doesn't always catch your words clearly."

"Oh no." Cyrus's eyebrows buckle.

"Hey, it's okay. Why don't you read it back now and just see how it sounds? If there's a bad mistake, you can correct it."

I show him how to edit the text, and he changes one word, then slumps back with relief. "Phew."

"Yeah." I smile. "You really like this girl, huh?"

"Yeah. She's Abigail. She's my friend."

"Do you think you'll become more than friends?" I keep my voice casual, my insides tossing and turning as thoughts of Dani hit me hard.

"Maybe." He shrugs. "I liked it when she held my hand."

"That was exciting, right?" I grin at him.

"I don't want to have the sex, though." He shakes his head. "That's your job."

I snicker. "Why don't you want to have sex?"

"It sounds yucky."

I nod, suddenly deciding I don't want to go there.

"But I know you... that you have sex and you like it." He grins. "So you should... you do it."

My laughter is dry as I shake my head, gathering up the Uno cards and shuffling them. "I need to find myself a woman for that."

"What about Dani?"

I purse my lips. "We're not together anymore, brah. You know that."

"Yeah, but you still... you think about her all the time. I know you miss her. Just like... just... I missed you when you were away."

"I know," I have to admit.

"So, you should... go see her." His face lights up, like he's just come up with the best idea. "You go see her and she'll see you, and you... you can have all the sex."

I wince. "It doesn't work like that. I can't just..." I shake my head, my sigh deep and heavy. "She has to want me too, you know? That's how it works. You both want each other. You *both* love each other, and then you can be together."

Cyrus thinks about this, then nods and leans back in his chair, staring at me like I'm overcomplicating things or something, but I'm seriously not.

"Hey, uh..." I check my watch and rise from my chair. "I don't have time to play another round. I need to go and pick up that stuff for Mama, and then I have to get ready for work."

Dad hooked me up with a job at the construction company he works for. It's just some manual labor stuff to see me through the summer. I had my interview with his boss, and the guy is keen to take me on, train me up as a project manager... after the summer. So, I've been digging ditches and sweating up a storm on various construction sites. The heat has been brutal, which is why the foreman at this week's job has been running early morning and evening shifts.

I'll be working through until after 3 a.m., but I don't mind so much.

"Okay, Ty." Cyrus watches me walk out of the room as I call my dad, who tells me he'll be home in an hour, so I don't have to take Cyrus with me.

I'm kind of relieved. I love my brother so much, but I'm done for the day. And now it means I can collect Mama's stuff from the store across town and have dinner out that way. I won't need to come back home before my shift. I'll just grab myself a burger and eat it in the car.

Cyrus will be okay on his own, but I text Mama to let her know as well. She'll no doubt call him in twenty minutes or so to make sure he's still in one piece.

Lacey's at a sleepover tonight, so at least that's one less person to think about.

Stepping into my room, I spot Rook curled up on a sunny patch of my bed.

"Hey, boy," I greet him, kissing his head and giving him a little pet before getting changed into my work clothes. I pause by my mirror, gazing at the ticket shoved into the frame.

"Dani," I whisper, wondering if she's going to be at the concert.

Tobin texted me last week, reminding me about it, making sure I'd booked a flight. I gave him an ambivalent answer, not wanting to commit to anything. If I do go, I'll drive up. Yes, it takes about twelve and a half hours, but I need the time to prepare myself. And I wouldn't mind the peace and quiet of driving all by myself with no one to take care of but me.

I just want to hit the road, get some space. I'll stop the night somewhere, probably sleep in the back of my car at a truck stop or something, I don't know.

I've been meaning to do a road trip. I had grand plans of visiting both Zander and Wily, but they haven't come together. Family commitments and work have taken over, and I'm trying to scrape together every penny I can.

Because I need to get on a plane. Get out of this country.

Now that Dad's back to work and pretty much recovered, I'm not needed as much as I was. Mama even told me the other night that I seemed restless and I should figure out what I really want to do.

I couldn't admit it then, but I'm going to have to at some point, right?

I can't stay here forever. And I can't keep missing Dani Hill.

She made it clear she wasn't ready for a relationship.
*She wasn't ready then. She might be now!*

That familiar hope flutters inside of me, but... I haven't heard from her in over two months. Not one text. I've even sent her the odd one, just to let her know I'm thinking about her, and she's sent nothing back.

If she's at the concert, then I really shouldn't be.

I want her to enjoy it. I want her to have fun with her friends. I'll no doubt put a damper on things.

I should stay here.

Maybe work an extra shift or two.

My boss has already approved my time off. I requested it in a moment of weakness. And now, in my moment of strength, I can tell him I don't need it anymore.

I just have to keep my head down and focus on saving.

Then find the courage to tell my family that I need to get on a plane and see the world, because the longer I stay here... the more I feel myself shriveling up.

With a sigh, I pull the ticket off my mirror and drop it toward my trash can. It flutters through the air and ends up on the floor beside it.

Shaking my head, I finish getting ready, refusing to look back at that ticket. Refusing to acknowledge how much my choice hurts.

But I can't go.

The whole getting-over-Dani thing won't be done any faster by seeing her again. It'll be like throwing myself into a fire and expecting not to get burned.

I have to stay in Dallas next weekend.

That's the only thing I can handle right now.

# CHAPTER 50
## DANI

I dropped the groceries home to Mom and spent the evening with Elsa. We watched *The Little Mermaid* and sang along to all the songs. It was fun. We giggled, and I held her tight throughout the scary bit at the end.

As the final credits were rolling, she was turning into a limp teddy bear in my arms, and I carried her downstairs so her parents could coax her through her nighttime routine.

"Night, Aunty Dee."

"Good night, Elly. Love you." I kissed her and headed up to my room.

I had grand plans of reading my book, then drifting into a peaceful sleep.

It didn't come.

I tossed and turned most of the night, then was jolted awake by a nightmare around 4 a.m.—it was a mean one, filled with a thumping drumbeat, cackling faces, and dead eyes staring up at the ceiling and not blinking.

Clutching the covers to my chest, I lay in the darkness, panting and sweating and too afraid to close my eyes again. I lay there until the sun came up, torturing myself with memories of that night.

Seeing Reef again brought it all back. I practiced the breathing techniques the therapist taught me along with the list of affirmations we'd written together.

I said them over and over until my body stopped shaking and I could sit up.

Bypassing breakfast, I snuck out of the house and went for a really long walk.

I didn't mean to end up at the cemetery, but here I am, gazing down at Atlas's gravestone.

"Hey." I take a seat on the grass. The sun has already dried it off for me and is threatening a scorcher of a day. A fine sheen of sweat is covering my body, and I wipe the back of my hand across my forehead.

Picking at the grass, I try to think of what I really want to say to this man.

I've visited him a few times since I got home. The therapy has really been helping me work through my grief. I hadn't realized I'd just been burying it under this pile of denial. Atlas was perfect. I was scum. And that was that.

Therapy has helped me unearth the truth.

Atlas was far from perfect.

And that night I left the party, I was protecting myself.

Unfortunately, that move had fatal consequences, but I am only responsible for the choice I made that night, no one else's.

If I could turn back time, would I stay?

Yes. Because I may have been able to stop Atlas from

taking those pills. I might have even seen who gave them to him and been able to stop them.

But that's not my reality.

And the truth is...

I sigh. "You treated me badly." My voice shakes every time I admit this to him. But at least I finally can. "I had every right to walk away from that conversation."

My head bobs as another sigh rushes out of me.

"I bumped into Reef yesterday. Remember him?" I smile. "Of course you do. You loved that guy." My nose wrinkles. "I never fully understood it, because I never liked him. Not really. I pretended for your sake, but..." I shudder. "There was just something about him that didn't gel with me and..." My body goes still, the blade of grass in my hand starting to tremble as a thought hits me. "You know what? I think it's because I was missing Tyrell. Reef kind of filled that spot in your life when Ty left, and I just didn't rate him. I could see that he didn't bring out the best in you. Ty always did. He was your silent conscience or something. He kept you in check and... well, Reef didn't. And I guess that was one of the reasons why I never really warmed to him."

I tip my head, looking up at the morning sky.

"Wow, you know I... I've only just figured that out now." My laughter is dry. "I guess I've always cared about Tyrell. Always liked him. And now I..." My swallow is thick as I stare at Atlas's name on the stone. "I love him. I miss him."

Biting my lips together, I start to bob my head and really acknowledge this. Really own my feelings over the whole Ty situation. It feels weird saying all of this to Atlas, but maybe it's also cathartic.

"I've spent weeks trying to deny this, but it's just been growing inside me." I tap my chest. "I want Tyrell. And I thought I couldn't do a relationship, and maybe I still can't." My shoulders slump as I mutter a soft "Shit."

Squeezing my eyes shut, I pinch the bridge of my nose, the scents of summer whistling around me as I try to figure out what I'm trying to say.

"It'd be so unfair of me to mess him around like that, but..." My eyes pop open and I stare at the gravestone, tracing each letter of Atlas's name with my gaze. "I think I was made to love someone. Like romantically. I don't want to be single for the rest of my life. I only said that because I was scared. I was *terrified*, and I..." Biting the inside of my cheek, I release a shaky huff. "Maybe I'm not so much anymore."

Plucking a fresh grass blade from the ground, I run my fingers over it, my throat swelling as I keep talking.

"I wish you'd never left me. I wish you hadn't taken those damn drugs. I wish you hadn't started hanging with Reef and those other musicians. I wish you could have stayed that sweet, bright-eyed guy from high school." I smile at his inscription—*Beloved son and friend. Forever in our hearts*. My nose starts to tingle, and I look to the sky, the white puffy clouds floating above me as I croak, "I was so in love with you, Atlas. And I would have stayed loyal to you through thick and thin. But... you died. And you told me to fuck off when all I was trying to do was help you."

I eyeball his name, picturing his abashed grin.

"I'm sorry that I told you to go to hell. I didn't mean if, of course." I huff. "And I'm sorry that I did fuck off. Deep down, I knew you needed me, but I was so mad at you. And now…"

I shake my head, but my voice comes out all soft and easy… because I've been practicing this.

"I forgive myself for that. I was just trying to protect myself, and I can see that now, and I forgive me." I bite my lips together, tears burning my eyes as my lips wobble into a smile. "And I forgive you, because you did screw up that night. You screwed up a lot of times before that too. And I shouldn't have tried to make you perfect in my mind. I only did that out of guilt. And it's held me back. So…" I suck in a breath. "I forgive you, and I'm finally ready to let you go." Tears fill my eyes then, one spilling over and trailing down my cheek. "I love you, Atlas, and you'll always be a precious part of my memory… my story. But it's time for me to go and write a new one. For real this time."

Wow. I can't believe I just said that.

I did it.

I told him, and it wasn't as hard as I thought it'd be.

I'm ready to move on.

I'm seriously ready.

With an awe-filled laugh, I rise from the ground, brushing off the back of my shorts.

"My therapist is going to be so proud of me." I laugh again. "And I didn't realize I was ready to say all that to you. I thought bumping into Reef again was like this trigger and I was set back, but… it was more like the final switch I needed. The final button to be pushed." Kissing the pads of my fingers, I then rest them on his gravestone. "But I'm okay. I can do this. It's time for me to say goodbye now." I smile, my chest swirling with this warmth I wasn't expecting. Like the weight I've been carrying all this time is starting to burn away... dissolve... I don't know, but I kind of like this feeling.

"Goodbye, my first love. Thanks for all the good things you gave me. And thanks for having such an amazing best friend, because... I think it's time for me to see him again."

That warmth expands, spreading through my body as I nod and let out a watery laugh.

"I love you, Atlas." I place one last kiss on his gravestone, my voice a husky whisper as I finally say, "Goodbye."

Then I turn and walk away.

I don't look back like I usually do.

I place one foot in front of the other and I make it all the way to the car, feeling lighter with each step.

# CHAPTER 51
## TYRELL

It's nearly four in the morning when I creep into the house. Everyone will still be sleeping for another few hours, and I don't want to wake them, although I'm desperate for a shower. Hopefully me clattering around in the bathroom won't disrupt anyone. I stink after a labor-intensive shift.

A soft meow catches my attention, and I glance down as Peaches follows me into the house. "Where have you been, girl?"

Lifting her up, I nuzzle her against my cheek before placing her back on the floor.

I need a hot shower, a cold drink, and then sleep. Lots and lots of sleep.

Padding through the kitchen in my work socks, I try not to trip over Cyrus's cat as she weaves between my legs, then nearly jump out of my skin when I reach the living room and find my parents sitting there.

"Holy shiii..." I let the word trail off because Mama don't like cussin'.

It's kind of become a family joke in a way. Anytime anyone gets a little mouthy, we all put on a drawl, wagging our finger and saying, "Mama don't like cussin'." It's especially great when we get to do it to *her*.

"Mmmm-hmmm." She gives me one of her looks, and I sag into the wall, leaning my shoulder against it and looking between them.

"You guys good? Why are you up?"

They're both looking at me in a way that's setting off alarm bells.

Shit, I am so not in the mood for a serious talk right now, but it's obvious they set an alarm so they could be sitting here when I walked in from work.

There's no getting out of this. They mean business, and that shower's gonna have to wait.

"Sit." Mama points to the ottoman on the other side of the room from her. She can obviously smell me.

"You sure I can't shower first?" I mumble, taking a seat on the worn-out leather.

"This is important, and you always shower for way too long. Then you'll want to crawl into bed, and this conversation won't happen."

I scrub a hand down my face as Peaches curls into a ball at my feet.

"Now, boy, we need to talk about this."

My insides pinch when Mama picks up a piece of card from the coffee table beside her. I squint my eyes, trying to figure out what it is... until I notice the QR code and sigh. My concert ticket.

"Dad found this on the floor, next to your trash can. Please tell us it just fell off your mirror." She waves it in the air, and I glance at Dad, wondering why he was in my room.

He raises his hand. "I was only putting laundry on the end of your bed."

"You guys don't have to do my laundry for me," I mutter.

"Oh, stop." Mama frowns. "He did a load for everyone, cleaned out all the baskets, so just say thank you."

I sigh. "Thanks, Pop."

He nods, then glances at the ticket and raises his eyebrows at me. "You weren't gonna throw that out, were ya?"

With a soft groan, I cover my face with my hand.

"He was," Mama says to Dad before turning on me. "Boy, what is wrong with you? This could be your chance to get her back. You have to go."

"She doesn't want me, Mama." I drop my hand to frown at her.

"That's not true. She said she wasn't ready."

I flick my hand in the air. "And what makes you think she's ready now?"

"I don't know, but you can't keep moping around here. You have to go and do something about it."

My eyebrows wrinkle as I release a sharp sigh and look to Dad for help. But he's siding with Mama on this one.

Shit.

"Your time off work has already been approved. You are going to this concert."

I open my mouth to protest, then internally kick myself. Shit! I totally forgot to speak to my boss about not needing the time off anymore. How the hell did I do that?

As soon as I got to work, I got busy and it slipped my mind. Shit!

"Look." Mama sighs. "You know I love you. And I know that I can't boss you around like I used to, but... Tyrell, you will regret it if you don't go. You have been miserable all summer, and I can't stand it! You keep smiling and trying to pretend that you're fine, but you're not. You're not happy, boy. And it's breaking your mama's heart."

"Mama, come on." I cringe, hating the way her eyes are starting to glass with tears. "Please, don't. I just..."

"Just what?" Dad asks after my words turn into yet another heavy sigh.

"I... I don't know."

"Son." Dad shuffles in his chair. "You can't keep going like this. You're breathing and you're going through the motions each day, but you've lost your spark. We can feel your constant tension and unrest. Now, we're assuming that it's just about Dani breaking up with you. But is there something we're missing here?"

Closing my eyes with a sigh, I figure that I've just been given the perfect opportunity and I have to fucking take it, because I may not get a better one.

"I can't stay in Dallas." I hold my breath and force myself to look between them.

Their expressions are both unreadable, dammit.

*Just keep going. Get it out.*

"I love you. All of you. So much. And I get that family loyalty is very important, and I really want to be there to support you all."

"But...," Mama prompts me.

"But..." I lick my lips and have to look down at the

carpet for this part. "I want to travel the world. I need to get out of here and explore and experience other cultures and see other places. It's this burning inside me that I can't extinguish." I tap my chest. "I've tried! I've tried to forget about it and want other things, but I always come back to this... this dream. This *need* to spread my wings and go."

My expression crumples as I dare to look up and see just how much I'm hurting them.

Dad's smile is sad, but he's smiling. And Mama's got a tear trickling down her cheek now. She swipes it away before moving forward to the very edge of her seat.

"You always did have an adventurous spirit."

Dad softly chuckles. "When you were a boy, you were obsessed with wanting to know what was out there. You used to talk about how you wanted to be Indiana Jones so you could go to ancient places and see the ruins."

"You've always gravitated toward anything outside of this place." Mama looks at Dad. "Maybe I didn't want to admit it, but I think I knew this day would come eventually." She sighs. "I can sense it in you. Flitting off for one summer ain't gonna cut it. Am I right?"

I wince and nod. "Yeah, Mama. I want to *live* overseas. I want to immerse myself."

"How will you make money?" Dad asks.

"Well, I'll need to save a bunch more before I leave, and then I'm hoping to get work. There's lots of jobs that I can do—waiting tables, working in ski lodges. There's probably some construction work I could pick up. They'll often hire people from overseas for short-term positions. I was thinking I'd travel until I needed to earn some money, then find a job for a few months, save up, and then move on to the next place."

Mama winces. "What about your degree? All that study? Was it for nothing?"

"No." I shake my head. "And I've still got this job lined up for the year ahead. I'll do that, learn what I can. I'll work hard. But I have to know that travel is on the horizon. And eventually, when I get it out of my system, I'll settle down, and that's when I can get that nine-to-five, you know? I'll become a project manager for some construction company and..." I huff, wishing that sounded more appealing.

Is Mama right? Was all that study for nothing?

"So you're just gonna roam the planet, working under the table?" Dad raises his eyebrows at me.

I rush to justify myself. "I won't do anything illegal. I'll make sure I'm working for honest people. They can pay me with food and board if they want to."

Dad flicks his hand through the air. "People do work off the books all the time. I'm not judging. I just want you to think this through."

Rubbing at my tired eyes, I shrug, not sure what to say. "I know this all sounds risky and unstable, but I'll make sure that I keep enough money aside to get home again. If things go bad, I'll always have that option."

Dad's lips twitch, and he turns to catch Mama's eye. "He's a good boy, Nina. He knows what he's doing."

"I know that. I *know* that, but it doesn't mean I won't miss him like crazy." She tuts and gets up from her chair, rushing across to me and wrapping her arms so tight around my neck, my eyes start to water.

"Mama, it's okay. I'm not leaving right now."

She lets out a laughing sob and lets me go, ignoring my stink and perching her butt on the ottoman. I shuffle along to make room for her, disturbing Peaches. She stretches before wandering down the hallway, her tail swishing.

Mama reaches for my hand, curling her fingers around mine and giving them a squeeze.

I glance at her before looking at Dad. "Are you sure you guys are okay with this? I thought you'd be really upset. That's why I haven't said anything."

"Why would we be upset?" Dad frowns.

"Because you... you need me. I mean... I know it's hard work looking after everybody, and I always feel like I have to stay close by in case—"

"We love having you around," Mama cuts me off. "But not to your detriment. Tyrell Jackson, we would never stand in the way of your dreams. We love you, boy." She almost looks wounded that I didn't already know this, so I wrap my arm around her, kissing the side of her head in quiet thanks.

Wow.

I mean... this is really gonna happen for me. I'm going to see the world!

*Why doesn't this feel more exciting?*

I sense Dad's eyes on me and force a smile. "Thanks for your support. Both of you. It means a lot."

"Of course." Dad's eyes narrow, and I dart my gaze back to the safety of the floor. "You thought she was going to go with you, didn't you? You had high hopes."

I sniff, eventually nodding. "Yeah."

"Aw, baby." Mama touches my cheek.

"I just wanted someone to share my experiences with, you know? I thought..." I swallow. "She was it. The one." I sniff again, my throat swelling until it's painful.

"Well, maybe you'll fall in love with a girl overseas." Mama pats my thigh, forcing a bright tone that none of us can buy into.

I throw her a pained frown, and her shoulders sag.

"I know, baby. She really caught your heart, didn't she?"

Clenching my jaw, I try to nod, but I can't seem to do anything.

Mama stands with a tut and walks to the coffee table. Snatching the ticket, she brings it back to me. "You have to go. You have to at least try, because what if she's ready?"

"What if she's not?"

"Then you go without her. But if you don't find out for sure where she stands, then you'll never be able to truly let it go."

"I'm guessing the second you see each other, you'll get a gut feeling." Dad nods, glancing at Mama with a tenderness that's so blatant it makes my heart squeeze. I want to look at my woman that way.

I want to look at *Dani* that way.

The fact that I can't stop thinking about her has to be a sign, right? I just can't seem to let her go.

Staring at the ticket in Mama's hand, I hesitate.

"You'll get closure or you'll win her back. Either way, you have to do this, boy." Mama's voice is borderline pleading.

*Do I really want to put myself through that?*

*What if she's moved on and I'm the fool who's been clinging to this unrequited love?*

*But what if she's hoping to see you there? What if she's ready for you?*

With my heart in my throat, I take the ticket from Mama and stare down at the QR code.

This is it.

My chance.

And I have to take it.

"You won't regret it, son," Dad assures me while Mama leans down and kisses the top of my head.

"Now go shower before I faint from exposure to toxic fumes."

"Hey, you were the one who had to do the talking now," I tease her.

She laughs, pushing my shoulder with a soft "Go on witcha. Get clean."

I stand and pause before leaving the room. Looking between my parents, I give them a heartfelt thank you. "Your support means the world to me. You know that, right?"

"You mean the world to us." Dad smiles at me.

"We're proud of you." Mama pats my cheek. "And I'm gonna miss you like crazy, but as long as you keep sending me photos and giving me updates, I will survive."

She starts singing that Gloria Gaynor song as she collects Dad's empty mug, then hers, before heading into the kitchen.

I share one last look with my father before nodding and heading to the bathroom.

I'm gonna survive too.

My heart kicks out of place as I glance down at the ticket in my hand.

It feels like a chance. A whisper of hope.

Damn, it feels like fucking everything right now.

# CHAPTER 52
## DANI

So, I drove up to Nolan this afternoon, sporting the jeans with the little rips and the top with the deep V-neck.

"And make sure you pair that with your black leather jacket. You know the one I love?" Tobin had instructed me.

When he spots me coming, he lets out a squealing cheer. "Yes, girl!" Running over, he picks me up, spinning me around and kissing my lips once before taking me in.

"You did everything I told you to. And your hair!" He makes me turn so he can get a decent look at the soft locs I got done. It took a few hours and cost a ton, but they should last me around six weeks, and I really love the new look. It makes me feel like a new woman, and I really needed to do something different after saying goodbye to Atlas.

Holding my cheeks, Tobin gives them a little pat and bats his eyes at me. "Daddy's so proud."

I laugh. "Thank you," I say, then reach up to hug Jed.

"How you doin', girl?" he softly asks when he releases me.

"Yeah, I'm great." I tug at the back of my jeans and look between them.

Their frowns are so skeptical that I have to blow out a huffing breath. "What? I am. I'm doing really well."

"You seem on edge." Tobin rubs my arm, sharing a concerned frown with Jed.

"What do you expect me to be?" I swallow and scratch the side of my nose. "I mean... is he here?"

*Please be here. Please be here!*

"Not yet." Jed glances around as if Tyrell might suddenly materialize.

I can't help following his gaze, my heart in my throat... until I see Nix skipping toward me with a bright smile.

"Hey, you." I laugh, pulling her into a hug. Oh my gosh, I had no idea how much I'd been missing her!

Squeezing her tight against me, I make her hug me for a few more seconds than she wants before letting go.

"How are you?" I smile at her, and she gives me a little smirk.

"I'm doing good." She throws a thumb over her shoulder. "In spite of having to live with this tree over here."

I glance up at the man standing behind her. He is tall and very handsome, his smile lopsided as he throws an arm around her shoulders.

"Don't listen to her. She's secretly in love with me. Can't get enough of climbing trees, this girl." He winks as Nix elbows him in the stomach, and he makes a big show of pretending that it hurts.

Nix rolls her eyes and introduces us in a droll tone. "My peeps, this is Darian, who should not be living at Basketball Base, but his dumb ass failed one of his papers last year, so he's been catching up in summer school. Meaning... that six-bedroom mansion I was supposed to be enjoying all to myself has been overcrowded."

Darian frowns and points to himself. "It's *my* place. And my sister never should have agreed to let you live there without discussing it with everyone first."

"None of you were supposed to be there!" she argues back, flinging her arms wide, and that's when I see it.

That spark. The way she's trying to fight a smile as she argues with this guy.

Wait. Darian. That name is familiar now that I think about it. Is he the one whose eyebrow she shaved off?

My lips part and I gape at her for a second, narrowing my eyes as I try to see if one of his eyebrows looks uneven.

They're both oblivious to me staring at them, too busy bickering with each other.

Tobin sidles up beside me, watching in bemused interest. "I think our fairy might have found herself a place to call home."

"You think?" I glance at them and wince. There's no way I'd want to be in a relationship like that, snipping at each other the whole time.

"Can't you feel the sexual tension?" He bulges his eyes at me.

Jed rounds my other side, getting in on the conversation. "Fairies do live in trees, you know."

"They're totally doing it," Tobin quips.

"You sure?" I cross my arms, still watching them and then having to bite my lips against a laugh when he takes her wrists, spinning her around and pulling her back against his torso. He leans down to whisper something in her ear, and she can't fight her grin.

"Oh yeah, they are definitely boinking," Jed agrees with his boyfriend, who gets the giggles.

"Boinking. Baby, I love you."

"I love you too." He reaches for Tobin's hand and pulls him close, and I remain on my own, trying not to notice how cold it is with nobody beside me.

My eyes scan the milling crowds around us, desperately seeking out the man I couldn't handle being with.

The thought of seeing him makes my stomach trill.

I wasn't ready two and a half months ago. That's why I walked away.

But I've had time.

Time to work on myself.

Time to let go of what happened to Atlas. To forgive myself for the part I played in it. To forgive *him* for what he allowed to happen to his body.

I'm feeling stronger and more secure than I ever have.

Yet this ache still beats inside me.

I'm whole on my own, but I'm not complete. And I'm pretty sure there's only one person who can fill that space. Or at least one person who I *want* to fill that space.

And he's not here.

"I don't know if he'll make it," Tobin warns me softly. "I really tried to get him here, but..." He shrugs. "Sorry, Dani Girl."

"That's okay." I shake my head and walk beside him toward the growing line waiting to get into the stadium.

"It was my choice to break up with him. He doesn't owe me anything."

Jed's arm comes around me, and he gives me a squeeze. "You're gonna be all right. You're strong. You're tough. You can handle anything."

I nod, forcing myself to agree with him.

# CHAPTER 53
## TYRELL

I'm fucking late.

I didn't mean to be. It was just one thing after another, from heavy traffic to an engine mishap and my stupid phone crapping out on me. It just went dead, and I have no idea why. I've tried charging it, banging it against my steering wheel, begging for it to come back on, but nope. It shut off and is being a total asshole about restarting.

I'll have to buy a new one at some point, which is pissing me off because I don't want to spend the money on it. Unless some tech genius can fix it for me. I'll try to stop somewhere on the way back tomorrow and see what I can do.

Fuck!

These are all the worst omens, reminding me that I shouldn't have come.

As I sat there in that garage with my knee bobbing while I waited for the mechanic to fix I don't know the fuck what, I could feel my chaotic insides breaking down. I nearly bailed after I saw the cost of the bill. Paying it with gritted teeth, I emptied a chunk out of my savings account and drove back toward the interstate.

I had a choice then: Turn back to Dallas or keep heading north to Nolan.

I don't know why, but I headed north, and I'm not sure if it was the right decision.

Ever since I decided to drive up here, I've been a stressed-out mess. Dani is consuming me at every turn. I'm going to be seeing her tonight. I think. If she came. I didn't have the guts to text and ask Tobin, and since my phone's not working, I have no idea if he's given me a heads-up.

Shit.

Picking up my pace, I jog across the stadium parking lot. I had to park like five blocks away. The streets are crowded for this thing; everyone in Nolan seems to be here.

The music is already blasting, the sound so familiar it makes my chest hurt.

Atlas used to play this kind of music.

Electric Reverence was one of his inspiration bands. It was just a small indie group back then, but he always raved about them. There was some connection there, but I can't remember what it was.

I should have remembered that when Tobin and Jed bought us the tickets, but I didn't. In fact, it didn't click until Lacey was looking them up and getting all jealous that I was going and not taking her with me.

"One of them used to live in Colorado Springs," she told me, lifting the screen and showing me an image.

I didn't recognize them, but something sparked. A memory clicked, and I pictured Atlas raving about this new indie band and their killer sound. Him and that bass player friend of his.

Rhett or something.

Shit, I can't remember his name.

All I know is that walking into this stadium with the flashing lights and thumping beat is taking me back in time.

Back to a grungy bedroom next door to my house and a teenage boy with big dreams. He'd sit on the edge of his mattress, strumming his guitar and talking about how we were going to travel the world. He was going to play on stages with thousands of fans screaming his name, singing along to his lyrics.

"It's gonna be epic." He grinned at me, strumming his guitar and playing some complicated riff with his agile fingers.

I believed him. Back then, I had no doubts he'd become a rock star. Back then, I didn't think he was capable of ending his life so recklessly.

But it happened, and now I'm standing in a crowd, watching some other guitarist play a complicated riff while the audience thunders and cheers.

Tobin and Jed bought us tickets in the area right in front of the stage. I could muscle my way through there, but it's already so crowded, so I linger at the back, wondering if Dani's down there with them. Wondering what I'll say to her if she is.

Wondering...

Wondering...

Wondering...

"Tyrell!" someone shouts, and I turn to my right, grinning when I spot a familiar mop of messy blond hair.

"Hey." I grin, giving Carson a quick bro hug before smiling at Nylah. "I didn't know you guys were gonna be here."

"We managed to snag some tickets last week." She's all triumphant. "Had to pay premium, but... worth it!" She points to the stage, raising her arms and dancing.

I share a quick smile with Carson before he steps up behind her and starts moving his body in time with hers. Wrapping his arm around her waist, they get lost in the music, and I sway beside them, unable to stand still.

The beat is pretty addictive.

"Hey, Tyrell!" Blake jumps up beside me, kissing my cheek and grinning.

"You guys too?" I spin and pull both her and Grady into a hug. Damn, I've missed these guys.

"Nice to see you, man!" Grady pats my back, yelling above the music. "I didn't know if you were coming."

"Yeah, I left it to the last minute to decide, and then it's been a shit show getting here, but..." I spread my arms wide. "I'm here."

"How long are you staying for?" Blake asks.

"Just the night."

"Boo!" She frowns while Grady shakes his head.

"Bullshit, man. You gotta spend a few nights. There's still some space at Football Frat; the last two guys don't move in for another week yet. You can have your old room back."

"Really? It's still free?"

"Yeah, Lincoln doesn't get back from his summer break until after next weekend. You can have his room— your old room—until then."

"Wait, did you just say Lincoln?" My eyebrows bunch.

"How the hell did you pull that off? Is Carson moving out or something?"

Grady laughs and yells above the music, "We've had to instate a *No Fleischer* rule. Every guy in the house had to sign an agreement and everything." He rolls his eyes while I tip my head back with a laugh.

"So, you'll stay?" Blake beams up at me.

"Yeah. Why not?"

"Yay!" She raises her hands in the air, then jumps across to Nylah.

"Thanks for the invite." I lift my chin at Grady.

"Anytime, man. You'll always have a place with us."

The idea of being back at Football Frat feels like home.

And I've missed home.

My insides kick with pleasure, the angst at possibly seeing Dani starting to fade as I focus on my friends and having a good time with them.

Guess she's not the only reason I couldn't resist coming back.

I've got family here too. They may not be blood, but they're mine, and I didn't realize how much I was missing them until right now.

# CHAPTER 54
## DANI

The concert was amazing, and as the rest of the crowd disperses, we line up to enter the after-party. I still haven't seen Tyrell, and I can't admit to anyone how much that's killing me.

He didn't come.

He obviously didn't want to see me, and I hate that I hurt him enough to scare him off for good.

*So just text him! Find out how he's doing.*

On impulse, I pull my phone free and just do it, sending him a message before I chicken out.

*Me: Missed you tonight. Was hoping to see you at the concert. I've been thinking about you a lot lately. Maybe we can catch up sometime. Hope you're doing okay.*

I bite my lip, reading it back and wondering if I should press Send. It feels like an explosive text, each of those words potentially tearing a hole right through my defenses.

Do I really want to say that to him?

*Yes! Press Send!*

"Dani, let's go." Tobin grabs my wrist, pulling me forward, and my thumb bumps the send button, the message going through.

I watch the box appear on my screen, holding my breath and toying with the idea of deleting it, but Tobin's pulling me into this after-party and *ugh*!

Slipping the phone into the back pocket of my jeans, I let that message linger in the sphere or wherever the hell it goes. It'll be on Tyrell's screen by now. He's probably read it already.

And great, now I'm going to spend the rest of the night obsessing over whether or not he'll text me back.

Shit, I shouldn't have sent it.

I'm about to pull out my phone and delete the message, but Tobin won't let me.

"Get off your phone and be in the moment, please," he singsongs, introducing me to some hot guy in leather pants with a neck tattoo.

I force polite conversation while Jed and Tobin gush to the woman beside him about how much they loved the concert.

It's painful and awkward, and when I spot Nix and Darian moving farther into the room, I take off after them.

They veer left, and I'm about to follow when I end up bumping into Reef.

Oh great.

"Hey... again." I stutter to a stop, my tone far from enthusiastic as I give him an awkward smile. "Uh... nice job tonight."

"Yeah, thanks." His eyes are kind of glazed; he obviously lit up just before entering the party. Although maybe it's not just weed. There's a dangerous energy coming off him, a vacant, lax smile... and the way his eyes trail down my body is making me squirm.

Who knows what the hell he'll say in his current condition? I'm pretty sure he was as close to sober as he could get when I bumped into him that other day and he made it clear that I let Atlas down.

I don't want to know what his high brain thinks about it.

I shift away from him, searching the room for my friends, and end up bumping into another band member. The drummer. His hair is still wet from the exertion on stage, and yep, he stinks.

"Hey." He grins down at me, looking just as wasted as Reef. "Who's this?"

"This..." Reef rests a hand on my shoulder. "This is the girl who used to go out with Atlas. Do you remember that guy? He was like the best guitarist I knew." His words are slurred and offbeat.

"No fucking way!" The drummer gives me a dopey smile. "You're Atlas's girl?"

"Well... I... I was." Past tense. It always used to be so brutal that I'd keep it in the present. *"Yes, I am Atlas's girl."* It didn't matter that he was dead. I was his, always and forever.

But I just said *was.*

And it didn't hurt.

Because I *have* finally let him go.

I was Atlas's girl, but he's dead, and I don't belong to anyone.

I'm my own person. A woman who wants a man but doesn't need one.

*I want Tyrell.*

The reminder is a soft whisper, and I turn to look for him, one last desperate bid to see if he actually made it tonight.

But I don't see him.

With a swallow, I resist the urge to check my phone. It hasn't buzzed or anything, so he's either not seen it, or he's ignoring it.

"Yeah, this one here, she..." Reef's scoffing laugh gives me chills. "She got all shitty with Atlas the night he died."

My head pings back. "What are you doing?"

"She told him to go to hell," Reef keeps talking, pointing an accusing thumb my way. "And then took off and just left him there, all brokenhearted."

I gape at him while the drummer beside him lets out this awkward laugh.

Reef narrows his eyes at me. "He should be alive."

"Yes." I nod. "He should. But then he took those pills."

"Because he was upset!" Reef growls. "And he wouldn't have been that way if you'd stayed."

I shake my head, drawing on my therapy sessions and scrambling to find that calm she told me look for. The place where I could logically and unemotionally assess the events of that night.

"He was upset anyway," I reply in a small voice. "And this is not the time or place for this conversation."

"I think it feels pretty fucking familiar, don't you? You gonna yell at me too, make me feel so shitty that I need to get me a little something to take the edge off?"

I grit my teeth.

"I didn't know how else to help him." Reef shakes his head, looking at the drummer like he'll get it. "He was gonna lose his shit, man. I had to give him something."

"What?" The word comes out of me as a soft whisper, my heart slamming into my rib cage as his confession registers with brutal clarity. "What did you do?"

Reef turns to me with an accusing glare. "I helped him out, because you left."

"You helped him out?" I repeat, an explosion of rage firing through me. "You mean gave him those pills!"

"Hey." He raises his hands like I'm being the unreasonable one. "He needed to chill out. Find his Zen. You riled him up pretty bad, and I didn't know what to do."

"You... you killed him," I rasp.

"Fuck off." He shoves my shoulder. "No, I didn't. You did! You should have been there."

"You *were* there," I snarl. "And you're telling me you gave him the pills that ended his life! You asshole!"

"We don't know that's what it was. He'd had a lot that night."

"Those pushed him over the edge!" An anger so hot and evasive I don't know what to do with it fires through me and I lunge, my hands shooting out like rockets as I shove this stoner with all the force I can muster.

He stumbles back a step, growling at me when I pounce forward with my fists.

"You were his friend!" I scream at him, pounding his chest. "He looked up to you!"

He grunts, shoving me away, then rounding on me with a punch I didn't see coming. His knuckles connect with my cheek, and I let out a shocked gasp as my head snaps sideways.

# CHAPTER 55
## TYRELL

I've finally made it into the party.

It took about fifteen minutes of sweet-talking the bouncer to get my Football Frat buddies in with me, but he finally relented when Grady offered to get him tickets to the opening game of the season.

They exchanged numbers, and Grady will deliver.

"Nice work." Nylah grins at him. "I'll get Dad to hook those up for ya. Now..." She looks around the party. "Let's go have some more fun."

Carson's lips quirk into a smile as he wraps his arm around her waist and pulls her forward.

I spot Jed and Tobin within seconds, and my heart kicks out of place.

Is Dani here?

Did she make it?

I should go say hello to her old roommates—they can probably tell me exactly where she is—but they're so wrapped up in conversation that I decide to bypass them and head farther into the fray.

And that's when I see it.

There's a movement of bodies, a gasping, rushed steps backward as people get out of the way.

I frown, stepping forward to investigate.

And everything turns into slow motion.

I spot the side of Dani's face and have enough time to register that her hair has changed. It looks amazing! And then I see the fierce expression on her face, the way she lunges forward with her fists and starts attacking the guy with the long, straggly hair.

Why does he look familiar?

A breath catches in my throat, then turns into a thundering growl when the guy shoves her back, then fires his fucking fist into her face!

For a second, I can't make myself believe it.

But the way her head snaps back sends a red haze splashing across my vision, and I can't stop the roar busting out of me.

"Get away from her!" I push people aside in my bid to reach her.

I am so fucking enraged right now that I can't even see straight. This white noise is buzzing in my ears, and the second I'm within reach, I snatch the guy's fist before he lands a fresh one on her.

"Get the fuck away from her," I shout, shoving him backward.

I've got a good five inches on the guy, not to mention a fair few pounds of muscle—seething, ready-to-break-something muscle. When he goes to stumble away from me, I pull him back, landing my elbow in his face so he knows what it feels like.

His head lolls to the side, this garbled laugh coming out of him as blood coats the edge of his mouth.

I can't believe he fucking hit her.

What the hell went down between them to cause this?

I'm not even sure I want to know, but I want to finish him for hurting her.

"You little fucker!" I fist his jacket.

"Tyrell!" someone barks behind me.

It's Grady, forever the voice of reason.

I spin back to glare at him, but my eyes catch Dani, swaying on her feet. Blake's beside her, trying to get a look at her face, and I immediately release the asshole to make sure she's okay.

"Hey." I bend down to try and check her cheek. "You all right?"

"Yeah." She nods but is obviously really shaken up.

"You're bleeding." My chest spasms with a mixture of worry and rage as I lightly brush my thumb below the cut he left on her cheekbone. He must be wearing a ring. That fucker!

Turning back with another snarl, I'm about to go after the guy again, but he's now in the clutches of Grady and Carson, who are dragging him away for a "chat." I have no idea how that's gonna go down, but I trust them to get to the bottom of it.

"Let me go!" he's shouting as security muscles their way through the crowd.

"Step aside, please!"

"Excuse me," the other one barks. "Let us through."

"She attacked me first!" The guy tries to wrestle free of Grady's and Carson's hold on him, but they're not giving an inch.

They are just as pissed as I am.

"I attacked you because you're an asshole!" Dani moves around me to point at the guy. "He was too wasted to know what he was doing. You should have protected him!"

"You should have been there!" he argues right back, and my insides run cold.

Are they talking about Atlas?

"You gave him the drugs that killed him! That's not on me." Her voice breaks. "And it's something you'll have to live with for the rest of your life!"

Fuck. They *are* talking about Atlas.

Who the hell is this guy?

Oh shit. I do recognize him. He was in Atlas's band. He was the bass player tonight!

He growls at Dani, his eyes glazing with something dark and dangerous. I move to form a barrier between him and her, staring at him with my own dark look.

My fingers curl into fists, and I swear if security wasn't here, I would be pummeling the living shit out of this guy.

He gave Atlas those pills, and he's accusing Dani of not being there for him?

I should fucking end this guy right now.

"We've got this," Grady warns me, his look one of calm control as he subtly raises his chin and silently tells me to focus on Dani.

Before I lose the thread of self-control I have left, I spin and wrap my arm around her, bundling her out of the room just as Jed and Tobin run into view.

"Oh my—" Tobin gasps. "What happened?"

"I'm okay." Dani snuggles into my side, looking anything but.

"She needs to get checked out," I tell them. "I'm gonna take her to the hospital."

"The police are on their way," someone informs me. "An ambulance too. We'll let the paramedics have a look at her and assess the situation."

"Okay." I nod. "Is there someplace we can wait for them?"

"Yeah, of course." The woman ushers us into a side room, and Tobin, Jed, Nix, and some tall guy who I think is on the Nolan U basketball team follow us in there, quickly gathering around Dani and softly demanding details.

I want them too, but I'm not about to force them out of her.

Helping her into a chair, I take a seat beside her, silently warning the others to back off and give her some space.

The tall guy—Dar-something. Darius? Darian... Darian Gomez, I think—backs off, finding a spot against the wall.

Nix completely ignores me, pulling her chair closer so she can sit opposite Dani. Tobin and Jed do the same.

With a soft sigh, Dani rests her head against my arm like it's the most natural thing in the world to do.

I go still, not wanting to move an inch in case she suddenly becomes aware of what she's doing.

With a soft sniff, she shakily shares her story, reminding me all about Reef and the influence he had over Atlas.

He and my boy became tight after I moved to Nolan

U, but I had no idea what a terrible influence he was having on Atlas. I thought it was the other way around, and I hate myself for going there.

When she gets to the part about him accusing her of breaking Atlas's heart, I want to get up and thump him all over again.

"What a fucking assbucket," Tobin spits.

"I want to maim that guy." Jed shakes his head, sharing a raging look with me.

Oh, what I wouldn't give to walk back into that party with him and pummel the shit out of Reef the Stoner. We could take turns, one punch each until he's out cold and bleeding.

I'm not usually a violent guy, but I will make an exception for any man who punches a woman in the face.

I can't believe he fucking tried to make her responsible for Atlas's death when he was the one who *gave him* the pills that night.

How did the police not follow that up?

It was an obvious OD, and rather than thinking foul play, they just put it down to a reckless rock star not taking care of himself, downing dirty pills that were laced with fentanyl.

Did Reef know they were bad?

Fuck. Either way, Reef never should have given anything to Atlas. Is there any way he could get charged for that?

Surely there has to be some consequences for his actions.

The woman pops her head into the room. "The police are here. I'm sending the paramedics your way in just a second."

"Thank you." Tobin raises his hand at her while Dani squirms beside me.

She's already spent after telling us the stor,y and now she's gonna have to do it again.

Shit. I wish I could protect her from that.

But all I can do right now is be the guy she's leaning against. And like hell anyone is gonna stop me from doing that.

# CHAPTER 56
## DANI

I have to suffer through my story a second time, but the police officer interviewing me is really nice. She has a calm, quiet voice, and her partner is an old guy with gray hair and grandpa vibes. They're both very kind and compassionate, and they're not going to charge me for attacking Reef. Thank God. But they have taken him to the station for questioning.

Hopefully the truth will come out, and he'll get some kind of consequence for giving Atlas those pills that night. There has to be some kind of charge for that, right?

He aided Atlas in his overdose. Surely he'll get time for that.

"Unfortunately," the officer sighs, looking at Tyrell, who just asked the very question I was thinking, "I wouldn't hold my breath. It's been a long time since your friend OD'd, and it will be very hard to prove that those pills were the final tipping point. I don't think there'll be enough submissible evidence."

"So he just gets away with it?" Tyrell spits.

The officer gives him a pained frown, and I shake my head, hating that life can be so fucking unfair sometimes.

I can sense Tyrell wants to argue this further, but I grip his shirt, giving it a little tug and shaking my head. It's over. Atlas is gone, and nothing will change that.

He huffs and scowls at the officer. "Can you at least check that he's not carrying any dangerous drugs on him? Maybe he can get busted for possession or something. And you can charge him for assault while you're at it. Look at her cheek." He points at me.

The officer nods. "We will be looking into all of that, I assure you."

The paramedics arrive, and the officers leave them to it. The one who tends my cheek and makes me look into this flashlight thing a few times before finally relenting is nice. He's worried about a concussion, but in the end decides it's mild and hands me two Advil. I down them and hope the effects kick in soon. Nevertheless, he tells everyone around me what to look for over the next few days.

If my headache gets any worse or I start feeling dizzy or nauseous, they have to take me to the hospital. Everyone promises they'll do exactly that, although I won't be with any of these people in the next day or two.

Tobin and Jed are flying back to New York tomorrow, I think, and even though Nix has offered to let me stay the night at Darian's place so I don't have to drive back to Colorado Springs tonight, I'm still hesitating.

Because the only person I want to be with right now is sitting beside me.

"What do you want to do?" Tyrell softly asks, his voice

a husky mumble while everyone else starts discussing my plans for the night.

"I want to get out of here," I whisper back, then shift my head to look up at him. "Can you take me... somewhere? Anywhere."

He nods, his brown gaze a gentle caress. "Where are you staying tonight?"

"I was planning on driving back to Colorado Springs." I wince.

"Maybe you should take Nix up on her offer?"

"Yeah." I purse my lips. "Maybe."

His lips curl into a soft smile. "Come on." He gives me a gentle nudge with his arm. "Let's at least get out of this place, and I can drop you to her house later."

"Okay." A spark of hope skips through me when he rises from his seat, then reaches down to offer me his hand.

I take it, because there is seriously nothing else I want to do right now.

As I rise from my spot on the couch, Tobin catches my eyes, his lips twitching into a grin as he flicks his fingers, ushering us away before anyone else notices.

Within seconds, I get a flurry of texts.

*Jed: Tell him you love him.*

*Nix: You better kiss that boy before the end of the night. Do you want me to wait up for you?*

. . .

*Tobs: I need deets, but they must include - we're back together!*

The only one I respond to is Nix, because she asked me an actual question.

*Me: No. You take care of you. I'll let you know how the rest of my night pans out and if I need a place to crash.*

*Nix: Fingers crossed it'll be in his bed!*

I wince, the thought making my stomach spasm. I'm a ball of nerves as I amble beside Tyrell. I don't know where his car is, but I follow him without thought because it's Tyrell and I trust this man.

"You sure you're okay?" he asks me when we turn down another road. The streetlights illuminate our way, casting long shadows on the sidewalk.

I shake my head but answer, "I'm okay."

"You don't have to be brave for me, you know. You can be whatever the fuck you want. You can cry or scream or yell or... not say a damn thing. Whatever you need."

I smile at that, loving the complete absence of pressure. I can be what I want, and he'll accept it.

Just like he always does. So accepting. So respectful.

Brushing the back of my finger down his hand as it swings past me, I softly check, "How are you feeling?"

A breath snorts out his nose, his voice gravelly and gruff when he replies, "I'm raging. Trying not to be a dick about it, but..." He growls. "I want to break that fucker's fingers!"

"No. You're not allowed to do that."

"Yeah, yeah, I know. I'll get arrested."

I snatch his hand, pulling him to a stop so he can turn and look at me. Gazing up at him, I touch his face with a smile. "No, I mean, you can hold him down and *I'll* break his fingers."

He snickers, his smile blooming as he cups my cheeks. "You're so tough."

"Not really." I sigh, flinching just a little when he brushes his thumb across my aching cheek.

"Sorry," he mumbles, letting me go and taking a step away from me.

I immediately feel bereft and desperately want to reach for his hand again. Instead, I thread my fingers together and softly confess, "I'm not okay either." I close my eyes, shaking my head and trying to word this perfectly. "I mean, I'm okay. I'm coping with life, and I feel much more secure and calm than I did... back when..." My voice trails off, and I give him a pained frown.

He nods, tucking his hands into his pockets and looking to the ground with a sad smile.

"But I miss you," I rasp, then let out a watery laugh. "I keep trying to convince myself that being single is the way to go, but then something will happen and all I can think about is telling you. Texting you or sharing it with you."

His eyes round just a little, like he wasn't expecting me to say this.

"And I should have." I nod. "I did this epic road trip to

New York, you know? To visit Jed and Tobs, and it was great. I had a good time." My nose starts to tingle. "And I would have had a much *better* time if you'd been there with me. We could have blasted Whitney on the freeway. Sung until our voices were hoarse."

The right side of his mouth curls up, then grows into that full smile I love so much. "I would have taken the back roads. More time with you."

My breath catches and I reach for his hand, playing with his long, strong fingers. "I've been so afraid."

"Of what?" He takes one of my locs between his fingers, spinning it back and forth.

"Of being in love with you."

He goes still, and I dare to check his expression. His lips are slightly parted, his eyes all wide and... hopeful?

"Would that be so bad?" he whispers.

"Yes."

"Why?"

"Because I could lose you. And the thought of having to get over you or live without you was all just... too much."

"You're already living without me." He lets my hair go so he can cup my cheek. "And I want to stop missing you too. I want to stop mapping out this life for myself that has this big hole in it, because you're not there."

I know that feeling. Oh shit, I know that feeling so well.

"Let's just be together." He leans down, catching my gaze and practically begging me, "Please, baby. Just be with me."

"But what if—"

"No what-ifs," he cuts me off. "We can't do that to

ourselves. We have to live in the what *is*. And what is..." His voice trails off as a smile curls his lips again, his eyes lighting with this affection that is just so damn sweet. "What is... is that I love you. And I want to spend my time with you. I want to text you when I see something funny, and I want to call you just so I can hear your voice."

My insides bloom with this warmth that's so addictive, I'm not sure I ever want to move from this spot. Stepping right up against him, I wrap my arms around his neck and rise to the tips of my toes. "I want to kiss you when I see you." I brush my fingers across the back of his neck. "And I want your arm around me when I'm watching a movie on the couch. I want to thread my fingers between yours when I'm walking down the street."

"I want to travel the world with you. See every sight and sound and culture. I want to experience all of that. With you."

My smile grows a mile wide as I whisper, "Me too," then pull his head down so he can kiss me.

# CHAPTER 57
## TYRELL

I don't know how long we stand on that street, but the second her tongue brushed against mine, I was lost to her.

It's not until we get a honking car and a few friendly catcalls pulling us apart that I finally come to.

Dani rests her forehead against my chest, hiding her embarrassment with a soft giggle.

"Want to get out of here?" I rub my hand down her back, talking against the side of her head.

"Yes." She squeezes my waist, and I take her hand, pulling her to my SUV with hurried steps.

Grady and Carson said I could stay at Football Frat, so that's what I'm doing.

I hope someone's home, because I don't want to have to rummage around out back, looking for the fake rock that has the spare key in it.

Driving probably a touch too fast, I arrive at Football Frat within eight minutes and pull up to the curb.

Lights are on in the living room, and Dani winces at the house.

"Is there room for you..." She glances up at me with hooded eyes. "I mean... for us?"

My only response is a wolfish grin.

Yes. I am so ready for an *us*!

Jumping out of the car, I run around in time to close the door for her, then snatch her hand and pull her up the front path.

This bubbling sensation is brewing in my belly as I try to wrap my head around this awesome, amazing thing.

Dani wants to be with me.

She wants to take this risk with me.

She wants to live with *what is* with me!

"Come on, come on," I urge her up the stairs and she starts to laugh.

"Boy, you're acting like an excited puppy."

"I'm an excited hound dog." I turn to wiggle my eyebrows at her, and she snorts, laughing into her hand.

"Who says you're getting laid right now?" she teases, and I pause on the front step, my hand on the doorknob as I slowly look down to check if she's serious.

Her expression is impossible to read, so I tell my eager dick to chill the fuck out and go for casual.

"We don't..." I shake my head, forcing the words out. "We don't have to have sex. I'm just looking forward to hanging with you. Whatever that looks like."

She grins at me, rising up to kiss my lips. "You're a good man, Tyrell Jackson."

Turning the doorknob, she walks inside, and I sag

with disappointment. Fuck. I really thought we were gonna get busy. I've been craving her for weeks.

But it's not just about sex, right?

I love all of her, whether we're doing it or not.

I just want to be with her, and sitting around or even just falling asleep beside her will be good too.

"Oh, hey, you guys!" Blake pops up off the couch, her face alight with excitement when she sees me standing right behind Dani.

I settle my hands on Dani's shoulders and acknowledge Nylah, Carson, Blake, and Grady. "Hey. You all good?"

"Yeah, we only got home a few minutes ago. Thought we'd watch a movie to unwind." Grady points at the TV.

"You want to join us?" Nylah asks.

My stomach clenches, but I keep my mouth shut, letting Dani make the decision.

"Sorry, we're kind of busy." Dani points back at me with her thumb.

Nylah narrows her eyes at us. "Doing what?"

"Having all the sex," Dani sings, snatching my hand and dragging me up the stairs while my friends holler and whoop behind me.

Blake's laughing her ass off, flopping into Grady's lap while Nylah cheers us on.

I cringe, letting Dani pull me up the stairs, but catching her around the waist as soon as we reach the landing. Lifting her off her feet, I enjoy her squeal as I run down to my old room.

The bed's not even made, just a blanket covering the mattress, and we tumble onto that thing, rolling from one side to the other as we make out, our kisses frantic with passion.

I suck her neck, then work my way back to her lips, my hands gliding all over her, my fingers itching for her smooth skin.

She's the first to wiggle her fingers under my shirt, and I follow suit, feeling her up over her silky bra.

Her tongue continues to destroy mine, only taking short breaks to lift my shirt over my head. Then she wriggles off her jacket and the shimmery thing she's got on underneath.

I groan, pressing my nose between her breasts, then kissing a line up to the base of her chin.

She rolls sideways so I can unhook her bra, then scrapes her fingers over my scalp as I kiss and suck her nipples until they're puckered and slippery.

"Mmmmmm," she moans, bucking her hips against mine, making it blatantly obvious that she's been as dry as I have these last few months.

I haven't even looked at another girl, because she's it. The only one who's been able to ignite my heart. And I'm having her. Enjoying every inch of her.

"Yes, yes," she pants as I move to unbutton her jeans. She brushes my fumbling fingers aside, helping me out and stripping off her pants.

I do the same, kicking the fabric off my ankles. My belt buckle hits the floor with a thud, and I roll my naked ass back to face her.

She grins down at my dick, wrapping her fingers around it with a playful smile. "Hey, buddy. I really missed you too."

I grin. "He's been pining for you, baby."

Brushing her locs over her shoulder, I kiss the skin I've just exposed, hissing with desire when she squeezes my head.

"Really pining," I choke out, enjoying her rumbling laughter as she flops onto her back and pulls me on top of her.

As much as I want to plunge right into her, I take my sweet time, working her body into a messy frenzy with my tongue and fingers. She comes with glorious wails, her body jerking, her legs snapping together as she writhes on the bed.

She's all things wet and slippery by the time I make it back up her body and I start nudging my dick against her opening. It's one hungry MOFO and wants in.

"Got any... pro... tec... tion?" She gasps out the words, still flying high off the orgasm I just sent ripping through her body.

"I fucking better," I growl, lurching off my bed and checking my wallet.

Oh, thank fuck!

I kiss the condom packet before peeling it open and wrapping myself. I can't wait for the day when I don't need one of these things, but for now...

Crawling back up the bed, I nestle myself between her thighs, carefully lining us up before slowly easing into her.

She takes me one inch at a time, her head tipping back, her mouth popping open as I fill her. I check that she's good before starting to slowly move in and out of her. I can't take my eyes off her face.

She has such a beautiful face, and when her eyes pop

open and she catches me gazing at her, she stills beneath me.

Touching my face, she rubs her thumb across the bottom of my chin and smiles at me. "I love you."

My heart skips a beat. I stop moving, my hips pressing her into the mattress as I turn my head to kiss her palm.

"I love you too." My voice is thick with emotion.

Her smile grows a little wider, practically glowing as she basks in my adoration.

Because I do.

I adore this woman.

My woman.

My Dani Girl.

**ONE YEAR LATER...**

# CHAPTER 58

## DANI

Tyrell and I have been solid for a year now.

One full year!

And now we're sitting at the airport, surrounded by our friends and waiting to board a flight to London. We've decided to start our journey in the UK, and we'll see where life takes us from there. We've been saving our asses off for the last year, both working full-time in Dallas and squirreling away as many pennies as we can. We both took on second jobs, so we've been working constantly, but it's been worth it.

Our budget is going to be tight, but thanks to Tyrell's parents, who let us live in their house for free, and a bunch of family handouts on both sides, we're leaving with a fair chunk of savings and will make this adventure last for as long as we possibly can. We've mapped out a potential route, but we're not setting anything in stone.

We're living in the now.

In the *what is*.

And it's working great for us.

I check the flight board, then my phone, biting my lips together and giggling at the jittery anticipation jumping in my stomach.

We're going to have to go through security soon, but we're making this farewell with our friends last for as long as possible. Jed and Tobin have already caught their flight back to New York. Tobin cried, and I had to fight my tears as we hugged it out in the domestic terminal.

"Stay in touch, okay?" I patted his back.

"I'm expecting regular posts and texts." He sniffled while Jed drew me into a hug.

"Proud of you," he murmured against my ear before shaking Tyrell's hand.

Nix and Darian took off after that goodbye, and now we're down to the Football Frat crew, who all wanted to stay until the bitter end.

By the time this is over, I will be done with goodbyes, that's for sure.

We said goodbye to my family last month when we stayed with them for a long weekend, then said goodbye to Tyrell's family a few days ago before flying to Denver and meeting up with the entire Football Frat clan, plus my old roomies, in Nolan. It was the best reunion...

I look around at them all, marveling at the changes that have happened in this short year.

Jed and Tobin got married at the beginning of the summer. Tyrell and I attended their flash New York wedding. It was such a swanky affair... and I loved every second of it. Jed's uncle funded the event, and Tobin took advantage of his very kind offer. He really has a flair for big events like that, and I felt like a first-class lady step-ping into the expensive hotel for a rooftop ceremony. The view was stunning. But all I could really focus on was the loved-up looks on my friends' faces.

When Jed said, "I do," Tobin's eyes glassed with tears, and he totally lost it when he was trying to say his vows. Jed squeezed his hand, his expression glowing when he whispered, "You can do it, baby. I love you."

"And I love you," Tobin blubbered. "I never thought I could get so lucky to meet such an amazing man."

I leaned my head against Tyrell's shoulder, thinking exactly the same thing.

I am the luckiest lady alive.

Although, I'm pretty sure Satch would argue that point. Wily proposed to her at Christmas, and she's now sporting this whopping great diamond, which is seriously jaw-dropping. They're not getting married until after she graduates, which is still one more year away, but I can imagine it will be a huge event. The media has been all over it. People love a feel-good story, and the rise of Wily Wilson in the NFL has been a thing of beauty. He worked his ass off last year and is all set to start next season. He's pumped, and I'm happy for him. And Satch has been coping with the publicity really well, as far as I'm aware. Wily's a king in front of the camera, all smiles and flirty banter. Satch stands with the other football wives in the team suite, blushing every time a camera swings her way. You can tell she's nervous, but then she'll spot Wily waving at her and her face will light up. People love, love, *love* their cute vibe.

My eyes dart to Blake, who's sitting beside her brother. She's on Grady's knee, her leg swinging back and forth as she looks at something on her phone. Grady's talking to her, pointing at the screen and grinning. She laughs, curling into him before reaching up to press a kiss to his jawline. He just graduated from Nolan U, and I'm pretty sure he's about to start an internship at some environmental place. I can't remember, but it's got to do with saving trees or forests or something. Blake's still got three years left at college, and they've found a little apartment together. I'm pretty sure Grady's job is mostly online with site visits scattered throughout, so he'll probably be away a lot, but at least he gets to come home to her after each trip.

"No!" Zoey puts her hands on her hips, then wags her little finger up at her father, who's giving her a very dry, unimpressed frown.

Leaning forward, he takes her little hand and replies, "Yes, lil' bug, you will, because if you're really that hungry, you'll eat the snack food Mommy made for you."

Zoey's expression buckles. "But chocolate," she whines, pointing to the shop just next to the chairs we're waiting in.

"But carrot sticks," Zander replies, forcing enthusiasm as he pulls them out of Zoey's bright pink backpack.

She huffs, scowling at her father before turning around to eye up the rest of the group. Her gaze lands on Wily, who's fighting a grin... and she starts to move toward him.

"Don't you dare," Zander warns him. "If you buy her chocolate, I will end you, man. I am not kidding."

I bite my lips together, sharing a quick look with Tyrell as we fight our laughter.

Poor Zander is exhausted. I'm guessing having six-month-old twins will do that to you. Cole and Logan were born right at the end of Zander's first season with the LA

Chargers. They arrived a month earlier than expected, and he nearly missed the birth but managed to fly home in the nick of time.

Since then, it's been a whirlwind of diaper changes and late-night feedings, plus looking after a precocious Zoey, who's getting more ballsy by the day. Seriously, that girl has got herself personality to spare, and as she puts on her best smile and swans toward Uncle Wily, you can see it in full effect.

"Come on, man," Wily whines. "Look at those baby blues. How am I supposed to—"

"Find a way," Zander growls.

Carson stands up with a snicker, snatching Zoey into his arms and walking away with her before Wily can fold like a deck of cards. She yells out a few protests until he says something quietly in her ear, and then she giggles.

Leaning back with a sigh, Wily blows out a breath and shakes his head. "That was close."

Zander ignores him, eyeing up Carson with a suspicious glare.

"Don't worry." Nylah touches his shoulder. "He's just taking her over to the mechanical helicopter thing."

Closing his eyes with a relieved sigh, Zander nods. "Okay. Thanks." He looks around the group. "She's been going crazy for sugar the last few months. And with us so distracted by the twins, she's getting away with everything. We're trying to rein her in." Scrubbing a hand over his forehead, he leans forward with a big yawn.

"When does she start kindergarten?" I ask.

"Not for another year, but she'll be going to preschool four days a week as soon as the summer's over, so that'll be good. She's so ready for more days."

"How's Sienna doing?" Nylah settles down beside him, rubbing his back like a mother hen.

"Yeah, she's amazing. Such a good mom." He glances across at us. "Sorry she couldn't make it. We had a really shitty night. Cole just wouldn't settle, and then he woke up Logan. We finally managed to get them both down around four, and Zoey was up, bright and bouncy, at six."

"Ouch," Satch softly whispers, wincing and giving Wily a worried frown.

"It's going to be okay, baby." He brushes his lips across her forehead, and she gives him a doubtful look.

I perk up in my chair and point at her. "Are you...?"

She presses her finger to her lips, cringing and giving away the fact that yes, she's pregnant, and no, this was seriously not planned.

She still has her senior year to get through.

"I know," she mouths at my pained frown, shaking her head but then fighting a smile.

Oh my gosh.

I rise to my feet, quickly scuttling across to her and crouching down by her chair so we can have a whispered conversation.

"How far along are you?"

She leans into me, keeping her voice as low as possible. "Only six weeks, so we don't want to say anything yet."

"What are you going to do about school?"

"I'm going to do as much as I can. I've already scheduled a meeting with an academic adviser so we can figure out the best way forward. I seriously never expected this to happen. I thought we were being so careful."

Resting my hand over hers, I give her a reassuring

smile. "You're going to be great, and Wily will be such a good dad. I'm really happy for you guys."

She grins. "I hope I can do this."

"You totally can. You're amazing."

Her teeth sink into her bottom lip. "My parents said they'll move to Arizona for a few months to help out after the birth, so that'll be cool."

"At least the baby's due after the football season."

"Yeah." Satch blows out a breath. "And about two months before finals."

"You'll get through. Especially if your parents are around to help. You're super smart. You've got this."

"Thanks." She smiles at me. "Only you and Sienna know, which means Zander probably knows, but I really want to keep it quiet for now. As soon as the media finds out, they'll be all over it." She makes a face.

I give her a sympathetic laugh. "The joys of being engaged to a celebrity, huh?"

She groans. "Thank God he's not an A-list actor or something."

"True," I say emphatically, then sense Tyrell eyeing me up with a questioning frown.

I glance at Satch. "Can I tell him? I'll wait until we're on the plane, if you want."

She smiles and nods. "Sure."

"Thank you." I kiss her cheek, then remember to ask, "How are you feeling, by the way? I mean, like, physically."

"Really good, actually. Minimal nausea, no puking. I felt kind of guilty admitting that to Sienna, but she was so happy for me. She wouldn't wish her pregnancies on anyone."

"I wonder if it will be her last."

"I really hope so. For her sake. Her body takes such a thrashing."

"But then she gets a beautiful baby out of it."

"Two." Satch giggles, then groans. "Oh man, I hope I don't have twins."

"I'm sure you won't," I assure her, then stand up when Carson saunters back with a much calmer Zoey.

"Man, I am so hungry for carrot sticks." He looks at Nylah. "It's the only thing I feel like eating."

Nylah gives him an impish grin, then looks at Zander. "I don't suppose you have any, do you? Because I could seriously go for carrot sticks too. They are *delicious*."

"Count me in!" Wily raises his hand. "I love those things."

"Yeah, I'll take one too." Tyrell gets in on the action.

"Wait!" Zoey yells, wriggling out of Carson's arms. He pops her down and she goes to the bag, pulling out the carrot sticks and looking around at each of us with a wary frown. After a beat, she pops the bag open and announces, "I will hand them out."

She then goes around the circle, allowing us to have one stick each before plunking down by Zander's feet and finishing off the rest of the bag.

Zander winks at Carson, giving him a grateful smile, then jerking up in his seat when he spots something behind us.

We all turn in time to see Sienna pushing a double stroller around a group of travelers. Her smile is broad and beautiful, and she looks like a million bucks considering she got no sleep last night.

"I made it," she sings, parking the stroller by my feet

and giving me a tight squeeze. "I had to come and see you off. I was dealing with major FOMO."

I laugh as Zander wanders over to her, kissing her lips as soon as she's released me. "How'd you get here?"

"I Ubered. The hotel's not too far, and the guy was really good about having to buckle in the boys' car seats and fold up the stroller."

Zander gives her a surprised smile, then peeks into the stroller, grinning down at his babies. "They're both asleep."

"Yes, miracles happen," Sienna murmurs before bending down to pick up Zoey. "Hey, lil' bug. Good girl. Did you eat all your carrot sticks?"

"Yep!" She gives her mom a proud smile before hugging her, then looking into the stroller and telling us all to be quiet. "They're sleeping. Shh." She points at Wily. "Don't be loud."

He zips his lips, which causes Blake to snort and start giggling.

"Stop." He nudges her and she nudges right back, and Grady gets jostled around as his girlfriend tussles with her brother.

Their play fighting is on the cusp of escalating when he lets out a patient sigh and lifts her off his left leg and settles her onto his right so she's out of easy reach of her brother.

Wily grunts at him. "Spoilsport."

"Man child," Grady clips back.

They share a quick side-eye, and then all eyes dart to the departure board as a muffled announcement comes over the speaker.

"That's us." I walk toward Tyrell with an excited grin,

the anticipation buzzing through me nearly too much to handle.

We're doing it.

We're actually doing it.

"Okay, hold up!" Zander calls us all to attention before the farewell hugs ensue. "I can't say goodbye to you guys without at least having a plan of when I'm going to see you again."

Tyrell pulls me against his side, smiling at his friend. "We'll be back. We're just not sure when."

"I hate how we're all so scattered now." Zander winces. "This weekend we just spent together was the best, and I want to do that again. We should have a set date when we always try to get together. Like families do at Christmas."

"We definitely can't do Christmas." Sienna shakes her head. "That's too hard with football and family commitments. We need to choose a weekend that doesn't have anything else on. And preferably after the Super Bowl." She leans against Zander's side, and he wraps his arm around her.

"That's it, then." Blake bounces on her toes. "The weekend after the Super Bowl. Let's just make a plan to get together, and whoever can make it will."

"But everyone has to really try to be there." Wily points around the group, his finger landing on us. "We'll give you an exemption for this coming year, but the one after that, you better show."

"We should get married then." Satch bobs on her toes. "Give everyone the best excuse, you know? Can't miss our wedding."

"I love it." Wily grins, leaning down to kiss her, then

pulling back with an excited gleam in his eye. Oh yeah, they're gonna have a baby at their wedding! That's so sweet!

"And then the year after that? What will our excuse be then?" Carson drawls.

"Christmas." Nylah shrugs. "Let's just make the weekend after the Super Bowl our annual Football Frat Christmas. We can bring gifts, celebrate how awesome we all are. Make it a long weekend every year."

"A Football Frat Christmas," Zander murmurs with a smile while Zoey raises her hands in the air.

"Christmas! I love Christmas," she yells.

"Done." Sienna laughs, kissing her cheek. "I'm excited already."

And so am I.

As much as I don't like planning ahead, the idea of *knowing* we're going to see these guys each year sends a warm lick of pleasure right through me.

Tyrell grins, sharing a smile with me before we pull apart and start our final round of goodbye hugs.

We're heading off on this adventure together, but we always have a home back here... and these Football Frat Christmases are going to be the best.


**And they really are.**
**Which is why a decade later, they're still going strong.**

**And their ten-year celebration is a special one, because
*everyone* will be there... if they can get their tribe of
children organized, not lose anyone... and rebook a
canceled flight or two.**

How many kids do you think this crew has between them now?

Get a snapshot of Football Frat family life as everyone tries to make it back to Nolan for a Valentine's Day Christmas...

I can't wait to celebrate *The Holiday Play* on Valentine's Day with you!

*And if you'd like to find out more about the upcoming Nolan U Basketball series, keeping reading...*

# THE NEXT NOLAN U SERIES...

Throughout the Nolan U Football series, you have been given little tastes of the characters for the upcoming Nolan U Basketball series, and very soon it will be time to go back and find out all of their stories.

I can't WAIT for you to read all the things they've been up to, and experience each of their romances.

You'll get the chance to start their journey in July, where we'll head to Mac's family lake house for some *Summer Heat*...

Charli and Darian have just found out they have access to a six-bedroom house in Nolan for them to see out the rest of their college years. They are stoked, and wanting to find the perfect roommates for their year ahead. So, of course they'll start with the basketball team and of course they'll run a few secret tests to make sure they pick the perfect people to live with.

They head to Finn MacAlister's lake house for a week of "tryouts" and there you'll get to know these basketball boys (and Charli) better. Plus, you'll find out how the Top Four are chosen.

You'll also get to see what went down between Darian and Nix, and experience the "eyebrow shaving" incident. Squee! Seriously, the heat between those two is intense and I can't wait for you to feel it.

**So, if you want to be a part of this new series and be the first to read "Summer Heat," then make sure you're signed up for my newsletter.**

**You'll gain access to the Nolan U Locker Room, which is an exclusive page on my website (password protected) that has a bunch of fun stuff for you—bonus scenes, character interviews and first-looks at everything that's coming up.**

**If you're already on my mailing list, you will have been given the password by now, if not... SIGN UP HERE:**

**www.katyarcher.com/nolan-u-locker-room-sign-up**

# NOTE FROM KATY

Dear reader,

Wow. You made it. Were you as emotional reading this story as I was writing it? I knew this one was going to hit me in the feels. Atlas's death had a big impact on both Dani and Tyrell, and it takes time to work through the grieving process. But the way they helped each other... how protective and sweet Tyrell was... Oh man! It got me good.

I also adored the way Tyrell was with his brother, Cyrus. He's going to be the sweetest, most patient dad. Which brings me to *The Holiday Play*. The reason I set this one ten years into the future is because I wanted you to see what all of these characters are like as parents. Zoey will be fourteen in this book, so you'll also get to see what she's like as a teenager, plus watch Zander, Wily, Carson, Grady and Tyrell bet the best dads and uncles ever!

For one whole weekend, we will get to experience the highs and lows, the joys and chaos that is the extended Football Frat family and I cannot WAIT for you to enjoy every page of it. Bring on February 14th! And don't forget to enter the giveaway for the chance to win one of the three prizes 🎁

If you enjoyed *The Perfect Play*, I would so appreciate you leaving an honest review on Amazon and/or Goodreads. Even just a star rating is helpful. You don't have to write anything if you don't want to. But star ratings and even short reviews really help validate the book, letting readers know it's worth a shot. It also tells Amazon and Goodreads that this book is worth shining a spotlight on. I know there are a bunch of readers out there who love college sports romance just as much as we do. If you can help me reach them, then that would be freaking fantastic.

Thanks for the assist!

I'd also like to thank a few key people who have been instrumental in helping me get this book ready for you— Megan, Kristin, Beth and Rachael. Thank you for all of your hard work. You are seriously *amazing* and I appreciate all the time and energy you give me. I love these books so much and you are an instrumental part of that.

My IG peeps—I want to give a special thank you to all the people who helped me brainstorm ideas for first date deal breakers: @shaelynrae11 @makaylapaige2015 @roni3713 @janepelham @phia_eilice @authorcmklein

@fastpitchfan12 @airamjustairam @lala_lifeguard004 @amandabs926
Thank you for all of your awesome ideas. You were such a huge help.

Trudi—what would I do without you, chica? You will always be one of my faves 🤍

My review team—thank you, thank you, thank you. Your reviews always blow me away. I love how much you love Nolan U. It makes my heart sing.

My readers—you are so freaking amazing! I love you and appreciate you so much. Thanks for reading the Nolan U books and loving them so much 🤍

My creator—you made me to live in the *what is* and I embrace that. Thank you for this fantastic life you've given me. I love you so much 🤍

xoxo
*Katy*

# BOOKS BY KATY ARCHER

## NOLAN U HOCKEY

Hockey House V-cards (prequel)
The Forbidden Freshman
The Heart Stealer
The Game Changer
The Love Penalty
The Only Goal
The Forever Game

## NOLAN U FOOTBALL

The First Play (prequel)
The Forever Play
The Off-Limits Play
The Surprise Play
The Illicit Play
The Perfect Play
The Holiday Play
*(Releasing on Valentine's Day 2026)*

## NOLAN U BASKETBALL

*Releasing in 2026 - 2027*
Summer Heat (prequel)
Off the Record Training
Out of Bounds Affair
The Kissing Experiment
The Wild Shot Player
Hate to Date You, Roomie
Loving You in Overtime

## NOLAN U - GEN 2

*Starting in 2027*

# CONTACT KATY

I love to hear from my readers, so feel free to email me anytime. You can also find out more on my website.

EMAIL: katy@katyarcher.com

WEBSITE: www.katyarcher.com

And if you want to connect with me on social and see pretty reels and teasers from the books, you can find me Addicted to College Sports Romance on...

INSTAGRAM
@addictedtocollegesportsromance

FACEBOOK
@collegesportsromancebooks

TIKTOK
@katyarcherauthor

www.ingramcontent.com/pod-product-compliance
Lightning Source LLC
Chambersburg PA
CBHW022235020726
47496CB00004B/907